MAELSTROM

BY DAVID NIALL WILSON

"The Grand Sabbat."

They were still staring at the words, trying to figure out just what the hell they might mean, when Flash suddenly let out a loud hiss.

"Hey!" he said, his voice sharp and low, "I think I heard someone! Let's get the hell out of here."

Cursing again, Weasel slammed the little book closed and stuffed it quickly into its box and back into the bigger volume. He reached up and jammed the book home between the true gospels, hoping that he'd gotten it back in the right order, but not caring enough to try and straighten it if he hadn't.

They could all hear the sounds now, shuffling uneven footsteps that seemed as loud as gunshots in the ominous silence of the empty church. Hearts racing, they tumbled out of the office, barely remembering to pull the heavy door closed behind them.

The huge statue over the pool seemed to be staring directly at them as they crossed the silent expanse of the huge room, the accusation in its eyes now malevolent and deep. The feeling of being watched was intense, making the hairs on the back of Nick's neck stand up, the nerves he'd worked so hard to maintain at an even keel, to crack and crumble.

DEDICATION

I want to dedicate this book to The Who, ZZ Top, John Cougar (before he was Mellencamp) and all the bands I saw during my years in the US Navy out in San Diego. This is for Mark "Ping" Johnson, Mike "Hand Man" Walsh, Don Paresi, Bruce Bray, and all the rockers I've played music with, shared dark nights on the streets with, and who helped me build just the right rock and roll nightmares for *Maelstrom*. Last but not least, this is for Mark Rainey and the old *Deathrealm* Crowd who are no strangers to the Cult of Light and Starry Wisdom in all its incarnations.

ACKNOWLEDGMENTS

I'd like to thank, first and foremost, Roy and Liz from Bad Moon Books for finally making this novel a reality. I'd like to add special thanks to Alex McVey for the wonderful cover art, the readers from the old Horror Mall boards (you know who you are) who read an earlier version and helped me make the work stronger. I'd like to thank my family, Trish who really is the best part of me, Bill, Stephanie, Zach, Zane, and Katie, who give me a reason to feel important when life gets me down, and the amazing folks at VectorCSP—where I spend my days ministering to the IT needs of one of the best companies in the world. In short…this book is blessed.

INTRODUCTION

This book represents such a very long period of my creative life that I hardly know how to explain it. It was conceived on board a US Navy ship. During that period of my life, nothing mattered more than the music. I wrote, yes, but I lived and breathed rock and roll. My stereo, or someone's stereo, blared around the clock. Headphones filled the rest of the hours, and every chance we got we piled into Mark Johnson's "Magic Bus" and headed off to the Stadium in San Diego, CA, to see a show. We always parked at the corner of rows 3 and D in the parking lot, so we could find our way back. That was always in question—it was a different, wilder time; and I wouldn't trade it for anything.

I remember seeing The Who, John Cougar, and Loverboy on the same night. My clearest memory of that night happened in the van, right after the concert, when a dancer we'd picked up and taken with us—sitting in her new Loverboy pink tube top—burst the stunned after-shock silence of The Who to say… "Loverboy…they were the BEST." I will never forget that. It was in that moment I realized that rock and roll really was magic, and not everyone "got" it.

When I decided to write about a band, I brought to bear everything that mattered to me at the time. Big flashy shows, lyrics that meant something, vocals against a solid blues backbeat, guitars that flickered with power (Thank you ZZ Top for that image). I wanted the experience of the concert in the first chapter to feel "real"…and I asked my friends to contribute. There's a line about thousands of fluttering bats that belongs to Gary Markum (who became Big Mac Markum in a couple of other stories).

Along with the music, I had a lot of life to include in this. At the point where I started this novel, I'd written and sold This is My Blood, which was a high-concept, very difficult novel. I'd written for White Wolf, writing to "spec" and for Star Trek; but I'd never just sat down to tell a story I could invest myself in. This was the first, and it's taken literally decades to get it to print. This includes snippets of my childhood, insights into my family, lyrics I actually wrote for a band—Mystyque—that never came to be. This has demons and magic, an evil preacher, sex and violence, Lovecraftian evil, and, at its heart, good characters pitted against the darkness. That's what it's always been about—which side are you on, and which side will win.

If you're reading this, you already invested money in my work. I hope you'll enjoy it, but more than that, I hope I'll do my job—taking you to Lavender, California, to the cemetery and The Church of New Light—to Nick's home, and to much darker places. I hope you'll hear the music in your head. Maybe you'll see all those old Bic lighters swaying in a wash of The Who's music that's so loud, hairs move on your arms.

If any of that happens…I've done my job. Hope you'll stop by my website, or my Facebook page, or Twitter, and let me know…

—David Niall Wilson

CHAPTER ONE

One moment there was light; the next there was nothing. The lights snapped off and darkness swallowed the huge amphitheater whole. All sound ceased for one long moment, cut short with a collective indrawn breath. The heady aromas of sweat, perfume, cigarette smoke, and burning hemp permeated the air. Adrenalin pumped and brains were charged; the moment was a still-shot photo against a backdrop of slowed time. Every eye in the building focused forward. It was going to be awesome.

Nick pressed the length of his body as tightly against Ruthie's soft curves as he could get—so close that he could feel where her short skirt stopped and her legs flowed downward, could make out the syncopated rhythm of her heartbeat in the almost total silence. He was aware of her, but his focus was on the stage.

It wasn't visible in the darkness. Only the glimmer of hundreds of Bic lighters, waving back and forth in a flickering, undulating motion, disturbed the eerie vastness. It was hypnotic and powerful. His heartbeat thundered in his chest and vibrated up to resonate through his mind, amplified by the forced silence.

Every muscle was taut; his nerves were on edge. Though it remained invisible, the distant platform pulled against the massed bodies with a magnetic attraction that threatened to press the back of the crowd forward so tightly into the front that they would become a single, human, particleboard conglomeration. Nick grinned into it all fiercely. This, he knew, was it—what it was all about. This was the night.

An odd, half-whining, half-rustling echo rose from all sides at once: the sound of the wings of a thousand bats, rippling, multiplying, growing until the air resonated with the sound. All those thousands of eyes, seconds earlier gripped by the black nothingness that obscured the stage, darted upward in sudden confusion, watching, unwilling to miss a single sight or sensation. In those seconds of diversion, lightning flashed. The air went suddenly white, and the echoing rustle became a roar.

Nick snapped his eyes back from the ceiling to the stage, but all he could make out was the glaring, strobed image of the flash. Sound undulated around him, caressed and pounded him, moving between the hairs that dangled across his forehead and vibrated against his scalp.

Then the glare cleared, and they were there. *Maelstrom*, chrome-studded leather glittering in the wash of brilliant, multicolored light. They had snapped into existence like an invasion force from another world. The guitars wailed; the drums pounded, and the incredible volume of the vocals embedded their message in the base of his skull, rising rhythmically through his mind. Slowly, the corners of his mouth twisted up in a demonic grin.

"Righteous!" he screamed, his words lost in the cresting sound of the band and blending subtly with the unchecked bedlam that was the crowd. "Awesome!"

Devon Storme grinned out into the fuzzy expanse of writhing, screaming humanity. His eyes flashed with the fiery glitter of complete control. Slowly, each move a theatrical symphony of motion, he raised his eyes until they faced skyward. His silver hair, long and straight, flowed in an iridescent cascade from his shoulders.

He howled. As the microphone in his hand carried the sound to the amplifiers and mixers, it rose in volume and power and shot from the towers of speaker columns to echo off the acoustically perfect rafters, carom wildly from the walls, and lift the audience to an even higher emotional level. It took them to "the edge."

From where he stood, concentrating his energy on the pitch

and the resonance of that one long screaming note, he couldn't hear the overpowering sound he was creating. The monitors on stage were set for a much lower decibel level. He judged how he affected changes in the crowd by their motion. Each variation of sound flowed through the seething mass of bodies in waves. It was exhilarating beyond any other high. They were his, his and *Maelstrom's*, and they were in for the night of their lives. He snapped his eyes downward, focusing on an abstract point near the center of the crowd. With the lights glaring in his face, he couldn't make out any individual faces beyond the first three rows, just a twisting, swaying mass of energy and emotion. Without warning he brought his hand up, then back down, and pointed his finger into the crowd. He tossed back his hair and launched into the first song. Behind him the guitars screamed and the bass rolled like thunder. He rode the eye of the storm and fired his words like bolts of energy into the eager targets below him.

"Ride upon the dragon's breath,
The essence of the Mistral Wind,
Take the pathways sealed to man,
On astral wings ascend.
Ride the serpents coiling scales,
Find the freedom of the air.
Alone upon the dragon's breath,
Ride it if you dare!"

He felt the psychic pressure of their eyes, all of their eyes, riveted to his face, his body. Every leap or twist brought screams of adulation, ripples of movement. The crowd, entangled in his words, had become an extension of the band, a huge, monstrous body of flesh with the music at its core, the band as its brain.

The song ended, but the steady backbeat of the drums never faded. He smiled out at his disciples and tilted his head to the side in a patented gesture that said, "Hey, let's party!" It was a universal body language that was eloquent in a way that even the music fell short of.

"Are we happy tonight?" he asked, voice crashing and echoing, otherworldly and hypnotic. "Are we ready for the *Storm*?"

He swung his hair about and swept the crowd with a leering scrutiny that hushed what little sound remained. "We are all here, you know," he continued. "The Mechanic, on drums."

His voice faded into the resounding beat. A tremor of snare and symbols rang out, then another, a building crescendo of crashing, rhythmic thunder. Cresting on the wave of an avalanche of syncopation, The Mechanic's hair spun, and sweat flew from his brow, sparkling like small rivulets of light. Then the thunder faded slowly, returning to a steady, deceptively intricate backbeat. Stepping forward once again, Devon smiled.

"Beside me rides The Force, rhythm guitar." A crackle of distortion rocked out and wove itself into the rhythm of the drums, small flourishes and eddies of notes rippling through the steady, droning resonance of the chords.

"And Tommy Thunder on bass!" he snapped, ushering in a pummeling, bone-shaking rush of deep, rich notes, perfectly timed with the drums, but so closely woven with the chords and notes of the guitar that the two might be a single instrument, the sound born of a single thought.

The music was gathering speed now, and Devon threw his hands over his head as he cried, "Lightning!"

Beside him, the short, blonde-haired guitarist moved slightly forward and launched into a flurry of notes that hit the amphitheater like a waterfall of sound, bursting through the structure of the music but disturbing nothing, flawlessly running harmonic foot races with bass and drum, and speeding through the rhythm like quicksilver.

Louie "Lightning" Rivers was hot. Devon knew it; the crowd knew it, *and Lightning* knew it. Devon's smile widened yet again. The music was there—right on the edge, and the crowd was eating it up, absolutely entranced, with the band's hole card yet to be played. It was time to bring on the show-stopper of all showstoppers.

Stepping further to one side, just out of the spotlight, he grabbed the second microphone that awaited him there. He raised his arm above his head, a sign to the lighting crew, and the spotlights dimmed, replaced by a greenish glow that was brightest at the center of the stage.

"And the Storm," his voice echoed, reciting in deep, mystical tones, "rose to tear and rend. Thunder crashed, Lightning flashed, and the night was taken—taken by..." he hesitated as the music slowed, a seductive blues beat that pulled at the collective limbs of the crowd with invisible strings, forcing them into sinuous motion, "Gail Force!"

She slipped from the shadows with lips parted and eyes aglow and gyrated across the stage to stand, writhing and twisting in perfect unison with the waves of sound. Her nearly bare body glowed in the green radiance from above. The lights wound about her, like a giant luminous serpent, tightening its grip. Bodies swayed in time; all eyes were on her as she sent her passion flowing outward, dripped the honey of pure sexual abandon from her skin, flung it from her hair and out in a shower to soak them all. Then she stepped to the microphone, and she sang.

Nick could just make out the haughty, arrogant form of Devon Storme as he stepped forward once more to stand at Gail's side. They were like fire and ice, moon and sun. A perfect complement, one to the other.

It was like a dream. Nick's mind blended one light with another, all light with the sound; and before his eyes a goddess danced, just for him. He continued to press forward, oblivious of his surroundings. The trip was hot. He felt the LSD pump through his veins and tasted it sizzling at the back of his throat, reminding him what network was responsible for the program. WLSD—better living through modern chemistry. Yeah. He hoped he'd be alive when it was all over, but for the moment he was trapped, adrift in the frenzied emotion, twisting in the grasp of *Maelstrom*.

"Awesome," he thought again—or had he spoken? The moment was lost, and he couldn't quite recall, nor could he remember why he would care. All around him his friends shook, danced, and stared up at the stage, lost in their own private worlds, off on their own trips.

He felt Ruthie press back against him firmly, never letting the contact between them break, or lessen. Her touch, the feel of her body, her scent, every sensory perception wove itself to the vision of Gail Force, toying with his fantasies, driving him right to that edge, that magical Jim Morrison world where anything was possible. His teeth ground together compulsively, and the odd numbing dryness at the back of his throat persisted. Every ten minutes or so, a sizzling crackle shot from his throat to his ears and back down his throat.

Fried, he thought, grinning. *What a night!*

The music shifted, slow and sensuous, fast and frantic; and it twisted them first one way, then the other. It was magical, the hold the songs had over them, an escapist's dream. The world, its problems, its mundane realities, all had been scraped away to show the bare, essential emotion of the moment. Three hours seemed like three years until it ended, and then it seemed all too short.

Devon and Gail crooned, then screamed, all in perfect harmony; Lightning Louie's solos grew, if possible, faster and more complex as the night wore on. His guitar spoke, cried out, sang, and screeched at the perfect controlling touch of pick and fingers.

It ended, just as it had begun. The lights flashed out; the crowd was stunned to silence, and their next vision was the stage, barren and empty, as the house lights rose from a dim haze to a confusing brilliance. Nick's mind told him that it must be the same stage that met his eyes; he *knew* it was the same, and yet in some subtle, impossible way it was not.

The fluorescent lights glared; the wooden platform was snarled with wires and dead amplifiers, and the garbage—the refuse of 40,000 screaming fans was stuck to the floor in puddles of spilled soda, beer, and sweat. All of these things registered themselves among Nick's thought patterns, and then were rejected. It was cheap, disgusting, and way too empty. Time to roll.

Ruthie seemed to sense the snapping of the spell, and she peeled herself reluctantly from his embrace. He wondered if it had been the same for her; if she had been dreaming that they were making love, melting to one, flowing together in a molten blob of passion. She looked around at the others, then at Nick; her eyes filled with nervous guilt—with uncertainty.

Ruthie was on Nick's wavelength: he felt it. She was tripping like a rocket, and unlike Nick and the others, it made her feel conspicuous and alone. He smiled at her, willing the sparkle in his eyes to tell her that he was just as far beyond control as she was, just as fucked up and out-of-sync, and that it was okay.

Tripping, he knew, could bring people together, or drive them apart more quickly and completely than any other experience. It forced you to the edge. On the edge you can be pushed just as easily as you can fall—or jump.

"Wow," Weasel commented, breaking the silence and tossing his stringy black hair out of his eyes with one hand. Sweat splashed the rest of them, and he watched the droplets fly, grinning. "Hot trip," he added. "Guess we'd better vacate, though. The air's getting pretty dead in here."

"Well," Flash tossed in, his eyes bright and full of energy, "we can't go home, that's for sure. My mom and dad would fucking *freak* if they saw me like this. I mean, they already think you guys spend your nights killing old ladies for their bread money and drinking blood. You send me home tripping, mom makes me a sandwich and I tell her to make it stop flopping and breathing so I can eat it…? Nope. No fucking way."

They all laughed and turned toward the doors, where the last dregs of stoners and drunks were weaving their way through the huge exit and into the after-concert bedlam of the parking lot.

Outside waited a surreal world, much different from the confined inner space of the amphitheater. Thousands of cars in various states of departure moved in a slow-motion mechanical dance. The four friends wove their way through small groups of people gathered around the tailgates of trucks to wait for traffic to clear, passing through waves of sound as they moved from the range of one stereo to the next. Some played Maelstrom; others ran the gamut of the safer, more traditional sounds of Morrison or Zeppelin, and the newer, more trip-intense groups like Nine Inch Nails, or Seether. A few adventurous folks even braved the radio and its endless stream of prattle and pseudo-pop nonsense.

They passed through it all in silence, waiting; and they were not disappointed. Flash, as everyone knew he would be, was the first to break the silence, tossing off the words they all wanted to hear.

"Good night to raise the devil," he said, his voice wavering in a horrible impression of Vincent Price. "Shady Grove night?"

Nobody answered, at first. They glanced at one another tentatively, waiting. None of them could face their parents yet, and empty rooms without music, alone, were not real possibilities as long as the drug held them, which would be most of the night.

The shaded paths and whispering mists of the graveyard were a challenge: one that they knew only too well. Every time Flash and Nick were tripping, they somehow ended up there.

Nick said he was looking for ghosts. Ruthie was watching him now, the gleam in his eyes, and the far away smile on his lips. She could believe, when he was this way and when the trip gave her the sight, that he might find them. She wasn't certain if she wanted to be there if he did—some of the real-world ghosts of his life were powerful enough to be frightening. Like his father.

He drew her though, almost like *Maelstrom* had drawn them all. It was a Shady Grove night; that much was certain, and it was going to be wild. Ruthie drew a little closer to Nick's side and shivered.

The van was still surrounded by wandering kids, open cars, trucks and vehicles of all types, and sound. A thousand stereos blared in melodious discord. This, along with the acid, kept them quiet. They moved in a tight bunch: it seemed safer.

Using the memorization ritual he'd perfected long ago, Flash led them unerringly back to where "The Magic Bus" was parked. He'd purposely put it in plain sight of the parking lot markers 3 and D.

"Welcome, friends," he chanted, spinning slowly to grin at them in his best sideshow manner, "to the third dimension. It is a dimension of sight, and sound. Your coach awaits, the night beckons, and it's going to be a long, long trip...buckle in, and prepare for blast off."

"The rap" had started. Maelstrom had warmed them up, reality was gone, and they all laughed and rushed with the pseudo-energy of LSD-25. When Flash got started, the words flowed on and on, unending waves of profound gibberish. It filled the void, breathed life into dead air.

Sometimes Weasel and Nick joined in—it was like a war zone then. Ruthie was always amazed, unable to catch up or take part, and glad that they were content to leave her out of it, an observer yet still a part of the experience.

Mostly it was just Flash, but tonight Weasel was giving him a run for it. Nick was silent, holding her tightly against him and dreaming. Ruthie waited it out, waited for the cool breeze and shadowy silence of Shady Grove.

The two of them sat in the very back of the van, and she leaned between his legs, cradled in his arms. He reached forward slowly, cupped her breasts in his hands and massaged them sensuously to the beat of the music that now blared from the van's massive stereo.

Weasel had taken the reins, steadily feuding with Flash and keeping him alert. Driving on acid was like a video game, and all of them were acutely aware of what happened to the losing spacecraft in video games. Flash managed it, again, and they rolled out of the lot and onto the freeway, one of a stream of thousands of drunk, stoned, and rowdy vehicles in a river of rushing metal.

Weasel popped another tape into the stereo, and, like a minor flashback, *Maelstrom* belted out their trademark song, "Tailspin," Gail Force screeching in a high-pitched, soprano whine that belied the otherwise melodic qualities of her voice. The memory of the last few hours snapped vividly back into focus.

Nick's hand, as his thoughts returned to the band, and the concert, drifted toward Ruthie's thigh and continued its sensual massage.

"Yeah," Flash screamed, flooring the van and passing a long string of cars as if they were motionless, "bring on the night!" The highway, in silent agreement, complied. It would be a long trip.

CHAPTER TWO

The last car arrived at nearly eleven, sliding through the shadows and into the concealment of the old barn, and nosing its way in among the others that were already there. The headlights glared brightly in the dim interior, flashed off, and seconds later the darkness gave way to the light of flickering oil lamps, bobbing up and down like will-'o-the-wisps as those who held them moved through the shadows.

All thirteen were present. The time for waiting or hesitation was past. Midnight would mark the start of the Solstice, and the darkness beckoned to them with a giddy rush of power—a premonition of darker, wilder things to come.

No clouds marred the perfect ebon of the night sky. The wind ran invisible fingers through branches and leaves, bringing the rustling, whispery voices of the trees to life. Those voices whistled brightly, and then trailed off into the night to die in the limitless expanse of countryside spreading out on all sides.

Their wait had been long, impossibly long. So much had gone into preparation, planning, and perfect execution. It was the night of a lifetime: a one-in-a-million chance at more than any of the thirteen—individually—could ever have dreamed of. It was going to be perfect.

They carried various bundles under their arms; two held what appeared to be nothing more than a long, lumpy carpet, rolled haphazardly for the journey. Halfway down the winding trail that led from the old farm to the high, imposing iron gates of the graveyard, the bundle began to squirm.

The two continued on their way, ignoring the movement, controlling their burden with ease. From one end of the roll a shoe poked out, slipped free, and fell to the ground. One of the others, trailing behind, bent to retrieve it, securing it in some deep fold or pocket in his robe. They picked up speed as they neared their destination. Anticipation was a palpable force, prodding them onward with fiery jabs.

They wore dark robes that swept the ground as they walked, rustling in eerie counterpoint to the leaves above them. The robes rose to full hoods, which were carefully pulled up, and over their heads and down in front, obscuring all but the glint of their eyes as they caught stray glimmers of moonlight. The robes brushed the signs of their passing into oblivion, dragging through the dust and tall grass as they passed.

Their movements were fluid, the actions of a single purpose, silent, swift, and exact. Tension crackled about them, heightening their senses until each sound, each step, registered like thunder. From the bundle carried between them, lost, hysterical sounds filtered through—weak and totally without hope. The sounds died unheeded in the endless void of night.

As they approached the cemetery, the ominous spiked bars that formed the fence surrounding the rear wall impaled their shadows. Bright moonlight washed over the gate. The first to reach the entrance swung the gate easily inward. The old locks and chains had rusted away years before, and they passed inside, winding their way through the shady plots and ivy-draped stone monuments.

This rear section of the graveyard was the oldest. The vines and shrubbery were marching slowly forward to reclaim the graves there, unwilling to relinquish the control to man completely. The path was overgrown in spots, but not impassable, and they moved down it with practiced ease. When the undergrowth gave way to an open clearing, they slowed and spread out.

A pair of gravestones stood in the center of the space, ripped from their proper resting places decades past. Across their top lay a large slab from some even more ancient, distant burial plot. The three formed a low bench of chill, molded stone, which appeared somehow untouched by fungus or dirt. An altar. In its center the stone was darkly stained.

The rolled bundle was carried from the shadows and laid across the stone. Candles were brought forth on all sides, leaping to life and flickering eerily. Five sets of hands held these aloft, five figures moved to place themselves at the cardinal points of the circle. A pentagram was formed.

Two of those remaining moved slowly about the circle, caught up in a strange, mincing dance step. The rhythm they created followed an intricate pattern. As they danced, they reached into leather bags worn at their sides and sprinkled scented herbs and powders to flutter to the ground. It took several minutes to complete this ritual, but none of the others moved until the entire circle was carefully covered.

As the two neared each of those holding a candle, they chanted a short, monosyllabic incantation. The candle bearers answered in the same, toneless voice, standing rigid as the dancers circled them. At each point a larger handful of the powder was tossed to the wind, offerings to the five spirits—the gatekeepers.

The other six stood about the stone altar, one each at the head and foot, and two on either side. They stood in silence and stared straight ahead, concentrating.

When the dancers had finished, they joined the two at the ends of the altar. Those at the points of the star bent to place small braziers on the ground, and the cloying, sticky-sweet scent of incense rose from each. The scented smoke swirled about and among them, and its intoxicating aroma formed images of mist and air that hovered at their backs and sides.

The two at each end of the altar grabbed the bundle and removed the cords that bound it, uncoiling it in a single, swift motion. The cloth fell away to both sides, draping over the stone slab and baring the form of a young woman. She was bound with a bandanna for a gag and packing twine on both arms and legs. She rolled wildly back and forth in her restraints, trying to force the gag from between her teeth.

Gretchen felt herself rolled roughly to her back. She drew in the sudden rush of fresh air with heaving gasps of breath, and tried with every ounce of her soul to scream. The cotton gag gripped her jaw too tightly. She twisted to one side, turning blindly about and trying to roll off of the stone slab in a vain bid for salvation. She saw eyes leering at her from above, lost in the folds of deep, dark robes: eyes that began to glitter, then to smile, as she struggled. Again she tried to scream, but it was far, far too late.

Strong hands gripped her ankles, released the cords from them quickly and efficiently and drew them roughly apart. Her remaining shoe was removed and leather straps wrapped tightly about each ankle. She kicked out as she felt the chain of her ankle bracelet dig into her flesh from the pressure of the strap, but they were too strong. She moaned into the gag, as the straps were pulled taut over the corners of the stone, forcing her to straddle it, her legs spread wide and bound together beneath.

Her wrists were next. The process was repeated at the head of the table, her arms being drawn in a loop behind her back and around the stone, and then bound in place. There was little slack, making struggle difficult; but still she tried. Her muscles rippled, tight—rigid with the effort; her skin beaded with sweat, plastering her clothing to her thighs and breasts. Her heart hammered like a drummer gone mad, and her eyes glazed with terror.

Then she saw the blade. It hovered over her, mesmerizing in a blue-white flash of the moon's waxing light. Then it flickered downward and slid up the side of her blouse. She drew herself as far away from the cold steel of the blade as possible, trembling. She tried to hold herself motionless as the knife sheared through her blouse, slicing it like a razor blade through paper.

Through tear-fogged eyes she saw the blade sweep back, grazing her now bare breasts with the feather touch of icy metal, to slice into the material of her skirt. That was gone then, too, and beneath it she wore only her stockings. These were cut away as well, leaving her naked and shivering, her skin awash with tiny goose bumps, sheathed in a clammy coating of fear-soaked sweat.

She fought, writhed, and squirmed about on the stone, scraping her arms and thighs with the effort. The leather straps mocked her efforts, and the gag only cut deeper into the sides of her jaw.

Her captors began to chant. They danced in a slow-motion whirl that was dizzying and disorienting. At odd intervals they reached out, running cool hands provocatively over her flesh, trailing across her breasts and over her thighs. Teasing at her fear. She tried to pull away, to retreat from the obscenity of their groping hands; but her efforts met only cold stone, and it held her, helpless and vulnerable, presented to them for their pleasure. Bile rose in her throat, and she bit it back.

The dancing slowed, and then stopped. One of the robed figures stooped and brought forth a chalice, brimming with some dark liquid, a drop of which dribbled down the side and over his hand. Reaching down to grip Gretchen painfully by the hair, he tilted her head back and poured a mouthful of the strange brew carefully over the top of the gag. She tried to spit, tried to turn her head to the side and force the drink from her mouth; but he held her too tightly, and she could not spit past the cotton of the bandanna. She felt heat as the sickly sweet mixture trickled down her throat, and at last she was forced to swallow, wildly gasping to regain her breath. She drank it all, and tears filled her eyes until she saw nothing but a blur.

Next, the figure raised the cup to his lips and drank deeply. It traveled quickly around the circle. Each of the robed figures took a deep draught and passed it along. Gretchen felt the warmth and sweetness in her throat spreading into a fuzzy numbness and working its way through her bloodstream. She still shook her head, still struggled; but the movements had grown slow and dream-like. The shaking of her head only spread the webs of confusion gripping her thoughts more thickly.

Hands caressed her skin. They covered her with some sort of ointment, a cool salve that tingled through her pores and soaked into her nerves in cool, soothing waves. She wanted to scream. The helpless violation drove like a sharp spike into the back of her brain and ordered her to fight, but she had no strength for it. Whatever had been in the drink had erased her control over her limbs. Now the tingle of the ointment melted through her skin, layer by layer. She smelled the pungent odor of the stuff wafting up, as her breathing grew ragged, and then deeper.

Her skin was warming, glowing, and electric with sensation. An inner fire erupted and sent a spasm of shivers spinning through her each time a finger, or a hand, made contact. Her head spun. She fought an already lost battle for control of her own body. The clearing faded. Thought faded. She arched to seek the probing hands as the figures chanted. The writhing struggles on which she'd concentrated melted to a hot, molten swaying motion that coincided to the steps of their dance. Hands rippled over her flesh, leading her, teasing her.

Until it had already happened, she was not aware of the first as he entered her. She tried to scream then, but the drugs dulled her concentration, and each sensation shot through her like icy fire. The false chemical pleasure rippled across nerve endings and twisted her to its will. The ointment wormed its way further through her bloodstream and drew forth reactions she had no defense against. Her body bucked and pressed upward; her voice whimpered and moaned, crying out as each pulled free and the next took his place. Her mind wept.

She had no way of keeping count, but after a seemingly endless succession, after she had been prepared, a last figure stepped forward. He stood close by her side, and she watched him, panting, unable to move or draw back from his presence. She stared up at him. The utter helplessness and hopelessness of the moment washed over her, and she shuddered. She felt their seed dripping across her inner thigh, and the combined sweat of them rubbed deeply into her skin.

Then she saw a bright glitter, a flashing flutter of silver. Fascinated, she watched it as it rose high above her, another star in the endless night sky, and then plummeted, its speed unreal and dizzying. Confused, she pressed herself up off the stone, anticipating yet another touch—another sensation.

The blade sank deep into her flesh, bursting her heart and cascading the circled figures with droplets of blood. They drew back their hoods, bared their faces to the caress of the moonlight, and returned to their dance. On the stone slab, the blood still oozed slowly from Gretchen's cooling body to drip steadily, puddling on the ground beneath their feet.

They began their chant in earnest, and the dance became

wild—reckless and with abandon—a tribute and sacrifice to the waning moon. It was done. Their eyes flashed with the fire of dark desire. It was done.

CHAPTER THREE

Somehow, Flash managed to steer the van through the twisting glow of flashing lights and rushing landscape without a hitch. It seemed as though they'd been driving for hours, days even; and the memory of *Maelstrom* and the concert were fading away behind them rapidly.

Nick and Ruthie knew that they were nearing the cemetery when they heard the crunch of gravel under the tires that signaled their turn onto Shady Grove Lane, a winding one-lane drive that brought one from State Highway 13 to the front gates of the Shady Grove cemetery.

The images induced by the acid were slowing, losing their otherworldly intensity. This was the part of the trip that Nick always found most memorable. When the peak receded, the sizzling sensations in his throat came further and further apart; and his mind seemed to reach a state of absolute clarity. Every thought deepened and took on more meaning. It might not be true, he knew. More likely he'd just fried so many brain cells that simple things began to appear profound. It didn't matter. It was a beautiful night, somehow made more so by the trailing wisps of the drug, and he was going to enjoy it.

Pulling her a little tighter into his arms, he stroked Ruthie's long golden hair absently. He saw the headlights bouncing ahead when they went over a particularly large pothole, then darkness again in a lazy, roller coaster-like motion. The momentary light had caught on Ruthie's hair, making it ripple like spun gold.

She was a cute girl, a little lost at times, a bit too insecure, but in her own way more special to him than any person besides his mother. He knew that she was scared when they tripped, afraid of being alone with him when she was so vulnerable, yet unwilling to be apart.

The others never brought girls with them. Nick liked the sensation of responsibility. He kept his eyes open and watched over her. She was a slender girl. The acid accentuated this impression, giving her the flighty frailty of a small, delicate bird. She tugged at him, not just physically, but at some inner strings that others seemed unable to find, or to grasp. Special.

He liked having her near him, and this night in particular he had wanted her there. It was a special night for him. He wrapped his arms further around her and gave her a quick hug, reassuring her that he was aware of her and that she was in his thoughts. She pressed back against him and snuggled in a little deeper.

Turning her head slightly, she looked up into his smiling eyes and shyly smiled in return. She didn't speak, knew that such a moment was better in silence. Nothing said at times such as this was nothing said wrong. She laid her head back against his chest, her cheek pressed tightly where she could feel the beating of his heart, and lost herself once more in the music.

They passed through the cemetery gates at last and turned down the left fork just inside, skirting the edges of the newer plots and the gatehouse. They preferred the older sections, near the rear of the grounds, and Flash headed slowly in that direction. Their usual spot was a pull-off from the main trail beside a huge, musty old mausoleum that provided a good parking space as well as cover from the gate behind.

"Well, kiddies," Flash piped up, "Next stop funland, ghouls, ghosties, eerie phenomena of all shapes, sizes, and nightmare regions. Please watch your step, and the flight departs for all parts homeward in two hours. Thank you for flying Magic Bus Airlines..."

They stopped moving with a lurch, reminding them all to be thankful that Flash had pulled it off again, that they were in one piece, alive, and ready to roll. The music blared louder with the engine off, echoing strangely in the enclosed metal shell of the van. Without another word, Flash reached out and killed the stereo, leaving a strobing echo of the final song, "Reach for the Light," ringing through their ears.

"Wow," Weasel commented with his usual profundity. Shaking his head from side to side as if to free it of the sound, he continued, "Heavy."

"Pretty wordy for a fucking rodent," Nick answered, rising slowly to a crouch and extricating himself from behind Ruthie to reach for the door. He stepped out into the cool night air and turned to give Ruthie his hand, drawing her out and close to him in one motion. The others catapulted from opposite sides of the van in unison, whooping like banshees. In what seemed only seconds, the four of them stood in a group, looking about themselves with interest.

"Ghost hunt?" Flash called, eyeing Nick and Ruthie, who stood pressed tightly together, gazing into one another's eyes.

"Not tonight, I think," Nick answered. "I'm going to walk around, you know? I feel like just letting the night happen, letting it flow."

"Yeah," Flash answered, "we know." He fixed Ruthie with a leering half smile, cocked one eyebrow up and waggled his finger at her. "You watch him close, Ruthie girl, real close. Moonlight, it gets him totally weird, you know? Never can tell what *appetites* or *lusts* might grip him. In fact..."

"Cut," Nick said, waving his hands, "the shadows beckon." He grinned, but his arms held Ruthie tightly and comfortingly. "We'll catch you two on the return flight, Cap'n. Beam us up when you're ready to launch."

Grabbing Ruthie's hand, he began walking away slowly, already scanning the shadows and alcoves of the old tombs for anything of interest. His mind was not on ghosts, though, not really. The pressure Ruthie was returning on his hand told him that she knew it too.

He felt her shiver slightly, pulling closer. Tonight was special: the concert, the drugs, and their friends—perfect. *Maelstrom* were Nick's idols, and now there was this—the graveyard, the silence. He had planned it so that he could give the whole night to her, a slice of his life she could share. He glanced down and saw that she was smiling fiercely, the drugs bringing her emotions much closer to the surface. She was almost crying, she was so happy, and he had to look away before his own eyes teared up.

Ahead, the line of ancient gravestones met with a climbing wall of vines and shrubs, growing up, over, and around the larger of the old monuments and eventually crashing against a wall of trees. Among the waving branches and shuffling, dried leaves of those trees the shadows were at their strongest—so Nick told himself as he approached them.

Oddly, and he had noticed it before, beyond the tree line there was no feel of death. It was as if the graves, with their expensive carved stones and sun-bleached plastic bouquets were more of a monument to the mundane trivialities of life than to a meaningful afterlife. He couldn't picture a spirit choosing to remain in such a place; it was like a museum.

There were graves among the trees as well, some with small tree trunks growing from their centers, others covered over in leaves and debris. The names on these older graves were generally longer and sounded more distinguished. Here and there a Spanish name cropped up—more so than in the newer parts of the cemetery. These were the final resting places of the true founding fathers of San Valencez and Lavender California. These men, women, and children had known the twin cities when they were merely plots of ground and a few scattered vineyards. He wondered briefly if they would approve of what had become of their land. He wondered if they would be sorry that no one remembered them.

They were nearing the place he sought, and his pulse quickened. He'd discovered what he called "the altar" several years earlier on one of their first ghost hunts. There was, he was certain, some far less ominous reason why it was there than virgin sacrifice, but he preferred his fantasy.

"The altar" was a stone slab, supported at both ends by a pair of headstones that had been placed in the center of a clearing. There were dark stains on that stone, dark and rusty brown. He could almost feel the weight of time pressing down on the ancient stone, could almost hear the chanting and see the priests as they offered scantily clad young women to elder gods.

This was the place where he'd wanted to end this night. First the trip, then *Maelstrom*, all on the night of the Summer Solstice. It was a magic night, for him, anyway, one that was destined to be stamped in his memory. He wanted to do everything he could to add to that, to embed it in his mind. He wanted the memories to be perfect.

He had also planned for Ruthie to be there. She was becoming a larger part of his life, and possibly of his future. It was important to Nick that she knew *all* of him, every aspect of his life, the easy to understand and the difficult to deal with. He knew he was a moody person, probably right on the borderline of weird, by most standards. If she couldn't cope with that, he needed to know now, before he committed too much.

Nick was not one to harbor delusions about life. He wanted to know everything there was to know about people—wanted them to care enough to know about him. His own home was a perfect example of everything he feared in life; he had no intention of adding another broken family to the statistics in sociology class.

The problem was that half the people you met didn't want to know or be known, and a good percentage of those who did want to know ended up being consumed by the need to take advantage of that knowledge, once it was theirs. He hoped Ruthie wouldn't turn out to be one of these; it was important. He was beginning to think that he was in love with her.

He watched her as they walked, smiling as she shyly averted her eyes. She was looking about with interest, obviously fascinated in a morbid sort of way, but scared too. He squeezed her hand again to reassure her. She looked a little like one of those actresses in a Night of the Living Dead movie, as if she expected every snap of a branch or rustle of leaves to usher skeletal fingers up through the ground to grasp at her ankles and trip her up.

He noticed each time she started or flinched, but he didn't laugh. There was a twinkle in his eye when he slowed his steps and pulled her closer, letting her know that he understood how she felt. She managed a smile in return. There wasn't much farther to go, and he wanted her to be happy about it all, not scared. It was their night, hers as well as his.

The foliage ahead was thick and menacing. The moonlight pierced it only in scattered shafts, forcing shadows to impossible lengths and ghastly shapes, punctuating the pitch-dark cores of the deeper shade.

Suddenly they stopped short, startled by a sound in the distance—engines? Nick's first thought was that Flash and Weasel were driving around somewhere behind them, but it sounded like a *lot* of cars, like an entire parking lot of cars had started up all at once. He glanced at Ruthie, who shared his confusion, and they listened carefully as the sounds grew louder, then fainter, and finally faded away.

"A funeral at midnight?" Nick muttered. He started pushing ahead again, a little more quickly, snapping off branches and trampling shrubs as he went. Something had just gone on, or was still going on, and he wanted to know just what the hell it was. The trip was fading to the wide-eyed aftermath of leftover speed that would carry him into the wee hours of the morning, and his mind felt fresh and clear.

Ruthie, eyes wide, was obviously in less of a hurry to bust in on whatever goings-on might be found in a darkened cemetery; but she plugged gamely along at his heels. Given the choice of staying behind to wait for him in the darkness, Nick supposed anything would have been preferable.

Nick plowed through the brush unerringly, heading for the altar. He ducked around hanging branches, skipped over roots and fallen limbs, leaving Ruthie slightly behind, then catching himself and waiting impatiently for her to catch up before continuing.

The moon had dimmed somewhat as it passed from the night sky into the gray, half-light of early morning; but there was still plenty left to illuminate the clearing. Nick stopped dead in his tracks as he caught his first sight of the altar.

"Shit," he breathed, holding up an arm to stop Ruthie from coming any closer. "Jesus fucking Christ!"

There was a woman tied to the altar in an obviously painful, spread-eagled position. Her hair flowed back and over the end of the stone table. Her face, contorted in a grimace that was half smile and half agony, was turned to the sky, as if in supplication.

Blood, dark and still dripping slowly from the stone, had puddled on the ground beneath her. A lot of blood. He turned, trying to shield Ruthie from the sight, knowing what the remnants of the LSD would do with *this* fucking nightmare; but he was too late. She'd already moved around to his side and was staring in silence, slowly shaking her head back and forth.

Her eyes grew suddenly wide, then dim and glazed with shock. Her throat constricted; her abdomen twitched, and Nick knew the scream was coming a moment before it began to rise. He leaped to her side, hand reaching to clamp off the sound, too late.

The scream erupted, echoing through the graveyard like the pealing of a church bell, or the wailing of a lost spirit, loud and accusing. Belatedly Nick clapped a hand firmly over Ruthie's mouth and pulled her quickly back into the shadows.

"Don't scream," he ordered, keeping his voice calm and level. He could see the beginnings of hysteria churning in her eyes, and there was no time for it. "We have to get back to the van. Something happened here, something bad. We have to get the others, and we have to be quiet. Whoever did this might not be gone."

That last bit caught her, if none of his other words sank home, and it yanked her back from the brink—barely. It helped, also, that he was holding her, he thought. He only wished there was time to think about that.

"Nick," she choked out, her voice a strained whisper that yearned to break back into a scream. "That woman, I know her."

"What are you talking about? Who is she?"

"Mrs. Steiner," she answered. "She works at the school. I...I think her name is Gretchen. She was always so nice, and she..."

Nick silenced her again, gripping her shoulders insistently and turning her back the way they'd come. There would be time to seek explanations later. Now there was only the van, Flash, Weasel, and safety.

All that existed in the next few moments was flashing ground, shadows, and barely dodged headstones as Nick led her as quickly and quietly as safety would allow, supporting her when she stumbled and whispering encouragement to her every few seconds. Though it had seemed to take forever to reach the clearing, it was not that far to the van; and soon the light grew brighter and the old mausoleum where Flash had parked came into sight. The others weren't there.

Nick hurried to the driver's side door and reached inside, giving a quick blast on the horn. This was a signal they'd developed on earlier "ghost hunts" to make each other aware of interesting "finds." He knew that it would only take moments for Flash and Weasel to arrive.

Opening the back of the van, he helped Ruthie inside, seated her on the plush shag carpet and leaned her back carefully against the rear wall. He held her there, kneeling in front of her, and let her lean against him. He could feel her trembling, could feel his shirt dampening with her tears as convulsive sobs racked her small frame. Then she pulled back slightly, looking up at him with red, pleading eyes.

"It was the trip, wasn't it? Wasn't it!" She was nearly babbling, "I mean, that couldn't have been a body, Mrs. Steiner, could it? She couldn't be dead, not here, not like that. Nick, what's *happening*?"

"I don't know," he said, eyes bright with a mixture of fear and intensity that threatened to frighten her again. He softened his expression when he saw her start to pull back, cursing himself for not paying attention to her fear. "I'm going to find out, though."

"Don't go." She said, reading the interest and fear and determination from his eyes in a glance. "What if they come back, or..."

"I'll be all right," he said, almost sharply, rising at the sound of approaching footsteps. "I just want to get a closer look, to know what the hell happened there. I'll take Flash; Weasel can stay with you. Make sure he keeps the motor running. We'll be back soon...I promise."

She would have pressed the issue, he could see it in her eyes, would have tried to stop him, to hold him close to her; but he was too quick. Before her eyes could capture him fully, he slipped back out through the door, spinning into a whirlwind of questions from Flash and Weasel, whose grins faded quickly when they caught their first sight of Ruthie, huddled up and sobbing in the back of the van.

Nick made his patented "cut" sign in the air, and they fell silent, waiting. After a pause, "What's up, Nick?" Flash asked. "She looks like she *really* saw a ghost."

Nick wasn't ready to try and tell them what he'd seen. "Not yet," he said. "Weasel, stay here with Ruthie, okay? And get the engine running; we may be getting out of here fast." Glancing over at Flash, he smiled grimly. "You and me, buddy, the altar. I'll fill you in when we get there."

They took off in silence, but it was obviously not an easy thing for Flash to pull off. Nick knew he was acting strange, didn't even know why he felt he shouldn't say anything; but somehow he knew it would be better if Flash just *saw* what he'd seen. Nick very seldom tried to take charge, though he was the recognized leader of their little group; and he knew that despite his curiosity, Flash would know it was serious enough to listen. The two of them had been best friends since the sixth grade; they understood one another pretty well.

They covered the ground much more rapidly this time. Without Ruthie's hesitance and with the memory of what awaited them still fresh in Nick's mind, they were able to slip through the shadows like wraiths. Nick was outwardly calm. That was what he'd wanted Ruthie to see, and now he wanted the same from Flash. Somehow the idea that others needed him to hold himself together helped, gave him a more solid purpose.

His mind was anything but calm though. His heart was beating far too rapidly for comfort, accelerated by fear and even further by the ragged remnants of the LSD; and his thoughts were keeping pace, jumbled and confused. It was one thing to dream about bursting onto the scene of a satanic ritual, casting aside high priests as he went and saving the virgin beauty from being sacrificed; it was quite another to actually step through the trees in a cemetery and find the grim reality of those dreams facing you.

His stomach was queasy with the memory of the blood, and the eerie, half-grinning countenance of the woman's death.

Somehow that expression was wrong: it was the most desperately *wrong* thing he'd ever seen. It didn't fit any concept of death as he understood it; it didn't even fit into the pattern of his world.

They approached the clearing and Nick reached a hand out to slow Flash's advance, and shot his friend a warning look. There was no way of knowing who might have heard Ruthie's scream, or where they might be now. He was even less certain of what they would find when they arrived. His eyes must have conveyed some of his fear to his friend, because he slowed as well, his movements becoming careful and nervous.

They slipped up to the edge of the line of trees circling the clearing, parting branches to get a better view of the altar. Nick had prepared himself for the shock, despite having already seen the body; but he was *not* prepared for what he saw now. The altar stood, dark and bare, shadows playing around and across it in laughing, mocking dances of darkness. Empty.

He gaped, spinning rapidly about to meet his friend's expectant gaze. Flash's eyes grew wide for a second, then skeptical, as he swept them back over the altar, the clearing, and to Nick again.

"Are you putting me on, man?" he asked finally. "I mean, were you two out here doing some heavy hallucinating, or what? I don't see anything."

Stumbling into the clearing without answering, Nick walked slowly across to the stone table. It looked just as it always had before, no body, no vacant, staring eyes or dangling hair, only stone, cold and empty. There wasn't even any fresh blood marring the surface; it was brown and stained and dirty, like the rest of the stone, except for a few clear, white bits showing through that caught the moon's dying light in a white, ethereal glow.

He reached out and touched it, doubt creeping slowly into his own mind, but doubt that left few options but insanity. No way could he and Ruthie have been seeing the same damned thing if it was the drug. The body had to have been there. He bent to inspect a shiny object on the ground, retrieving it and holding it up to the light where they could both see it better.

It was a small pin, a cross, surrounded by an odd design he

didn't recognize. As he examined it, he noticed a sticky wetness on his fingers. Still not speaking, he turned and held his hand, with the pin in it, to Flash.

His friend looked at him in momentary confusion, then reached out and touched the sticky liquid, holding it to his nose. In one movement he registered what it was and spun wildly, checking the clearing to be certain they were alone. Nick put a hand on his shoulder to quiet him, and gestured once more toward the line of trees. Once they were out of sight, he hurriedly and quietly told Flash what had happened, why he'd dragged him back to the clearing.

"If this is true, man," and Flash's eyes left no doubt that he now believed it, "we may be in serious shit! We'd better get the fuck out of here."

In the distance, they heard a single engine start; and that was all it took. They broke and ran, ran for the van and their friends, for sanity.

As they spun away from the clearing, a small, shiny object worked its way from Nick's jeans pocket, falling to the ground unnoticed in a glittering arc. It was a small pocketknife, a souvenir, and emblazoned across the face of it was a single word. *MAELSTROM.*

They reached the van in record time. Flash pushed Weasel almost forcibly from behind the wheel and Nick dove into the back, slamming the door behind him. He gathered Ruthie into his arms as Flash hit the gas, lurched backward in a skidding spin and pointed the van at the gate. They exited Shady Grove in a cloud of dust and flying gravel, headed as rapidly as was safe, and a bit faster, toward the main road.

They were five miles from home before anyone spoke, and when it happened, nobody answered. The sound died. In grim, frightened silence, they drove on. Nick and Flash were deep in thought, Ruthie in helpless fear. Weasel fixed each of them at different times with his questioning stares, but he never got his answers. It would wait for the daylight.

The last trails of drug-induced euphoria were nearly gone, and sleep was next. Sleep was the cure, at least temporarily, for madness. Nick hoped, fervently, that his father would have gone to work before he arrived. A confrontation at home was the last thing his frazzled nerves needed. He hugged Ruthie a bit closer and leaned back, watching the play of the streetlights on the ceiling of the van and trying not to think.

CHAPTER FOUR

Jeanette Leatherman bit her lip and held her comments as her son stumbled through the door, wide-eyed and haggard, and mumbled his greetings and goodnight in a single spurt of hasty, nervous words. Without even waiting for her response, he headed immediately for his room.

Thankfully Ed had gone on to work, dark promises of beating sense into his long-haired freak of a son floating behind him like the first warning clouds at the birth of a brewing storm. Jeanette knew from long years of experience how Nick would take such an attempt at "setting him straight." His eyes would grow dark and smoky; his chin would take on that familiar line of sullen tension, and he would bear the punishment in silence.

She knew that silence and feared it, not for herself, but for Nick and for Ed. The boy's hatred was tightly bound behind that silent anger, but even the tightest of bindings had its limits. For probably the millionth time, she wondered why it had to be that way.

When she'd met Ed, he'd seemed so perfect. He'd been protective, and calm, fun to be with. Now she had to really force her mind to remember that man at all. He had gone, and she had no idea when or where.

As she heard Nick's door slam behind him, his steps echoed by those of his dog, a huge black Doberman he'd named Lizzy, Jeanette sighed and went to the kitchen for coffee and a cigarette. She knew the Ed she'd married had dropped off for an extended stay in one of the thousand whiskey bottles he'd visited over the past few years, an extended stay that had likely lost him forever.

Now she was afraid that it was on the verge of costing her her son, as well. Nick would barely talk to her when Ed was around, and to Ed he said nothing at all unless spoken to. When Ed was gone, Nick let loose tirades, floods of bottled emotion that frightened her almost as much as Ed's violence. There was an accusing tone to Nick's voice when he was calm, a sense of betrayal in the depths of his eyes that rose to the surface whenever they locked with her own. She had often thought that, if she were not around, the two of them would have killed one another by now.

Loud music, muffled by the plaster walls, erupted from Nick's room. She knew that, in some warped way, the music was meant to try and help him sleep. She knew about the drugs, though not which ones, or how much he did; and she knew that sometimes they made it hard, or even impossible, for him to rest. Ed's alcohol to Nick's drugs. Was it all her fault?

Nearly in tears, she walked along the hall to her own room. She needed a shoulder to cry on, but it looked as though, once again, her pillow would have to do.

A whimpering and scratching sound caught her ear as she passed her son's door, barely audible above the raucous strains of what she knew through repetitive exposure was an album by a group called *Maelstrom*.

"Nick?" she called. "Nick, are you asleep?" There was no answer, but the whining became more insistent, punctuated by a sharp bark. Jeanette opened the door a crack and a wet black nose popped through, followed by a large paw that pulled the crack wider.

Lizzy slipped from the room and sat, watching Jeanette with deep, sorrowful eyes. The music was nearly unbearable in volume, and Nick was lying face down on his pillow, dead to the world. Slipping quietly to the stereo, she turned it about halfway down. When she saw that he didn't move, she left, closing the door softly behind her and continuing on down the hall to her own room.

Glad to be free of the painfully loud noise, Lizzy trotted along at her heels. When Jeanette plopped down wearily across the bed, eyes moistening with the beginnings of the tears she had been fighting so hard to prevent, tears of confusion and futile, undirected anger, a wet nose pushed itself up under her arm. Lifting it with a flip of her head, the dog wormed her way underneath until she was close enough to lick at Jeanette's face, wiping away the tears.

Rolling over, she almost managed to lose the tears in hyster-ical laughter. Somehow sensing that the moment had improved, Lizzy leaped to the bed at her side, dropped heavily into a lump of fur and placed her head softly between Jeanette's breasts, where she could look up at her.

The sight of those concerned, loving eyes staring at her was all that it took.

"Stupid dog," she said, hugging its neck and laughing. "I have reasons to cry, okay? Just leave me alone."

Lizzy showed no sign of compliance, shuffling a bit closer and attempting to lick her face again. Closing her eyes and hug-ging the soft furry body tightly, Jeanette allowed herself to drift off. There would be an answer, somewhere. There would have to be. Whatever it took, whatever the cost, she knew that it was going to be up to her to find it.

In seeming agreement, the Doberman also slept, one paw lifting to rest protectively across Jeanette's waist. When she woke, she thought drowsily, she would have to figure out what to do. It had just been going on for too long.

CHAPTER FIVE

The day was starting out to be a hot one, a real scorcher. It was also threatening to be damned long, and a surefire bet for a headache. Straker swept the area with an intensity belied by the casual slump of his shoulders and the cigarette that dangled lazily from his lip. He was concentrating, working—it was something he was good at.

Most people passed over Ken Straker in a crowd without noticing the brightness in the recesses of his eyes. They were deep, thoughtful eyes, at first glance friendly and lazy, that could gleam with a nearly predatory glow when he was actually onto something, following a lead. Most of those same people would be shocked if presented with his record, as well. It was impressive.

At the moment, Inspector Straker was not impressed with either himself or his record, not to mention the investigation at hand. He'd already spent three hours in the sun, the bluecoats another before that, all increasingly hot hours, and all equally void of any progress. At that moment they had nothing more to show for their time than some splotches of blood, a few bits of trampled ground, the imprint of a size nine Nike sneaker, and air. Mostly air.

He began what was probably his twentieth circle about the stone table that hour alone, lost in thought. This time, on a whim, he moved a few steps toward the perimeter of the clearing, letting his eyes wander in and out among the trees and the midday shadows.

It was funny how *clear* the area was. It didn't really look as though someone had come through with a rake or a lawn-mower, not recently. It had the feel of years upon it, the mark of age. It might have been this way for years, centuries even, given the names and dates on some of the headstones; and the trash piles along some of the trails in the surrounding woods spanned several generations of rowdy evenings and secret meetings of the normal sort, beer cans—rubbers. *Jesus,* he thought, *even I wouldn't have had sex in a fucking graveyard.*

There was no such refuse here, no scrawled graffiti on the stone, no cans or bottles. Somehow, though it had the mark of the perfect party zone, this place had stood, virtually untouched as the years washed over it.

He wondered, and not for the first time that day, how they could possibly have never found this place before. There had been more raids than he could remember on out-of-control parties here among the tombstones, even a couple of incidents of teenagers digging up old graves for a prank. Some prank. No mention had ever been made of secret altars or hidden glades though. It was strange.

Heaving a sigh of resignation that boiled in his gut like smoldering flames, threatening severe indigestion to keep his now pounding headache company, he started back through the trees toward the entrance to the cemetery.

He watched everything as he went. Seldom was there a moment when he was able to refrain from recording a situation in detail. This was as likely a route for a departing psycho as any, he supposed. Assuming it had begun with a car or truck of some sort for transportation, it would have been easiest to park among the graves and head in toward the altar from there. His eyes picked up the sparkle of the knife before he'd taken two steps.

"Well," he muttered, "what have we here?"

Reaching into the pocket of his jacket, he pulled out a small plastic evidence bag and a pair of tweezers. He lifted the knife carefully, deposited it in the bag and held it up to the light.

There was no sign of rust; the blade's owner had been there recently, no more than two days before he guessed. The inscription, *Maelstrom,* seemed to indicate a youngster, probably male. Even in the craziness of the modern music scene, women—girls—didn't usually carry knives.

He tucked the bag back into the folds of his jacket and continued on. He found several places where feet had scraped the ground, a few broken twigs and branches, but nothing definite, nothing he could use. He moved out of the older section and wandered back and forth across the newer graves, still searching. Nothing.

Near one of the larger mausoleums he found a short skid mark in the gravel of the drive. A maintenance vehicle could have left it as easily as anything else.

"Damn," he muttered, heading for the front gate where his own unmarked sedan was parked. Here he was, sweating his ass off, wandering around a graveyard with nothing more to go on than a kid's knife, a brutal ritual murder, and questions.

If it hadn't been for an anonymous tip, they wouldn't have even found the damned altar, if it *was* an altar. The body had been found that morning down at Sunrise Beach, buried to the neck in white sand and covered in feeding crabs.

There had been the damndest grin on the woman's face. Straker could still see it as clearly as if it were there in front of his face. It had been evil, almost demonic, and it was a damn sight different than any dead person's face he'd ever seen. That would include a lot of faces…too many.

The initial report from the Medical Examiner's office showed traces of several narcotic substances in the woman's blood, what little there was left. There were signs of repeated sexual abuse, and the one knife wound, the official "cause of death," a single puncture, straight through the heart. The body was nearly white, bloodless, more like a thing long dead than a freshly slain, beautiful young woman.

The facts were committed to the files in Straker's mind, tucked away to put into place like a complex puzzle when he had enough pieces in hand. He wasn't there yet. He wasn't even close. He kept coming back to her face, the smile. It was that smile, he knew, that would stick with him. What in God's creation could they have done to make her smile in the face of death, and why was there no pleasure, or laughter, in the expression?

In earlier years, it might have made him shudder to think about it. Instead, he burped. The indigestion he'd feared earlier had become a churning reality, and he knew that lunch was now out of the question. *Damn,* he thought again, *damn.*

"See what you can do with this," Straker told the young lab tech, handing over the knife in its plastic, protective baggie. "I'll be getting some coffee."

"I'll get right on it, Inspector," the boy grinned back at him. "If there's anything here to find, I'll find it. Pretty slim chance, I'd say, though. You really think the guy who did this was carrying this?"

"I don't know what the hell I think," Straker said, turning away. "Just give it your best shot." As he moved down the hall he reflected on how much things in the station had changed over the years.

That tech, for instance, Bates was his name. Straker remembered hauling him in for juvenile crimes more than once, what seemed only a few short years before, and here the kid was, college degree in hand, working at his side. It was a hell of a world.

He knew the last thing his stomach needed at that moment was an infusion of acidic station house coffee, but he was going to have it anyway, indigestion be damned. He dropped by the front desk and picked up his messages, then moved on down the hall to the small coffee lounge at the end.

There was a beat up Mr. Coffee in his office, but he wanted company, a set of ears to bounce the hopeless jumble of bullshit he'd compiled so far off of, in the hope of gleaning some clue, something he'd overlooked. Sometimes, just the act of talking about a case would straighten it out in his mind.

He set the pile of assorted memos, mail, and phone messages that had accumulated while he was out of the office on one of the small round tables, and went across to the coffee urn to fill his cup. It was a San Valencez Dragons cup, the local college team. Straker had played linebacker for them, even showed promise of going pro, till his ankle gave out. The cup had seen a lot of years and too few washings. Nobody but Straker would even touch it.

There was nobody else in the room. Probably, he mused, they were all still out enjoying the lunch his grumbling stomach had denied him. Not everyone got the chance to have their appetite surgically removed by a psycho.

He sat in front of the papers and began sorting through them absently. There were several "call me, we'll do lunch" type memos from various people wanting something, a notice of an upcoming bachelor party, and at the bottom, a phone message sheet with the Captain's name on it, scratched out, and his own written in its place in bold, red letters. It was a request for an interview on the murder from a local reporter, a Ms. Pamela Green.

"Damn," he muttered. He hadn't released anything on this, not yet. Hell, he hadn't even had time to sort out what he had, let alone prepare a press release. In fact, his orders had been to keep this as quiet as possible, no reports of any activity beyond the ordinary.

How had she known? She even had his by-God name, and he'd only been assigned to the case that morning. "Damn," he repeated.

He pushed the rest of the papers and messages aside and sat back, his brow furrowed by a darkening scowl. He sipped the coffee slowly and tried to relax. He let it all tumble about in his head, hoping a few of the pieces would fall into place. One thing was certain, if nothing else: he had to head off this reporter quick. The case was grisly and frightening, exactly the kind of sensationalist crap he didn't want tossed to the press before he had something to go on.

His experience told him that, if it were indeed a psycho they were dealing with, publicity would only feed the sick forces that motivated him. There seemed to be a kind of "Hey, Ma, look at me," thing with these guys, and he didn't want to egg the killer on to new crimes.

Besides, he needed to be a bit more certain what the facts of the case actually were before he proceeded. It might be a psycho; it might be a *bunch* of psychos. It might be a bum. Newspapers, with their instant decisions and caustic commentary, could foul up an investigation faster than almost anything else he could think of. It wasn't going to happen to this one.

He rose from his seat, resignation creasing his already haggard face, and headed back to his office. The memo flapped in his grip like an annoying insect, increasing his ire with each step. His stomach had degraded from normal indigestion to a churning mass of spiked worms.

Yep, he told himself, *this day was going to be as fucked up as a football bat, no doubt at all.* He started his Mr. Coffee and sat in his thickly padded leather chair to stare at the telephone. He knew he couldn't put this off any longer, but he'd be damned if he was going to hurry.

"Herald Star," a friendly voice piped up at his second ring, "Janet speaking. How may I direct your call?"

"Pamela Green, please," he sighed. "This is Inspector Ken Straker; she's expecting my call."

"One moment, please."

As he listened to the disconnected whirring of switches making contact and lines buzzing as he was shifted from one set of lines to another, he wondered about operators. Did they have a damned school where they worked on developing those cutesy, bright-as-a-bell fucking plastic voices, or did they only take those who were naturally too cheerful for such jobs?

This time the answer came on the fourth ring. "Pamela Green, may I help you?" The voice was deep and rich, a speaker's voice. Straker immediately liked the sound of it, despite his irritation.

"Inspector Ken Straker here," he said. "I have a memo requesting an interview?"

"Yes!" Her exuberance was obvious in the tonal change of her voice, and he was irritated all over again. "I'd hoped you'd agree to talk to me. When can we meet? Have you any leads?"

God, Straker almost groaned at the sudden lurch in his intestines. "Miss Green, it is Miss, isn't it? I hope you'll understand. I've only been on this case for half of one day, and already I've seen a beautiful young woman murdered, walked around in a graveyard in ninety-degree heat, and missed my lunch.

"I have nothing concrete, and if I did, I certainly wouldn't be calling up to prematurely spread it about in the evening Herald.

There are killers loose in our town. I intend to catch him, them, or whatever, lock them up, and throw the key far, far away. When I have done so, you will be first civilian I notify."

This mild tirade met momentary silence. He almost smiled as he imagined her face. He had never met Pamela Green, never even seen a picture of her; but he thought she probably fit his mental image of a woman reporter pretty closely. Thin, bossy, hair probably tied back so tightly that she wore a permanent scowl from the pain. He hoped she wouldn't take it too hard, but he had a lot to do.

"I see," she finally answered, much more calmly than he'd expected. "Well, Inspector, I admire your dedication; I also share your sentiments. I guess that perhaps I should have made my reasons for calling a bit clearer from the start. It must have seemed a bit strange to you that I knew so much so soon? I mean, I'm a reporter, but there are limits, even for us. Don't you wonder how I know what I do?"

Knowing that his own answer would not stop her from telling him, and a little curious besides, he remained silent. She went on.

"Gretchen Steiner, the woman you saw murdered, was my best friend, Inspector. I was the one who let your detectives in this morning to search through her things in the apartment.

"When she wouldn't answer her door last night, I thought that something might be wrong. Her car and her bicycle were both out front; that alone was strange enough to make me worry. I figured at the time that she must be out on a date, though it was odd that she wouldn't have mentioned it ahead of time, or just out for a walk. This morning she didn't answer again. I'm her ride to work.

"She gave me a key to her apartment last year when I watched her cats for her. I went in, just to see if she'd overslept, or if she was too sick to get out of bed. The front room, as you probably know by now, was a shambles. Her cats, she had three and loved them like children, started meowing and raising hell as soon as I came inside. They hadn't been fed. That was when I called the police.

"I don't believe that your officers would have answered my

questions, even if I'd asked them, but I overheard two of them as they left. They were talking about a phone call that had tipped off an investigation on some sort of ritual murder. I want to know if there's a connection, Inspector. This isn't for the paper, yet, it's for me. If I wanted a story, I had enough to put it in this morning's edition."

It was Straker's turn to be silent. This was not what he'd expected, and it also seemed likely to prove the biggest break to come his way since he'd started that morning. He hadn't paid that much attention to the name of the person calling in the report—he'd assumed it was just a passerby. She hadn't told the officer at the desk that she was a close friend, only that she thought something might be wrong. When they'd discovered the body and made the connection, her name must have gotten lost in the shuffle.

"I'll tell you what, Miss Green…"

"Pamela," she interjected, "please."

"Pamela, then. If I can get your word not to release anything before I give the go-ahead, I'll keep you up on what I know. I've lost friends myself. I'll want to question you, as well. You seem to know more about our victim than even her employers could provide, and, being a reporter, I'd guess you pay more attention to things than most folks. Maybe you've noticed something you aren't aware of.

"You think about your friend, all right? You think about anything odd she might have done lately, anyone she might have been seeing, anything at all different from the norm. Even the smallest thing might be important. And, Pamela?"

"Yes?"

"Thank you. A story now could have ruined my investigation, such as it is. I appreciate your cooperation. We'll get him, you can count on it."

"I hope so, Inspector," she was obviously fighting hard now to control the tremor in her voice, "I really do."

The click of her receiver echoed for a long time in his ears as Straker slowly placed his own phone on the hook. His stomach had calmed some, and he was beginning to reconsider lunch. Rising, he flipped off the coffee without touching a drop, and walked slowly back into the hall. Pastrami was sounding good. He wondered what the hell could happen next.

CHAPTER SIX

The failing rays of the evening sun washed brilliantly over the pure white stone of the Church of New Light. With its turreted, arching doorways and freshly cleaned windows of multicolored stained glass, the church was an imposing structure by any standards.

The windows in particular were special, each pattern of colors laid out in a complex, intricate design that went beyond even the panoramic scenes they depicted. The angles were set so that, when various stages of sun and moonlight struck the glass, further wonders of effect and beauty were created among the various statues and stonework that adorned the interior of the building.

Above and behind the polished mahogany pulpit, imposing and magnificent in its tragic splendor, hung a huge bas-relief of Christ, eyes set at an all-encompassing angle, and features locked into an anguished but beneficent grimace of all-forgiving love. At sunset, when the fading rays reached the proper angle, they refracted through the lens-like surfaces of the red panes of stained glass in the rear wall of the church. This sent beams of crimson light flashing the length of the building to stain the carefully molded and polished surfaces of the statue a glowing, blood red.

As the sun continued to fall, lowering to its nightly meeting with the earth, the "blood" appeared to trickle down, winding its way among the contours of the statue until it reached the baptismal pool below. Here there were crystals set into the stone of the pool, which caught the reflected light and spread it through the water of the pool. At times like this, it appeared that the water, symbolic of the blood of the son of God, had transformed from holy water to actual blood, flowing down into the pool to cleanse the sins from those troubled or lost souls who found themselves in need.

It was a beautiful work, created by the local sensation, D'Alberto, and it had appeared in some of the finest artistic and architectural journals in the nation. The elders of the church, and the City Council of Lavender, California, were very pleased with it.

Horace Goldbough, minister and evangelist, founding father of the Church of New Light, dedicated the work himself. He built his following from a small parish to a thriving evangelical phenomenon in only a few short years. He did it through faith, largely in himself, through the charismatic smile and deep gray eyes the Lord had given him, and through a burning desire to exalt himself above all others—to *be* someone.

Every Sunday he appeared before the massed souls of his "flock," putting on one hell of a good show of being a humble servant of the Lord. Behind the mask of his half-amused, half-compassionate smile, an expression that invariably drew attention to his eyes, a full-blown, egomaniacal leer usually lurked.

He was as hooked as those who followed him, as caught up in the act as his audience. It was the immediate rush of power, the control that accompanied a fiery sermon or a triumphant baptismal address, that drew him back again and again, like the call of a truly addictive drug. Morality had never been a question. His job was a simple matter of supply and demand, like any commodity on any market of the world. Horace Goldbough was in demand, and he was fond of gloating over this fact at every opportunity.

At the present moment, however, seated at the edge of the baptismal pool and watching the trickling red light show wind its way in crimson streams about the savior's ankles, he was pondering other things than his control over the "sheep" of his congregation. He was feeling an unfamiliar twinge of nervous fear, though the anxiety had a way of feeding his exhilaration, and he was uncertain how to deal with it. The fact was that there was absolutely no action he could take that would in any way work toward allaying his fears.

Brenda would come around soon. She never worried. Ever. In the ten years they'd been associated with one another, he couldn't recall a single moment in which she had been anything less than in complete control.

That was one of the things that made him nervous. Brenda was beginning to be a problem. Horace didn't like to be controlled, and he didn't like to be manipulated either. As his plans moved toward their culmination, his own position became increasingly more precipitous, his confidence and patience more strained.

He knew that he would have to deal with her soon. Somehow. The only problem was that when he looked deep into those green, bottomless eyes, he sensed that she knew what he planned, even that she looked forward to it. Damn the woman! She was like a snake, coiled and deadly, and he was getting very tired of cowering like a rat, wondering when the hell she was going to strike.

The huge oaken doors behind him cracked open with a loud, tortuous squeal. There was a whisper of silk rustling as she slipped through and closed it behind her. Horace remained as he was, motionless, his eyes lost in the bloodred depths of the pool in front of him.

Although he had chosen not to turn, not to look at her, his mind filled in the blanks with practiced ease. She would be standing there, her arms clasped over her breasts. Her gown would be green. She always wore green. She told him that it was for the effect it brought out in her eyes and her hair, an effect that she was very adept at taking advantage of; but he sensed it was more, another part of her mystery.

Horace didn't look because the sight of her, full-figured and exotic with the green silk clinging provocatively to the many curves she placed in the path of its downward swoop to the floor, was enough to give her the immediate upper hand in any conversation. He was not in the mood to be put at a disadvantage, as much as he might wish—no, *hunger*—for the sight of her.

"You are quiet," she observed. He sensed her gaze dancing over his back, her mind questing for his thoughts. "Are you having misgivings, love?" The scent of jasmine leaked through his defenses, and he felt her delicate fingers as she walked them slowly across his shoulder. As she slid sinuously down his side, pressing tightly against him and coming to rest on the stone beside him, his thoughts grew murky. Dazed, he heaved a heavy sigh and turned, sacrificing himself to her eyes.

"No misgivings," he lied easily, "just a small case of the nerves. Things are a bit shaky right at the moment, wouldn't you say? So much rides on everything we do."

"Shaky?" She asked, eyes distant and thoughtful. "I would hope that the shaking is a prelude to an explosion, love. I have worked—*we*—have worked, for a very, very long time toward this moment. Here," she reached out and gripped his shoulders, her grip surprisingly strong, and began to massage them, kneading the pressure from his muscles, releasing the knotted tension like broken strands of sprung steel, "let me help to ease your mind. We've been through a lot, you and I; and yet still, even now, we must wait."

"Perhaps," he managed without allowing any catch in his voice to betray him, or his need, "we might better spend our waiting time elsewhere? This is no place—or time—for one of my congregation to walk in and find me here, with you. It is not yet time for that."

"I hoped you might want to—talk." She smiled, a quaver in her own voice betraying the tension she would not admit to. He marveled as he realized that she was as nervous as he, and as much in need of release. The intensity of her emotion was incredible, intoxicating.

"I brought wine," she added. "Come, let us celebrate, you and I."

He rose without chancing another word, holding out his arm to help her rise and slipping it as casually around her shoulder as his raging hormones would allow, and leading her away from the pool and toward the back of the building. His Volvo was parked out back, a tan sedan, very conservative, with personalized license plates that read "Nu Light." He would have preferred a Ferrari, but the show must go on.

Under only the slight pressure of their half-embrace, he felt

Brenda tremble. The tremor reverberated through his nervous system, caroming from each of the vertebrae in his spine to lodge in his groin. Simultaneously he tightened his grip on her shoulders and quickened his steps.

At the door he stopped her with a gesture. Her eyes, the depths of which he was very familiar with, were calm as usual on the surface; but beneath he sensed a need, very nearly a helplessness that was new—new and incredibly erotic.

He quickly scanned the area surrounding the parking lot and the street beyond. Even under this much pressure, he had enough sense not to be seen sneaking out the back of the church with a woman. Seeing no one, he grabbed her arm in a painfully tight grip and shoved her roughly toward the car. She didn't protest, as he had known she would not. Too much depended on complete secrecy, at least for the moment.

Besides, at moments like these, the moments he dreamed of alone in the dark hours of the night, the moments that drove him against his own common sense at times to do her bidding, even when his very sanity screamed for him to end it, to run away and never turn back, the precious moments where he was in control of her, not the opposite, these were worth any price. Damn her, she was an opiate, addictive and maddening. It was going to be one hell of a long, hot drive.

Looming behind them, quiet and solemn, the church glistened in the last rays of the evening sun. Through the windows, the stone eyes of Jesus stared out, trailing after them, boring their own brand of pain and guilt through windows, shoulders, bone and blood, clawing at his heart. He brushed the image aside and soothed the pain it left behind with a glance at Brenda, a short dip into her eyes.

It was enough. All thoughts of fear, or the church, or anything but her disappeared in that single flash. He drove quickly, letting the glimpse of her strobe like a video echo in his mind, eating its way through him like molten lead.

The drive, as it turned out, was more interminable than just long. He wound them at a completely mindless pace down the twisting length of his private drive, punching the button that would raise the garage door and skidding to a halt inside. As they rose together, leaving the cushioned comfort of the Volvo's plush interior to melt together in the lightless room beyond, surrounded by the mingled fumes of gasoline, oil, and jasmine, the wait and its pain dwindled and erased itself from reality as if it had never been.

Fumbling the key from his pocket, he managed to slip it into the lock and open the door, dragging her inside. As the door slammed shut behind them, he spun her into his arms and lifted her without a word, carrying her through the kitchen, down a lushly carpeted hall, and into his bedroom.

Her skin was hot, burning like fire through the sheer silk; and her hands were all over him, probing, urging. She didn't speak, but the low moans that escaped her with each step he took, and the wild abandon of her eyes communicated her need eloquently.

He stopped by the bed, held her squirming body close and stared deeply into her eyes, drinking in the elixir of passion and helplessness in their depths. Smiling, he threw her to the bed and watched, fascinated, as she arched, even in flight, pushing her body toward his touch.

He reached for her, gripped the shoulder straps of her gown and ripped downward, shredding the material with strength born of sheer, animal urgency. He dragged it from her with a growl and tossed it aside. She cried out, a whimper, but not of protest.

Dragging himself from the bed with an effort, his entire frame trembling, Horace moved to the dresser along the far wall of the room. He was fighting to savor the few moments, *precious* moments, of control. Clutching at the handle of his top drawer, he yanked it open, sweat slicking his fingers until they ripped painfully on ornate designs carved into the dresser's wood surface. There was a red-tinge, a film of milky, hazy crimson, sliding across his vision, warping his sight.

In the open drawer, a matched set of rough leather straps lay on top of the purple waves of his pastoral gown: an obscene reminder of the twin paths of his life—of his mind. He grabbed them and spun to where the object of his perversity lay, pressing her hands to her own body and twisting about on the sheets of his bed.

Her hands wove intricate trails of passion from her breasts to her thighs; her eyes were wild—beyond coherent thought—animal.

Growling deep in his throat, he leaped onto the bed at her side, grabbing first one ankle, then the other, and binding them securely to the foot of the bed with the leather straps. She seemed not even to notice the restraints, beckoning with hands and lips and eyes, licking herself with the pink wetness of her tongue, desperately reaching out to drag him near. Somehow he resisted long enough to tie her arms in place with the remaining straps, before he complied.

The dim light flickered across the rippling surface of her well-muscled torso, glittering like rows of tiny jewels. Her skin radiated a heat that threatened to melt her to him, and her eyes, those eyes he loved and feared, rolled almost completely up into themselves, momentarily powerless.

He smiled through the haze, reaching for her hair and took it in a cruel grip. He lifted her roughly. She twisted and raised her body to meet his groping, probing hand, pressing herself against every available inch of his skin.

For now, she was his. He was in control. For the moment, and for the night, it was all that mattered. Outside, the moon was rising to its throne. Later, much later, her screams were loud, long, and very, very satisfying.

CHAPTER SEVEN

Straker was not pleased. His coffee was almost cold, his stomach was churning, as usual, and the damned fingerprints, against all the odds, had been on the knife. He stared at the mountain of paperwork in front of him. The lab report was perched neatly atop it, but Straker didn't want to see any of it. He was remembering the first time he'd met the boy whose fingerprints were on that knife, Nick Leatherman, Ed Leatherman's son.

He'd had those prints on file for a couple of years now, ever since he'd had to bust the kid for possession of three joints and a six-pack. At that time, he'd made a judgment call, something he did often, especially in juvenile cases. He'd seen something in that boy's eyes, something way too adult for such a young man.

Their conversation during questioning had been a tense, frightened string of macho bullshit: a boy's foolish attempt to prove his manhood by rejecting authority in any form. Straker had played along, guiding the boy to a grudging truce by offering a man-to-man level of interaction that had finally seemed to be getting through. Now he had to wonder, faced with this new evidence, if the boy had heard a word he'd said.

There were no illusions in Straker's mind of turning young lives around with a few stern words and a couple of bits of sage advice—not in this world. He'd only been concerned, as he always was, that the boy understood the broader concept of what he was getting at. The idea was that a man had to take into consideration all consequences before making a life-forming decision—like smoking pot. In Straker's mind, dope was a bad decision, a losing bet.

He knew Nick had probably continued to party, even to do drugs; but he also thought that he'd seen something, maybe in the way the boy finally confessed everything, or the way he calmly waited for his punishment, that said that he knew that there were limits, and that he was aware of them. Straker had been certain that time would mature the boy, and that he wouldn't develop into a hard case.

Straker's career was built on a string of such glimpses, insights into the minds of others. He had very seldom found himself in a position such as this, where one of those insights might prove false. It wasn't a pleasant thought, but it was hard to refute the facts. The knife had been found very near to the scene of the murder, and it hadn't been there long.

Straker reached wearily for his phone, then stopped. He'd known Ed Leatherman for over nineteen years. He could predict the response to even a suspicion of trouble from the man's son, and he decided on the spot that it would be better and safer if he were to go in person—safer for everyone involved.

Heaving a heavy sigh that somehow managed to reignite the fire in his gut, he downed the last bitter gulp of cold coffee from his cup and rose. It was going to be a hell of a day.

He tucked the lab report into one pocket and a half-eaten pack of Tums in the other, and headed out to his car, still trying to bring a picture into focus where the Leatherman boy and a brutally butchered young woman were both featured, and still unable to manage it.

"Damn," he thought out loud, "Why do they play in graveyards? Whatever happened to the woods, or out back of the power plant? Damn."

When Nick awoke, his head was still fuzzy from the lingering effects of the previous night's chemicals, and disjointed visions left over from fitful dreams. Horrible visions. He knew, vaguely, that he needed to do something, that they would *all* have to do something, and soon; but it wasn't clear what that "something" might be.

His thoughts drifted to Ruthie, how she was taking it all, what she was thinking. It was then that the poster caught his eye: a full-length portrait of *Maelstrom* that hung on the wall above the cluttered surface of his desk. In that instant, it all flashed back to him; and he practically fell out of bed in his haste. He ran his hand back through the length of his hair in a totally inadequate attempt at untangling it.

He had to call the others, Flash, Weasel, Ruthie…somehow, someway, they had to straighten this mess out before it went any further. He snatched a fresh pair of jeans from where his mother had piled them on his dresser and slipped a faded black *Metallica* T-shirt over his head, then headed for the door.

Lizzy had heard him as soon as he left his bed, and dropped to the floor from where she was perched on his parent's bed. She trotted to the door to stare at him. He knew it was crazy, stupid, even, but when she looked at him like that he was certain he could detect human expressions. This one was disapproval.

"Sorry, girl," he muttered, turning toward the door. "No time to make up just now. I've got to get going."

"Nick?" His mother's voice floated tiredly out after him. He heard more than weariness in those tones: sadness? Pain?

"That you, Mom?" he stalled, hearing her soft footsteps approaching and noting the quizzical tilt of Lizzy's head.

"Yes," she said, coming into sight down the hallway, "you aren't going out again, are you? I was making supper. I… Nick, I never *see* you anymore."

His heart gave a familiar little twist. He read the warring emotions behind her guarded words with practiced ease. What was worse was that he knew she was right. It had been a long time, maybe too long, since they'd spoken closely or spent any private time together. Ed had seen to that, Ed, Seagram's Seven, and years.

He knew that she felt trapped, and he also knew, though he still wasn't quite ready to admit it, that none of it was really her fault. He could even acknowledge, if only to himself, that he was the one being a coward, abandoning her when she needed his support. He just couldn't stop himself.

"I can't stay, Mom, not now," he said softly. Forcing a grin to his lips that fooled neither of them, he went on, "Something came up last night; I have to go and find Flash and Ruthie."

Nick saw her eyes brighten almost imperceptibly when he mentioned Ruthie. He knew that she approved of Ruthie almost as much as she disapproved of Flash and Weasel.

"I'll be home soon, really." He tried to put his feelings behind the promise, to let her know how much he still cared beneath his veneer of disinterest and rebellion; but the effort didn't even scratch the surface of the wall that had come between them.

She only lowered her eyes, mumbled goodbye, and turned slowly back toward the empty kitchen. He might have gone after her then, might have tried to hug her as he had years before, let her cry on his shoulder; but the doorbell rang, and the moment was lost.

Instead, the ache of things lost was lodged firmly in his chest; and he turned away as well. He went to the door, pulled it open, and found himself staring into a set of deep, slate-colored eyes that he knew only too well.

"Hello Nick," Straker said, smiling thinly and without humor. "Can we talk?"

The anger, the rebellion that seemed so much a part of his life these days, began to rise, to flood through him; but he stopped it cold. Cop or no cop, this man had been straight with him. In a time when his life could have tipped either way, when there seemed like no one left he could turn to, this man had been there. Besides, none of the tough-kid routine had ever seemed to faze Straker. Only the truth had gotten through.

"Is something wrong?" he asked finally, "or are you here for a social call?"

Straker didn't comment. He handed Nick a piece of paper, some sort of evidence report, watching for reactions as the realization of what it was, what it could mean, flashed through Nick's mind.

My knife? Nick thought back rapidly. Shit, he hadn't even known it was gone. Reflexively, he reached for it, knowing that Straker wouldn't be there unless the pocket was empty. The curious, searching gleam in Straker's eyes made his blood chill and thicken.

"What do you want?" he asked at last, stepping slightly back from the door.

"Just to talk, for now," Straker replied. "Can I come in?"

Without waiting for an answer, he brushed past Nick and started down the hall toward the kitchen, where Nick's mother stood, watching him with an empty, hollow look in her eyes.

She knew Straker, and she knew where and why she had seen him last. More trouble was just a bit beyond the limit of what she was capable of handling just then. She stumbled back down the hall toward her room, slamming the door behind her as she went.

Lizzy tried to follow, almost getting her nose caught in the crunch of wood as the door slammed. After a couple of half-hearted, unanswered scratches at the door, she turned and trotted to the corner of the kitchen, plopping down heavily and lying her head across her front paws—watching.

Nick and Straker sat at the kitchen table across from one another. Nick's eyes were dull, and he kept shifting them down to gaze at the swirled patterns of the tile on the floor, or to the intricate webwork of cracks spreading down from the corner of the ceiling. Anything to avoid that gaze. Straker's expression was alert, but not accusing.

"I guess you know what I'm after, Nick," he began. "You, maybe some others, were in the Shady Grove Cemetery last night, or the night before. I want to know why, and I want to know what you did while you were out there."

"I don't know what you're talking about," Nick mumbled, knowing the lie was hopelessly inadequate, but working to buy some time. "That knife was stolen in school days ago. Why would I go to a graveyard, for Christ's sake?"

"I don't know," Straker continued, his eyes never blinking. "I also don't know how someone could steal your knife without smudging your fingerprints or adding any of their own. Maybe you'd better check your memory a little closer, son, because this all makes you look pretty guilty; and I'd like to think that you're not."

"Guilty?" Nick's brain finally flashed on the entirety of the situation, what he might be implicated in. His heart sank. "Guilty of what?"

"You don't know?" Straker bored deep with those eyes, and

Nick felt his bravado wavering. "You didn't by any chance see anything a little odd did you? A body? Some blood? A bunch of people who didn't belong? You know, Nick, back in those trees, at the altar?"

"I..." Nick clamped his jaw down tightly and firmly. No way was he getting baited into blurting out words he hadn't had time to consider. Not when it was this important. This was starting to look bad. "What altar?" he asked, voice level and emotionless.

"Well, the one we found your knife beside, of course," Straker went on calmly. "Maybe you're missing the seriousness of this, son. I can't do a thing to help you if you fight me. Right now, you're the only suspect we have, and the crime isn't trespassing in a graveyard, it's murder. Now are you going to tell me what the hell happened last night, or not?"

Nick didn't answer. His mind was whirling, and he knew that any attempt he made to describe the previous night's events, even leaving out the acid, would seem warped and disjointed. No way would Straker believe he was telling the truth. He might listen, that much Nick would give him; but the man had a job to do, and it was too much of a chance for Nick to take.

All he wanted at that moment was to go, to run away and keep running. The knowledge that all these thoughts and more must be plastered all over his face for a man like Straker to read, didn't help things any, either. Murder?

Straker was just about to speak again, to press harder, when the front door slammed loudly open and Ed Leatherman came walking in on them like a dark cloud, settling silence over the room as if a soundproof curtain had shut it off. Nick's last drop of blood froze in his veins.

"What are you doing here, Straker? You in trouble again, Nick? You'd better talk to me boy, better talk fast."

Straker rose, meeting Ed's hostile advance with a cool stare. "Just some routine questions, Ed, nothing to get riled about."

"Then get it on out of here." Ed, at least two inches taller and twenty pounds heavier than Straker, scowled at them both, then noticed the paper sitting on the table in front of Nick. He reached out quickly and grabbed it, reading slowly. His frown deepened.

"Shady Grove? That's the rich-folk planting ground out east of town, ain't it? On 13? What the hell would you be doing out there, Nick boy, finding out that those blue blood bastards die, just like the rest of us?

"What's the problem here, anyway, Straker, trespassing?"

Nick was really frightened now. Murder, jail, those were surreal images in his young mind, unknown creatures lurking in the haze at the back of his thoughts. His step-dad, now, he was real, very real; and Nick knew only too well what he could expect in reaction to the one word he expected Straker to speak next. Murder. He was priming his muscles for a lunge at the door when Straker answered.

"No charge, Ed. I told you, this is only a routine questioning. You know about the killing out there yet?"

"Killing? Ed's eyes lit up with a sudden spark that nearly unsettled Straker's experienced nerves. "What killing? Didn't see nothin' in the paper about no killing."

"A young woman," Straker said, lighting up a cigarette, "gym teacher from the local high school. They raped her, cut her up with a knife. It looks to be some sort of a ritual murder, real weirdos. We know the kids sometimes go there, to drink and party.

"Hell, Ed, I went out behind the old power plant when I was a kid for the same thing. Times change. It just happens that Nick here lost his knife at Shady Grove; I thought he might have noticed something, or someone, anything that didn't seem to belong in a graveyard. We're pretty well stumped on this one."

Nick relaxed visibly and sent a silent thanks to both God and Straker. Ed Leatherman was a man of two pleasures, alcohol and violence. Nick had been on the wrong end of that violence too many times.

"Yeah," Ed was almost grinning now, reminiscing. "I been to the power plant a few times myself. Used to go down by the gravel pit a lot too. Had a hell of a time down there, once or twice.

"Satan worshipers, huh?" he swung his gaze back to Straker as if just remembering he was there. "Damn. What next? You need any help, deputies, whatever, you come on around. I don't much like the idea of psychos roaming around my town, even out with the dead rich folks. You need me, you come runnin'."

"I'll do that," Straker said, heading down the hall toward the door. "You keep in touch, Nick," he called back. "We may still need to talk."

Ed watched, suspicious as always in the presence of anyone not directly under the pressure of his own thumb, or anyone in authority, until Straker was out the door and it had closed behind him. Feeling that the moment was still in the balance, Nick reached

for the refrigerator, pulled out a cold Budweiser, and popped the top. As Ed spun to the sound, Nick handed him the beer. His heart was pounding; what would happen next?

"Damned crazy town," Ed snapped, taking the beer. "You get you one, too, Nick. I think maybe it's time you and me had us a talk—straightened some things out. Seems like you've grown up a bit since we did that last."

Nick did as he was told, swallowing quickly and gratefully. Such times as this were rare. Ed had never pretended to like the idea of being a father. He liked even less being the father of a "long-haired, dope-smoking punk," and it was not often that he decided he had a moment to spare Nick for anything other than a screaming tirade or a beating.

There was no question of one thing; Nick hated the man, hated him actively nearly every waking moment of every day of his life. It made it harder that something inside him, buried deep, yearned for more times like this, no matter how great the rift between the two of them might be. It sprang from a deep-seated wish for normality, for acceptance and a life that seemed just out of reach, no matter how far he stretched his groping fingers.

When Ed said for him to get a beer, something had snapped into place, another form of control he supposed. It had made him feel closer to the man, a part of something. He had always wished it could be that way, for his mother's sake as much as his own.

He knew that she had met a different man, or perceived one, those long years ago when she married Ed. She'd seen a good man, or created one from her imagination and dreams, a man who would have been a good father. Ed had fooled her; now she fooled herself. Nick was on his own. That was just the way of it; nothing ever seemed to change.

Ed, (never Dad, not to Nick) headed for the back porch without looking back, taking a long pull off his beer. Nick followed, wondering what it would be about this time. He wanted just to leave, to be gone, to free himself from the burdens of maintaining his calm in the face of Ed's volatile temper.

The instilled control of years was too great to allow it. He followed obediently, grateful that he had the beer to occupy his lips and hands. It helped hide the trembling that shook his entire frame.

He slipped through the back screen door before it had a chance to snap closed, following Ed out onto the deck that overlooked their backyard. Ed turned as he reached the rail, watching Nick approach with the calm, deadly intensity of a snake watching food cross its path. Nick forced himself to appear calm, but he doubted that it did much to fool Ed.

"Me and you come from different worlds, boy." Ed began, taking another swallow and turning to look out over the yard.

Nick only nodded.

"Time was when I'd have said anyone with hair like yours and listenin' to that clanking, screaming bullshit you call music was a fuckin' queer. Fact is, at the time I'd've been right. Like I said, times change."

He stopped for a longer, contemplative sip of his beer, checking to see what kind of reaction his words were bringing out. Nick only returned the stare. Against his own will, he was curious now. What in the hell was this asshole getting at, anyhow?

"Seems that my way of looking at things might not be exactly right anymore." Ed spun all the way around and stared out over the yard. "See, when I was your age, I had me a black leather jacket and a crew cut, listened to Jerry Lee Lewis and Merle Haggard. My dad, he'd of bet his ass I was on my way to prison, or worse. Hated everything about me. He never understood; maybe I don't either."

"When I saw you in there with ol' Straker, it reminded me of some things. It reminded me of that other time, with the dope. I was ready to kick your ass that time, for sure. It reminded me of other things too, though. It reminded me that I was a punk kid once, been in trouble a time or two.

"I'm not saying I'm sorry for anything, Nick," he turned back to fix Nick with a stare that dared him to deny it. "Maybe it wouldn't matter by now, anyway. You've had a rough time in life so far, kid, and I've been a part of that.

"You just keep this in mind. I might not like you, might beat the piss out of you a few more times before I'm through, don't know. You ever really need me, though, after I'm done beating the dumbass out of you, I'll still be there. Get out of here now. I got me some thinking to do. Don't be gone all night, either; and stay out of that goddamned graveyard."

The words swam through Nick's head. Why, of all times, why now? Philosophy, for God's sake, from a drunken redneck. Too much. Too fucking much.

Nick took the easiest route and headed for the front door, nearly running by the time he reached it, and slammed out into the front yard. Ed had been right about one thing, there was nothing left to be said. Nothing that would change things. Nick knew that much was true. Most likely he'd come home a little late, find the man in a drunken rage, pissed at himself for what he would think of as a moment of weakness, and get his ass kicked. That was just the way it worked.

With his mind full of confusing thoughts, and the late-evening sunshine sending his shadow out to trail behind him like a black cape, he started out to find his friends. There was a queasy feeling in his stomach, the combined fear of his meeting with Straker and his confrontation with Ed. As he passed by the fence that circled his backyard, the popping top of another Budweiser punctuated his retreat. He began to run.

CHAPTER EIGHT

Brenda sat in silence, brushing the long black strands of her hair in long, even strokes. Her skin still tingled from the caress of the shower. The scent of jasmine permeated the air, emanating from the bath oil and the open bottle of perfume she'd left on the dresser beside her.

She loved flowers, their touch, and their scent. She'd adopted them as a trait, odd odors, incense; it was all a part of what she liked to think of as her mystique, the aura of "difference" with which she surrounded herself.

She knew how to use that mystique to control those around her, knew also that she was attractive, beautiful even, and how to twist that to her advantage. Men, especially, fell under her spell without any considerable effort on her part. Subtle shifts of her eyes, the casual tilt of her head, a slight movement that allowed the material of her dress to expose a fraction more of her thigh, she knew all this and more.

It wasn't enough, never had been; and she was well aware of this too. It was all too easy, too trivial. Her needs exceeded her grasping control; her appetites burned her with an intensity that threatened, at times, to consume her like a flame. She was uncertain whether she dreaded that, or yearned for it.

The brush slid easily through her hair, scratching lightly across her back. Horace was in the next room on the phone. She thought of him, and she smiled.

Horace Goldbough was the one person in the entire world she would claim any true affection for. He knew how to feed her fires, how to build them until they engulfed the world surrounding them with their searing heat. It was, of course, not enough. Horace could feed the fire, but he couldn't quench it. Perhaps, she thought again, as she had so many times before, he could help her to reach one who could. That was her prayer.

She heard the rustle of his robes as he rose from the phone and looked up, smiling at his reflection in the mirror above her as he entered the room. He was staring ahead, not at anything in particular, a satisfied smile adorning his lips. Something from the phone call he'd just finished? A lingering memory of her—of the past few hours? Both?

"It would appear," he commented dryly, "that our efforts have been received favorably. A diversion has been placed into our hands, a very adequate diversion. We were not alone in Shady Grove the other night. Our company may or may not have seen anything, but I believe I know just how to handle this."

"Tell me," she said, still brushing. He sat very close to her, on the edge of the dresser, well within the spell of her "presence," and began speaking. Her smile did not so much widen as deepen. Lights danced in her eyes and she brushed harder. Now and again she tilted her head to favor him with a glance of approval.

It was good to find that his sources were so widely scattered, that his influence was in no way inconsequential. He was a surprising man. Unbelievably, the fire began to wash through her again.

As if sensing this, he leaned closer, finishing the final details of what he had planned in a seductive whisper, lips pressed to her ear, his breath hot on her skin. The plan was perfect, devilish, and she knew that it must have been inspired by the power she sought. Perhaps it was even an omen.

Horace reached out a hand, brushed a stray lock of hair from the side of her throat; and she reached up, gripping his hand tightly. He returned the pressure of her grip and pulled her to her feet with a deceivingly gentle tug. The fire, moments earlier battled down to smoldering embers, rose to claim her, sweeping him along in its wake.

This time she melted into his arms, lost before she could begin to fight. Seconds, lucid fragments of the reality that receded so rapidly, told her that she must stop—break free. He was controlling her too easily, and that was the one thing that she feared.

Her needs, her appetites, were strong, stronger than her will, by far. She knew that she could not allow them to rule her, not yet. She couldn't turn over control of her leash to this man—that was for another. He was not the one.

None of these warning thoughts could cool the heat of her skin, or calm the whirling lights that confused her eyes and made her captive to sensation. He swept her into his strong arms and returned her to the bedroom, where he laid her upon the sheets with surprising gentleness and slid the clothing from his own body in a single, easy motion.

He lay beside her and leaned in to kiss her deeply. She moaned, wanting him inside her, trying to scoot up the bed and away, but he grabbed her by the hair and guided her, moving her to the rhythm of his own pleasure. She nearly sobbed in frustration, but she submitted.

In the molten lake of her passion, she floated, needing him, needing the release that could be provided only by his body. It could save her, save her from drowning, release her to reality for just a little while longer.

There was one who waited; in him she would drown. For now she complied, moved as he directed, burning for completion. It was a long time before he allowed it. She passed out in the clutches of a scream that shook her frame to its roots, his—his alone.

He watched her for a while after, then curled her possessively into his arms and slept as well. The morning would bring too many things for him to think of all at once. He had to be awake then, prepared. Church was at eight.

CHAPTER NINE

Hector Clearwater's eyes glittered brightly as he stared over the table at Brenda Beauchane, and he had to make a concerted effort not to drool. There was unadulterated lust in that gaze, longing, even. This was a normal response, and she ignored it, taking it for granted. He was, after all, a man. What she wanted was to hear him speak, to hear his thoughts on her proposal.

"So," he said finally, coming to the reluctant conclusion that she was unimpressed by the impact of his famous smile, or the proximity of his finely honed figure. "Reverend Goldbough is finally agreeing to appear on *Clear it Up*? What changed his mind? Surely one such as he," the smirk that invaded his features was perfectly timed, instantaneous, a trademark feature of his show; its meaning was to be interpreted as a shift from his previous, conciliatory and serious attitude, which was a ploy, to his outright search for blood, "is not concerned with such an earthly thing as the money we have offered?"

"I'm sorry," Brenda answered in her most condescending voice, "I must have been less than clear." Alarming little sparks flitted about in the depths of her eyes as her anger suddenly blossomed, and Hector actually sat back a bit in his seat as he listened. "Reverend Goldbough is offering you a much better story than your planned assault on his personal righteousness. He is willing to come forward and face the rock group *Maelstrom* with proof of their evil—actual evidence. He is willing to make your program and its audience the battleground for a confrontation with the minions of Satan himself. The money is not a factor, Mr. Clearwater."

"I suppose," Hector grinned, "that he'll bring in his equipment for such a battle—tape players that play backwards at varying speeds and such—to support these claims? Perhaps a demonic chant in ancient Swahili that he has detected in some recording, at great personal expense and effort?

"Really, Ms. Beauchane, I much prefer the personal attack. This topic is old and a bit tired, don't you think?"

Now her eyes actually flashed, and Hector nearly started from his seat in alarm.

"Listen to me!" she snapped. "In Lavender, California, this very week, a ritual murder took place. At the scene, and you can confirm this with local police, a boy's pocketknife was found. The knife is inscribed with a single word, Mr. Clearwater, *Maelstrom.*

That knife was purchased that very night at a concert: again, *Maelstrom.* The knife was found by police beside a stone altar in the very deepest part of the Shady Grove cemetery, the site of the murder I mentioned earlier. Police have neither announced the ritual aspect of the killing to the public, nor brought this boy into custody. There is no explanation available of the boy's presence in the graveyard on the night of the murder and rape of a local high school teacher, Gretchen Steiner. Am I getting through, or are you still having trouble keeping up with this?"

Now she was talking. Hector's professional "scent" for a story was primed and ready, his nose almost twitching. This was good stuff, maybe *really* good. If he could persuade the musicians to appear, and if he could control the flow of questions and answers in just the right way, it might just be spectacular.

Of course, Hector knew that nothing could be officially pinned on the group. There were plenty of cases already decided that relieved them of responsibility for deviant behavior attributed to listeners of their music. Hector was not naive enough to think he'd be doing the community any favors. More likely the publicity would be enormous, shooting *Maelstrom's* next album to the top of the charts. That was fine with Hector. Everyone had the right to make a living. He just wanted the chance to get his people, the general public, the housewives and Christian grandmothers of America, into an uproar.

"The local police," he asked quickly, "they let this information out? It's public knowledge, or..."

"We have our sources, Mr. Clearwater," she smiled. "The police have released publicly only that Ms. Steiner was murdered under strange circumstances. They've withheld the boy, the knife, and all information on the actual circumstances surrounding the murder 'pending further investigation.'"

"One in your line of work must realize what might happen to that boy in his community if he were suspected of Satanism and ritual murder? Perhaps if you act quickly enough, you can get the Police Inspector handling the case, Straker, I believe his name is, to appear as well. It might prove very interesting to ask him publicly why he has not held the boy on suspicion, or even brought him in for questioning, despite the evidence."

Brenda knew then that he was hers. She leaned back and watched calmly as his mind shifted into high gear, sorting facts, putting the puzzle pieces into place. It was what he did best; planning a public attack designed to not only humiliate and question the character of his unsuspecting guests, but also to give her, and Horace, time to finish their own task.

The whole thing was a masterwork of intrigue, orchestrated by one type of genius and passed into the hands of another. Hector Clearwater had been hounding Horace for years in sordid attempts to con him onto the show. There were more than enough topics for discussion concerning The Church of New Light.

Clearwater had come across with claims of Horace conning elderly women out of their life savings in the name of his "movement," of promising miracles that never happened. He'd even gone as far as to send investigators out to check up on the missionary work the church sponsored. Fortunately for Horace, though not for Hector, this aspect of the church was clean. Horace was a shrewd man; he knew there had to be a certain amount of legitimacy to what he did, and the missions were very real.

More and more as the years passed, she had coaxed and cajoled Horace into cleaning up his act. The claims Clearwater might have made in years past would easily have been

substantiated. Now the tracks were covered, and all the investigators would find was a modern saint. It was imperative that no
attention be drawn to their more important work.

Horace was naive. For all his wisdom, for all his intellect, he
still believed that he and she sought a common goal, and that
they were working in a partnership. She knew better. The ritual
was hers alone. Long years had gone into the research, years
and what some men would call her soul. Her virginity had been
the first, perhaps the least, of those things she'd sacrificed. She
wasn't about to share the prize with Horace, or anyone.

There was also the hunger to be considered, the fiery need
that consumed her whenever she felt the dark forces move.
Horace sensed the forces as well, on a lower level, and he knew
her needs. He was coming to a point where he could nearly
control them. She allowed him this fleeting control and concentrated on the future, the outcome that he could neither interpret
nor foresee. She used her physical form as a distraction. He was
as addicted to her as she was to the feel of his control.

When the details had been smoothed to their mutual satisfaction, and Hector Clearwater had attempted a few more half-
hearted passes, she left him, a huge grin of satisfaction plastered
across his greedy face. Horace would be nearly ready to leave
the church, and she hoped that he would not leave her long to
wait.

The night ahead promised to be a busy one. The powers
were shifting, and there was precious little time in which to
take advantage of them. She felt the familiar tug of desire lick
at her limbs and sift through her consciousness. Her veins
throbbed—her nerves heated and burned. She needed release
to cleanse her mind.

Horace was the only one she could turn to, and the idea
of such a binding was both disturbing and exciting. She drove
toward Lavender and the church as slowly as her tingling skin
would allow, skirting the edges of the legal limit. The journey
would stretch interminably, she knew, but the wait at the church
itself would be worse. The air there bothered her—the "aura" of
the place. Despite Horace's almost blatant hypocrisy in matters
of the spirit, his followers believed. They had filled the building

with their faith—the strength of their "God." It was contrary to Brenda's purpose—her own belief—the temple of the enemy. It wasn't a place she could long abide, and with the impending ordeal so near, the walls of the church magnified her need to incredible proportion. Fuming and panting, she drove on, fighting to concentrate on the centerline of the highway and the wheel.

Pamela Green sat, staring at her phone in indecision, biting off the last of her nails in frustration. Straker had promised to keep her informed, and she believed that he meant what he said. For some reason, maybe the calm, reasonable tone of his voice on the phone, or his no-nonsense beginning to their talk, she trusted him. It was just the waiting that was killing her—the not knowing.

It was maddening to just sit back and wait when she knew that whoever had killed Gretchen was still on the loose, still stalking the streets of Lavender. Her job was investigation, digging up the facts. It was all she could do to stay away from it.

Who would be next? She shivered, unwilling to face such a question honestly. Unable to contain herself any longer, she made her decision and snatched the phone from its cradle before she could change her mind. As it rang, she caught herself biting the nails on her free hand again and dropped it nervously to her side. A bad habit.

Just as she was about to give up in frustration Kendall Straker's deep, gravelly voice snapped into her ear. "Hello, Inspector Straker here."

Releasing a deep breath that she hadn't even been aware she was holding, Pamela replied. "It's me, Inspector. Pamela Green? I don't mean to bother you, just nervous, I guess, but I was just wondering if maybe you'd learned anything…you know…about Gretchen's death?"

"I've found a few things," he admitted. "There's nothing that I really feel like discussing over the phone, though." He hesitated, and she imagined him glancing down at his watch. "Ms. Green, would you care to discuss it over dinner? I'm starving, and Giovanni's is having their lasagna special tonight."

She hesitated for only a second before agreeing. Her apartment, normally a cheerful, comfortable retreat from the world, was beginning to weigh on her like a blanket of oppressive silence. She needed to get out, to talk to someone—anyone.

Pamela had few friends. She was far too busy with her job to spend much time on the town socializing, and reporters, she had found, drew the worst of lots when it came to associates. Everyone she worked with seemed in a hurry to climb their personal ladder. Sincerity was for novelists and starving poets; the newspaper business attracted only sharks.

"That would be nice, Inspector. I haven't eaten much today—nothing in fact. Would you give me, say, an hour to get ready?"

"On one condition," he said, and she could tell that he was smiling, "call me Ken. I get that "Inspector" crap all day long; it gets tiring after a while."

"All right...Ken." Pamela found herself smiling too, despite her anxiety. "I'll see you in about an hour." After giving her address and hanging up, Pamela sat there for some time, staring at the wall, lost in thought. If she didn't find out something that would put her mind—and heart—to rest soon, she would develop ulcers.

Rising, she turned her thoughts to Kendall Straker, lasagna, and the shower. With the prospect of a night out to prepare for, somehow the apartment seemed less bleak—less empty. Even the shadows seemed to recede a bit.

When Nick arrived at Ruthie's house, she opened the door before he'd even finished his first knock. She'd obviously been waiting, and he took her immediately into a tight embrace, saying nothing, just holding her close. The silence held for a while—no words were needed, but there wasn't enough time to waste. Pulling back, but not away, Nick spoke.

"We've got to find Flash," he said, his face a mask of anxiety and purpose. "Inspector Straker—you know, the guy from the police department?—came by to see me this morning. He had my knife, the one I bought at the concert. I dropped it out in Shady Grove, right near the altar. If we don't find some answers to what was going on there real quick, I could be in some serious trouble."

Nodding, Ruthie closed the door behind her and grabbed his arm, letting him lead her off toward Weasel's "shack." The shack was an old wooden storage shed that sat in Weasel's backyard. Several summers earlier, Weasel's dad, Chuck, had given the boys the use of the building on the promise of cleaning it up and keeping it that way. Since then, Nick, Flash, Weasel, and a few select friends had redesigned the place, turning it into a sort of clubhouse—a home away from home where adults never came.

Of course, over the years their responsibilities had somehow grown to include the backyard, painting the fence, cleaning the garage, etc., but it was cool. Weasel's parents never invaded their privacy, and on several occasions they had chipped in and helped when the boys wanted to find a particular new item— the paneling they'd gotten from the "seconds" lumber yard and the carpet they'd picked up used when one of the law offices downtown closed.

The shack had become a fortress against the adult world, a bastion of rock and roll that was barricaded against the onslaught of mundane reality. Nick had a feeling he would find the other two there—no way were they sitting at home and brooding, waiting for a curious parent to bug them about what was bothering them. He needed their help now, more than he ever had in the past.

Flash's van was parked in the street out front, and Nick breathed a sigh of relief. Before they even reached the end of the driveway, the sound of the stereo blasted out of the backyard at them.

The stereo was one of Weasel's projects. Ever since he'd gotten a Radio Shack electronics set at age ten, he'd been a whiz at wiring and sound equipment of every type. He'd been building radios, speaker systems, and little battery-operated shock-sticks to annoy the girls at school for years. The stereo was his masterwork.

The original unit had come from Murphy's Thrift Store in San Valencez. It was huge, glowing dials, two-inch VU meters, and a power knob that was as big around as an apple. It had been ten dollars, and it had worked on only one channel. The volume knob had been scratchy, and the turntable had had no arm. Fifty dollars and two weeks after he'd carted it home it had boomed out its first tunes from the shack, which was now a crisscrossed jumble of wires, speakers, and cables. The sound was deafening.

Nick pushed the door open, leaned inside and gave Weasel the sign for decreased volume. They'd developed the signs as a kind of game one night, a way to communicate when the stereo was too loud for talking. They had come in handy on more than one occasion since then.

As the music lowered to a dull throb, Nick ushered Ruthie inside, leading her to where his own private beanbag throne awaited. He sat down, pulling her down between his legs and wrapping his arms about her protectively. When they were settled, he turned to the others.

"We got trouble, man," he said. "I dropped that knife I bought, you know, the *Maelstrom* blade from the concert? They found it right out by the altar. That guy Straker was at my doorstep this morning, asking questions. He wanted to know who I was with—what we saw."

"Did you tell him?" Flash asked quickly, worry creasing unfamiliar lines across his almost perpetually smiling face.

"Of course not," Nick said, shaking his head. "I played dumb. No way I was saying anything until I had a chance to talk it over with you guys. Besides, Straker never got to finish his questioning. Ed walked in right in the middle of it all. Even Straker seemed a little nervous after that.

"Then things got really weird. Straker and Ed, they've known each other for years—not like friends, though. Straker covered for me. He didn't tell Ed a thing, not really, nothing more than that I'd been out at the graveyard.

"Ed got really strange then. I was all ready to light out, thought for sure he was going to kick my ass; but he didn't. He gave me a fucking beer, man, can you believe it? Started spouting his philosophy of life and family right there on the back porch like we were old friends."

"Ed?" Flash asked, incredulous. "You talking about the same

Ed we all know and hate? The man whose brain came without the instruction sheet? The king of the drunken red-necks? Ed?"

"One and the same." Nick assured them. "He told me to get out when he was finished, and I went. At least I left there without a black eye and with my head in one piece. Anyway, that stuff isn't important. What do we do next?"

"You still got that pin you found?" Flash asked, deep in thought. "You know, the one from that thumper church downtown, the 'Church of New Light,' or some shit?"

"Is that what it is?" Nick asked, reaching into his pocket to fish the small pendant out. "I'd forgotten all about that thing. I wonder if Ms. Steiner was a member? Maybe she dropped it."

"She was a Baptist," Ruthie cut in, her voice quavering as the reality of what they'd seen returned. "She went to my church. I remember because one day my dad got slapped on the way home for commenting on how well one of her Sunday dresses fit..."

Nick pulled her tightly against him with one arm and held the pin up to the light where they could all see it. The tiny gold cross caught glimmers of light from the one window and twinkled mysteriously, daring them to discover its secret.

"What the hell," Nick muttered, "would something like this be doing in the back of a graveyard? And who could have dropped it?"

"I don't know," Ruthie said, turning slightly to face him, "but maybe you should have told the police about it? I mean, isn't it a clue?"

The three boys looked at one another, and then back at her, the same expression painted on all three of their faces. The police were not there to help. Too often they were the enemy.

"I'm afraid that might have been a mistake," Nick answered her softly. "What if they'd found some way to use it against me? Like, for instance, that I didn't rush right down to the police station and turn it over as soon as we found it.

"Besides, they'd love to pin something like this on me. Maybe not Straker, but he's only one man. I'm exactly the type of 'bad kid' they'd like to make an example of.

"In any case, I never had the chance to mention it. Like

I said, Ed walked in. Maybe Straker would be cool about it, maybe he'd even help; but I'd rather not chance it. I want to check this out myself. It's *my* ass on the line here."

"You're right about the cops," Weasel cut in, "but what else is there to do? I mean, we aren't detectives; what good is that pin gonna do us?"

"I'm not sure yet," Nick confessed, "but I'm going to do my best to find out. This is the only thing we have to go on that the police don't, and this little pin may just save my butt before this is all through. I'm kind of fond of it—my butt, I mean."

They all laughed then, though it sounded a bit strained; and Weasel leaned forward to turn the stereo back up. Reaching around behind the speaker cabinet at his side, he retrieved a small plastic bag and a brass pipe. He lit it quickly, inhaled deeply and leaned back to let the smoke trickle up and out his nostrils. Then he handed it to Flash.

The smoke filled the small room quickly, growing to a haze that impaired their vision and fogged their minds. As he felt the familiar giddiness relax him, Nick took Ruthie's shoulders gently into his hands and turned her to face him. Gazing into her frightened eyes with an expression that he hoped seemed calm and in control, he pulled her forward to where he could speak into her ear and be heard.

"Everything is going to be okay," he said. "Nothing can come between us—I won't let it. Don't worry."

Since he could think of nothing else to say that would in any way help, and since the scent of her perfume was winding its way, along with the smoke, up his nostrils and through his senses, he quit talking and began gently nibbling on her ear.

Responding, Ruthie slid her cheek over his lips slowly and chased his tongue with her own, meeting his kiss with a small burst of passion that surprised him. Ruthie was usually very shy and reserved, especially when the others were around. Now she pressed against him so tightly that it was difficult to get his breath.

Flash, seeing that the two entwined on the beanbag were getting a bit more serious than usual, turned to Weasel and made a quick flurry of signs to the effect that they should go out in search of a Pepsi or something. Weasel followed Flash's gaze, grinned, and nodded, rising and heading for the door.

Nick paused momentarily and looked up as Flash was just reaching the door. He mouthed a quick "thank you" that was lost in the din of the music. With a final thumbs up, Weasel closed the door behind them; and Nick heard the locking bar slide into place. He and Ruthie weren't trapped; they could exit through the hidden trap door in back, but nobody could walk in on them unannounced.

Turning his eyes back to Ruthie's, he drank deeply of the emotion he found there. She was beautiful, and somewhere inside, in places he generally avoided in his own mind, he found the courage and the words to speak, feeling the rightness of both time and place, feeling her need.

"Ruthie, I love you." The words were short, simple, but the meaning and reaction they brought were as complex as a map of the stars. She stared at him for a long time, searching his eyes, testing him for falsehood. At the corners of her eyes, tears formed slowly, welling up and spilling down her cheeks; and with a soft cry, she threw herself into his arms.

He kissed her again and let his hands roam down her body. Again he was surprised as she began a slow, groping search of her own. For the first time in their relationship, when Nick's fingers reached and fumbled with the buckle of her belt, then to shift beyond, she didn't stop him. She pressed herself up to meet his touch and kissed him more deeply, as though drawing courage from the act.

Smiling, she reached down and unfastened her belt for him, then gripped her jeans and slipped them quickly down and off in one quick movement. Nick could only watch. His heart raced, but time seemed to have come to a standstill. He dropped his pants quickly and slipped out of the rest of his clothes, then pulled her naked form against his, feeling the electric touch of skin on skin, the scrape of bone on bone where their hips met.

"Nick," she gasped, barely able to control her voice, "I...I've never...I love you too. Don't hurt me?"

He stroked her hair gently, the old glitter back in his eyes.

"Never, Ruthie, never." He slid over her like a soft wave.

It was a long time before they slipped out the back and went after the others.

CHAPTER TEN

Devon Storme was kicked back on the couch, one leg hooked up and over the back cushion, thumbing idly through the latest issue of "Rock Talk" magazine. The feature article was a *Maelstrom* exclusive. He never failed to marvel at the surreality of it all. Here was his face, plastered over several glossy pages, mixed in with tawdry shots of Gail and the others, grimacing and leering lewdly into a camera he'd never seen.

There was one shot in particular that kept catching his eye. It was a full-page shot of his face, sweat flying from him in all directions and his eyes aglow with reflected light from the overhead spots. It made him look like some sort of demon. He chuckled, flipped through the pages, and shook his head.

Any of his fans seeing him as he was at that moment would have been shocked—excessively under-awed. His hair, which was actually dark, chestnut brown, not black, was combed carefully, reaching just to the collar of his shirt. Without the makeup his features were still striking, but more serious. He wore faded Levis and a black T-shirt with an M. C. Escher print on it.

From down the hall he heard his sister, Gail (that relationship, carefully hidden, was another secret that would have driven the fans crazy) strumming softly on an acoustic guitar and humming along. Occasionally he caught a short phrase or a refrain. She was working on lyrics for a new song.

Without the harsh bite of the amplifiers and the frenzied accompaniment of the band, she had a sweet, melodic voice. The music provided a pleasant, soothing background; and Devon was slightly more irritated than usual when the jangling of the telephone interrupted the chorus.

"I'll get it," he called out, sliding off the couch and heading across the room in one smooth movement. The magazine, forgotten in his haste, dropped to the floor, his own demonic visage glaring up from the floor.

He snatched the receiver from its cradle irritably and snapped, "Yeah, Devon here, what's your pleasure?" His voice had slipped into its "stage" tones without conscious thought. It was a habit learned on long days of road travel. You never knew who might come up with your number, no need to let any cats out of the bag.

"Dev?" The voice on the other end was the unmistakable New York twang of their manager, Sammy Rosenman. Sammy sounded anxious over something, but that was nothing new. Sammy was always nervous—it was his job.

"Yeah, Sammy; it's me," Devon said, his voice leveling off. "What's the problem? You sound like someone's got a gun to your head."

"In a way," Sammy continued, "I guess they have, Dev. This may be bad, real bad. You know that show, 'Clear it Up,' the talk show on Wednesday nights?"

"The one where that greasy asshole brings people on and makes fools of them? What's that guy's name, anyway, Hector something-or-other…?"

"Clearwater." Sammy finished. "Clear it Up with Hector Clearwater. Anyway, here's the deal. The guy has some crazy notion about having *Maelstrom* appear on his show. They have a weirdo church out in California, "The Church of New Light," I think, is claiming that you and the band are leading their children to Satanism, or some such crap.

"Clearwater wants you guys to face the minister of that church, one Horace Goldbough, on national television next week. He claims he's giving you a chance to defend yourselves, but you've seen how he operates."

Devon paused, a thoughtful expression on his face that would have increased the strain on Sammy's nerves a hundred times over had the little manager seen it. Finally, he answered.

"What do you think, Sammy?"

"I tell you, Dev, I really don't know. I don't trust the guy;

that much is damn sure. On the other hand, national television coverage never hurts record sales, no matter the outcome. How do you think the band would react? I mean, those guys can get a little out of hand, you know?"

"They'd love it," Devon said, grinning at the prospect himself. "Louie's been chomping at the bit to go after one of these holy-rollers, ever since that time last year on tour when that guy called us demons outside the stadium in Toledo. He'd jump at the chance to get a crack at one of those guys, one-on-one."

"Well," Sammy replied, still hesitant, "I'll go ahead and see about setting it up, then. I hope you can control them, Dev. It could get really hairy with the promoters and the record people if they don't stay cool with this guy Clearwater. He may be an asshole, but he's a *sharp* asshole, and he's trouble with the biggest damned capital T you ever saw."

"If I can't calm them down, Gail can," Devon assured him. "The Mechanic's the only one we really have to worry about in public, anyway; and he's like a puppy dog when she's around. The others only cause trouble when he leads. We can handle it, and it sounds like it might actually be fun. We've needed something to break up the monotony for a while now."

"It's yours then," Sammy sighed. "I'll get back with Clearwater's producer, and I'll call you tomorrow with the details."

The line went dead, and Devon spun, retrieved his magazine from the floor and tossed it on the end table. The sun was setting outside, and he rose, moving to where he could look out over the lake below. They had a beautiful view of Lake Quantal, one of the smaller bodies of water that surrounded the Lake of the Ozarks; and it was moments like this when he could fully appreciate it.

Even the name of the lake, Quantal, meant solitude. The quiet place. It fit. Solitude was the main reason he and Gail had wanted the place, giving up several tempting offers of New York penthouses and California beach cottages in favor of it. After fifteen years of life on the road, living in vans and trucks, sleazy hotels and bars with no privacy, they'd needed it. After twenty-seven years, he could barely remember beyond the last ten. There wasn't much worth remembering. Success had hit them full force, and it was definitely a "high," but it came with a price. Life at the top was not always as pleasant as dreamers wished it.

He let his thoughts drift. The "Rock and Roll as the choir of Satan" thing was an old, old battle. It was almost surprising, after all the crap that had gone on before, that it was still a topic worthy of a television talk show's attention. Maybe they had another angle—Clearwater was no fool.

Maybe not, though. Rock music had always had its share of persecution. In Devon's life, there had been no lack of self-righteous idiots with the notion of condemning his music. It had started in his own home.

His father, one of the elders in the local congregation of the First Revivalist Church and Mission of Oak Lane, Oklahoma, had been one of the first. If the presiding Holy Father, the Not Quite Right Reverend Lee Caldwell, had had his way, Rock music and anything associated with it in the remotest context would have been outlawed within a hundred miles of the town. He wouldn't have wanted it outlawed entirely—without rock music and other modern sins, what would he have to rant and rave about on Sundays?

In fact, not too many years back, Reverend Caldwell's son, Thomas, had made the news when he'd launched a personal war on the "Choir of Satan" out in California. Reportedly, after the incident and the following "reality check," Reverend Caldwell had revised his teaching somewhat. Devon had no way of knowing, nor did it particularly interest him.

He and Gail had left home when she was twenty and he eighteen. It had been a messy, angry departure—a rending of what had been a tentative family bond, at best. They'd never returned, not for a visit, not for reconciliation. Not that they hadn't made the attempt. Gail had tried to call on more than one occasion. There had been no answer. Devon figured it was just as well.

Considering the situation between her and their father, especially after his mother had died, they had been better off on their own. Without the buffer of their mother's common sense, and with the grief of her loss eating at him with no room for respite, their father had chosen his own deep end and jumped off.

No music. No after school activities at all, in fact, unless they had wanted to hang out at the church and sing in the choir.

"That music, it's corrupting you," the man had said, shaking an angry finger at them both. "Why, Gail girl, look at the *clothes* you wear. No self-respecting Christian would suffer this, nor shall I."

In the end, both Devon and Gail had seen his efforts for what they were. He was unable to control his *own* desires when she was around. If they hadn't left he would either have molested Gail, or driven hot nails through his own hands in order to fight the urge. Neither alternative was inspiring, so the two of them had set out on their own. It hadn't worked out badly at all.

Gail had always been a few years older, maturity wise, than her years and looks would indicate. She was shrewd, capable, and not above using the talents God had gifted her with to make her way in the world. She'd managed to land a job dancing, and Devon had gone to work for a local department store nearby. One way or another, they'd always managed.

Soon they'd been able to save a little, picking up odds and ends of equipment from pawnshops, thrift stores, wherever it became available. They'd ended up with a couple of beat up old guitars, a handful of microphones and cords, and a slightly battered but still serviceable PA system. It was in those early days, working together to scrape up a living and make a life, that the music had grown strong.

Devon had always been good with words. It was one of the few gifts he had from his mother. Both of them sang well. That was from their father, from grueling hours of forced choir practice in the loft above the First Revivalist Church and Mission. Though the memories of those days were not all pleasant, they had served the two well when they set about developing their own harmonic blends, the threads that would become the first of the tapestry of sound and artistry that was the backbone of *Maelstrom's* eerie, heavy blues style. It was a time, also, that had brought them closer together.

There had been a lot of stops before *Maelstrom*. They'd been through other bands, one after another, slipping from town to town and bar to bar, before the fateful night they'd met "Lightning" Rivers and The Mechanic in a backstreet club in Pittsburgh.

Devon and Gail had been biding their time for a couple of weeks, playing with a local band called *Blue Onyx* in a shady little club near the outskirts of the city. The other members of that band, two of which were older black men, were content with what they had and with where they were going. Nothing, and nowhere, as far as Devon had been concerned.

At first it was fine. It was a chance to learn, and the full-time members of *Blue Onyx* had no lack of talent or experience between them. It had also been one of the first rare opportunities to work a few of their own songs into the act. There was something missing, though, and both Devon and Gail knew it. There was no inspiration motivating the band, no emotional flow. They were precise, clean, and very, very, ordinary. Their main purpose in playing, it seemed, was to insure that they had the price of their drinks.

Lightning and The Mechanic had been traveling with a longhaired, makeup artist Led Zeppelin imitation billing itself as *Resurrection*. When the pair arrived at *The Pirate's Den*, where *Blue Onyx* was playing an extended, lifeless gig, they'd just been fired from their band for about the hundredth time. In true "Lightning" style, Louie had launched them both into a headlong drunk that raged over half the city, finally leading to a meeting that could only be defined as "fate."

Even for *The Pirate's Den*, it was a very dead night. Most of the patrons in attendance were either blitzed out of their minds or involved in their own private little dream worlds. The band was only there for background noise—it could have been elevator muzak for all they cared. It would have been another night of depression to add to a growing string, if Louie and The Mechanic hadn't wandered in—stormed in, actually.

With a single look around to assess the situation, a conqueror surveying a land he wished to ravage, Louie cut loose with a resounding whoop and made a beeline for the stage. Unable to think of any good reason to attempt evicting them, the management had turned their eyes aside and served the two men big strong drinks in the hope of keeping the peace.

Devon watched with amusement from center stage, where he leaned casually on his microphone stand. It was the most excitement they'd seen in weeks. Gail sat on a stool off to the side with her guitar and a second mic—her eyes were smiling as well, though she carefully hid it from her lips. Both nearly laughed when The Mechanic tripped over a chair in his enthusiasm and showered whiskey over both himself and Louie, all the while waving his free hand at the stage and shouting "Freebird!" in a booming voice.

Devon looked at Gail, then at the others on the stage, and shrugged. What followed was perhaps the only memorable performance of *Blue Onyx's* short career. They did not play Freebird. What they did play was a version of "Train Kept A Rollin'," similar to that done by The Yardbirds, but deeper, and with more bite.

Devon and Gail wound their voices together in an intricate harmony that they'd discovered somewhere near the bottom of a bottle of cheap mescal years before. Devon's record collection was an odd assortment, and they'd learned a little bit from each one.

The others in the band, half lit on cheap wine and somehow catching the feeling of the music, shared their enthusiasm for once. It all came together in a tight, unbroken rhythm that seemed to pulse out and seep through the corners of the club. Even Jo Jo, the huge black man who played bass, began to bob his head and boogie.

Standing now, two tables away from the stage, his eyes darting back and forth from Devon to Gail, and back again, Louie listened. He had his hand clamped tightly over the protesting mouth of The Mechanic. He'd slapped it there when the bigger man attempted to shout again, almost pissing him off. Louie was oblivious. When the music ended, the after-silence cloaking them all in its tingling embrace, his eyes locked on Devon's in wonder.

"Hey," he called out, breaking the silence, "that was hot.

What the hell are the two of you doing *here* for chrissake?"

"No better offers," Devon had answered, grinning down at him. "Who are you?"

"Louie 'Lightning' Rivers, at your service," the short dark-haired man answered, rolling up on the balls of his feet in his excitement, "best damned guitarist in the world. This is The Mechanic," he swept his arm to the side, gesturing at his companion, "master of the 'pummel skins'."

A skeptical glint rose to Devon's eyes at that point, though he still smiled. "Big words. I'm Devon Caldwell, that's Gail, my sister, and this," he swept his own arm to one side, then the other, "is *Blue Onyx*."

Turning a glittering eye on "Junior" Gordon, the emaciated speed freak who played guitar for the band, Louie let his smile slide a bit wider. "Hey, man," he said, pointing to the battered Les Paul slung over the little man's shoulder, "you let me borrow that axe for a few minutes, and I'll buy you a double whatever-the-fuck-yer-drinking. What do you say?"

Junior shrugged. Free drinks were free drinks. Besides, nobody else was around, and he was bored. He handed over the guitar and headed for the bar, not even looking back as Louie strapped in and moved to adjust the amp. He carefully avoided any warm-up licks or sound. Turning back to Devon, he said, "Let's run that last one back once, what do you say?"

Shrugging, Devon motioned to Bozz, the drummer, who hit the intro without hesitation. He was the only band member who really seemed to care about the music, other than Devon and Gail, and he smiled even wider when Louie motioned that he should pick up the beat.

What happened next was nearly indescribable, and it was halfway through the first verse before Devon recovered from it. Notes rippled off the old guitar like a waterfall and showered over him: sweet, pure, and at least twice as fast as Devon would have believed possible. Gail had put her own guitar down after the first flurry, content to sit and watch in amazement. When his head cleared somewhat, Devon closed his eyes and let his head fall back. He grabbed the microphone and sang.

His voice rose in a wail that would have made a demon

run in fear, rose with a power he'd never unleashed before that moment; and the chorus sailed across the room, cresting in the center like a wave of blues and crashing down on the few, catatonic patrons who still loitered about the bar.

On the second chorus Gail joined in, and it clicked—just like that. Magic. The Mechanic, still on the floor below, had been stomping his feet wildly and was staring up at the stage, captivated by Gail's face. Apparently "Lightning" was nothing new to him. Devon couldn't stop the grin from nearly splitting his face in two. Jesus, what a moment.

They'd played for nearly an hour that night, The Mechanic even joining them for a couple of songs when Bozz left to get himself a drink and a little rest. They played old blues, new rock, even a couple of soul numbers—nothing that came to mind seemed to be beyond them.

When the bar closed, they all left together. Devon invited the other two, who were staying with *Resurrection* in a hotel downtown, to come to their place and jam. They accepted, and within a week they'd formed Maelstrom and quit their jobs, throwing it all into one big shot. It had turned out to be a very good bet.

Two weeks later, at their first gig, a longhaired, freckle-faced redhead had approached Louie after the show, with his eyes ablaze. He said he'd never heard lead played like Louie's. Louie, of course, had agreed. Then he said that Louie had never heard rhythm guitar like *he* could produce, and he'd pulled out a cassette tape. Seeing something he liked in the kid's eyes, Louie listened to the tape. It was nothing short of great, and "The Force" had signed on for "the tour."

All of that was years, tours, albums and memories away. *Maelstrom*, after seven years of nearly nonstop work, was by far the hottest thing on the music scene. Between Devon's production of the show and faculty with lyrics, Gail's haunting voice and awesome body, and the pure magic of the mesh between the musicians, a sound beyond the "commercial crap" on the radio had been found, honed and perfected.

Now they were going to go on television, defend themselves against pompous words and hellfire preaching; and the idea bothered Devon much more than he could understand.

The worst he expected was a standoff. The preacher, of course, would cry sin and devil worship, ranting and raving about the fiery pit that awaited them. The band, probably with Louie in the lead, would laugh back at him, calling him an idiot. It was all seemingly harmless entertainment.

So, Devon thought, *what is it that makes me want to call Sammy back and tell him to forget the whole damned thing?* He held the urge in check. The others would kill him if they found out he blew a chance like this.

With the annoying bite of worry snapping at the back of his thoughts, he turned on the stereo. Led Zeppelin rose from the speakers to fill the room with sound, and he let himself slip back into the pages of his magazine, pushing all thoughts of television talk shows and evangelists from his mind. He could break the news to the others that night at rehearsal. Damned if he was going to let some grinning idiot of a talk show host ruin *his* Saturday afternoon.

It was not long before the soothing notes of the music and the unadulterated praise of the magazine article cleared his thoughts. He read on, swinging his leg over the couch again and laying back with a plop. For the moment, Hector Clearwater, Horace Goldbough, and Satan could all go fuck themselves. He lost himself in a calm haze of melody and rhythm—drifting into a doze on a pleasant bed of sound.

CHAPTER ELEVEN

The roar of voices died to a babble, then to a pulsing hum, then to an almost oppressive silence. The air was charged with emotion and crackling with faith. The sonorous, droning strains of the huge pipe organ flanking the pulpit of The Church of New Light seeped through the acoustically perfect hall with growing power, and reached out to wrap around the gathered congregation and hold them fast.

Horace, seated in an ornate wooden chair behind the altar, allowed his mind to drift. The time for fiery speech and flogging the masses would come later. It was a familiar ritual: first the singing; then prayer, which would be led by one of the doddering "elders" of the church; then a selection of hymns from the choir. It was all orchestrated to build tension, to bring the crowd to an emotional peak at just the right moment. There were proper and improper ways of staging an entrance. Horace was a practiced master of the art.

The initial singing got their blood flowing and their minds on the right track. It brought them all together in a tight, emotional bonding that could be stretched and manipulated, once it was in place. Then the prayer would drone out, a group appeal for forgiveness. They would pray as one, but each would search his own heart, truly wishing for forgiveness of whatever lack or sin they might feel the weight of, under the close scrutiny of God.

The prayer was the method of injecting the moment with an aura of solemn reverence, to elevate the hour to come above the mundane reality of day-to-day existence. It was a way of confirming that the time belonged to God, not to man.

Then the choir would sing. All of the wonder, the bottled emotions that had been waiting to spring forth at the end of the prayer would be held in check. The music would go on, and on. Eyes would wander and bodies would fidget in uncomfortable wooden seats. The stage would then be set for the most important moment, the *coup de grâce.*

Just as they became certain that the choir's endless performance was their personal punishment for a life of sin, when their minds were numb and their eyes nearly glazed over from boredom, Horace would take the pulpit. He would sweep them with his eyes and lash out at them in his sensuous, booming voice. He would sling righteousness at them in the tones of one who believed he might detect a flaw in their faith, a wavering among his own followers.

Immediately at the disadvantage, caught like a group of inattentive children in school they would sit there, stunned; and they would be his. He would assault them with the ferocity of his tirade until he assumed complete control. It would happen just like that—he knew it. It always had.

Horace still remembered the days when things had not been so certain. The present, glorious Church of New Light had not been built overnight. It had been a long, arduous road, full of pitfalls and rife with stress. Anything less and it would never have come as far as it had.

Horace thrived on challenge and adversity. He had always been focused on his central goal, more power. He had a deep-seated hunger for complete control of others. It was his strength.

His ability to manipulate others was now developed to a consummate skill. It had sprouted at a very young age, and he had sharpened it to a razor's edge. Even his parents had seldom been able to catch him in any falsehood: his lies rang with too much sincerity; his eyes were deep and full of the warmth of honesty and truth. It had all served him well.

His choice of evangelism as a career had come at a young age. He had always been able to bring out the guilt in others, to fan the flames of deep-rooted insecurity and cultivate the desire for redemption. Somehow, the details of his own sinful ways were overlooked in the process; he'd never been called on them.

Ironically, it had been his mother, whom he'd secretly loathed for her lack of imagination and spirit, who was responsible for launching him on his road to success. She'd been addicted to the Sunday morning evangelical programs, never missing a service. She preferred them, in fact, to live services, claiming that they allowed her more privacy in her worship.

And it didn't stop there. She bought every "holy" object they offered up for sale, contributed to every mission and cause that they pronounced worthy. She was buying a ticket—a ticket to heaven. She truly believed that she could buy off the devil from her sinful soul.

Horace remembered how his father would rant and rave at her when he discovered some new unnecessary purchase or extravagant donation. She'd always cried during these "scenes," showing her control of her spouse by lowering the flames of his anger to the licking, aggravating embers of guilt—as often as not bartering off the pleasures of her body against his ire. It was okay; she could always donate more money later in repentance.

Horace learned from them both. He had little respect for either of them, though. They had paid his way through college at great personal sacrifice, and though he appreciated the outcome of this, it was nearly the last time they ever saw or heard from him. They just had nothing he was looking for.

College proved to be another easy challenge. His neat appearance and hard work earned him a near perfect reputation with both staff and students alike. His best courses were Speech and Psychology. He was gifted with a quick and eloquent tongue, and he quickly added to that arsenal the ability to group words together in phrases that would bring about calculated emotional responses. As soon as he had worked it into a believable act, he began to volunteer to speak at local church functions and revivals, missing no opportunity to take the stage and practice his control.

At age twenty-six, a Master of Arts in Theology firmly in hand, Horace had his last name changed legally to Goldbough, a word play on the book "The Golden Bough," which was a history on pagan beliefs and rituals. He then packed his bags and moved to Lavender, California, where he was offered the position of minister in a small Baptist church.

Horace had his eyes set on bigger things, but he knew also that for it to be perfect he would have to control the situation from the start. California was where he wanted to be, and he counted on his training and keen eye for an opening to control, to bring himself the success he desired. His expectations had proven well grounded.

Lavender was a relatively small community, a suburb of the neighboring metropolis of San Valencez. When he arrived, Horace found that the previous Reverend had been a bit complacent—almost idle. This worked in his favor in the long run, much as did the choir's recital during Sunday services. Lavender had waited, unsuspecting, calm and secure in their lackadaisical spirituality.

Horace hit them like a righteous storm, sweeping them away before him like leaves in the autumn wind. It was almost too easy to believe. He'd begun by planning, talking to the citizens, putting together a "program" that would lead them all to his feet. His first sermon, beginning with a sort of casual, diversionary chat, had finally worked its way to the key words, "You all seem like quiet, God-fearing folks."

His eyes had flashed then, his hands had gripped the scarred wood of the old pulpit until the knuckles went white and the wood actually vibrated from his emotion. This was his moment, the time to claim his own; and he sent his voice booming out, crashing from the faded plaster walls of the old building, resounding from the arched oak timbers above him.

"But then," he cried, "so did the Pharisees, the men who *persecuted* our Lord. So did Saul, even before he was blinded by the light of our savior; and so did Judas, until the day of his betrayal, the day he sold his faith in our Lord for a few pieces of silver. Friends, I do not want to seem to be faithful. I will not let my *appearance* of faith drag me down.

"None among us, no, not one among us, has earned the glorious salvation we have in *Jesus*. Not one among us owes him any less than his everlasting *soul*! Let us pray."

They had been hooked. Everyone in that room, every member of the congregation, sat teary-eyed and tense, sinking lower and lower into their pews as he told them of their sin, of their lack of gratitude, of their failure in faith. Horace pulled them each out of their happy, satisfied little worlds of self-righteousness, plucked them forth one by one, and bared to them the reality of their own perfidy. It was compelling, emotionally charged, irresistible—and completely false. It did not matter.

Thirty-eight of the forty-two people present came to the front of the church when he called for recommitment—for repentance. Of those thirty-eight searching souls, fourteen were baptized that very night. The collection plates brimmed—overflowed. Horace collected more that night than the church had seen in several months. It had begun.

The word spread quickly. More and more people came each week, trying to squash in among the already packed pews and standing at the back of the church, barely contained by the walls. Horace had had to go to two, then to three services each Sunday, and two during the course of the week to accommodate them all. It didn't take much time after that before he was able to start the suggestion circulating, the thought that they needed a new, bigger church.

Within two years of his arrival in Lavender, the first set of plans for the new building was drawn. In the meantime, while funds were raised at an unbelievable pace and the proper location was being discussed, "providence" stepped in. An aging lawyer, touched by one of Horace's sermons, came forth to donate a huge old farmhouse that had belonged to his family for decades. A quick shifting of the inner walls and some hurried construction to outfit the place with pews and an organ, and the second church came into being. It had been accomplished for next to nothing, most of the work having been voluntary and most of the supplies donated.

Horace supervised it all with plastic smiles and fervent blessings, at the same time looking out for his own interests and those of the newly dubbed "Church of New Light." The farmhouse was put under the sole proprietorship of this new church, with Horace as cosigner. He was already looking forward then, counting up the money the sale of the place would bring when the new church was built. It had gone a long way toward making his dreams a reality. Through this all, his congregation grew.

About a year before the third church was to be completed, Horace had met Brenda. She appeared at his services one day, green gown elegant and trailing the floor behind her, eyes flashing. He noticed her immediately, of course, but he had "truly" noticed her when she came forward to take the communion.

Communion was the one religious ritual that Horace truly enjoyed. The Church of New Light celebrated communion in a similar manner to that of the Catholic Church. It was a rush, a stimulating example of his power to see his parishioners, rich, poor, famous—all kneeling humbly at his feet. That day Brenda had been one of the first among them, and he had been forcing his features to remain solemn and pious as he let his eyes wander over her supple, slender figure and the long dark tresses of her hair, molded to the muscles of her back. He had been just on the verge of a bit of sinful fantasy when she looked up and caught him for the first time with her eyes.

He stared at her, kneeling beneath him, exotic, beautiful, and compelling. He almost allowed himself to return her gaze for too long—almost allowed his entire congregation to catch him in a moment of open lust. Almost.

Brenda lowered her eyes, releasing him with a snap that he would have sworn was audible, though no one else seemed to notice. His hands trembled as he reached down and placed the wafer between her full red lips. It was then that he felt the first soft, erotic touch of her tongue. She ran it in unmistakable, lingering warmth over his fingers before she pulled back, making way for the next in line.

Horace thanked God at that moment. He thanked God for his loose fitting robes, and that his erection, which was so stiff it was painful, was invisible to those around him. Only he knew, and she—whoever she was. He'd stepped back as quickly as he could without attracting undue attention to himself, and returned to the pulpit, leaving the rest of the ceremony to the church elders. His mind had been awash with confusion, his skin hot and itching—every nerve tense.

Some inner strength had gotten him through the rest of that

service. He sang, his voice breaking only once, delivered the final prayer, and took the ever-present, all-important collection, all the while making a willful effort to avoid further contact with those eyes. It was the greatest test of his control that he'd ever faced, the roughest contest he'd ever won.

That hour had passed in a sort of semiconscious blur, and he exited the main area of the church as soon as he possibly could, claiming to have been struck by a sudden headache, and retired to his office. It had been an ache, all right, but his head was fine, if a bit muddled.

When all of the other cars were gone, even the altar boys having finished their cleaning duties and rushing off to their afternoon's activities, there had come a knock on his door. It had been soft, and yet sure. Almost demanding. Horace rose, breathing deeply to steel his nerves; and he opened that door.

There had been no words between them. She'd stood, eyes blazing, drawing him closer without a movement or a word. Her arms swung wide and invited him to enter. He'd been powerless to resist. Pulling her into the office and bolting the door behind her, he'd spun her around and accepted her invitation.

Before that moment, Horace had been naive. Innocent, even, if such a word had ever been applicable to him. He'd known his share of women, discreetly, and he'd known pleasure, as well. None of it had prepared him for the intensity of passion she evoked in him. He hadn't been prepared for the searing heat of her, and yet he had withstood her initial assault in the church, and now he had claimed her for his own.

If he had found himself unable to quell or tame his own desire for her, he found he was at least capable of controlling hers. She moved to his touch, sighed, moaned, squirmed as if heaven itself had been thrust upon her. Long hours later, lying together in a heap of vestments, silk, and sweat, he'd held her close and looked into her eyes. As if suddenly aware of the moment, he'd asked, "Who are you?"

Now, years later, he realized that through it all that was the one question she had never fully answered. Where had she come from? He only had a vague idea—uncertain thoughts ran races with his jerky questions. His lust for her always won the race, barely. It didn't really matter where she'd come from, only that she had come.

The church around him snapped back into focus as it became unnaturally quiet. The sudden silence was his cue and he rose, almost mechanically, and dragged his mind and his concentration back to the present. Below him, eyes upturned and breath indrawn, they waited.

He laid it on thick—this was an important week. He told them that there were powers, powers of Satan, of evil, unseen and moving among them. He could not, of course, publicly decry those forces, not by name. That would be playing *his* game...Satan's. He would, though, he promised, face them down within the week.

He told them all of his challenge to Satan, of the television battle that was planned. He had not, of course, heard from Brenda yet; but this he did not mention. He had absolutely no doubt that the eyes that had ruled his own thoughts, body, and soul for so long could handle the likes of Hector Clearwater. How could they fail?

Even if by some twist the program never happened, he still could take it all and put it to his advantage. The idea was not truly, of course, to attack rock and roll at all, not the musicians, or even the boy, Leatherman. It was a diversion: a tactic to cloud the eyes of police and reporters long enough for the final part of the game that he was so deeply enmeshed in to play out. It was unfortunate for the boy, but that was not Horace's concern.

As he wrapped up the sermon with a heated harangue of the devil and all his minions, followed by his signature call for support and prayer from his followers, Horace went back onto automatic pilot. He went through the motions of the closing hymns and the prayer without sparing them an ounce of concentration. His mind was already planning, looking ahead to the night to come.

There were powers building, unseen, malignant, and thrilling. Even as he reached out to place the bread of communion in each mouth, even as the wine trickled down his own throat and warmed his senses, he felt the flow of forces he could barely conceive tingling over his skin and wedging into the ends of his nerves. It was all so close, so very close.

The wine was bitter, dry and tangy. He wished that he could turn up the bottle and use the liquid pseudo-fire to clear his thoughts, if just for a few moments.

As he moved to the great wooden doors, paying idle compliments and making inane prattle sound holy, shaking the hands of people he knew, and those he didn't, ushering them from his world with as much haste as possible, he noticed a tear in the sleeve of his robe. He frowned and held the material up for a moment in consternation.

His pendant was missing. It was a small, gold and enamel cross that had been presented to him on the day of the christening of the new church building. He thought back quickly, trying to remember when he had last noticed it; but for some reason he couldn't bring the moment into focus. It was lost in the seemingly endless stream of smiling, enraptured faces, the drying sweat of the grips of hundreds—thousands—of hands.

Behind the church, he sensed Brenda waiting. He felt the draw of her on his senses, felt her heat as if her skin was pressed tightly to his own. It seemed that the morning would never end, that the people would continue to flow through the doors forever; but at last it was over.

He closed the doors and headed back through the church, bypassing his office and heading straight for the parking lot and for her car. He moved as slowly as his legs could be forced, until he was within sight of her; but the smoldering hunger in her eyes wore him down. Cursing himself for a weak fool, he broke into a run. Damn her; damn her and those *eyes*!

CHAPTER TWELVE

Brenda pulled into the crowded parking lot, skirted the building and circled around back, out of sight. She knew that she was early, that church services wouldn't end for another thirty minutes or more. She'd just needed to move, to get out of the house—now she was faced with the frustration of waiting. She bit her lip and fought to clear her mind and regain her failing control.

That control was slipping fast, running through her fingers like water. She only hoped that she could make it last. It *had* to last. She had done far too much, come much too far, to allow her own mind to fail her now.

She forced her mind back through time, using the images and memories to flood in and straighten her vision. If she couldn't control herself in the present, she could refocus on the past—the beginning. It had started so far away, so long ago, that it seemed surreal and impossible. Of the youth that had spawned her, the first steps along her journey through life, there remained only a foggy blur, insubstantial dream visions.

At age seventeen she'd met a man named Tom. Only Tom, no last name—she vaguely wondered why she'd never asked for a last name. Tom was older than she, forty perhaps, though his eyes had hinted at more. He'd been an attractive man, in any case, and when they met, she'd been stoned.

College had been next on her agenda; she'd planned to use it as an extension of years in high school spent on music and parties. She'd had vague plans to study Philosophy, or English— maybe to become a writer. Nothing had been concrete; it hadn't seemed important. Tom changed all of that irrevocably.

They met at a party she'd been invited to attend by a college freshman she'd met at a bookstore. It seemed like a good way to begin her transition from little girl to adulthood—a step up in the world. There had been a great many interesting people in attendance, and nearly all of the conversations she flitted through were deep, or seemed so through the haze of drugs and alcohol that she'd entered into.

She'd just become disenchanted with a group heavily entrenched in a discussion of magic and occult mysteries and turned away from them, when she found herself face to face with a middle-aged man of medium build, and fell directly into his eyes.

She noted that he was dressed well, though in clothes that normally would have been better suited to a younger man. On him they wore well, seemingly painted to a well-muscled body that moved with a sureness and grace she had seldom seen. It was his eyes, though, that held her.

They were not normal; she'd been certain of that, even in her drugged and drifting state of mind. There were dancing lights and prismatic ripples leaping about on the deep green of their irises. There were reflections of things that she was certain were not there to be reflected—almost causing her to turn and look to see what had caused them. She noticed all of this in an instant, though it seemed more of an eternity; and he took full advantage of the moment.

She would have tried to yank her gaze free of those eyes, might even have turned and hurried off, but before she could do more than open and close her mouth dumbly, the man smiled, placed his hand softly on her forearm, and led her to a small couch at the side of the room.

She allowed him to lead her, hardly aware on any conscious level of the movement. Even now, years and miles and worlds away from that time and that moment, she was uncertain whether she could have pulled away at all. She doubted it.

"My name," the man said at last, his voice deep and mellow, very pleasant to the ear, "is Tom. You are Brenda?"

She nodded, not even able to voice the question of how he knew her name. It didn't seem important, and she wasn't certain that she wanted to know, in any case. He continued to speak after only a short pause, his smile widening.

"You seemed somewhat skeptical a moment ago," he commented, nodding in the direction of the discussion they'd just left behind. "I take it you have no interest in the occult, then?"

It was an odd question, and somehow compelling. It suddenly triggered her ability to speak, and she startled herself by blurting out "I don't know." She blushed then, letting her eyes fall toward the floor, trying to pull them free and collect her thoughts.

"It just seems too matter-of-fact when *they* talk about it, so trivial." She looked over at the group she'd just left, and she couldn't imagine, after examining them more closely, how she'd ever gotten caught up with them in the first place. "I've always read that the occult was dark, mysterious, wonderful—that's how most writers portray it. Or dangerous.

"Those guys," she indicated the group with an almost rude toss of her head, "seem to think scientists should capture a witch or something and dissect it—her. It takes all the *magic* out of the magic. Am I making any sense?"

Tom was smiling again, though she didn't know if he was smiling with or at her. "I know exactly what you mean. I find them a bit tedious myself.

"What would you say," he continued, winking at her conspiratorially, "to someone who claimed that he could not only prove that there's more to it than drunken discussions, but who offered to show you the occult first hand?"

She'd flinched at those blunt words, pulling back slightly; but his smile somehow held her in place. Placing his hand on her arm again, he went on hastily.

"I don't mean to scare you. I only meant to say that I know things: things these young people here do not. I have—friends, let us call them—many of whom practice various occult arts on a regular basis. I'm not saying that I believe in any of it, spells, rituals, astrology...nothing of the sort. I'm only offering you the chance to meet some of them and see for yourself. Much more satisfying, I'll guarantee, than a discussion among those who are only casually interested."

Brenda had stared at him for a long moment then, trying to decide if he were serious, kidding, or trying to pick her up. Her first impulse, as always when anything serious arose, had been to get up and run—to find some meaningless conversation somewhere far away from Tom and his offer, and to forget that it had ever happened. That was the way to avoid commitments—to avoid the chance of being hurt or taken advantage of. It just hadn't been possible this time. She'd made the mistake of looking once again into those powerful eyes, and found herself trapped. She sat there, mouth open and eyes vacant like a love-struck schoolgirl as he went on talking.

"Tonight these friends of mine are getting together. Their place isn't far from here. I was thinking of going there to observe—would you like to join me?"

She'd tried to shake loose then. Warning signs and visions of rapists and monsters of all sorts flashed through her mind, but the urge to see what he was all about was too strong. "I guess," she'd answered shakily, trembling, "but I can't stay too late, I..."

He smiled again, and the entire room took on a sort of skewed aspect, as though it was blurred and he was the single focus. That was her first taste of power, of control that could brush aside the wishes and will of one person in lieu of another. She was still talking, but he wasn't listening to her words. He rose, drew her effortlessly after him with only the touch of his hand on her arm, and moved off through the crowded room toward the door.

At the time it had seemed strange. Now, after years among those with that same power, to varying degrees, Brenda saw that he had known all along that she would do as he said— that he had assumed it. Nobody else in the room even acknowledged their passing. They'd walked right past the boy who brought her to the party. Brenda had purposely looked right into his eyes and seen absolutely nothing. It was as if she and Tom weren't there.

The night had just reached its darkest point when Tom pulled her car up in front of a dingy brown house near the outskirts of town. He'd insisted on driving, and she hadn't protested. Actually, she hadn't been certain that she *could* protest. After shutting off the lights and killing the ignition, Tom got out, locked the door behind him and came around to help her out as well—almost gallantly. It was pleasant, she'd thought, to receive such treatment after her awkward experiences dating boys her own age.

She looked about herself with nervous interest as the fresh night air brought her back from the strange daze she'd been in. There was no movement in the street, no lights, no traffic. Long shadows formed of displaced moonbeams reached from the darker recesses like groping talons, seeming to inch toward her. Even the house they approached seemed deserted. Dust swirled about the steps and up the edges of the front wall, until it dispersed into a series of tiny whirling clouds. She almost expected an owl to hoot, or a wolf to howl—maybe some bats.

"Come," he said, still smiling. "Don't let their little stage setting frighten you. Everyone here gets a little caught up in the act. You know, the *mystery* of the thing. They say a haunted-looking house helps put them in the proper frame of mind for this sort of thing. In any case, they are a lot less likely to be bothered out here."

Brenda nodded; unable to think of anything to say that wouldn't sound silly, she followed him up to the door. She didn't know what she was getting into, but she knew that *anything* going on inside would be preferable to standing in that eerie, moonlit street for even another minute.

Her pulse quickened as Tom placed an arm gently across her shoulders. Something about him, his nearness and his touch, sent tiny pricks of energy racing through her. Shivering, she moved forward and stood quietly at his side, as he knocked on the door in an intricate rhythm that she couldn't quite catch. Almost immediately the door began to creak slowly open.

Incense floated out to her, the scents of jasmine and sandalwood mingled in the chill air, blending subtly with the musky odor of rotted wood and dying plants that permeated the old place. It was a very earthy combination, in some way extremely sensual. It was, in fact, very nearly erotic the way it captivated her mind and rippled through her senses.

She nearly cried out when Tom pulled gently on her arm to start her forward again. The combination of his touch and the incense had nearly driven her over some weird, psychic edge.

Once inside, there was no light at all. As the door closed, she caught glimpses of robed figures—several of them—moving about the space inside. Now it was all a lightless void and she was adrift in it—adrift in a sea of incense. Hands reached out and grasped her firmly but softly by her shoulders, and a voice whispered—the lips only inches from her ear, though she'd not even sensed another's presence.

"Don't be afraid," the voice instructed. It was a woman's voice, soft and melodic, mesmerizing. "I will help to guide you. Come with me...first you must be cleansed."

Still trembling, but more curious now than afraid, her confidence bolstered by the appearance of another woman as her guide, Brenda moved on into the darkness. She made it through what must have been several rooms and a couple of hallways without bumping into anything. It gave her the odd impression of walking through an immense, pitch-black cavern—or through space.

Wisps of fine material (or was it spider webs?) brushed against her face as she went, but for some reason even the latter image didn't really upset her. It was the aura of the place, the feeling that things were happening beyond the normal; it all seemed just another part of the experience. The hands on her shoulders pulled her to a stop and reached around her sides to begin fumbling at the buttons of her blouse.

"What," she reached down to stop them, panic returning in a sudden wave, "What are you doing?"

"Shhh..." the voice was still soft and soothing, and the hands did not hesitate in their movements, despite her protest. "It's necessary. Don't worry." A hand gently grasped her wrist and pulled it out into the darkness. She felt it slip past soft material, felt the erotic tingle on her skin once more as her fingers brushed flesh, felt the heavy fleshy weight of a woman's breast as her hand was clasped against it firmly.

"We are all equal here," the voice continued. The woman released her grip on Brenda's wrist, but left it to linger where she had placed it, rubbing herself softly against the fingers until Brenda felt the nipple growing taut beneath her touch.

The woman's hands returned to the task of removing Brenda's clothing, but this time she didn't struggle—except with the heat—the raging emotions—that the contact of her hand on this woman's breast aroused. It was a dark passion, thrilling and overpowering.

She felt her blouse, her jeans, and then her undergarments fall away. Soft caresses followed as a sponge, warm, wet, and scented with the same jasmine that perfumed the air, was run swiftly over her skin. She closed her eyes, leaned her head back and arched forward to meet the caresses. It was all she could do to keep from moaning as the soft massage of the sponge and the warm liquid moved over her body, her breasts, her stomach, up and down and up again, across the skin of her thighs. She nearly whimpered when the trail led between her legs and lingered, moving upward with excruciating slowness.

Before she was aware that the bathing had ceased, a silksoft robe was drawn over her head and slid down her naked form to ride easily on her shoulders. It fell down her legs and brushed lightly across every curve of her body, to trail along the floor, lost in the endless shadows.

She felt her nipples harden, rising to meet the caress of the robes; and her breathing had become short and choppy. The woman's hands returned to her shoulder, just as before, and she was pressed onward into the darkness.

They continued like this for a few moments, and then something changed subtly. She realized that it was light. For the first time since entering this strange, ebony otherworld, this house that seemed as large as a cathedral, she saw the faint flicker of yellow light ahead. The shadows clutched at it, as if jealous of the invasion; but it flickered on, growing more and more intense as they neared it. After the consuming darkness, it was nearly painful to look upon, as though the light was assaulting her eyes. She blinked once, then twice, moving forward all the while at the urging of her unseen guide.

"Sit," the voice directed her, close up against her ear again. She did as she was instructed, caught up in the sensations of the moment and nearly overwhelmed by curiosity. The scents, the electricity of the woman's touch, the silk and the darkness, all of it filled her at once—overpowering the fear she knew she should feel—making her one with the moment.

All thoughts of the earlier party, even of her life before her strange transit of darkness and sensation, were blurred. Only that which she felt, saw, and experienced at that moment existed. She relaxed and concentrated on each new sensory input, unwilling to let any of it pass unnoticed or untested.

All around her she heard and felt the rustling and shifting of other robed bodies. The woman who had bathed her earlier, who had led her through the darkness and comforted her with her touch, was now faintly visible, seated at her side. Brenda turned for just a moment and the woman glanced at her with a pair of deep, glowing green eyes; then the light receded and it was dark again.

A voice spoke loudly into the silence—and yet not too loudly. It filled the air but did not jangle Brenda's nerves, seeming to come at her from every direction at once. It was as if the entire circle of hooded faces spoke and their issuance was a single voice—a joining. She listened carefully, searching the line of darkened hoods, but could discern neither what was being said nor who was saying it.

The chant droned on and on, endless and deep. Images formed in Brenda's mind, fleeting visions that she couldn't quite capture and hold, teased at her thoughts. She understood none of the words being spoken, if they were indeed words and not merely incanted tones; and yet they reached down into some dark recess of her psyche, some chamber far beneath her mundane consciousness, and drew forth their own meanings.

The images in her mind clarified for longer periods. Flickering shapes crossed and recrossed a surreal video screen in her head—within her being. The shapes were somehow very sense-oriented, erotic, and they reached out toward her, as though they were vaguely aware as well, as though they wanted her.

She shuddered, caught up in the dark beauty of it all, and shivered as she realized her own desire for their touch—for unity. From her left, a silver cup, barely discernible in the dim light, was passed.

"Drink," the woman whispered, her lips so close that Brenda could feel the hot breath on her neck. The woman's tongue flicked out, for only an instant, caressing the lobe of Brenda's ear; and a convulsive shudder racked her entire frame. The light brush of the other's fingers as she passed the cup from hand to hand, sent fiery tendrils of desire down Brenda's arm to clench in the nerves of her breasts. She would have prolonged it, grasped at it even; but the hand was gone as quickly as it had arrived, and she held only the cup.

Not wanting to do anything to mar the wonder of the moment, wanting to experience all that was there to be had, she raised the drink and poured a small amount of the liquid between her lips. It was sweet, sticky, and smooth at the same time. It was a strange, heady taste, but not unpleasant.

"Pass the cup," the woman said, and once more Brenda did as she was told, eager to move on to the next step, whatever that might be. She was never certain, upon reflection, whether she even noticed the numbing encroachment of the drug—the fogging of her thoughts. The chant continued, omnipresent in the darkness, hypnotic.

The woman's hand had slipped free of the darkness then, grasping Brenda's forearm and urging her to rise. The floor swayed dizzyingly and her balance felt off, as though countered by weights of lead. Somehow she fought herself steady, and the woman's hands pressed her forward.

Though she could see nothing, she knew somehow, deep down, that she was approaching the very center of the circle. The chanting truly surrounded her now, where it had only seemed so before. It had a new quality, a harmonic lilt that spoke of many voices, many sources. At the center of the room, the hand on her arm halted her and the voice returned, still haunting, still soothing.

"Sit, lay back, and do not be alarmed. No harm shall come to you. He is here. Do you feel him, flowing about us? *Filling* us?"

Brenda had felt something: a force, or an aura, a dark, velvet presence that threatened to blot out all else, to overwhelm all sensation. Then, at last, she felt the woman's hands again as well, searing her skin with the intensity of their caresses. She felt her robe slip up, sliding softly across her skin, across the erect nipples of her breasts, and then off—cast into the darkness.

The hands dropped to her knees as she settled back on the floor, beginning an upward finger-walk of passion. Brenda squirmed then, not away, but up, pressing herself into the touch, seeking the probing fingers. Her mind reeled and she relinquished control of the moment.

Jasmine filled her nostrils; soft lips brushed her own, and tendrils of silky hair fell across her cheeks. Any remaining vestige of thought was erased by the woman's kiss: soft, erotic, like nothing she'd ever experienced. Brenda was vaguely aware, after that, of a progression of different touches, each discernible from the others, each a new level of pleasure.

She felt the first entry—the taking of the maidenhood she'd so long protected as a bastion of her individuality—the gift she'd found none worthy of—in a blast of what seemed to her to be dark light—a blacker flash in the already all-encompassing darkness. She made out several faces, barely visible in the flickering half-light. They were not human faces. They were the faces of those in her vision, those she'd seen during the chant.

Her memory faded after that. She awakened alone, fully dressed, about a block beyond the party she'd left with Tom. She'd been sleeping in the front seat of her car. Beside her, like a message from an alien world, had lain a book. The book. On top of it had been a note signed simply, "Tom." She had never seen him again.

Brenda,

You have passed the doorway. Great things are expected of you, things beyond your wildest imagination. You will understand more when you have studied the book. Powers move on our Earth not generally recognized by those around us. Such a power awaits you.

Yours in darkness,

Tom.

After shaking the cobwebs from her head and secreting the book in her purse, she'd started the car and driven home, her mind reeling with half-remembered pleasures and dark dreams. When she reached the privacy of her room, within her apartment, both doors locked from the inside, she sat, opened the book, and read it for the first time, cover to cover.

She had been transformed again, then, though she hadn't truly realized it at the time. Somewhere in its pages, she had changed. It was a book of ritual, and a book of promise as well. It was an instruction in the ways of darkness that left nothing at all to the imagination. The rest of what had come had been up to her, her task. The reality—that which she had striven for and yearned for, at times begged for in the darker crevasses at the back of her mind—was about to become very real.

A rap on the window of her car caused her to nearly start from the seat, her dream-like memories fading quickly. She almost struck her head on the wheel as she spun. Horace stood outside, concern etched in the lines around his eyes, and he was staring in at her oddly. Slowly, she lowered the window, allowing the cobwebs to loosen themselves from her thoughts.

"Are you all right?" he asked as the crack in the window widened. "I've tried for over five minutes to get your attention!"

"Sorry," she answered. "I...I was remembering. The memories were very...strong. Vivid. We must go. There is so much to do, so little time to do it, and..."

She said no more, but she saw in the smile and glitter that invaded his eyes that he knew perfectly well what else she needed, what she craved.

Without another word, he entered the car and brushed her leg with his hand as she slid across the seat to allow him behind the wheel. She shivered and bit her lip. The tiny trickle of blood that ran down from the cut this caused, blended with her saliva and gave it a faint taste of salt. Heat rose like a brush fire to engulf her reason.

Tight-lipped, filled with a dark anticipation of his own, Horace stared straight ahead and drove. It would be a long night: a night of power; and there was so little time.

CHAPTER THIRTEEN

When Straker pulled up in front of Pamela's apartment, he had no idea what he should expect. His impressions, first of a schoolmarm librarian type, and later of a warm, caring woman, warred in his imagination. He'd been on "blind dates" before, spoken to a few of them on the phone prior to that first meeting, as well. It was an amazing thing how often the most feminine and attractive voices ended up emanating from three hundred pound frames. When Pamela Green opened her door, he was surprised; and he found that he had trouble in keeping himself from staring openly.

Tall and slender, dressed in a mid-length skirt and loose-fitting cotton blouse, Pamela came out the door and down the sidewalk in a rush. Her hair, teased back in a wild, untamed fashion, looked as likely to have been caught in a whirlwind as to have been put that way by design; but it set her features off perfectly. She was younger than he'd thought. If you were to stretch the probabilities of time a bit, she could have almost been his daughter.

"Figures," he mumbled to himself. "I finally get a blind date who's a looker, and she turns out to be from the wrong freaking generation."

He got out and walked around to open the door for her, holding it wide. He slipped his eyes quickly up and down her figure, lingered a bit too long on her legs, and she caught him, sending a blush straight to the roots of his hair. She smiled, but it still put him at an initial disadvantage he didn't care for at all.

"Nice evening," he commented, plopping back in behind the wheel. "The breeze is a change after all that heat. Heat and I don't get along too well, never have."

Searching his face for something and apparently finding it, she smiled again. It was a very pleasant smile, full of honesty and warmth. It helped to put him back at ease.

"It is," she answered finally. "It seems like summer gets hot pretty quick here, then stays that way. I'm from back east; it would still be cool at home."

He tried to guess her accent, but failed. He was usually pretty good at placing folks; it irked him a little that her background was evading him. Her voice had polish, a sort of educated flash that spoke of long years in good colleges. Again, he was impressed.

"I see," he said. "I've lived here in Lavender all my life...you never really get used to it. The heat, I mean."

They rode in silence for a time then, neither really knowing what to say. They'd passed the talking about the weather segment—the awkwardness was quick to follow. Even the streets were silent, almost barren of traffic. At that hour, most people were either caught up in the traffic on the freeway or already sitting down to dinner.

Turning the nose of the car into the driveway of Giovanni's, Straker noticed that there were a few patrons ahead of them, but not too many. That was good. He hated to wait for a seat, but he was already uncomfortable enough without adding the weight of an empty room to his problems.

It wasn't until after the waiter had come, taken their order and gone, leaving them to sip glasses of red wine, that he finally turned to her and broached the subject of why they were there.

"So, Pamela," he still felt slightly uncomfortable not saying "Miss Green", "you and Gretchen Steiner were close friends. You still smile, and it's a very attractive smile, but maybe you'd like to talk about it? It's never easy to lose a friend..."

A sudden shadow crossed her features, and he went on quickly, hoping he wasn't blundering through this quite as badly as he was certain that he must be. "I only meant it might help to talk," he said. "I was hoping I might gain some insight from it, some clue as to what might have happened that night—anything that might help.

"If you can think of any change, any slight difference in her manner, the way she spoke to you, anything at all that was not like her. I'm at a loss on the motive of this murder, and motive is usually our strongest stepping stone."

"I'm sorry," she smiled again, weakly. "I'd be happy to tell you about Gretchen; that's why we're here, isn't it? It's just that, well, we *were* very close—like sisters. It hurts a lot.

"She and I met, I suppose, because we were the only two people on the block who weren't from here and who didn't know anybody. She came here straight from San Valencez University, to teach Physical Education over at Lavender High. That's what she'd always wanted, to teach.

"I came here to make a name for myself, to try and build the type of journalistic reputation that could lead me to bigger things, a magazine, or a major newspaper. We both had our dreams.

"One day we met on the street. I was out, pretending as usual to be jogging. I had a new set of expensive workout clothes, a Jane Fonda tape waiting on my video player in the apartment, and a set of sneakers that set me back nearly a week's salary. Gretchen was out running.

"When I saw her, I tried—foolishly, I might add—to match her pace. It was less than two blocks before I had to stop with a cramp, breathing so hard I thought I'd pass out on the spot. For some reason, she stopped too—stopped and helped me.

"When we found out that we were practically neighbors; she offered to coach me along on my running. It was the first gesture of friendship I'd received in Lavender, and I snapped it up. We became friends quickly after that. Pretty simple story, actually. I run five miles a day now. She did that."

"It shows," Straker commented. "It sounds as if Miss Steiner was a pretty friendly lady. That makes this even tougher to ask, but I have to do it. Do you have any idea, even a glimmer of an inkling, why anyone might have wanted to kill her?"

Pamela shook her head, almost violently, as if trying to shake free of her emotions and continue. After a few moments, she did so. "She was so…special, Ken. This is hard for me to describe…to put into words that make sense.

"Gretchen was a very simple, pure woman, in many ways

naive to the world. She was twenty-seven years old, unmarried and still looking for Mr. Right. I'd bet a month's pay that she was a virgin, though I never had the courage to ask.

"Her life was her kids at school, her cats at home, and running. She used to tell me about the running, how she'd done it since she was a little girl—her dad was her coach. She said she wanted to run in a marathon someday...I guess some dreams just never make it, do they?"

Her voice broke then, and she reached for her wine glass, trying to use it to mask the emotion. Straker averted his eyes for a second out of politeness. As he swung them back to meet hers, they passed over the curves of her firm young breasts. She seemed not to notice this time.

Deciding that it was his turn to give up something, he spoke into the growing silence. "We did find one clue. There was a small pocket knife, obviously not the murder weapon, but lying right beside the...altar."

He hesitated over that last word. It still didn't sit well with him that such a place existed within his own jurisdiction, and he didn't want to upset her any more than was necessary. *But, damn it all,* he thought, *it was a double-d goddamned altar.*

"The knife belongs to a local boy, a kid I know. I have reason to believe he and some friends may have been in the graveyard that night. They may have seen something, heard something."

Pamela's eyes lit with immediate interest. He saw her intuitive and investigative skills snapping into place, and he almost smiled.

"Have you questioned him?" she asked quickly. "Is he in custody? You don't think he..."

"Hold on, Pamela," he said, raising a hand in mock surrender, as if fending off an attack. "One question at a time, please. This is supposed to be dinner, not a press conference.

"No, he is not in custody. I have no real reason, other than the knife and the suggestion that he may have been in the cemetery, to suspect him of doing anything wrong. I tried to question him, might even have learned something useful, but his father—stepfather, actually, stomped in on us.

"He's a violent man, drinks too much. I got out of there as

quickly as I could, after I'd calmed him down. I could go back with a warrant, I suppose, but I don't believe that the boy is guilty of anything, just scared. If I went in there officially, the town would be on his back like a pack of dogs, on what was left of him, anyway. I'm afraid his father would get him first, and that wouldn't be a pretty sight. Frankly, I'm a bit stumped on this one."

"What could a boy of that age have wanted in a graveyard in the middle of the night?" Pamela asked, curious now and leaning forward. The scent of her perfume drifted up to fill his nostrils. Her eyes were glittering, alive, and he was glad to have her back after the emotional bout a few moments before.

"It's no secret to us," Straker answered slowly, "The Police Department, I mean," he explained quickly, "that local kids have used Shady Grove for some time now as an evening party spot. It's out of the way, seldom patrolled, the perfect place for a little illicit gathering—for adolescent encounters of all sorts. Teenagers today seem to have a morbid fascination with death. To them the graveyard is 'cool'."

"But," she pursed her lips in an oddly attractive expression, "how did this...this 'altar,' ever go unnoticed? Especially if it's such a popular spot? I mean, even an irregular patrol would have noticed something like that...and what about the custodians? The place does have a custodian, doesn't it? Hasn't anyone ever reported it?"

"They have, in a way." Straker answered, staring off to the side as though distracted. He turned back suddenly and continued. "I found one report, digging through the records, that was overlooked somehow. It seems that one Abner Kiley is the caretaker of Shady Grove, has been for over fifteen years now.

"One time in October, about three years ago, he came across our 'altar.' It had fresh blood on it then, too, but it was never taken seriously. The back part of that cemetery is very old, almost completely overgrown in parts. You'd think you were walking through a jungle. It borders very closely on a public hunting ground, and it seems that when Abner found his blood, it was smack in the middle of deer season.

"He just assumed that someone had killed a deer, gutted

and quartered it on that makeshift stone table, and hauled it off through the cemetery because the driveway was the most convenient route. Made sense to us, and there were no missing persons reports at the time.

"According to the report, all old Abner was concerned about was the trespassing. The two upright stone slabs beneath that altar are gravestones. They're old, and there's no way to know for sure where they were stolen from, but someone used to be buried under them. Abner takes his responsibilities pretty seriously, and he just didn't think it was right. We upped our patrol schedule for a week or so, made a few more passes than normal through that area, but it eventually slid through the cracks. We just don't have the manpower to reach out that far very often."

"Then this isn't the first...sacrifice?" Pamela shuddered, reaching again for her wine glass, taking a long sip, then setting it back down. After a couple of seconds she snatched it up again, downing it in a single gulp and reaching again for the bottle. "How many?"

"There's just no way of telling," Straker answered, making a purposeful effort to keep his voice steady. He hadn't meant to return to any topic that would disturb his companion. "The only evidence at this point is in the accumulation of bloodstains on the stone. They've been there far too long even to tell how many animals, or humans, might have left them. I took some scrapings and sent them on the FBI lab in Los Angeles, but I'm not holding my breath.

"My own guess is that there have been strange things going on behind our backs here in Lavender for a long time, maybe several years. We might have never noticed at all, but this time they chose to involve someone from the town, and this time they got caught."

Pamela stared down at the table for a while, collecting her thoughts. It was a whole new picture now, a different ballgame altogether, and it was a horrifying reality to consider.

"That makes it a lot worse then, doesn't it Ken? I mean, someone who's been here a long time must be involved." She was speaking slowly, thinking her way through it. "Probably several of them. That doesn't make it much easier to find them, but easier than if they were coming here from somewhere else, leaving behind their garbage, and going away again. What's next, then?"

"I'm not sure," Straker confessed. "I'm still hoping to learn something from the boy. If I can get past his father and get him alone for a few minutes, I think I can convince him to be straight with me. He's a little odd, but he seems to have his head on pretty straight, otherwise, especially considering all the shit that he's been through. Kids in his situation pretty often turn out bad— the pressure's enough just growing up, as I remember it."

Their food arrived then, steaming heaps of lasagna, garlic bread and fresh garden salad. Pamela surprised him by reading his mind and ordering a second bottle of wine. The first was nearly gone, and he could feel the warmth of it flowing through his system.

The conversation lagged as they shoveled the hot, spicy food into their mouths. He was surprised to find how hungry he was, as if the appetite that had evaded him since this investigation had begun had returned to him all at once. The case was starting to interfere with his system, his routine, and that was something he hated almost as much as psychos.

I can see it now, he thought, a grin spreading across his face before he could stop it, "Inspector dies of bleeding ulcers. Indigestion, or Satanic possession?"

They finished their meal in relative silence. There was little more to be said that would be of any help, and each of them were lost in their own speculations. While Pamela was nearly a decade and half his junior, he was finding her company surprisingly comfortable. It served, if nothing else, to remind him just how long it had been since he'd spent any time in the company of a good looking woman. Too long, that much was certain.

She was bright, pretty, and exactly what he wished he'd invested a larger part of his earlier life on. What he had done instead, was to take off, noble purpose in hand, and marry himself to the police force. It seemed so right at the time, so important. The eradication of all of the "bad guys," the righting of things that were "wrong."

Noticing his mood swing, Pamela derailed her own train

of thoughts and asked, "Why do you do it, Ken? You look like you've been up for days, almost obsessed. When was the last time you had a good night's sleep? A decent meal?

"I guess that I really don't understand it, how can you survive it? I mean, you have to let it all wash over you and then go on, time after time. I know that I'll survive what's happened here. Gretchen is gone, and I'll have to learn to live with that in my own way. But you, you must have seen this sort of thing a hundred times, and yet you go on. How?"

"Is this an interview?" he asked, smiling up at her bleakly, wondering how she'd read so close to his thoughts without his saying a word. He decided to answer the question, one that he had been asked before and brushed aside, if only to try and clear it up for himself.

"I grew up in a rough home," he said, rolling his wine glass between the fingers of both hands and staring down into the swirling red liquid. "I saw a lot of things happen, and a lot of people that meant a lot to me were hurt. My father drank, my mother had boyfriends, and my older sister never did quite learn how to cope.

"I guess, when it all comes down to the root of the matter, she's my reason. Annie. She grew up with nobody to watch out for her. I was too young, Mom was never around, and Dad was too drunk. When she grew up, and she was a pretty girl, she became just another part of the problem. It was as if she never had a chance.

"She turned to drugs; I never even noticed. She was gone from home more and more, and then one day she was just gone. They found her in the park that night—dead. She'd overdosed, been raped, robbed, and I saw her there before they took her away. I had to go, you see, someone had to identify her. Dad was out drinking, Mom was with some guy I'd never seen before and didn't have time to be bothered. I was fourteen."

"You don't have to tell me this," Pamela said, stopping him. Her eyes were awash with sympathy, with a shared pain that seemed to lift his spirits somewhat. Her hands were wrapped tightly around her wine glass. "I didn't know."

"It's okay," he said, taking a drink of his own wine and

smiling at her. "I've never told anyone this. Maybe it's high time I did. Maybe I never even told myself why I do it. Somehow that made it easier. Just bottle it up and forget about it.

"There isn't much more to tell, in any case. I saw Annie there, knew that the people who'd done it to her were loose— that they would do it again to someone else's sister, or someone's mother. I remember one of the investigators, a fat old man named McCloskey. He pulled me aside and gave me a bit of wisdom that's stuck with me all these years.

"He said, 'Fucking psychos, kid. They're everywhere. We'll get the ones who got your sister, count on it, but you watch out. There are a lot of them out there. You watch out for the fucking psychos, you'll be all right.'

"I left home soon after that, finished high school by hook and crook, and moved over to San Valencez. I worked there as a waiter for two years, attending courses at the Community College until I had enough behind me to get on the force.

"I moved up pretty fast, and when there was an opening back here in Lavender, I took it. My first Detective post. I guess I've been fighting my own little war with Officer McCloskey's psychos ever since. I'm a bit of one myself now, I suppose. It comes with the territory."

She didn't say anything at first, only stared at him and sipped her wine. It was as if she were sizing him up, pitting him in her mind against the type of people who might have killed her friend. She smiled, and he guessed that she believed he might find them after all.

"I'm sorry to hear about Annie," she said quietly, playing with her empty glass before filling it yet again. "I guess I really don't know how that would feel. You've been—alone—ever since?"

"I've had friends," he admitted, "even a couple of girlfriends. In the end, they all lost—or won—depending on your outlook. They all lost to my obsession. My job is a tough master.

"Every time someone gets killed or raped and the case is put in front of me, some kind of responsibility thing grabs hold of me. If I don't stop them, who will? Does that make any sense?

"Now your friend is dead, probably killed by one of the 'fine upstanding citizens' I'm sworn to protect. It's up to me to make sure that it doesn't happen again."

"I can see that, I suppose," she said, pouring the last of the wine into both of their glasses equally, "but if it helps any, I feel responsible as well. And," she added, fixing him with a deep, thoughtful stare, "I feel a great deal better about it all knowing we are on the same side. Now that we've talked, I mean. Thank you for dinner."

He smiled, but he didn't speak. They finished the wine in silence and returned to his car. The mellow effects of the wine were still lulling his senses, and the night was crisp and clear. He didn't want to break the spell of the moment.

He parked the car in front of her apartment and helped her out onto the sidewalk, wistfully remembering similar times with older women, but not really disappointed. She caught the look, smiled, and pecked him on one cheek. It was very similar to a father-daughter kiss, and afterward she hurried up the walk. At the door, she turned and called back to him.

"Thanks again, Ken, and don't worry. We'll get them, always, because we're right."

He only wished it were that simple. Then the door opened and closed, and she was gone. The empty night loomed ahead. Straker nosed out onto the street and pointed the car for home. Somehow he knew he'd be able to sleep this time.

As the moon and its mysteries assumed control of the night, he drove home, and climbed between the sheets. For once he slept peacefully—peacefully and without dreams.

CHAPTER FOURTEEN

Straker stared down at the memo in his hand, his intestines coming to a quick boil, wondering why every time a weirdo sent something to the force it wound up on his desk. The present annoyance was in the form of a small yellow phone memo. It was fastened securely to the front of a short stack of papers. Consent forms, actually, from the local television network. The memo was from one Hector Clearwater, a name that Straker was all too familiar with.

Damn the fool, he thought, slamming back into his chair in a sudden angry burst of frustration. *Does he think that murder is a fucking game?*

The memo was silent. It held no answers. Still fuming, he snatched up the phone and dialed. As the rings continued, he braced himself for what he knew was to come. This wasn't going to be a pleasant conversation, not at all.

"Hello?" The voice on the other end was cheerful, sunny, and bright. Annoying as hell at that instant. "Commissioner Stanley's Office; this is Mary; how may I direct your call?"

"Hello, Mary," he replied, "This is Ken. I have a message here that says I'm supposed to call John?"

"Yes," she agreed happily. "I have a note on that right here, Inspector. He's waiting for your call." Momentarily dropping the plastic lilt from her voice, she went on in more conspiratorial tones, "He doesn't seem very happy about it, either, Ken. He's been slamming stuff around that office all morning. What did you do?"

"It's a long story, Mary, way too long for the moment. I'll drop by some morning with donuts and tell you about it over coffee. You'd better put him on now; I wouldn't want to keep him waiting."

The line clicked once; a buzzer sounded as it transferred him, and John Stanley's booming voice crashed through the line in a sudden burst, nearly driving him back from the receiver in his hand. Grimacing in pain, Straker pulled it close again so he could hear.

"What the *hell* is going on, Ken? I've got phones ringing off the hook here. Even the double-d goddamned by God *mayor* has been on the line. Withholding evidence on a murder case? Satanists? And now they want to grill you on goddamn television like a rare steak in a barby-fucking-cue. Grill *us*! Don't you think, before you put my whanger on a butcher block and swing a cleaver at it you could at least give me some notice?"

Clearing his throat and envisioning the Blarney Stone, Straker cut in, hoping he could head this off before it got truly ugly.

"Hold on, John," he said wearily, "and calm down. You know me better than to start jumping down my throat without hearing me out. Have I ever put you in a spot like this before without warning?"

"Start talking and make it good," Stanley grated. "I don't have much time left before I'm going to be forced to act on this, one way or another; and I need my damn ducks in a row."

"You already know what case they're talking about, the Steiner murder. This is still an open investigation. There are too many questions unanswered to hazard a logical guess as to who, or even why the woman was murdered. Hell, everything from the initial call reporting the crime has been a series of riddles.

"As far as that knife, withholding evidence, you call it what you want. I can't arrest a kid for ritual murder because his goddamned pocket knife was found in a graveyard, and I'm not about to put him or his family through the bullshit that a line of questioning like that would stir up for no reason. If I had more on him, I'd bring him in; but I don't.

"As far as this 'Satan worship' angle, we never went public with that information at all—they got their information from somewhere else. We have nothing but an anonymous phone call and an altar with bloodstains on it to prove there was more than one person involved in the killing, let alone a group of religious weirdos. What would you have rather I did, John, called the fucking National Engraver and put out an all points call for a fucking exorcist?"

Static-filled silence greeted his outburst, and Ken nearly chuckled as an image of his friend's probable expression flashed through his mind. He and John Stanley had served together for a lot of years, hard years, walking beats as rookies in San Valencez, partners as detectives in Lavender, and the last few as Commissioner and Chief Inspector. They knew each other like brothers, close brothers.

"You know what I'm facing here, Ken," John said, sighing heavily as the steam leaked out of his tirade. "They're going to raise hell, literally, on this one. You and I, we have to come up with a story, a story we can both stick by; and it's got to be damned good—good enough to satisfy the public. Otherwise they'll nail our asses to the wall with big, square nails."

"So," Ken asked, already fearing the answer his next question was going to receive, "you want me to go ahead and accept the invitation to this television thing?"

"It isn't an invitation, really, Ken," John replied. "It's more of an ultimatum, don't you think? I mean, it's liable to be bad enough going on the show; what do you think this asshole would do to us if you refuse to show up?"

"I suppose you're right," he sighed. "I just hate letting this jerk ruin my investigation and not being able to do a damned thing about it. Whoever did that killing is going to *love* this."

Another thought occurred to Straker, and he voiced it. "The boy, John, Nick Leatherman? His dad's a mean tempered one, alcoholic and mean. I'm not exactly sure how he's going to take this, but I am sure that it won't be well. I'm not sure how I should handle that...any ideas?"

"Use your best judgment, Ken; you know your area and your people better than I do. I do think you'll have to bring the boy in, though. You'll want a chance to talk to him before that Clearwater asshole gets his mitts on him—after that it may be too late to learn anything at all. You don't think he had anything to do with our murder?"

"No," Straker said, feeling a sudden conviction in the words that he hadn't really been certain was there, "I just don't see it. I do think he's holding something back, though, something that would help me in the investigation. He acts as if he's scared of something, though I couldn't say what.

"I'll just have to try and find some way to get him in here without involving his father. That would be best. I hate to go behind the man's back, but I'll be damned if I'll be the cause of that boy getting another beating. The first suspicion that Nick is involved in anything that resembles trouble, Ed Leatherman may send him to that television program looking *really* bad."

"Well, like I said, do whatever you think is best. Just do it fast. And Ken?" John sighed again, as though he knew the situation was beyond his control and fading fast, "try and keep us, and your own ass, out of the hottest part of the water? Please? I'd truly hate to have to go home and tell Trudy I lost my pension to a talk show host after all these years."

"I'll do my best," Straker promised. "Tell Trudy I said 'hi'."

The phone clicked and Straker turned back to the papers on his desk, trying to frown them into nonexistence. Failing, he took up his pen quickly, before the urge to crumple the entire stupid mess into a ball and send it sailing for the garbage could really get a hold on him, and affixed his bold, thick-lined signature to the bottom of the consent form. This done, he took the stack, envelope, memo, and all, and tossed it angrily into the "out" basket on the corner of his desk.

His secretary, a rotating position between the clerks and typists that ran the bulk of the office's administrative business, could see that it got in the mail. Maybe they'd misfile it, or burn it by accident. He didn't really care; it was out of his hands now. For the moment he had to concentrate, to find some way to erase all thoughts of the coming televised ordeal by fire from his thoughts and get back to the investigation at hand. There were too many other things to be considered.

One thing was Nick Leatherman. He would need to see him as soon as possible, but how to go about it? Going to the

Leatherman house seemed a very poor answer. He supposed that the telephone would be his best bet, as long as Ed didn't answer it.

One way or the other, he needed to square his story with the boy's and get a clearer picture of what he knew. There were too many holes in what they'd learned so far, too many little glitches in any theory he was able to come up with. Asshole or not, Clearwater was no idiot. Not much would slip past the man's trained, predatory ears; and Kendall Straker wasn't about to play the man's fool without a fight.

Another thing, one that nagged at the back of his mind and would not let go of his thoughts, was the question of how one Reverend Horace Goldbough, minister of the Church of New Light and spiritual leader of the largest church in the area, had come by the knowledge that they had found the pocket knife in the first place.

While it was certainly true that rumor traveled fast, and while there were a few officers and staff members on his force that attended services regularly at the Church of New Light, it still struck him as very, very odd that the information had leaked so fast.

And why would a successful evangelist, other than the obvious publicity to be gained by the television exposure, be so adamant in the persecution of one boy, or one music group, even to the point of dragging the police into the frenzy? What did he want in return for all this effort—what did he hope to gain? And how the *hell* had he known about the damned knife?

Questions loomed on all sides, but no answers readily presented themselves. He picked up the phone again, flipped quickly through his Rolodex and found the Leatherman's home number. Steeling himself to drop the phone back into its cradle if Ed answered, he dialed.

The phone rang only twice before it was answered, and an agitated, feminine voice blurted out, "Hello?"

Taking a chance that he was calling at the proper time and that fate would back him up, Straker answered. "Mrs. Leatherman? This is Inspector Straker, Kendall Straker? We spoke a couple of days ago...is Nick there?"

"No..." the voice was hesitant now, and was that disappointment he detected in the tone? "No, he's not. Is there something wrong, Inspector? Has he done something bad? Is he in trouble? Ed..."

"Please, Mrs. Leatherman, don't call Ed." Straker was talking fast now, hoping she would agree with his thoughts—that he hadn't made a mistake in talking to her this way. "I don't want to make any trouble, not for you, and certainly not for Nick.

"I'll be honest with you, Mrs. Leatherman, I've known your husband Ed for a lot of years. We've never exactly seen eye to eye, and he can be, shall we say, a hard man to discuss things with.

"Nick isn't in trouble, not really, but I do need to talk to him. It's very important that I see him as soon as possible."

"He's not home." She repeated the words, nearly in tears, then continued before Straker could speak again. "Neither is Ed. There's a letter here, Inspector, from some man on a television show. Do you know what's going on, where they might be?"

"Christ," Straker blurted before he could stop himself. "Mrs. Leatherman," he sighed, seeing that, as usual, the easy road was closed and barred to him, "I don't really know exactly what the hell is going on myself. I do know that I've got to find Nick, and quickly. You say Ed's gone? Should he be home?"

"Supper is an hour late already," she said. "Ed never misses a meal or a beer, so he says. Ed and I've been married for a long time now, and he hasn't once missed supper without calling.

"He may not be the ideal husband, or father, but he's at least predictable. I think he saw that letter, and I think he may know where Nick is, too. I'm scared, Inspector."

"Damn," Straker breathed. It was worse than he'd thought. "Jeanette, you don't mind my calling you that, do you?" He was talking now to fill the gap while he thought, buying time as his mind slipped from plan to plan.

"No," she answered, obviously not caring at the moment *what* he called her, as long as he was willing to help.

"You stay there. If Ed comes in, try to keep him calm. Give

him a beer, if that will help. I'm going to come over there and wait for them with you. If Nick comes in, don't let him leave that house. He and I have got to talk, and now time may be even shorter than before.

"Whatever happens, try to keep your head. There are a lot of strange things going on. There are people in danger and the chance of a bunch of people being hurt, even killed. Am I getting through?"

"Yes," she said, seeming to brighten slightly at the promise of aid. "I'll be here, and I'll try to find Nick. I can call his friends, his girlfriend. Maybe one of them has seen him. They're never far apart, it seems."

"That's good, real good," Straker said as calmly as he could. "Make sure he knows that he's not in trouble. This time, he and I seem to be on the same side; and I need his help. I don't want to scare him—just need to talk. And, Jeanette?"

"Yes," she replied.

"Do you have any coffee?"

He didn't wait for an answer. Time was slipping away in an invisible stream, slipping away faster than it was supposed to. He got out to his car as quickly as possible and pulled into the slackening evening traffic. Another meal missed. He sighed, hitching his belt a bit tighter as he drove.

The moonlight was just beginning to splash across the city, the night to usurp the throne held for so many hours by the minions of daylight. It was a different world than that which the sun protected, a darker place. Things that seemed unlikely or impossible during the morning or afternoon hours, bloomed into sinister possibilities and strange realities under the shadowy cover of midnight. He let his foot push down a bit harder on the pedal.

Jeanette stood for a long moment with her hand resting on top of the telephone receiver. She'd just gotten off the phone with Ruthie's mother, Evelyn, and Ruthie was not home either. Neither were Flash or Weasel—she almost smiled at the names again, as usual, but couldn't quite pull it off. Had she ever been young enough to use nicknames like that?

She spent day after day in the house alone, except for the company of the dog, and yet it had never seemed so vacant—so empty. Finally gathering her wits back about her, she turned and headed toward the kitchen, going slowly about the familiar tasks of brewing coffee and cleaning up after the dinner.

She didn't know when Ed might be back, but just in case she scraped a generous portion of the dinner she'd prepared onto a plate and covered it with foil, placing it in the oven on warm. One thing was certain, when he did get there, he'd expect something to eat.

Hearing her move around, Lizzy came padding in to the room and nuzzled her leg with a wet, sympathetic nose. When the water was burping and bubbling through the tubes of the Mr. Coffee on its way to the pot, she moved to the kitchen table and plopped down into one of the vinyl-covered seats. She reached out affectionately to scratch the dog on her nose. Somehow the two of them had reached an understanding, as though she could gaze into the soft pools of Lizzie's eyes and see her own thoughts and emotions mirrored there.

She turned away after a moment and searched the blackness outside through the parted curtains for any sign of Ed, or of Nick. She found herself thinking about Ed, thinking more than was usual for her.

Ed was many things, most of them, she knew, were not really very good things. One thing he had always been, though, was dependable. She could always count on his being there, on his handling things, even if his methods were poor. That, she supposed, was the reason she'd accepted his proposal in the first place.

Young still, and with Nick to take care of, she'd needed someone who would be "there" for her. In those days Ed's hard, rough-edged ways had seemed to mask a steadiness, a maturity waiting to bloom as he aged. It had been that underlying dependability that had reassured her that things would work out between them, that they would be happy.

It had, of course, turned out to be only a barely controlled mask over even harder emotions, and violence. Ed was an angry, bitter man; but still he had been there. In her weakness, it had been enough. She'd stayed.

Now, sitting with only a dog for companionship, she waited. It occurred to her that, though she wanted him to be there, that she was nearly as frightened by the idea of his return as she was by the idea of the empty, brooding house. It was a familiar fear, not knowing what kind of mood he'd be in, not knowing what words might send him off on a tirade, or actually elicit a smile. It was a fear that she was at least accustomed to.

This void of the unknown that surrounded her was different. She remembered such moments in the past, hiding beneath blankets and fearing the sounds from her window, nights when she'd huddled alone and cried herself to sleep. They had been a long time ago, in a world that hardly existed—a little girl that had grown up and disappeared in the smoke of the years. She felt very tired. Even Ed, his beer, his temper, and his anger, was bearable in the face of nights like this. If only he, or Nick, would come home.

She was startled out of her reverie by the sharp rap of knuckles on the front door. Nearly stumbling from her seat in her haste, her heart hammering wildly, she hurried down the hall. She put her eye to the peephole and gazed out into the shadows.

It was Inspector Straker, was his name Ken? The oppressive weights lifted from her shoulders, at least slightly, and she flipped on the outside light and unlatched the chain that held the door tight. This was a good man; she felt it deep in her soul. He had helped Nick before, at a time when nobody would even listen to him, or to her; and he was there when they needed him again. At least she wouldn't be alone. Opening the door quickly, she stepped aside, nodding a greeting and closing it behind him.

"Neither of them has come home yet?" He asked the question gently, but it was obvious that he had already read the answer in her eyes. There was urgency in his words, a furtive nervousness that she caught flickering across his gaze.

"I've made coffee," she said, nearly blushing and furious at herself for it. She realized with shock that she'd not had company, least of all a man, in her home for months—possibly years.

Certainly not when Ed wasn't at home. "Let me get you a cup, and you can tell me what's happened."

"I'd like that," he said, smiling at her with a curious twist to his lips. It was not unpleasant to have him looking at her, and she did blush, this time. "Black, please," he continued. "I think it may be a long, long night."

Outside, where the breeze was picking up to a steady force, tossing leaves and sticks about and rustling through the branches of the trees, secrets were whispered; but nobody was there to hear.

CHAPTER FIFTEEN

Horace slid in behind the wheel of the rented car, checking his pockets and the folds of his robes to insure that he had forgotten nothing. Beside him, in the passenger seat, sat Brenda, her eyes bright and glistening, staring moodily off into the darkness. They were clothed in dark, velvet robes. Horace wore his vestments, as well, blending the two disparate faiths that bound his life in an odd parody of both.

He nosed the car out into traffic, and one by one, the others followed behind, staggering themselves so as not to gain undue attention. They had work to do this night, powers to weave and guards to set. This meeting was not as intense, perhaps, as their last, but each step was critical to the completeness of their task.

The night they truly awaited, the promised reward of service, was drawing closer rapidly. Horace felt it; they all did in varying degrees. It was in the aura of power that surrounded them, the sense of otherworldly presence that shadowed each movement. He felt it tingle through his veins and sensed it to the very core of his being. Energy crackled through the darkness and played in little dancing steps along the nape of his neck.

Brenda was lost in her own world, and he knew that she felt it too. She was the most sensitive of them all, the one with the longest connection to the forces they served. He avoided any physical contact with her scrupulously—even tried to keep his eyes averted from her as much as possible.

She was on edge, her nerves as taut as a piano wire strung too tightly. Her body seemed to tremble with suppressed energy, with frustrated anticipation. Her sensitivity, her nearness to the power, was her strength. It was why she had been chosen.

Horace wondered, deep inside, whether she truly knew what it was that she was working toward, what it was that was asked of her. He hadn't blindly followed her lead, as she thought. He'd done some reading, researched some things on his own that she knew nothing about. It had proven to be some pretty unorthodox reading material for an evangelist. He knew things now that he believed she did not want him to, things that shifted the balance of power considerably, though the outcome would still be the same.

He had also become familiar with his own part in the scheme of things, both what Brenda had planned, and the reality of the situation. She had misinterpreted a few nuances, or had been misled at some earlier time. It was as it should be. She would play her part, and she would be perfect. Perfection was all that mattered.

He only prayed that nothing would happen to come between them and their goals. The fear of failure rose above them, always, coiled like a serpent, ready to grip them in coils of power and fling them against the unnerving expanse of dark nothingness that lay beyond. It was not a possibility for consideration, but the itch of it remained in the recesses of his mind, goading him to concentration and care.

Care was the key, he knew. Careful, in fact, was much too simple, too weak of a word for what was necessary. They had to be more precise than an artisan, more secretive than a spy, more zealous than an apostle. It was a great weight, a heavy burden.

It bothered him that they had been discovered, even on the fringes, so soon in the ritual. The cemetery was an integral point in the design. Now it would be watched more carefully than ever before. Even their own private, secretive approach would hold more than its usual amount of danger for them.

At least, thus far, he and the Church of New Light seemed to have completely escaped any outside scrutiny. It was imperative that he not be watched, or followed. They would be undone if he were discovered now, and the consequences of that were too hideous and horrifying to even consider.

There were two remaining rituals to be performed, two

more pieces of a puzzle centuries in preparation. The first they would complete this very night; the other was the promise.

Horace drove on in silence, but a smile had invaded his face. He couldn't help himself. The moon had risen to her silent glory, casting an aura of silver light-fingers to pluck at the earth, lifting some shadows and lengthening others. Though the modern man in him knew it to be only a pale reflection, a re-telling of the tale of the day's brighter, seemingly more potent light, another deeper part of him, a primal instinct, spoke of other powers. The contrast of silver and darkness was a powerful sight, eerie and magical. Perfect for what was to come.

Farther back, behind even the last and most cautious of their procession, another set of lights had hit the road, trailing along slowly and steadily in their wake. They were far enough back not to appear a threat, but never so far that they lost the trail. Nobody in the procession had thought to keep a lookout; they were too confident that nobody was watching. Why should anyone be?

Ed steered the pickup easily with one hand, wondering just what the hell kind of weird shit Nick had gotten mixed up in this time. It was damned strange, all these fucking weirdos driving around in big groups so late at night, not the church-like thing to do, any way you cut it. It looked like a damned funeral procession, and, just where in hell, he wondered as he followed, were they heading, anyway?

Ed had lived in Lavender all of his life. He knew every road-way and path within a fifty-mile radius of the city, knew them like the lines on the back of his work-hardened hands. When he'd been a young man, sowing his oats, he'd done more than his share of exploring.

Actually, it hadn't ended with his childhood—Ed had never really grown up. Sometimes, late at night, even at thirty-eight years and rising, he still found himself and a six-pack sharing the lonely drive down to the old quarry, or out to the lot in back of the power plant.

He wasn't a part of that scene anymore, not really, but he liked to go there and remember. He'd sit and watch and drink as the young people came and went, the people he longed to be one of again and had lost so many years before. They played their little games, discovered the curves and secrets of one another's bodies, partied, all with an enthusiasm and abandon that he yearned for.

Memories of those times were the only ones he really had left. Everything else seemed cloudy to him, hazier with each passing year. He could vaguely remember the long hours spent in school, friends he hadn't seen in years, fights he'd been in, won, and lost. He even remembered a few of the girls, mostly the ones he'd taken out by the power plant, but a few he hadn't. All that mattered anymore was the beer, and the dreaming. Somehow he just wasn't cut out to handle the responsibilities of the adult world.

The column ahead slowed, and he braked to the side of the road, wondering what the hell they could be doing. They were turning, he realized finally, turning down the old Johnson road. Now his curiosity was *really* peaked. What in the hell could they want with *that* old place? There was nothing down that road but the old Johnson farm, abandoned since Ed was in high school, and a lot of open country.

He tried to sort out what he knew, to make a bigger picture of what he'd seen so far. There was damned little to go on, that much was sure. There was the letter.

The letter had come in the mail that afternoon, while he was still home eating lunch. He'd seen that it was from the television network, so he'd opened it. They wanted Nick to appear on that idiot television show, Clear it Up.

The letter had gone on to say how it would be in Nick's "best interests" to appear. It seemed there were allegations of strange goings on, accusations made by one Horace Goldbough of the Church of New Light. Damned religious faggot; why couldn't he leave decent folks alone?

Then there was good ol' Kenny Straker and that god-damned pocketknife. Ed knew he was no genius, had never claimed to be; but neither was he stupid. It hadn't taken him all that long, or too many beers for that matter, to see that whatever was going on, whatever all these assholes were up to, it was a giant bullet and it had Nick's name on it—*his* boy, damn it. It didn't look good, but that didn't matter. Family was family.

Ed was a man of action. It was the only response he knew, the only solution that would stop the itching at his mind. He'd started out after the first beer of his twelve-pack was empty, sliding into the pickup seat with the rest of them beside him, and hit the road. Popping the top of the second beer, he'd hit the end of the street and made the first turn toward his goal, Goldbough's home.

He knew where that asshole lived, knew the place only too well. He'd been around when Horace had first come to town, knew more about the "good Reverend" than most folks, he figured. More than he wanted to know, even.

For instance, he knew about that woman who stayed at the man's house, the supposed chaste leader of the good Christians of Lavender. He'd seen her often enough to know she was there more nights than not, and after careful scrutiny of her body and the way she moved it, he was certain that she wasn't there for any extended Bible study.

His plan was simple. Confrontation. He would finally speak his piece to the man who'd come into town like an avenging angel and swept the tiny "First Baptist Church" into the gutter like so much street trash with the first gusts of the whirlwind that had eventually deposited that big, fancy white building downtown. Ed had always hated the look of that place.

He figured it was about time the two of them met. He'd been planning to catch ol' Horace alone for a long, long time now— brooding over it, actually. It was one of the few loose ends in his life, one of the few roads he'd saved for later. There were things he knew about the "good Reverend" and the Church of New Light, and the trail of litter they had left behind as they grew, things he knew that even Goldbough, and certainly those who followed him, would be surprised by.

His mother had been among those swept along in the original flood of Horace's "Revival." When the church began its expansion, outgrowing the walls of the small First Baptist Church and spreading like cancer through the community, she had been one of the first baptized. It ate at Ed's insides to think about it.

He realized now that his father had been much the same then as he himself was now. It was not a thought that had ever occurred to him before, and for some reason it felt good. A connection to a past he'd thought lost. When Horace Goldbough and his church had blasted into their lives, it had not sat well with the elder Leatherman.

When Ed's mother had begun carrying her Bible with her everywhere she went and attending church first on Sundays, then twice on Sundays, and then on weeknights as well, his father had grown angry. He had certain ideas about the duties of a wife, and he believed she was neglecting those. It was a chink in the armor of his iron will, of his control of his family and home; and he couldn't abide it.

Ed remembered how hard his mother had tried, cleaning, cooking, doing extra little things to make his father happy. It was all in vain—a waste of time. Once Tobias Leatherman had made up his mind on something, he was like a wall of granite. You could chip away at him with all the logic and reason that you liked; nothing was going to change his viewpoint.

Ed saw that his mother had failed to look closely enough into his father's eyes, which were now, it seemed, his own. She had failed to see the true crux of the matter, the real problem.

His father wasn't about to become second fiddle to her church, not even if God and Satan battled in the front yard over his soul. His insecurity would not allow it. He had needed to be in control of his own little world, his family and his home. The outside world had been beyond his reach, but his home was not.

Ed had been too young at the time to really understand all of this. The understanding had come years later, a lifetime later. All he'd seen at the time was his mother's eyes, the fear and the pain that had filled them, and the yearning. He'd seen his father's eyes, as well, the anger and the fury that fired the man's every movement.

He'd also seen the beatings. He'd received his fair share of those, of course, but that was as it should have been. There were lessons that could be learned only one way. After a while he'd even caught himself a time or two, praying to the god that caused his mother so much pain, that *he* would be beaten. At least while it was happening, his mother was safe.

He reached the point in the road where the cars had turned down the older road and drove on past it, taking his time. He was betting they were there for a while, not for a joy ride; and he knew another road, an older road even than the one they were using. There was more than one way to get to that old farm, and he wasn't about to give himself away at this point in the game.

Besides, knowing the roads as he did and putting the gas to the floor a little, he could get there before they did, see what was what. Something told him it would be a bad mistake to follow them directly. It only gave him one route of escape, back the way he'd come; and it made the chance of discovery too great.

He'd meant to confront Goldbough at his own home, maybe get a closer look at that woman while he was at it. He'd wanted to demand the reasons why the man was attacking his boy, and by the way, why the simpering little faggot hadn't helped his mother.

She had never been a strong person, his mother. That was more than likely the reason she'd married his dad in the first place—probably why Jeanette had put up with him for so long, too. That, and the fact that his mother had turned up pregnant after a night of partying down by the river, had cemented the two into a family.

Ed had never really been clear on how the two had met. He'd only learned after years of piecing together bits of their fights and snippets of conversation how they'd come to be married. He knew two things for sure about that marriage. It was a mistake, and he was at least partly to blame for having been born.

The two had been an almost comically poor match. She'd been weak-willed, almost too easily controlled. His father had been strict, rough, and demanding. It was his mother's nature that had drawn her to the church in the first place.

It was possible, he thought, that the church had had an even stronger influence on her, in the end, than even his father, an even more demanding master. They had attacked her where she was most vulnerable, her submissiveness to the will of others, her insecurity. They'd taken that very weakness and thrown it in her face, making her hate herself for it; and at the same time they'd used it to manipulate her surely and steadily toward their own goals.

It *had* been Horace Goldbough and his church, after all, not Ed's father, that had been strong enough to drive her to her death. That much had been clear in the short note she'd left behind, the legacy of her final day. The note had said that she was weak, that she couldn't find a way to cope with the pain, couldn't find the strength to do her duty by God or her family. She'd said that her faith was too small, that she was unworthy of God's great gift of life; so she'd given it back. Even in the end, even in death, she'd taken the easy way out.

But Ed knew that this wasn't the entire story. She hadn't gone out quite that simply, even though his father had believed it implicitly. She'd asked for help, though not in so many words, begged for it.

Alone and seeking guidance, she'd come away destroyed. That was what the Church of New Light had offered her in her misery. Ed didn't know exactly what happened that day, his own memories were blurred, forever marred by the image of his mother's pale, over-white face, by visions of blood, dripping slowly into the bath water—the crimson pool of bath water in which she'd lain, cold and lifeless.

He remembered his first sight of the new church downtown. He could envision, even now, beer in hand and bumping down the dirt road through the darkness, the "artistic" play of light that had so excited the town. The dripping red display of blood that only reminded him of his mother. He wondered if Reverend Goldbough even remembered her, if the cocksucker had ever given her death, or her life, a second thought. If so, there was no indication of it, then, or now.

The road was just as he remembered it from years of hunting trips. It was a bit more overgrown than he'd thought it would be, but it was no problem for the big, four-wheel drive truck beneath him. He turned out the headlights and flipped on the soft yellow running lights on the bumper. He knew his way well enough, and he couldn't be certain of getting there first. No sense in letting them know they were watched.

Reaching out, he grabbed another beer, slightly warm, but still good enough, and popped the top, bouncing and bumping along through the trees at a good pace.

As Ed approached from the far side of the old farm, The Reverend Horace Goldbough and his followers wound their own trail through the moonlight, slowly approaching the old barn in single file. Unaware that anything was amiss with their plans, they proceeded, eyes flashing brighter and brighter as their goal neared. It was thirty minutes until midnight.

CHAPTER SIXTEEN

The van was parked in the back, directly beside the dumpster that bordered the parking lot of the Church of New Light. Nick, Ruthie, Flash, and Weasel sat inside, staring out the window at the gleaming expanse of the building's walls. The night's expedition was taking on a reality that had not figured in to the original idea—an idea that had seemed much better, and worlds simpler, when it had first occurred several hours earlier.

The surrounding streets were barren, void of life. It was like a scene from a bad "B" horror movie. The shadows, born of the tall buildings surrounding the church and the light of the waxing moon, stretched out across the parking lot and up the sides of the building, dark sentinels waiting to grab them and haul them off for their wicked thoughts. Even Nick felt a little less sure of their mission, confronted with the actuality of breaking into a church.

Knowing that if they sat there much longer, they'd just drive away, Nick broke the silence. "I guess we'd better move," he said, putting as much false courage behind his voice as he could to reassure the others. He needed their support on this one, more than he ever had before. "There's not that much night left. I'd hate to get caught in *this* fucking place.

"Besides, we have to get you guys all home before you get into trouble of your own. Anyone getting grounded or held up now would be a disaster—I need you all on this one."

They each nodded slowly, but it was clear that none of them was completely certain they were making the right move. It didn't matter, really, only that they make *some* move, do *something*.

"You're sure we want to do this?" Weasel asked, openly voicing the concerns they were all feeling. "I mean, breaking into a fucking ferchrissakes church...I don't know. It just seems, *wrong* somehow. Like stealing from the collection plate on Sunday, or taking the Bible out of a hotel. Isn't there any way we could get a look around the place during the day?"

It was an empty question needing no answer, and the silence that met it was complete. They piled out of the van, grouped quickly beside the wall of the building and waited for Nick to tell them what came next. For better or worse, they were in it now, up to their ears.

None of them were calm—that was completely out—but they weren't in the mood for backing down, either. As a group they moved across the sidewalk and down the side of the building, moving as quickly as they could into the dubious cover of the deeper shadows that ran along the edge of the church.

Nick hadn't really made any plans for how he would enter the building—it had all happened too fast for that, so now that they were there he was forced to improvise. He tried the first window they came to. It was locked tight, and the bottom panes were re-enforced in the rear by a wire mesh.

Cursing under his breath, he moved down the line, checking each window carefully, but all with the same result. The frustration was building fast; to be so close to possible answers and to be stopped by a fucking locked window was intolerable. Just as he was about to whirl away in disgust, resigning himself to the necessity of returning to the van for a tool he could use to break a window, he heard Ruthie call out softly from somewhere to his right.

"Nick! Nick, come here, quick." She was around the corner, at the side of the building where the ornately carved wooden doors led to the main parking lot of the building.

"What is it?" he answered, moving quickly to her side. "What did you find?"

She merely reached out and pulled on the door, which was unlocked, smiling at him shyly. In his haste to exit the church and to reach Brenda, Horace had neglected to lock the door behind him.

Grinning widely, Nick turned and waved at Flash and Weasel. "Come on," he called out, keeping his voice as low as possible. It was almost too good to be true, and that made him nervous. He didn't want to blow the whole thing by finding out that the door was only open because some caretaker was inside cleaning the church. The last thing he needed in his present predicament was to be caught breaking and entering a church.

The interior was lit by an odd, glowing luminescence that permeated the air, coming from everywhere at once instead of a single source. They quickly realized that what they were witnessing was a spectacle that few of even the faithful followers of Horace Goldbough and his church would ever see. The moonlight, seeping in by the same pathways that led to such pyrotechnical beauty when traveled by sunlight, was putting on a display of its own. The effect was muted, silver and eerie, but no less spectacular than that brought on by the light of day.

Nick wondered if it was an effect achieved by accident, or a private joke of Horace's.

Far above their heads, hanging in his position of perpetual suffering and forgiveness, the statue of Jesus shimmered with silver luminescence. A trickle of clear light seemed to be dripping down his leg toward the basin below, and no matter which way they moved, his eyes traced their steps—staring—accusing.

Trying to ignore it, to blank the dark significance of what they were doing from his mind, Nick motioned for the others to follow him. He wasn't sure exactly where they would find what he was after, or even *if* they would find it; but he was betting that the Reverend's office would be the best place to start. He followed the wall to his right, stepping carefully through the darkness to avoid tripping or making any undue sound.

They skirted the empty rows of pews, the altar with all its ornate tapestries and gilt-trimmed finery, and finally beyond the edge of the huge baptismal pool, checking doors and hallways as they went. Inside the main room of the church, nothing was locked. They found a storeroom, two coat closets, a row of small bible-study classrooms, and the stairs to the choir loft. Finally they came to a large, ornately carved door that was half hidden behind the back corner of the altar and the baptismal pool.

On the door, a brass placard announced in large, bold script, that this was the place they sought. It was the office of Horace Goldbough, the "Reverend" Horace Goldbough.

Nick had seen the man's name on the letter at home that afternoon. It had already been opened, so he knew he wasn't the first to read it, either. He'd been scanning it when the crunch of gravel at the end of the drive had announced his stepfather's return.

He'd seen enough of the letter to know that the man who worked in this office, the man who had founded this church, was wrapped up heavily in whatever was going on. God only knew who or what else was involved, but Nick had this to go on, and he was damned if anything, or anybody, was going to deter him.

He also had the pin that he'd found in the graveyard that night. He knew he had enough to tie the good Reverend into the whole mess; all he needed was a little more proof, enough that he could get someone to listen to what he knew without calling him crazy. Taking a deep breath to steady his nerves, he pushed inward on the door. It swung noiselessly on oiled hinges, swishing across the lush carpet with a barely audible hiss.

He felt a hand on his shoulder then, and Flash was at his side. "Are you sure you want to do this, man? I mean, I'm with you whatever; you know that. The rest of us, we'd probably get in a little trouble, but eventually they'd leave us alone. You, though, you're in enough trouble already."

"I know man, I know," Nick answered, smiling with all the courage he could muster, "but there's only one way out of this that I see, and that's through it. I have to find something, anything that can help me figure this thing out. Otherwise, it really doesn't matter; I'll still be in trouble."

"How about your friend Straker? Don't you think he'd help?"

"He would—will—but I need something concrete to go to him with," Nick countered. "He might be sympathetic if I went there now, but with no more than suspicions, what can he do to help? I've got to do this, man. You guys can wait outside, if you want."

Without a further word, or waiting for an answer, he turned toward the door, slipping quietly into the interior of the large room and pulling the small flashlight he'd brought along free from his pocket. Flipping it on, he moved to the left, keeping the light turned toward the floor so it wouldn't be visible through the windows.

He needn't have bothered. The windows were completely closed off, sealed by heavy wooden shutters that blocked even the bright moonlight completely. If the shutters hadn't been enough, the curtains were pulled as well; and they were dark and heavy. Nick wondered briefly what went on in here that Goldbough didn't want others to see, but he didn't have time to dwell on it at that moment.

The desk that filled most of the room's center was immaculately neat. There was no chance of lucking onto a stray memo or note lying about. He walked slowly around and sat in the heavily padded leather chair, reaching for the drawers to his right.

As he pulled each one open, shuffling quickly through their contents, the others followed him into the room. They spread out quickly, checking shelves and bookstands, any nook or cranny that might hold a secret. They moved quickly, but carefully. None of them wanted to disturb anything that might be noticeable the next day.

There was an oppressive air about the church, a weight that sagged down from the lofty ceiling and draped itself across their spirits. It might have just been the idea of the emptiness of the office, and the dark, brooding church beyond the doors; but somehow Nick didn't think so. There was an almost dream-like aura to the place.

Frustration settled in to twist his intestines as he finished sifting through the last of the drawers. Nothing. Nothing odd, nothing mysterious, nothing of any consequence at all. What he found was just what one would expect to find in the desk of a minister. Heaving a sigh of defeat, he pushed the drawer shut and rose, ready to tell the others it was time to get out before someone came along and discovered them. Before he could speak, he heard Weasel start to chuckle.

"Hot damn," the longhaired youth said, pointing to a gold-edged set of books prominently displayed on one of the shelves.

The volumes were carefully crafted leather; tiny gold ribbons that could serve as bookmarks dangled down the spines. They appeared to be new, untouched, as if meant for show only, not to actually be read. Weasel was snickering now, shaking his head back and forth in disbelief.

"What?" Nick hissed, crossing the room to stand and stare up at the books. He could see no reason for laughter—they were running out of time. "Have you cracked, man?"

"These books," Weasel said, "My dad has a set just like them, man. Look, each one is a gospel. There's Mark, Matthew, Luke, John, and Peter."

Ruthie had stepped up beside Nick, leaning her head softly on his shoulder; but she perked up at this. "Hey," she said, "Peter didn't write a gospel! There are only four of them in the Bible."

"Exactly," Weasel said, his grin widening even further. He reached out and grabbed the volume marked "Peter" from the shelves. "My dad has one of these babies in his office at work. He keeps his stash in it."

With a flourish, he flipped the book open. The first quarter of the book or so was covered in actual print, but the pages flipped quickly back as he thumbed them, and the true secret of the book was revealed. The center was hollowed out, the pages cut in an even, symmetrical oblong; and inside it was a small wooden box, like a jewelry case.

"You know where your father keeps his stash?" Flash asked, watching in fascination. "I knew he smoked, but he tells you where he keeps it?"

"Of course not," Weasel answered, fishing the small box out of its hiding spot. "I found it one day when I was bored—the books looked cool."

He flipped up the lid of the smaller box, and they all looked over his shoulder at the contents, breath indrawn. Inside was a smaller book, cracked with age and very brittle looking. The cover of the book was leather—but not the smooth, tooled leather you see in bookstores—*real* leather. It looked hand made. The pages, visible around the edges of the cover, were yellowed with age.

"What do you think *this* is?" Ruthie asked. "Maybe we

should leave it alone? I mean, look how *old* it is. It must be worth a lot of money."

Ignoring her, Weasel grabbed the old volume out of its niche in the fake gospel and flipped open the cover carefully with the tip of one finger. They all stared at the page that was revealed, unable to look away.

What confronted them was a hand-drawn illustration. It depicted the head of a goat that was inscribed carefully within the confines of a quickly scrawled pentagram. The sharp point of the star pointed downward, paralleling the triangle formed by the goat's beard.

The eyes would not release them. They were deep, staring back off of the crumbling paper with an intelligence and malevolent power that nearly brought the four of them to their knees with its intensity. The entire thing was done in odd, brownish ink. Nick had his own ideas on what that particular shade might be, but he decided, for the moment that it would be better to keep his mouth shut. He most certainly didn't want to know if he was right.

Weasel was the first to shake free, twisting his head back and forth and cursing softly. He reached out before anyone could stop him and turned to the next page. On this page, a second or inside cover, it seemed, there were only words, words also handwritten. Most of them were strange, seemingly impossible to pronounce, and meaningless. They read like names out of some fantasy novel, or the gibberish spouted by witches and wizards in some monster movie. Three words in the middle stood out clearly, though, and they were clear enough for all of them to make out.

"The Grand Sabbat."

They were still staring at the words, trying to figure out just what the hell they might mean, when Flash suddenly let out a loud hiss.

"Hey!" he said, his voice sharp and low, "I think I heard someone! Let's get the hell out of here."

Cursing again, Weasel slammed the little book closed and stuffed it quickly into its box and back into the bigger volume. He reached up and jammed the book home between the true gospels, hoping that he'd gotten it back in the right order, but not caring enough to try and straighten it if he hadn't.

They could all hear the sounds now, shuffling uneven footsteps that seemed as loud as gunshots in the ominous silence of the empty church. Hearts racing, they tumbled out of the office, barely remembering to pull the heavy door closed behind them.

The huge statue over the pool seemed to be staring directly at them as they crossed the silent expanse of the huge room, the accusation in its eyes now malevolent and deep. The feeling of being watched was intense, making the hairs on the back of Nick's neck stand up, the nerves he'd worked so hard to maintain at an even keel, to crack and crumble.

Outside the door, growing louder as they approached it from the inside, the footsteps continued. They were odd, offbeat and uneven, and the scraping on the gravel was very loud, as though whoever was there was dragging his feet clumsily. Then a voice cut through the darkness, almost stopping the beating of their hearts with its sudden outburst; and Weasel nearly keeled over in a fit of uncontrollable laughter. Nick leaned down, trying to shut his friend up, but there was a wide grin on his own lips as well.

The voice was singing, off-key and way too loud, keeping a sort of rhythm with the odd footsteps.

"S'nother late night, and...I had a drinkie.

I had a drinkie or two..."

The voice rose again a couple of seconds later, and they heard a muffled thud that might have been an elbow banging into the door. "You—hoo look tired, and you look thirsty; I'll share a little drinkie with you..."

There was the crash of broken glass then, and a low curse, but the singing stopped. The shuffling steps continued on down the wall and disappeared into the night, leaving them once more bathed in silence. When they were certain the man was gone, Flash turned to Nick and asked, "You want to go back, man?"

Nick saw that his friends would do whatever he decided, but he saw no reason to return to the oppressing confines of the church. He thought they'd probably found all there was to find here—maybe more than enough.

"Maybe we should get that book," Weasel said, glancing dubiously over his shoulder toward the office. "I could be there and back in just a second..."

Nick thought about it for a minute, but decided it was probably a bad idea. He glanced up at where the statue was still watching them. The spell of accusation had been broken somewhat by the lighthearted intrusion of the drunk. Turning back to the others, he shook his head.

"No, I think we'd better take our cue and get out of here while we have the chance. Ruthie has to be home in less than an hour, and my folks are probably waiting up for me."

His face darkened then, for just an instant; but they all caught it. None of them could mistake the meaning behind his words. If Ed Leatherman was waiting for him, it would not be pleasant. They had all witnessed the result of the man's discipline on many occasions.

"He's probably read that damned letter, too," Nick thought out loud.

"Letter?" Ruthie asked, her eyes showing her concern.

"I'll tell you about it in the van," Nick promised, pushing the door slightly open to check the parking lot. They slipped through the shadows without incident, sliding into their seats and sitting in silence for a few moments to be certain they hadn't been seen.

They waited in silence for Nick to explain, and finally he began to speak, telling them about the letter. It seemed almost like some kind of cruel joke when he thought about it. Here Straker was willing to almost blow the whole thing off, leave him alone completely, and this Goldbough clown had to stick his nose in it. The others listened in sympathy, none of them envying his next few hours. None of them would have traded the worst moment of their own life for even a good day with Nick's stepfather.

Flash started the engine and reached over to flip on the stereo and break the moody silence. There was nothing like music to put hope back into a hopeless situation. There was no doubt what station they would listen to—Flash had long since removed the tuning knob and glued the shaft in place with a large wad of chewing gum.

KROK, "the only Rock and Roll Station," blared out at them instantly, filling the "dead air" with sound. Flash had glued the knob in place after a visiting cousin had the nerve to tune the radio to a country station. When that same cousin had asked him why he did it, he'd answered that he believed his stereo would be demonically repossessed if he allowed that "red-necked country bullshit" to actually penetrate the speaker system.

Luckily the two of them had managed to compromise on an Outlaws' tape and gone on with their partying. They'd both been stoned, and neither of them was up to listening to their folks reminisce about the "good old days."

Now the radio spit out the final bars of the new Nine Inch Nails hit, and the DJ, Crazy Karl Walters, who worked the mid-shift "because it's the only time my 'friends' are awake, you know?" was rushing them forward into a stream of gibberish that ended in an introduction to a new single by *Maelstrom*. By the time they reached Ruthie's house, the heavy chords and harmonic vocals had transported them back to a semblance of reality, clearing their heads.

Nick got out with her, walked to the door and gave her a quick hug and a not-so-quick kiss that lingered for a long, long time. Without a word, he hurried back to the van and slipped into the backseat before she opened the door and went inside. It was always better if her dad believed she'd been out with a whole group of friends, rather than just one boy—Nick in particular. Nick and Ruthie's father had not yet reached an understanding over her—it was something he hoped to get around to soon. She waved quickly, smiling thinly and hurrying inside.

Flash tooted a quick note on his horn in salute and pulled back into traffic. He drove slowly, giving Nick time to pull himself together before they reached the Leatherman home. Nobody spoke. They let the music flow forth, loud and clear, washing away some of the daze created by their night's activities.

Curled up against the small couch-bed seat in the back, Nick was deep in thought. There were a lot of questions he had to answer, and he had to do it fast. For instance, what the hell was a "Grand Sabbat," for Christ's sake? For that matter, why would someone like the Reverend Horace Goldbough have a copy of the book? There seemed to be no answers available... none that would fit.

"Where do you think Ed could be?" Straker asked at last, when the silence between the two of them had built to unbearable proportions. Jeanette Leatherman, deep lines of worry creasing a face he thought was obviously too used to such an expression, was staring out the window into the darkness. Her slender hands were wrapped so tightly around her coffee cup that it was trembling—he was afraid it might burst from the pressure. In the cup, the coffee had grown lukewarm, then cool. She hadn't touched it.

"I don't know," she answered hollowly. "He's never stayed out like this, not without calling. It just isn't like him at all."

"He's a tough man, Jeanette," Straker said, trying his best to soothe her shaky nerves. "There isn't much out there that's going to bother a man like him. He'll be okay."

"I know," she replied, letting her eyes wander down from the window to find his, "I know. Sometimes, though," her eyes were full of a deep melancholy, a sadness he hadn't noticed before. "I guess you'll think me a very bad woman for saying this, but sometimes I wonder if I wouldn't be better off if something did happen."

She bit her lip as the words spilled forth, frightened for having said such a thing, but unable, and stubbornly unwilling, to take it back. Straker saw how her eyes darted about nervously, as though checking to see if she'd been caught; and his heart melted for her. She was such an attractive woman, intelligent, too. It was a shame to see her reduced to looking over her shoulder to see where the next blow was coming from.

He was about to comment, to tell her he understood where she was coming from, but he never got the words out of his mouth. They were both startled by the slamming of a car door outside and the crunch of wheels as the vehicle, whatever it had been, departed.

Jeanette half rose from her seat, a strange mixture of fear, hope, and surprise flooding her features. Her hand covered her mouth, as if to stifle a cry. It was obvious that despite Straker's words of hope, she still feared the worst, still feared that some disaster had befallen Ed, or Nick, or both.

The latch jiggled momentarily, then they heard the scrape of a key being inserted into the lock and the knob being turned. They heard footsteps. The door slammed shut again, and a second later, Nick appeared in the doorway. He stood there for a moment, taking in the scene before him in confusion.

"What's going on here?" he asked, moving to stand protectively at his mother's side and being caught up in an embarrassing hug the second he was in range. "Christ, Mom, you act like you thought you'd never see me again."

Turning to Straker, he asked, "Where's Ed? And what are you doing here, Inspector? Don't you have some criminals to chase or something?"

His mother moved in front of him quickly, staring at him as though trying to imprint his features in her mind. She didn't allow Straker time to speak, blurting out, "We don't know where he is, honey."

Nick's eyes jerked down to meet hers as he detected the lost, almost desperate tone of her voice. She was really worried about something, more worried than he'd ever seen her.

"He read the letter," she said, casting her eyes to the floor. "The one from that man at the television station. He left it on the table, and he hasn't been back. Not even to eat. He left the letter on the table."

Nick grabbed the letter and scanned it to make sure he remembered correctly what it was all about. Straker rose, putting a hand on his shoulder; and he jerked back, immediately on the defensive.

"Nick," Straker said quickly, his eyes earnest and almost pleading, "we have to talk. This television thing is no joke. Have you ever seen this show? That guy Clearwater cuts his teeth on ruining the lives of people like you and me...we have to see to it he doesn't get a chance to do that on this one.

"In two days we're both going to have to face him, him and about a half a million viewers who'd like nothing better than to see him out for blood. We have to get something concrete on this case before then, something we can divert him with, or you could be in more trouble than you realize."

"You think I killed that woman?" Nick asked, his tones low and measured, waiting.

"No, I don't." Straker answered instantly. "There's no real evidence to link you to anything but having been in the grave-yard. That won't stop Clearwater, though, and it won't stop an enraged public, either."

Nick sank back into the chair between Straker and his mother; the letter crumpled in his hand and he heaved a huge sigh of resignation. All the retaliation and rebellion faded from his features, and his voice was empty, almost dull, when he finally spoke.

"I was going to come to you soon, anyway," he confessed. "I think I know who did it—or at least who knows for sure who did, but I doubt that you'll believe me. I've been trying to get some evidence of my own, something to prove I'm right."

"Do me the favor of letting me decide for myself on this one," Straker answered, sitting back down and reaching for his coffee. "I'm ready to believe just about anything about now. Suppose you tell me what it is you've got?"

Starting from the beginning, skipping the part about the acid at the concert, he told them everything. He described the concert, the drive to the cemetery, his walk with Ruthie that had culminated in their macabre discovery in the back of the grave-yard, everything.

Reaching into his pocket, he fished out the pin he'd found, handing it over to Straker with a mixture of relief and nervous fear. As the Inspector was looking the thing over, he went on to describe his night's activities at the Church of New Light, and what they'd found there.

"You...you broke into a *church* Nick?" His mother's voice was incredulous, near to breaking down. "How could you..."

"What did you find?" Straker cut in, silencing Jeanette with a glance. His gaze was intense, concentrated, and for the first time since the whole mess had started, Nick began to think there might be a chance he was being believed.

"Well," he said, "I didn't find anything in his desk—looked through every folder and file drawer, too, nothing. We were getting ready to leave when Weasel—Uh, Tommy, I mean—saw these books up on the shelf.

"There are a set of five of them there, really fancy with gold edges and all. They were the gospels. None of the rest of us noticed, but Tommy's dad has the same set. Four of them are the real gospels, but there's one in the set by Peter. Peter never wrote a gospel. The inside of that book is like a little safe, or a hiding place.

"Anyway, inside it was another box, like a jewelry case, and inside that was another book, a really old one. It had a strange symbol painted in the front, looked like it might have been in blood. The next page had a title on it, 'The Grand Sabbat.'

"We didn't read any more or it. Some old drunk wandered by singing, scared the shit out of us. We put it back where it was and we got out of there quick."

"That's all you found?" Straker asked, his eyes dancing as if his mind were going full tilt. "You're sure you put the book back just where you found it?"

"Yeah, it's right where it was." Nick answered. "We didn't stick around to look for anything else. We just wanted to get out of there after that. I was hoping I'd find a knife or something."

"It may be enough," Straker said, slamming his hands onto the table in obvious satisfaction and rising. "Can I use your phone?"

"Go ahead," Nick said. He turned to his mother, then grabbed her hands, which were trembling, and held them firmly between his own. He knew she wasn't good at situations like this, and with Ed missing it was probably a little beyond her. Personally, he was glad his stepfather hadn't been there—if he had, he might never have had the chance to talk straight with Straker.

As he moved closer, pulling his mother into a hug that felt way too long in coming, he heard Straker behind him, dialing the phone. He almost smiled as he saw Lizzie, sitting in the corner by the door, watching the Inspector with big, wet eyes full of curiosity.

Straker held the receiver so tightly that his knuckles

whitened, waiting as the line connected, then began to ring. Pamela answered on the third ring, her voice heavy and slurred as if he'd awakened her from a deep sleep.

"Yes?" she said.

"Pamela?" he asked.

"Yes, who is this...Ken?"

"Yes, I'm sorry to wake you. This might be important, and I didn't know who else I could call that might be able to help me on this one. I don't want to get the office in an uproar yet. Can you take a quick note on this?"

"Just a second," she said. He could hear her fumbling about after a pen, and he smiled, stifling the image that immediately threatened to rise to the surface of his mind. He could see her, her wild hair even wilder, mussed by the pillows, sitting there in a flimsy white night gown. "Go ahead," she said a moment later, snapping him back to reality.

"I need you to find out about a book for me," he told her quickly. "It's probably rare, maybe not even in print except where handmade original copies are available. It's called 'The Grand Sabbat.' Have you got all that?"

"Yes," she replied, her voice brightening and gaining strength with each word. "But what is it? Where are you, Ken, and what's going on?"

"No time now to explain," he told her urgently. "You'll just have to trust me on this one. Call me tomorrow at the office; can you do that?"

"I can, but I'd rather know what's going on," she grumbled. "I'll call and we'll have lunch."

"Fine," he said. "I have to go now. I'll see you then."

Jeanette seemed to have calmed down by the time he returned to the table. Nick looked up at him, offering a thin, nervous smile.

"Now what," he asked. "Any ideas on where Ed might be?"

Straker shook his head. "I've known Ed a long time, Nick," he said slowly. "He's about as predictable as the wind. I wouldn't worry about him; he's a tough one, but if you two hear nothing by tomorrow, call me at the office. And Nick, you've been a big help. I appreciate it. We'll find whoever did this, count on it."

There seemed nothing left, for the moment, to be said; so he drained what was left in his coffee cup and headed for the door. Lizzie, who was not certain what was going on, followed him quietly, escorting him out.

"Inspector," Jeanette's eyes were losing the dim, lost look; and she actually smiled at him this time—a very attractive smile, "thank you."

Nodding, he stepped through the door and into the night. The moon lit the way with almost day-bright intensity. Sighing heavily, he got behind the wheel and headed for his office. There was always the couch, and there were only three or four hours to sleep before he had to be back at it. The night seemed endless, dark, and deep.

CHAPTER SEVENTEEN

The old barn filled up quickly. Vehicles of all types pulled into the cramped space, slid into line, and grew silent. Lights cut out, stereos cut off, and only moments after the lead car pulled in, there was nothing but silence. Next came the slamming of doors, the shuffling of feet, and the torches, flickering into life one after the other, slowly illuminating the old structure until it danced with unearthly shadows and fiery light.

Other than the sound of the torches guttering in the breeze, only the occasional slapping of cloth against flesh, or the scrape of footsteps on the dirt-strewn floor broke the silence. Everything was orchestrated down to the slightest movement— there were no words necessary.

Horace still maintained a safe distance from Brenda, avoiding her eyes and her touch as though each carried the plague. He moved toward the door first. The others slid into place silently, formed a single line behind him, each in his or her appointed position. Horace hesitated for only a second—there was much to do and little time to get it done. With a nod of his head, he moved off into the darkness, never once looking back to see that they followed. He didn't need to see them because he felt them.

Brenda followed very close at his heels, almost too close for safety. She gazed ahead with a manic, almost uncontrolled passion blazing in her eyes. She was just as aware as Horace of the consequences of an idle touch, a staggering step that might bring the two of them too close together. She fought herself and the rough terrain with every ounce of strength and control in her body, placing each step carefully in front of the last, keeping her eyes and her mind focused on the darkness ahead.

Her skin trembled as the darkness washed over her. It danced on the endings of her nerves, teased through the locks of her hair. The blackness surrounding them was as alive as she, exciting—irresistible. Already, just with the joining of those in the circle, with their physical proximity, the energy that permeated the air was tremendous.

All that held her steady was their goal—her goal. The burning was nothing compared to the promise of what was to come. This night was the beginning of her destiny. This knowledge became her focus, and she clung to it.

She and Horace were the only ones truly aware of the struggle. Her body twitched and jerked with a desire that she could not have bottled up with the most superhuman of efforts. She knew that Horace felt it, and shared it. He sensed the heat building in her in the air that separated them, could end it all by a slowed step, a touch, or a glance. He moved silently onward, and she prayed for strength for the both of them.

Behind, oblivious to what transpired between their two leaders, the others followed. They felt the building of the power, the tension of the gathering of forces unseen. For them it was enough.

This was the second to the last of the steps of *The Grand Sabbat.* All of those present, to varying degrees, knew the workings of the ritual and what it meant for them. It was an incredible moment, an historic occasion. Five of the six steps would be completed on this night. Six had not been completed successfully in the span of the last two centuries, not to the extent of perfection that they were achieving.

Tonight was the ritual of preparation, the blessing of the vessel, a night of prophecy. Tonight they would receive the final elements necessary for the completion of the sixth and final step, and its gift of power.

The next time they gathered the culmination of their efforts would become their offering, offered in return for power, for dreams, for the fulfillment of lust beyond the realm of humanity. They would be gods, walking among men. So they believed.

Before them, the gates of the cemetery rose, stark and imposing, silhouetted against the moonlit sky. The surrounding fence line, its wrought iron fingers groping skyward, sent long, spear-shaped shadows to cut across their path, striping the ground at their feet. They filed quickly through and disappeared into the overgrown trees and weeds at the back of the graveyard. The altar waited, and it was nearly time to begin.

Ed watched carefully from his vantage point on the hill, as the line of cars disappeared into the old barn and the lights dimmed. He kept the cherry of his cigarette low behind the dash of the truck, wanting to prevent it from giving him away. Not that those below were paying any fucking attention. Not that he really believed they would see him. Just being careful.

Something weird, he wasn't sure just exactly what the hell it might be, but something weird as blue blazes was going on down in that old farmhouse. He reached out absently and pulled another beer free of the twelve-pack. He popped the top. Flickering lights had come on in the barn now, and he saw them move toward the doorway, then out into the darkness. They were carrying torches, and the last of them, moving a bit more slowly, was leading some kind of animal, a pig? A sheep. Fuck, this was one wacked out bunch.

"Torches," he snorted derisively, "wonder what's wrong with a fucking flashlight?" He took a long pull off the beer. The group below wound down the trail that led off toward the back gate of the old cemetery, the one where that fucking altar was supposed to be. Ed had forgotten, right up until that moment, that the place even existed.

It explained a fuck of a lot; that was for sure. For instance, he was willing to bet he could show old Straker how his kill-ers had managed to slip away without leaving any signs, and how the body might have disappeared. They'd never gone into the newer graveyard where the boy and his friends had been at all. Shit, those kids had probably never even known the fuckers were there.

But this was all beside the point. The point was, and it gave him great satisfaction to realize it, he had them. All of them. He had their asses cold, and there was no longer any doubt in his mind who the killer was.

"Well I'll be God damned," he chuckled, taking another drink. "Fucking Church of New Light bullshit. A god damned minister." He chuckled at his own accidental joke, shaking his head and chugging half of the lukewarm beer in his can at a gulp. "I'll be double-d goddamned."

Behind the seat of his truck, on a rack he'd made himself back in the Lavender High School wood shop, rested his guns. His babies. Behind the rack, plastered on the window, were his NRA lifetime member sticker and his "When you pry it from my cold dead fingers" anti-gun control statement.

Turning casually, he took a quick inventory of his choices, running the situation through his mind. He had plenty of time; the assholes didn't even know he was there. There was the 30/30, the shotgun, and, hanging from a holster at the very bottom so that the back of his seat concealed it, the .357 slapped gently against his spine.

That one for sure, he knew. It was his insurance policy. Fuck American Express, he was fond of telling his buddies down at the bar, I got me that Smith & Wesson; and I never leave home without *it*. The gun had ridden there, right where it was, since the day he'd gotten it.

Ed wasn't sure what it was about guns, that gun in particular, but there was something about the feel of their weight in his hands, the solid, no-nonsense power they represented, that appealed to him. Whenever he went out to shoot it, the feel of the .357 bouncing against his hip had always given him an odd little thrill. He guessed it came from watching too many John Wayne movies. Didn't matter. He reached around and grabbed it by the belt, swinging it out and around to rest on his lap.

After thinking about it for a few more minutes, the length of time it took to swig down another beer, he decided on the shotgun as his second weapon. It carried more ammunition, and it was lighter. It wasn't that short of a walk to the cemetery gates, and he might have to get the fuck out of there quick.

Besides, he told himself, he was planning on getting down in close before he made any moves. He wanted to see the bastard's eyes, to make sure they knew who it was they were dealing with. The 30/30 wouldn't be as effective at that range.

He flipped open the glove box and began pulling out shells. He had every type of ammo he might need, and plenty of it. It never hurt to be prepared. He also pulled free the long, Bowie style hunting knife and its sheath, and strapped it to his boot. He was really starting to get into this.

He'd always loved war movies. He subscribed to only two magazines, *Soldier of Fortune* and the NRA's magazine. He'd read both religiously since high school. His biggest regret throughout his life was that he'd been born too late to go to any of the big wars—had never seen live combat. It was something he felt that he was born to, and now he was about to get a taste of it firsthand.

He popped the top on a last beer, guzzling half of it quickly and setting it on the seat beside him; he took the last few drags off his cigarette and crushed it out in the ashtray. Carefully sliding the door open, he got out of the truck, polished off the beer, and moved to the bushes on his right, letting loose a long and satisfying stream of urine and a loud burp.

When he was ready, he reached in for the gun belt and strapped it loosely around his waist, dangling on one side like a gunfighter. It rode easy on his hip, and he smiled. He took the box of ammo in hand and began to fit the bullets, one by one, into the small loops on the belt. Then he took the gun out of the holster and loaded it as well.

Grabbing the shotgun from the rack, he began shoveling shells in. Double ought buck. When it was full, he jammed as many of the remaining shells into his jeans pockets as he could without it interfering with his ability to walk. He pumped it once to put a shell in the chamber, slung the gun over his shoulder, and grabbed another beer. He popped the top with a flourish and closed the truck's door.

Below him the old farmhouse lay, covered once again by an oppressive blanket of silence. The procession had moved on down the road and out of sight long moments before, leaving him alone in the darkness. He chose a slightly different trail than the one that they had taken, not sure how much of a start they had, and, keeping concealed as best he could, he moved silently off into the shadows. He didn't want to miss anything.

They were ready. The torches had been placed at the proper junctures; the circle itself had been laid and consecrated with infinite care. They had chanted together the invocations, their tongues joining as one, flawlessly executing the age-old ceremony.

Horace stood at the head of the altar, his arms raised to the sky and his eyes blazing. His mind rushed with the power, reeled with it as it spun about them, twisting and tugging, relentless and unbridled. The swirling fog wrapped itself in and around his grasp, seeping toward the sky in jasmine-scented clouds. All was perfection. All was as it was fated to be.

Muzzled tightly to prevent any sound, the lamb was led forward. It had proved, beyond all likelihood, the most difficult part of the ceremony. Finding and purchasing such a beast, one that was pure and untainted in the manner required, was not something easily done. Not if one wanted to keep that purchase quiet.

The ceremony at hand, as had the last, called for blood. Not virgin blood, like that of the woman; not this time. The previous ritual had required it, as would the final ritual. This was different.

Strong hands lifted the animal's drowsy body to the surface of the stone, forcing it to lie down on the cold surface. Though its eyes were beginning to roll back to their whites in fear, as if in understanding of what was to come, it complied with a heavy sigh. It had been drugged and cleansed, prepared in accordance with the law of the ritual; and there was very little fight left to it.

As the animal laid its head softly against the hard, cold surface of the altar, Horace wheeled away, raised his hand and called forth the ritual in a rush of energy and passion that caught the others up like a whirlwind, galvanizing them into action. All around him, they began to circle, recreating the mincing, prancing dance that would call down, or draw up the one they sought, the steps that accompanied the words flowing forth from his mouth in a powerful, unbroken stream.

Although he'd spent days pouring over the book, his copy of which even Brenda was completely unaware of, Horace had never been able to find anything to explain to him the euphoria, the sensation of utter control that overcame him at this point in the ritual.

The words that were required of him were ancient, drawn from a very difficult tongue that he was certain had not originally been meant for the lips of mankind. He didn't know why he believed this, but he did. There were a lot of them, huge phrases and staccato rhythms that defied translation and boggled the mind at first glance.

He had tried, on occasion, to mumble his way through small passages during the day, to practice for the rituals to come. Whenever he did so, it was as if he spoke through mud.

His mind tripped over the intricacies; his lips stumbled horribly and mangled the sounds and the meter horribly. It had scared him, at first, had made him feel as though her were unworthy of his position.

When the proper moment came, though, when it was time for the final run-through, the one that counted, he was flawless. It seemed that only when all of the prerequisites had been met, when all the facets of the ritual were in place and the power flowed, could the words be properly spoken; and then they could hardly be denied.

They gushed forth, as if flying from his lips of their own accord. They never wavered, propelled by some force beyond his understanding, spoken by some other entity through the vessel of his vocal chords. Even the tones he used were alien, beyond his normal range, deep resonating sounds that modulated his voice in powerful, guttural syllables. It was a reminder of what they sought, that there were powers far beyond them, waiting to be unleashed.

Horace wasn't thinking about any of this; he was deeply entranced. The knife, which he wore as usual, strapped tightly to his waist with the ice-chill steel of its blade pressed against his skin, jumped to his hand at the proper moment with a life of its own, unerringly rising with the rhythm of the chant in a glittering, moon-spun arc of silver light.

Horace watched it rise, as if from far away, fascinated as arms that seemed to be his own lifted to the sky, their muscles bunching in intensely concentrated effort, then plummeted downward. The blade plunged deeply into the soft, yielding flesh of the sacrifice, tearing easily through flesh and bone and ripping downward to release the blood. It gushed forth, spraying his arms and his body with a crimson wave, washing the last of his mundane existence from his hands.

All eyes in the clearing were turned skyward; all heads moved in unison as the release of the blood shot through them, causing their bodies to convulse in sudden ecstasy. As the knife ripped through flesh, a wave of energy surged through the clearing, engulfing them all, completing the circle and binding them, one to the other, in a single ring of power.

Brenda dropped to her knees as the pulse ripped through her, then struggled weakly to her feet. She fought to maintain her balance, but her eyes caught two others, two glittering orbs that pierced her will with their own and drove her back to the earth. Horace!

He smiled at her, not releasing her eyes for even a second, and reached downward, dragging his finger toward him through the now pooling blood of the sacrifice. With a quick motion, he reached up and drew an inverted cross on his forehead with the sticky red liquid. His smile widened.

The others, caught up completely in the passion of the moment, moved before him in a prancing line. As each passed, Horace reached out and repeated the design on their faces. He continued until all of them were marked—except Brenda.

She had risen, unable to resist the chant, unable to halt the motion of her body. She joined the dance, falling in behind the last of the others. She did not close her eyes, they were locked with Horace's; and they drew her forward.

She came to him last, after the others had begun once again to circle, and she pressed forward toward the dripping liquid on his fingertip, watching as it flashed past her vision, leaving a video trail of red traces suspended in the air behind it. She felt it come to rest on her forehead, felt it draw back, and then across, felt the design burning itself into her skin.

She started to smile, and then stopped. Fear and outrage flashed across her features. It was not a cross he drew, but a star—a pentagram. Her eyes grew wider, and she tried with every ounce of strength remaining to her to draw back, but it was no use. Her mind screamed in negation, but it was done. Irreversible.

A tiny whimper escaped her as Horace reached out and grabbed her shoulders in an iron grip, a grim smile of pleasure painted across his features. She tried feebly to struggle, but even that movement, brushing her skin against his touch, feeding the fire, was too much. Her body tingled everywhere they made contact, afire with lust; and it betrayed her.

She pressed back into his grip and fell willingly into the icy pools of his eyes, as though drawn from herself completely and cast into their depths. It was to have been another! She was not to have been the voice, could not be.

Horace knew. She looked into his eyes, and she saw that he had known all along, had baited her into thinking she was in charge. She wanted to cry out—to scream, to stop him—it was too late. Far too late. The ritual was in motion, and the symbols were cast. He had won.

Strong hands gripped her ankles, her thighs, her waist, and she was lifted. The lamb had been removed from the altar, though she had no idea how, or when. Each spot where one of them touched her skin, each point of contact, was a searing point of light and heat. She felt as though her skin was melting into theirs.

They placed her gently across the bloody stone and released their hold on her flesh—all but Horace. He had returned to the head of the altar, and one of his hands rested on each of her temples. His fingers worked the skin, a subtle, rhythmic, undulating massage.

She felt the circle of bodies moving and spinning. The others danced, their steps choreographed by some otherworldly music, a dance as old as death. Under the ministrations of Horace's fingers, Brenda felt herself become a part of that circle, felt her body moving as well, writhing, sinuous motions that blended her to Horace's flesh, bound her to his will, sealed her to the ritual.

Helpless to resist, and unwilling, even in her failure, to give up their goal, she watched as the others circled. She knew as well as any of them, better, even, what came next. As she watched, she grew confused—something seemed different, wrong. The faces beneath the hoods, the shadowed bits and fragments that were visible, were not human—not at all.

Her mind flew back, back to Tom and his gift, back to that first night. They were familiar faces, familiar as old friends. They were the faces from her vision, the same prancing forms that had first initiated her to the power. Their touch was the same as well, the electricity of their caresses, the magnetism of their eyes.

Her head shook from side to side in a confusion of emotion and desire. Her thoughts clouded as the first moved forward, laying first his hands, and then his flicking tongue, on her soft, yielding flesh. He entered her in one swift movement, hot and violent, claiming her as his own.

Horace continued to massage her temples and to chant, watching with grim appreciation as she reacted to their energy and molded to the ritual. Her slender, exotic body wrapped itself in ecstasy around each of the others, throbbed with the shared passion of the circle. She was a match for them, more than a match, as the heat rose to consume her, to drive her up and forward, meeting each thrust with a more violent push of her own.

Each of them filled her, "the vessel," with more of the seed of darkness. The women teased and worked their tongues, tasting and leaving their essence behind. Each gave a piece of himself, a sample of his soul, to feed the one they served. This night they were truly one in his service; this night their Lord would speak. Horace knew this, felt it as he had never felt any truth before.

His would be the final gift, the final key to unlock the otherworldly door and free the one they sought. Brenda would speak—*He* would speak, through her. Horace would provide the seed of that voice.

Brenda had thought herself to be the chosen one, the emissary of the new darkness. He knew it now, had known it all along. Now she would be his, the first of many gifts he would receive before all was done. She would be his alone, her body, and her share of the power. She squirmed deliciously beneath his probing fingers.

When the others had finished, Horace turned her head to the side and drank in the expression of mixed joy and hatred, hunger and anger in her eyes. She pressed toward him, and he obliged her, sliding himself between her lips slowly. His seed must bring the voice, but she must desire it. She must coax it free of him without being forced.

No thought remained behind the eyes that watched him now. The heat had consumed her and the hunger was her soul. She licked him hungrily, possessed by lust, drawn by the imminent burst of power to come.

Her eyes, like the sheep's before her, rolled upward and disappeared behind the lids until nothing but the whites remained. She moved on the stone, her hands fondling her body, roving hotly over her skin. She moaned with unfulfilled need, with unquenchable desire; and Horace gripped her hair tightly. It was nearly done, seconds from perfection, and the circle spun with ecstasy.

Ed drained the last of the beer, crushed the can in one hand so violently that the aluminum ripped open and cut his finger. He barely noticed, tossing the can aside contemptuously and moving onward.

"Damn," he muttered. He'd been sitting for nearly a half an hour now, just watching. He'd seen movies, been to a few parties with the guys where they had slut pictures and shit, but never in all the years of his life had he witnessed anything to compare with the filth he'd just seen.

What those fuckers had done with that sheep, the dancing, then that woman *while* they danced, went beyond pornography, beyond even filth. It had disturbed him on a primal level, set his blood to boil. And that woman, she hadn't been complaining, either. The bitch had fucking *loved* it.

"Damn," he repeated, wishing he'd brought another beer along, or that he dared to light a cigarette. It was a moment of revelation for him. There were things in this world beyond anything he could have imagined—that much was painfully clear. He'd thought he was following a pack of religious weirdos, maybe out for a little dance in the moonlight and fake magic—shit. This was the most obscene thing he'd ever encountered, so wrong that it screamed in his face to right it.

When the woman turned her head to the side, giving the minister the damndest blowjob Ed had ever seen; it was too much for him to stand. It was enough, more than enough, and it galvanized him into action. These fuckers were psychos, plain and simple; and he was going to put an end to it. Now.

He was assaulted briefly by a wave of doubt. Maybe he should turn around, go back and tell someone, Straker maybe. He shook his head, sending the ideas scattering off into the shadows. He was here; he'd take care of it himself.

Rising to his feet, a bit unsteadily, he brought the shotgun around to rest at about a 45 degree angle to the ground and moved forward, slowly and surely, as though he were stalking a deer and didn't want to spook it. He didn't want them to see him too soon and take off, disappearing into the woods.

What he wanted was to get them all in his sights and gain control of the situation. He didn't know exactly what he planned to do when he had them, but he knew he wasn't letting any of them slip through his fingers, either.

"Should shoot every filthy man-jack of 'em," he muttered. "Damn."

He reached the clearing at the edge of the tree line at almost the precise moment that he saw Horace's body grow taut, the moment of completion. He saw the man grab the woman's hair even more tightly, hold her face pressed against him for a long moment, as if he were afraid something would spill free, and then release her. The robes fell across the man's body, and he stepped back slightly, his hands on the sides of the woman's head, massaging her.

Ed reflected that it was too bad he hadn't moved in time to keep that bastard from getting off. It would have been a capper for the fun to come, for sure.

An odd chant rose from the circle they'd laid on the ground, rising from all about them. Ed couldn't tell which of them, or if all of them, was speaking, nor did he care. It didn't matter; he'd had enough.

Stepping clear of the trees and raising the shotgun to his

shoulder, he cried out to them in a loud, angry voice.

"All right you bastards, hold it right there. Shut the fuck up and stand still, every damned one of you. Move one more perverted muscle, and I'll blow holes in you so big King Kong couldn't get off fucking them."

The steps of the dancers faltered at the intrusion of his voice, but the chanting, seemingly powered from elsewhere, from somewhere beyond the circle, rolled on and filled the air. Horace turned slightly, leered at Ed with an evil, indifferent expression that chilled his blood.

Pointing across the circle, Horace stabbed a finger into the night and said, "Take him."

Without further thought, without even acknowledging Ed's presence further, Horace turned back and continued his massage of the woman's head as if nothing had happened. That was it. That was the straw that broke the ol' camel's back. With a whoop and a rebel yell that split the night, reverberating from the trees, Ed leapt forward. He leveled the gun at the head and shoulders of the Reverend Horace Goldbough and prepared to ventilate him with a solid round of buckshot. He never got off the shot.

Rising from the stone, the woman turned to face him. It wasn't her face, though. A huge, leering demon's face gazed back at him, glaring out from beneath the mockery of the human flesh that tried to house it, framed by the wildly thrashing locks of her ebony hair. The figure stood, towering over them all with imperious arrogance.

Holding its arms out to him with its eyes blazing like a campfire doused with lighter fluid, it stood. Ed took a faltering step forward, and he tried once again to fire, to cut the madness off at its heart. His finger refused the commands of his screaming brain. The shotgun fell to the ground with a clatter, released by numb fingers. Forgotten. It bounced off the stones at his feet, and he stepped over it.

"Come."

The word spewed from the woman's mouth, full of venom and resonating with otherworldly power. Ed saw her lips move, saw her head tilt to the side in greedy anticipation of his compliance; but no woman possessed such a voice. No human, for that matter, could produce tones of such strength—such volume.

The command was repeated and he moved closer still. It was a hypnotic voice, compelling. His halting steps became surer. He fought with every ounce of his strength, the tendons standing out on his neck as he concentrated on one thing, running, escaping, but his legs carried him steadily forward.

Darkness enfolded him. The woman, what had been the woman, clasped slender, pale arms about him with frightening strength and held him like a small child as cold, too-red lips reached down, searching for his own. Her touch was like ice, like metal kept too long in the frigid cold, so chill that it burned. Her eyes, locked onto his, glowed yellow and feral.

Darkness swept through him, insanity filling him in its wake. When he was still, and staring blankly into worlds he'd never accept, she turned to face those who now danced again at her back.

Horace knelt, his eyes locked to the demonic gaze that now owned Brenda's eyes.

"As you command," he said, his voice a quavering whimper, all signs of strength and command having slipped away, "so must it be. What is your wish?"

The demon spoke, then, and they all listened. The words seeped through them, entered their being. They were etched into their psyche in ways beyond their understanding. Then there was silence, and the clearing snapped to reality with an almost audible release of power—a vacuum sucked in upon itself. The ritual had run its course.

As shadows once more rushed in to claim the small clearing, they gathered their implements quickly and filed out. Brenda's unconscious form, and the still-staring, slack-jawed shell that had once been Ed Leatherman, were lifted and carried along.

As instructed, Ed was put into a corner of the barn, bound and left, covered over with a pile of old straw. He would die soon enough, and his suffering would be a small enough price for what he had almost done, the harm he had almost caused. Nothing of the man he had been remained, in any case. There was nothing to save.

The line of cars, minus the one lone set of lights that had trailed them, wound its way back into the depths of the city. Horace drove, his body still shaking, his mind still awash with crazy anticipation. Brenda's head rested in his lap, exactly as he'd instructed the others to place it. After all, he smiled to himself, she was his.

On the horizon, the sun was just beginning to rise. He hurried home in silence.

CHAPTER EIGHTEEN

Pamela stared at the pile of books in front of her, a deep frown creasing her forehead. While her research had gleaned a good amount of information on the volume she sought, enough to set her nerves on edge and make her stomach queasy, no actual copy of the thing was to be found. None.

The church in Europe had banned it for being heretical and evil centuries earlier, only to have it spring up time and time again in indirect references and vague notes. Some held that it was now an oral tradition, handed down carefully from generation to generation like some secret doctrine of the ages.

As far as she could tell, the book dated back even as far as biblical times, perhaps further. No author was named, though the church, of course, cited Satan as its source. Cultists, those who read and followed the ritual set down in the book's pages, believed it to be the greatest of rituals, the culmination of their art. It was believed to be a gateway to the presence of the dark one himself, by whichever name he was called. A gateway to hell.

The purpose of the ritual was a bit vague, as well. Some of the sources she checked said it was a means of unleashing otherworldly power. Others said it was a gateway for ancient darkness, a pathway back to a world long sealed for some dark, malevolent presence. On one thing all of the references agreed, the powers unleashed by the book were too great to meddle with, beyond the control of any mortal practitioner of the dark arts. Even the secret societies that held the work in reverence never claimed to have seen the thing through to its conclusion.

Pamela shivered and closed the book in front of her with a

disgusted snap. Such things seemed more at home in a cheap horror film than in a history book, and the fact that she'd never known of their existence bothered her more than she cared to admit. How many dark secrets did the world around her hold? How many pits of human vipers still existed, waiting to claim their next victim?

What she really didn't want to dwell on was what this all meant to Gretchen's death. She didn't know how this book could possibly be related, but she was certain that the greater part of her didn't want to know. In any case, it was clear that she was on the wrong track, especially since Ken had said that time was short. The library had given up all it had to offer on the subject.

All that remained to her was to search the area's rare and occult bookstores in the hopes of at least getting a clue. It was obvious that this was not going to be an easy search—maybe not even possible. She had to meet with Straker for lunch in two hours, and she wanted to have something to tell him when she did.

She returned the books before her to the front desk and left the building, heading quickly down the street to her own office. She didn't have to be at work that day, but her desk would make a convenient, centrally located point from which to conduct her inquiries; and she felt more comfortable there.

The building was not empty, her apartment was. It was near the police department, as well, and somehow the proximity of one Kendall Straker and his men eased the weight on her mind.

She moved quickly past the front desk and through the newsroom, answering the few greetings quickly and shortly, and pushed her way into her own office, closing the door tightly behind her. Her office was the one haven in her life, beyond her home, the one place where everything was just as she wanted it.

There was a stack of new memos in her basket, along with some files and some research material she'd requested. She ignored it and reached immediately for the phone book in her bottom drawer. She flipped it open.

She found, to her dismay, that there were an intimidating number of retail bookstores in the area that claimed to carry an assortment of occult or magical texts. Some of them were obviously not the "real McCoy," advertising for freaked out cures and card readings in their back rooms; but the ones that seemed legitimate still ran over a good half page of the phone book.

She dialed the first one, making a check mark beside the name of the establishment in the book, and moving her finger on down to be ready with the next number as it rang.

The first two places she called were no help, specializing in newer texts, new age metaphysics and different brands of meditation and divination. The third, however, a used and obscure book dealer in downtown San Valencez, had at least heard of the book. It was a start.

"I don't suppose that you'd know where I might come across a copy?" she asked quickly, trying to hide her excitement.

"Ma'am," the book dealer had drawled back at her, "if you were to come across a copy of that thing around here, it would be nothing short of a miracle. The thing has been banned by the church since the early 13th century—they burned every copy they could get their hands on.

"Been a few copies circulating since then, all hand written, and almost never for sale. Collectors jump on the damned things so fast you hardly even know they were on the market. Rumor has it the Vatican has bought and burned another dozen copies over the years.

"Personally," the man went on, almost in a lecturing tone, "I can't see why the hell anyone would want the crazy thing. I mean, that's pretty heavy satanic stuff."

"I'm a reporter," Pamela explained, "I need it for research on a story I'm doing. You don't know anyone who might be able to find a copy of it, then, maybe someone you've forgotten? Say, in the next day or so? I'm willing to pay whatever is necessary—I really do need to see it."

She could almost visualize the man shaking his head, scratching his chin and thinking. After a long moment of silence, he answered her. "I don't know. I'm not making any promises, that much is sure, but I can do some checking around if it's really that important. There are a handful of dealers and possibly a couple of collectors on my mailing list who might have a copy, or at least access to one. Let me have a number where I can reach you; I'll see what I can do."

She gave him her home and office phone numbers with instructions to leave a message if she didn't answer. She also, on a last second impulse, gave him Straker's number, explaining that if she weren't available, that the man should try to contact the Inspector with the information, and that he would relay it to her. The man agreed, seeming to have gained some enthusiasm for the project, promising to do anything and everything he could to unearth a copy of the book.

Satisfied that she had done her utmost for the day, Pamela settled back at her desk to get ready to meet Ken for lunch. She fished a small compact from her purse, touched up her makeup quickly and ran her brush through her hair a few times. When she felt presentable, she reached again for the phone, this time dialing Ken's number. It was nearly noon, and she needed to find out where he wanted to meet for lunch, and, by the way, just what the hell was going on with all this secretive bullshit, anyway.

He answered the phone on the third ring, his voice sounding tired, strained, and tight. Listening with apparent interest to her account of the morning's research, he congratulated her on the progress she'd managed on such notice. When she reminded him it was time for their luncheon date, he suggested they meet down the street at a small cafe, The Boxcar, which lay about half way between them. She agreed, gathered her notes and headed back through the office and out onto the street in a flurry of motion.

Once she had something to go on, like the bookstore owner, she was like a terrier, shaking the information loose and running with it. The idea that all she could do now was to wait and see what he came up with, knowing it would not seem as crucial and important to him as it was to her, grated on her nerves. She wanted to be there, making the calls, pushing the man along. It was aggravating.

When she reached the cafe Straker was already there, seated by himself in a booth along the wall by the front window. He sipped a cup of his usual black coffee with an exhausted grimace on his face. He smiled when he saw her and stood to greet her, but it was obvious that his heart wasn't in the meal to come.

She sat opposite him, ordered iced tea and a sandwich, and then she let him have it, exhausted or no. He had yet to give her so much as a clue to what the hell was going on, and that coupled with the futility of her morning's research put a real edge to her tongue.

"All right, mister," she said, "just what in the blue blazes is going on here that you need to make mysterious, midnight phone calls and can't tell me why I'm chasing books about magic? Satanic books about magic, I might add, that have raised the eyebrows of more than one of the folks I've asked about it, wondering why I would want it. Has something come up that I should know about?"

It was either another sign of his weariness, or he was finally ready to trust her fully, but he didn't mince words this time. In as little time as possible, he outlined the events of the previous night, his visit to the Leatherman's, Ed's disappearance, and Nick's findings during the break-in at the Church of New Light. He then explained about the coming ordeal with Hector Clearwater, and his eyes wrinkled in disgust as he spat out that name. He finished by explaining that he'd just been on the phone with Nick's mother, and that Ed was still missing.

"I don't know why," he went on, "a hunch, I suppose, but I ran by that graveyard again this morning. One more look around, you know, like there might be something I'd missed? There was fresh blood on that altar—all over it. The place was pretty scuffed up, as if someone had gone over it with a snow-blower, or there'd been a tornado or something.

"I had the place torn apart—nothing. Not a clue as to who was there, or why. Just the blood. The guys back at the lab are doing an analysis on it now, but if no one turns up missing, we probably won't be able to match it to anything."

Pamela's voice raised a notch, and her voice caught as she blurted, "Someone else may be dead?" She stared at him with wide, frightened eyes; and he was almost sorry he'd spoken.

"Isn't this craziness ever going to end?" she demanded, not really expecting an answer. "I mean, in all the time I've lived here I can't remember a single murder closer than San Valencez; and now there's been two, just like that."

"Don't jump to conclusions," he warned her. "We haven't any evidence of a second murder. We've got little enough on the first."

She snorted in annoyance, taking a long drink of her tea to clear her throat. "So now you're going on television to be accused of withholding evidence. Are you planning on asking Reverend Goldbough about that pendant while you're there?"

"I don't know. I hadn't really thought about that yet," he said, reaching into his pocket and drawing forth a packet of Tums. Pulling the wrapper back a bit more, he popped two of the tablets into his mouth with a weary sigh. "I'm a pretty tough old man—I'm more worried about what they're going to do to the boy, Nick.

"I mean, with his stepfather missing and all, the last thing he and his mother need is trouble with the town; and that's just the kind of thing this could stir up. They need this guy Clearwater on their ass like they need new holes in their heads. Seems like it's up to me to drive them down there and try to keep things calm."

"You always take that responsible line, don't you?" she said, instantly regretting her words.

"I'm sorry, Ken," she went on, reaching over to rest her hand lightly on his arm, "I'm just having a hell of a time coping with all of this."

Her mind was racing. The television show put a whole new perspective on this—on all of it. While the issues being brought forth on the show were important, they were not the immediate concern here. What she wanted to know was what Goldbough was getting out of it? What was he planning?

"Ken, it's getting pretty obvious that Horace Goldbough is mixed up in this somehow. I mean, why else would he get involved—and right now?"

Straker stared at his coffee, watching it swirl and thinking about the acidic mess it was going to create when it washed away the effect of the antacid. "I've been wondering that myself. I wish I had enough for a warrant, or to bring him in for questioning, but with this show coming up it might not be such a good idea."

"What are you going to say, then?" she asked, buying time as the gears in her mind whirred and clicked over the facts.

"I won't know that until I see what they ask," he grinned, coming around a little, "but you can bet it will be the typical, straight-laced, hard-nosed cop answer. I'd hate to let my image slip."

It was good to see him smile again, weak as it was, and she laughed along with him. Promising to watch it all on television and give him a critical commentary later, she bowed out, wanting to get back to the phone and wait to hear from the bookseller. It was a long shot, she knew, but at the moment it was her strongest lead.

Straker thanked her for the information she'd already gathered and rose with her, watching quietly as she left. He watched a bit more carefully, he knew, than was necessary; but he couldn't seem to pull his eyes from the swivel of her slim hips as she headed briskly back out onto the street.

Sitting back down at the table, he ordered another refill on the coffee and fell into a brooding silence. He was still thinking about Pamela, hoping he'd done the right thing by involving a civilian and that she wouldn't make a mistake and do something foolish. The coffee arrived and he stared at it, the boiling sensation in his stomach nearly doubling as the scent wafted up and into his nostrils. He sipped at it anyway. It was going to be a long, long day.

Devon stood in front of the full-length mirror in his room, turning first one way, then the other, checking for any cracks or leaks in his usual "superstar" veneer. He was more than a bit concerned that he look his best for this one; national television was high-caliber advertising, and he certainly wanted his "A" game presented to their fans.

He heard shuffling about in the next room, and he imagined Gail, pulling on and off outfits, tossing first one and then the next of her favorites aside, trying for just the right combination, just the right feel. He'd tried his best to convince her to dress semi-conservatively, but he knew that whatever they did to tone their act down, it would make little difference.

His flashy personality and his sister's exotic good looks, coupled with their reputations from stage shows, co-lead singers of the "baddest rock band on the market," would precede them from film and magazine. Nothing would change the opinions of either fans or foes at this late date. Gail might as well show up in a leopard-spotted G-string. It was what they would expect.

The others, all of whom were more excited about the show than Devon himself, were to arrive in less than an hour. The only absentees were "The Force," who was on an extended vacation at his parent's beach house in North Carolina and had opted out, and Tommy "Thunder," who said he'd rather spend his down-time on the beach than arguing with reporters. They'd agreed to meet in the lobby of the hotel, where Sammy would shuffle them into a limo. Appearances could never be let down, not when you were in the spotlight.

Once they'd actually made a firm commitment for this appearance, Sammy had been a whirlwind of energy. No way was he going to let a single facet of this get out of hand, a single chance for celebrity or promotion slide by. He'd gathered clips together from the band's various performances, checked and corrected lyrical quotes that Clearwater's "thugs" had prepared for him to bombard them with during questioning, and through it all he'd given new meaning to the words, "sweating buckets." Sammy had always been the nervous sort.

What seemed to bother him the most was the lack of any sort of script. He had been unable to get any clear inside information on exactly what Clearwater was planning, and it bugged the hell out of him. It was obvious that it was going to be much more than your average "You are evil and you are leading our children to Satan with your horrible music" routine. Trying to figure out the angle was consuming the little manager's every waking minute.

It was beginning to bother Devon a little bit, too, though he wouldn't have admitted it to anyone, least of all Sammy. He was confident in his own ability to talk through any situation that presented itself, given the chance. That was the key, though, given the chance. Clearwater was famous for one-sided harangues, and Devon was pretty sure the rest of the band's patience would wear thin before they reached the far end of one of *those.*

His confidence couldn't erase the nagging doubt that itched at the back of his mind. They were being kept a little too much in the dark for his taste, and he hoped the others would realize it and keep themselves under control until they knew for sure what was going down.

Finally the doorbell rang, and he dumped his worries with a quick shake of his head, moving quickly to answer it. It couldn't possibly be Gail. She was still thumping around, changing outfits and fussing with her hair. She had to be at least another twenty minutes away from perfection, and they wouldn't see her until she was satisfied she'd achieved it. In fact, nobody should have been there yet.

He leaned down so he could see through the little peephole in the door and was assaulted by a long, wet tongue that filled the lens from the far side. Grinning, he swung the door wide. It was Louie and The Mechanic after all, and he decided that he was actually glad they'd come early. Then he saw what he hadn't at first glance, and he grimaced openly, his hands flying to the sides of his head.

The Mechanic held a bottle in one large, meaty hand, a Cuervo Gold Tequila bottle. In his other hand, a half-eaten lemon dripped juice up and down his arm and onto the floor at his feet. They were both grinning like idiots, and the bottle was 3/4 empty.

"Got any salt, man?" the big drummer grinned down at him, standing there and swaying back and forth like some kind of gigantic kid. "We ran out."

For a moment, Devon didn't move. He could only stand and stare in disbelief as the pair wove unsteadily back and forth, smelling like some sort of rotten brewery. Grabbing the bottle, which was closely followed by The Mechanic's burly arm and then his off-balance body, he dragged them both into the room with what would have passed easily as a snarl.

"Damn," he exploded, wrestling the bottle from The

Mechanic's weakened grip and backing out of reach, "what the hell are you two doing? Have you lost your fucking minds?"

"Hey," Louie's grin just widened, "if you wanted a drink, man, all you had to do was ask. Me and The Mechanic, we've already had plenty, you know." Almost as an afterthought, he said, "Why are you so uptight, man?"

Hearing the commotion from her own room next door, Gail chose that particular moment to make her grand entrance, still running a brush through her ebon mane of hair as if there were any chance she might tame it before they left. She took one look at the scene before her, Devon standing, Cuervo bottle held high and out of reach, his eyes flashing like those of some avenging angel, and the other two, unperturbed by his wrath, bobbing back and forth and grinning like a couple of idiots; and she lost control, bursting forth with a gale of laughter that nearly doubled her over and sent her sprawling to the floor.

Devon spun quickly, ready to snap at her too, the words "grow up" screaming to his lips, when he caught himself in mid stride, stopping cold. The words never made it to his lips. The look he found in each of their eyes only showed him a mirror of his own tension. They all had their own ways of coping; who was he to shove his down their throats?

"Fucking idiots," he muttered, not wanting to give the impression of surrender. He turned and headed for the small kitchenette, a chuckle rising to his own lips. There was just enough time, if he were extremely lucky, to pump a couple of cups of hot coffee into the two musicians before Sammy arrived and crucified them all.

Behind him he could hear all three of them laughing, and he grinned in spite of himself. The Mechanic was going into his puppy dog act, fawning over Gail; and she was drinking it all in as usual, flirting back and loving it. It was the band, the *Maelstrom*; and there was nothing left to do but be caught up in it.

Nick, against his mothers protest, had opted for a different approach. He hadn't dressed up for the show at all, preferring honesty to bullshit, as he put it to himself. He wore a faded

Led-Zeppelin T-shirt, slightly less-faded jeans than his usual, and a green feather earring that dangled almost to his shoulder. He might be going to put his neck on this guy Clearwater's chopping block, but he was damned if he was going to run from the asshole. He was pretty tired of the whole thing, but the secrecy was the worst. For him, that part was over.

The past few nights had been a revelation for what remained of the Leatherman household. Nick had found a level of closeness with his mother that was nearly as strong, and in some ways more comfortable, than he'd experienced at any time in his life.

They'd stayed up the last few nights talking, just talking and sitting, and waiting, waiting for Ed. A lot of subjects had come up, including the fact that neither of them was all that certain, at this point, that they really wanted him to come home. They talked about things neither had had the courage to bring up before. It was a learning experience for them, a growing experience.

Jeanette, after hearing how Nick felt about things, after finally letting him explain things to her as he saw them, without making excuses every few sentences for Ed, found in her son a level of maturity, an adulthood that she'd never even seen developing. She found that he had cared a lot more than he had seemed to, had she been honest enough to respect him, and that he had developed a strength of will and character that she could lean on without fear of being let down.

Nick, on the other side of the coin, was reaching a point that every young person reaches at some time in their growth. He was reaching the realization that his mother, besides being a shoulder to cry on, a cook, and the constant answer to all the trials of growing up, was also a person—a woman.

In some ways, he realized now, she was even a little bit like Ruthie. She was soft, feminine, and easily hurt. It was something to think about, a truth he'd never realized fully before. Children, it seems, always assume that the problems that assault them day in and day out are not present for adults, that there is a magic "growing up" line, across which you have money, a car, a job, and life is simple. It's quite a shock to realize that adults, if anything, have the harder road to travel, and that that is what they have to look forward to.

The day of the show they'd both gotten up early, despite their lack of sleep, and for the first time in years, he'd stayed home and let her make him breakfast. Over cups of coffee, another first, they'd continued to learn about one another, to discuss the future and what their next moves might be.

The possibility that Ed wasn't coming back was sinking in for both of them, ingraining itself in their minds. It was not, once you got down to it, very likely that he *was* coming back. That left a lot of holes to be filled, a lot of new burdens to be shouldered. It helped them to draw even closer together.

Ruthie stopped by at lunch, timidly ringing the front bell. She'd never been to Nick's house. Ed had frightened her far too much, and Nick had forbidden it. He'd brought a girl home once, years earlier. Ed had been full of nasty jokes, probing comments, and his eyes had never left the girls jeans. Nick didn't think the man had meant anything serious by it, but it wasn't a chance he was prepared to take.

Nick knew that Ruthie must have been worried sick, or she'd have never come; and he was secretly pleased at the light that bloomed in her eyes when he opened the door himself.

"I couldn't wait to see you," she said, almost crying. "I'm worried, about the show, about everything...can I come in? Is Ed here...?"

"Ed is gone," he said, surprised at how much more certain he felt of it just by saying the words. He grabbed her by a trembling shoulder and drew her through the door, propelling her ahead of him down the hall and into the kitchen. "He may never come back. We haven't heard from him or seen him since the other day, the day the letter came about the show. Even the police can't find him."

He felt her relax somewhat at that, and she left him quickly, hurrying to his mother's side with a sympathetic cry. "Mrs. Leatherman, are you all right?"

"Jeanette, dear," she answered, "call me Jeanette. I guess I'll finally be getting to see more of you, so there's no need to be formal with me.

"I'm fine, I guess, now that Nick and I have had a chance to talk things through. I'm glad that you're here, though. I'm afraid that I'm about to bore him to tears with my stories and my crying."

"Not at all, Mom," Nick said, smiling. "It feels good to really be, well, *home*, you know? It seems like it's been an awfully long time."

He walked over, put an arm around each of them and drew them close to his sides. "We'll get through this, all of it, one way or another. When we do, I'll have to take you both to dinner somewhere."

They were silent for a while then, lost in separate thoughts. Nick was thinking of the coming show, of what he would say and what would happen. Ruthie was thinking of Nick, and Jeanette of Ed, and Nick, and the whole parade of strangeness that was invading her little world.

Horace Goldbough, a glass of wine in his left hand to help steady his own nerves, was giving a set of last minute instructions to one of the church elders, Hiram Pierce, over the phone. He was explaining to Hiram, who'd been a steadfast believer since the early days, as far back as the first meeting in the old church, why it was imperative that he, not Horace himself, attend the broadcast session of Clear it Up.

"Hiram, you know how I feel about this show, this confrontation, but this is not something I can just push aside. I can't possibly let this poor woman down."

He was pouring it on, carefully modulating the emotions in his voice and exercising the famous control he'd built a career on, to its maximum potential. "She's a dear, dear friend, as important to me as my own mother, and her husband—Josh—he tells me that she's been calling for me round the clock.

"I don't mind telling you, Hiram, I'm worried for her. Her physician doesn't give her much time. She's not expected to last through the night, in fact. I have to be there for her, to pay my last respects. You do understand, don't you?"

Hiram's mind was gearing up. Horace felt it. The man was loyal, and much brighter than he appeared at first glance, but his mind took time to get into gear. Finally, the man managed an answer.

"But Reverend," he said slowly, thoughtfully, as though considering every word carefully before letting it escape his mouth, "I'm no speaking man, as well you know. I will be no match for those you were to face tonight. They will confuse me, as sure as God is my witness. I will disgrace you, bring dishonor to the church..."

"Not so, Hiram," Goldbough assured the man, "Not so. You will have help, you know, help that will not be available to those others. The Lord will be with you, as well as all of the information I have gathered for your use. There will be no need for open confrontation. The facts, as I have shown them to you, and your own faith, will be enough. You don't doubt that the Lord can see you through this, do you, Hiram?"

"If you say it is so, I'll believe it." Hiram answered, clearly *not* fully believing it. Horace could picture the big man shaking his head from side to side as he spoke, "But I'd feel much better if I knew that you were going to be there. This Clearwater fellow isn't going to be very happy, either; not after you signed all those papers. What am I to tell him when he sees that you have sent me in your stead."

"Just tell him the truth, Hiram; we'll sort it all out later," Horace lied easily. "You just give it your best shot, and everything will work out fine."

His eyes lifted and he saw Brenda, a glass of wine in her own hand, her eyes downcast, entering the room. She had the bottle in her other hand, and she refilled his glass before she sank onto the desk at his side. He ran an appreciative glance up her slender form to her eyes as he gave Hiram his final instructions.

Her eyes were as deep, as compelling as ever; but they held no more fear for him. There was a need in them now that never burned out, that was never fully quenched; and he was the only relief she sought. The fire in her was constant now, and when she was in his presence she was barely controlled. The expression in those eyes was a lost, abandoned one—an expression full of lust and frustration.

Placing the phone on its cradle, he reached for her, drawing her close. She moved pliantly under his touch, shuddering with released tension as his arms wrapped around her tightly, pressing her against him.

"Tonight," he said, running one hand down the smooth length of her back, releasing the silken ties that held her flimsy gown in place, "tonight we will complete it all. It will all be ours. Are you ready to rule at my side, my dear, or to be ruled?"

She didn't speak, only shifted slightly to allow the gown to slip down her shoulders and drop to her waist. She took his hands in hers and placed them eagerly on her breasts, pushing forward to meet them, the hunger leaping to her eyes.

"You know the answer to that already," she hissed. "There is still time before we must leave, rule me now. Take me."

For perhaps the last time ever, Horace did as she bid him, his eyes dancing as she sated his lusts. Soon it would be dark—soon it would always be dark. Smiling, he picked her up, carrying her to the bedroom and closing the door behind them with a decisive click, a click of finality.

CHAPTER NINETEEN

In the television studio, where lights were being trundled about on stands and tripods of every description, with cameras, microphones, and mixing equipment of all types protruding from every wall and dripping from the ceiling, it was a bit hard for Nick not to feel overwhelmed. They'd been there for about twenty minutes, and it was enough to make his head swim in confusion.

He and Straker had come in together and had immediately been taken into tow by a slight, redheaded young man with a clipboard and an attitude.

"Now, you justht stay right here, 'kay?" the guy lisped at them. "I'll let you know when we have everything ready for you."

Nick looked at Straker then and caught the man grinning. "I'm surprised he didn't say 'toodles,'" Straker said, keeping his voice low and dodging out of the way of a young woman with a tray full of coffee and sodas. "Christ! This place is like a damned ant farm."

Nick nodded and grinned. He looked around carefully, not wanting to miss anything or to be taken by surprise. It was going to be rough enough without surprises.

"You ready, Nick?" Straker asked him. "This is it. Whatever you do, don't let them blow your cool; don't let the assholes get to you. That's the only time they're really dangerous, when you're off balance and might say something you didn't really mean.

"They're going to try and make you, and probably me, too, say something that they can twist around and change into something else. You have to kind of anticipate what they're up to and compensate for it. If you just stick to the facts and remember they only have us for a one hour show, we can get through this in one piece."

Straker stopped talking when he saw that Nick was no longer listening. In fact, he was no longer looking at the Inspector at all—his eyes were glued to a spot somewhere beyond. Turning, Straker saw that a backstage door had opened across the room from them.

Led by a strutting Gail Force and made up like huge kids at Halloween, with their hair blown back as if from a storm and their mouths set in perpetual grins, *Maelstrom* was making their entrance. The stage crew, it seemed, was having a much harder time herding them into one spot, or getting them to stay there, or even to be quiet for that matter.

Nick was like a young colt, straining at its bridle. He was obviously having a hard time not calling out to them. He grabbed Straker's sleeve, pointing at the group and saying simply, "*Maelstrom.*"

Straker eyed the group of musicians curiously. The woman was a knockout by anyone's standards, though not as young as she seemed in all the posters he'd seen. Even with the strange hairdo and the odd costume she'd chosen for the night's festivities, she looked damned good. The other singer—he remembered that much from setting up security for their last concert—looked like a paler mirror image of the woman at his side.

The other two were grinning and looking around, bothering the cameramen and flirting with any woman that came within reach. They were having a pretty good time being a general nuisance, obviously comfortable enough with the backstage scene; and Straker grinned as he watched. From the looks of things, the two might be drunk. That would certainly serve Clearwater right, not to mention giving him more than a handful of trouble. Maybe this would be entertaining, after all.

His chances for further speculation were cut short pretty quickly. The band was collared, finally, by a harried looking junior producer, and hurried off down a hallway. Probably had a padded room with nothing breakable where they kept troublemakers. Straker found himself wondering if they'd get the same hospitality as the group of skinheads that had torn apart the set of the show the previous summer. Hector Clearwater had had some interesting guests. Not all of them had liked his attitude.

It was only a few seconds later that a young blonde woman came and directed Nick and Straker down that same hall-way, hustling them along as though they were late and it was their own fault. Everything sped up then, passing in a blur. Directions and last minute instructions were slammed at them from all sides; lights flashed in their faces and cameras were rolling about again, looking for the perfect angle. Before either of them could clearly make out what was happening, they were seated, closed in, and left alone again with half-heard and prob-ably misunderstood instructions on where and when to go when they were called. It was a nightmare.

Straker forced himself to remain calm, ignoring most of it and concentrating on keeping his thoughts straight. This was Clearwater's method, he knew, the method upon which he'd built his reputation. The man was in the position now of the ultimate electronic control freak. Everyone's actions but his own would now be orchestrated by small hand motions and the flick of certain buttons.

Clearwater would mold the entire program to his own design. The others would enter, exit, even answer the ques-tions he shot at them in his scattergun manner, at his whim. He could—and no doubt would—cut them off in mid-answer if things weren't going the way he wanted them to. It was more than an interview; it was a trial, a trial by fire, a losing battle. Straker knew what was coming; it was a lot like questioning a suspect. His stomach was already starting the initial churning that would lead to one hell of a case of indigestion.

Nick was separated from him by an invisible wall of noise. They could reach out and touch if they wanted, but no way could they hear each other speak. The acoustics were designed so that the audience was piped directly in where they could hear the response, and at the same time, their own words were fired directly into an exotic array of microphones guaranteed to catch every nuance, every under-the-breath curse that they let out. For the next hour, Straker realized, he would only be able to worry about maintaining his own control. He would just have to hope that the boy was up to the strain on his own. Somehow, he didn't think that would be a problem.

Suddenly, the flow of energy changed. It was noticeable as a slight disturbance at first, then a jabber and rushing about that seemed to indicate that something was wrong. The mood had shifted, but he couldn't tell immediately what the cause might be. He hoped Clearwater had fallen off his stool and gotten a concussion.

Whatever it was, the production crews were flying into a frenzy that made even their hurried motions of a few moments before seem slow in comparison. Straker searched the room, trying to keep from getting dizzy as they blurred here and there in front of him and around him. He thought, momentarily, of grabbing one of the scurrying idiots and questioning them, but thought better of it.

It was good that he hadn't bothered, because just then the hands on the big clock on the wall clicked to the 9:00 position, and all hell burst forth on the stage. Lights flashed all around them in unison, blinding the guests and filling the room with brilliant luminescence. The speakers picked up the show's inane theme song, which flashed out over the crowd and brought them to their feet in anticipation. The show was on.

Glancing down by his feet at the small monitor that was provided, just out of sight of the audience, Straker could see that the cameras were focused on Hector Clearwater and his plastic, guaranteed to bring the house down smile. Looking a bit closer, Straker thought that maybe that smile was a little flawed tonight, a little bit off. It was barely noticeable, but he saw a trace of what appeared to be annoyance in the man's eyes—possibly even cold anger. Whatever had just happened, it was clear that Hector wasn't pleased by it; and that was just fine with Straker. Once again he reflected that it was just possible the evening would be entertaining after all.

Hector Clearwater stood in the center of the stage and babbled his usual inanities at the audience, who of course thought every word was profound, and fought one *hell* of an inner struggle between the need to scream at the top of his lungs and the need to maintain the old iron control, let the show go on and salvage yet another impossible situation. Damn Goldbough, who did that pompous asshole think he was, anyway?

Back and to his left, sitting forward on his seat a bit nervously, with a sincere and absolutely clueless smile plastered across his face, sat one Hiram Pierce. Not Reverend Horace Goldbough, champion of Christianity and defender of the faith, not the evangelical savior of the entire San Valencez/Lavender area. No. What they had here was a doddering old fool in a severe black suit that would have fit in better at a funeral than a television appearance, who looked sadly out of place, holding his bible clutched so tightly against him that it appeared he planned on using it as a shield. Damn.

Behind the scenes in the camera booth, there was not a smile to be found. In fact, beyond Clearwater, who had to smile, Straker, who was growing clearly more amused by the second, and The Mechanic's half-drunken leer, there were few smiles anywhere in the building.

The Reverend Goldbough, presenting his most sincere apologies, had phoned in less than an hour before airtime to say that he would not, much as he had been looking forward to it, be able to attend the show, after all. He had given them some cock and bull story about a member of his congregation—one of the widows Hector had so often wrongly accused him of stealing from—was on her deathbed. The woman, he claimed, was calling for him repeatedly and was not expected to last out the night.

Naturally, he'd said, he had no choice but to go to the poor woman, to be there to console her in her last hours. It was lamentable to be sure, he'd told them, but surely excusable under the circumstances. Bullshit.

Then he'd pulled the capper, the pièce de résistance, so to speak. He wouldn't leave the show in the lurch. Oh no; he had made a commitment, and Satan had to be faced down. That much hadn't changed. He would, he'd said, send his most trusted adviser, his most loyal elder, Hiram Pierce, to speak in his stead.

As Hector, his voice a study of control and proper modulation with just the hint of an accent that would always remind people of his much-touted American Indian background, ran through the motions of presenting the opening sequence he'd prepared, ad-libbing the last minute change into place smoothly, if not happily, writers and producers scrambled about madly in frantic efforts to throw something together to cover the gap, to make up for the loss of Horace Goldbough and his magnetic presence.

The show would begin as planned, but in the case that the damage became irreparable, there was always the backup plan to turn to. This wasn't the first disaster they'd been faced with over the years; such things seemed to be about par for the course in this business. They were prepared to switch over at a moment's notice if things got out of hand, or if they just fell apart. Being taped live, it was a necessary precaution. Airtime had to be maintained so that the sponsors could get their fair share of it. That was just how things worked.

The members of *Maelstrom*, unaware that anything was wrong, were having a good time. Devon, Gail, Louie, and The Mechanic, gazed about themselves in amusement, waved at the crowd and chuckled among themselves. Although they were certainly no strangers to the stage or to the preparations that went into producing a show, they *were* new to the luxury of sitting back and watching as someone else was forced to do all the work.

Without the added worry of a microphone falling on their head when its stand finally failed the concert stress test, or a guitar slipping out of tune in the middle of a set, proving itself no match for a chaotic swing of Louie's hip, it was all a lot more fun. It was actually cool to see somebody else sweating for a change, especially if one of those sweating was an asshole like Clearwater.

Devon glanced over the shoulder of a passing stage assistant and tried to catch a glimpse of what was on her clipboard. He succeeded only in bumping the girl's shoulder with his chin, and she spun on him, her eyes blazing, ready to slap or scold whoever had been so clumsy. As usual, his smile managed to save him. It was obvious that she knew who he was, and it occurred to him that maybe Clearwater didn't have all the allies in the room that night.

"Sorry," he said. She ran off quickly without replying, but not before he caught her smiling in return. And blushing.

He returned his gaze to the stage, letting it wander down to the small monitor at his feet. It was sort of like the monitor speakers they used on stage to hear how they sounded, and he decided it could serve a very similar purpose here. His own turn on the hot coals wasn't due for a few minutes still. He glued his eyes to the small screen and watched carefully to get a clear handle on which way things were going, and how Clearwater was going to handle them.

Devon didn't mind being the center of attention; he was used to that. Even if that center point was the front line of Hector's attack, it was fine. He actually preferred to be the one defending the group—they might stand a chance of seeming intelligent that way. He had no intention, in any case, of going into the coming "battle" blindly. Louie and The Mechanic had that amply covered.

At that moment, a small gray man who looked like he'd rather be any place on God's green earth than here, was seated directly beside Clearwater, looking about nervously. With a clearly condescending smile that the little man missed and the audience could not see, Clearwater turned to him, and it was started.

"So, ladies and gentleman, since it would seem that the "good" Reverend Horace Goldbough has been, shall we say, sidetracked on his way to the show, we have with us Hiram Pierce, Elder of the Church of New Light, who will be standing in God's corner tonight. Hiram, what have you to say to our audience in opening?"

The little man cleared his throat and looked about himself in obviously growing fear. He had the appearance of a school kid asked to give an oral report, but who had forgotten his notes. Devon could almost imagine the poor guy crossing himself mentally as he closed his eyes for a second, cleared his throat a second time, and blurted out.

"I don't see it as a fight, Mr. Clearwater. I mean, not like in the sense of a boxing match, or a war. I'm not here to do battle, although the enemy is surely all around us. I'm only here to present the case of righteousness, to defend the minds of our young people, and to see justice done. That's how Reverend Goldbough put it to me, sir, and that's how I aim to present myself, no disrespect meant."

Then, as if the sudden realization had flashed upon him, that his words had just leapt electronically across hundreds of miles, that they would be recorded, rewound, and watched again and again, as he saw that mirrored in Hector's cold, reptilian eyes, his face grew red. Hiram clammed up then, quickly and completely, wavering between abject fear and righteous indignation.

Almost groaning, Hector flipped a switch somewhere below the desk in front of him, turned to his right and fixed his eyes in a quick salvage-the-moment attempt, on Straker's. At least the Inspector had had the good manners to show up when he said he would. Hector's staff had gotten a chance to check up on the accusations that the Beauchane woman had made, at least that much they had in hand. All of the things she'd said had turned out to be true. He was hoping that a quick shift in mid-stride could still pull this off.

"Inspector Kendall Straker," he said in introduction, spitting the words out in such a manner that it seemed to make them into an accusation, "Chief Inspector of the Lavender Police Department. Tell me, Inspector, is it true that you and your people are currently investigating a murder that was perpetrated in a graveyard?"

"Yes; that is true," Straker began, ready to launch into a small, prepared statement. He never got it out; Clearwater was back on the attack like a snake, giving no room for thought between strikes.

"Is it also true, then, Inspector, that you have withheld vital evidence from the public on this case, evidence that puts a possible perpetrator of one of the grisliest crimes in the history of our city in that graveyard on the night of the crime?"

Straker's face flamed, his plan of control flying out the window. Even Devon, watching him from the far side of the stage, caught his breath at the spark that leapt to the inspector's eyes at that moment. His whole frame shaking, gripping the arms of his chair in an effort to steady himself, he answered.

"Mr. Clearwater, I'm not sure what you think you're driving at, and I'm not sure that I like your attitude, either. I have not now, nor have I ever in many long years of serving the people of Lavender, withheld any evidence that could convict a killer. I also have no lead strong enough to bring such a killer, were I to have a viable suspect, to justice. If I had *either* of those things, I'd be out arresting that man or woman, not sitting here as you attempt to make a fool of me."

Unperturbed, Clearwater reached down and flipped another switch, cutting Straker's face from the screen while it was still red with anger, leaving that as the last image people would see of the man. He knew how to make every nuance of such a show work to his advantage—it was his finest talent. Without the slightest warning, he flashed Nick's startled face onto the screen. Straker was still trying to speak, off to the side, but the monitors and sound equipment had already shifted to Nick's microphones—the words were spoken to the air.

Nick, who had been gazing sideways at Gail Force's legs, was caught completely off guard. He didn't have a chance of regaining his balance in time to speak, and Clearwater had obviously been aware of it.

"This young man," he was saying, "Nick Leatherman, was in a certain graveyard a little over a week ago. No explanation of why he and his friends, whoever they might be, were there, but the evidence is clear. He dropped a pocketknife in the woods, very close to where the killing the inspector is so riled up about took place, didn't you, Nick?"

"Uh...yeah," Nick managed. He never got the chance to go on. He had been cut off as cleanly and effectively as Straker, and left to sit, staring blankly into the camera and no doubt looking as guilty as Charles Manson.

Hector felt the building rhythm, the control that made the

show work, falling into place, and was on a roll. He had taken over again, his own magnified voice shooting out over all the speakers with what Straker felt to be an exaggerated, overly gory account of Gretchen Steiner's murder. Above his head and clearly visible on the monitor screen, were photographs of the graveyard, the surrounding woods, and even the altar itself. How they had gotten out there and found the place so fast was beyond Straker's ability to imagine.

"Ritual murder, ladies and gentlemen, cults of devil-worshipping killers walking freely about in a community where peace and tranquility are the norm, a place where such a crime hits even closer to home than in the big city.

"As close to home as it *seems*, though," he went on, "all of the influences involved here are not Lavender's own. Not at all. The knife that was found in that graveyard wasn't just a Buck knife, such as a father might give his son for Christmas, or even a camping knife with a folding fork and spoon. It was a souvenir blade, purchased at a concert; and it was engraved with a *name*, ladies and gentlemen.

"The group whose name is engraved on that knife is here with us tonight, as well. In fact, it was on the very night of their concert that the murder took place. It was *from* that concert that Nick Leatherman and unnamed others left to make the trip that led them out the winding road to Shady Grove Cemetery."

The screen flashed from Nick's silent, confused face, to *Maelstrom* in all their present glory. Devon and Gail, predictably, managed to meet the cameras with charismatic, steady gazes. Unfortunately, the spell of this was lost on the crowd since Louie was busily engaged in watching some studio girl's ass, and The Mechanic was picking his nose.

"*Maelstrom*," Clearwater proclaimed, sweeping his arm in a gesture that encompassed all four of them, a smirk clearly planted across his face. "One of the most influential musical groups of this, or any time, living legends of rock and roll.

"Many of you may have followed them through the news, through the music journals. Magic, lewd sexual suggestion, alcohol, they have it all.

"The question is this," he said, slowing and sweeping the

audience with a sincere, big-brotherly glance, "are they the vehicles of Satan? Has their music led young Nick Leatherman, and countless other adolescent fans, to demonic worship? To Satanism?

"Are their barely cloaked sexual suggestions and mystic lyrics that seem to promise things beyond our 'real' world evidence of the devil's handiwork? That, ladies and gentlemen, is what we intend to find out here tonight."

Heaving a great sigh of resignation as his stomach settled slightly and his pulse returned to a semblance of normality, Straker sat back and waited. He waited for the show, the evening, and Hector Clearwater to just go away.

They were getting killed, tortured. Pamela's phone was on its fourth ring before she managed to peel her eyes from the screen in front of her and reach for it, dragging the phone onto the couch and pulling the receiver quickly to her ear. Her face was etched with deep lines of concern. It didn't appear to matter so much that the "good" Reverend Goldbough had bowed out on him; Hector Clearwater appeared to have the entire situation firmly in hand. Still watching out of the corner of her eye, she spoke.

"Yes, who is it?" she asked, almost hoping for a wrong number.

"Ms. Green?" the voice on the other end asked politely.

"Yes," she repeated, "this is Pamela Green. Who is this? May I help you?"

"This is Tom Dawson, from the bookstore, you remember? I said I'd give you a call if something came up about that book, *The Grand Sabbat*?"

He had her attention now. Forgetting the television for the moment, she gave him every ounce of concentration she could muster. "Yes? Did you find something, then?" She asked eagerly.

"Yes, I have," he answered slowly. "I did some checking around after you left the shop, made some calls. It seems, as far as anyone in the business can tell me, that there are two copies of that book in this area. One of them was purchased through very obscure channels a few years back, and the collector's name is being kept in strictest confidence.

"The other, and this is the truly odd part, was at a little shop right here in San Valencez, a place owned by a strange little old guy by the name of Tobias Langston. When I heard he actually had a copy for sale, I went on over and checked it out. It's authentic, all right, and it was actually available for sale, which is even more surprising. Like I said, all the copies are done by hand; and most of them are pretty old.

"This one is done on some kind of leather parchment that I've never seen before, and it has to be at least a couple of hundred years old. The man hardly wanted anything for the book, as if he was happy to part with it or didn't need the money, or something. I took the liberty of picking it up for you, though I have to tell you that after glancing through the thing, I can't imagine why anyone right in the head would want anything to do with it. Creepy stuff, for sure."

"I'll be right over to pick it up," she said, barely able to contain her excitement. "You will be open for a while longer, won't you?"

"I usually close up about now," he answered, "but I'll wait for you. Frankly, I'll be happy to get this thing out of my shop. I like books; they've been my life for a long time, but this one flat-out gives me the creeping willies. Besides, I have nothing else planned."

Thanking him, and with a final reluctant glance at the television, she grabbed her purse and headed for the door. It was only a short drive, and it seemed that it was but moments later when she pushed her way through the front doors of the small shop and hurried to the counter.

Dawson was seated in a comfortable leather chair a few feet behind the counter, reading quietly. He was not reading her book, though. She saw the small leather-bound volume sitting on his desk blotter almost the second she reached the counter, staring at it as if mesmerized. It was obviously what she sought.

The bookseller looked up then, taking in her features with a glance of appreciation before speaking.

"Glad you came," he grinned. "I was getting nervous with this thing lying around. It's as if it watches you, crazy as that sounds. I'll be happy not to have it to trouble me anymore. Here's the deal. I got the thing for fifty bucks. You throw in ten bucks for my time and trouble, and it's yours."

"Only fifty?" she said, surprised. She'd come prepared to spend a much larger sum. She had a small collection of signed and limited hardbacks at home, and she knew how expensive collecting could be, especially old and hard to find books.

"That was his price," Dawson nodded, obviously surprised himself. "Like I said, the guy seemed as anxious as I am to get rid of the thing; and money didn't seem to interest him all that much, one way or the other. You should see the oddball collection of stuff he's got there."

Pamela fumbled her checkbook out of her purse quickly, not certain why she felt so agitated. Probably the man's constant badgering about how the book made him nervous was getting to her. She had to admit, silly or not, that there was something about the thing that generated unease, a sort of slimy foulness that reminded her slightly of the drip pan at the bottom of her refrigerator, or the green mold she'd once found in a forgotten, half-full coffee cup. It rode in the pit of her stomach, and it made her a little nervous. At the same time, it drew her, demanding her attention.

"Thanks," she said, holding out the hastily scrawled check and her license for the man's approval. "Believe me; it is very important to me that I get a chance to look through this. I'd tell you why, but I'm certain you wouldn't believe me; and I'm almost out of time."

"Tough deadline?" he asked conversationally.

"Deadline?" she repeated dumbly, then remembered her story about writing an article and smiled at him. "You might say that."

As she grabbed the book and hurried back outside; she felt Dawson's eyes on her back, staring after her. She could just make out his face in the reflective surface of the glass doors—it wore a troubled, worried expression. He was fondling the check absently, folding it one way, then the other, as he watched her depart.

Pamela didn't wait until she got home to study her find.

It drew her attention, gnawed at her senses, demanding to be attended to. She opened the cover almost as soon as her car door was shut, and the grinning, brownish devil image leered out at her, foul and fascinating all at once. She tore at the page, flipping it to the next with a great effort of will, only barely freeing her eyes from those of the creature on the page.

"Jesus," she breathed, feeling a sensation of physical release as the demonic features were obscured from her sight. Face flushed, her eyes wide with horror and growing fear, she read on. It was a reading like no other she'd ever experienced, an obsessive scramble that led her wildly from line to line, word to word, words that screamed themselves out at her, binding themselves to her consciousness.

She did not make it through the thing easily. She fought with heart and soul every inch of the way across the oily, evil paper, across the blasphemies that unfolded, one after another; but it was of no use. When it was over, when the book lay at her side, closed, finally, it took her several long moments to get her eyes to refocus. Her mind wouldn't stabilize, whirling with impossible atrocities that still leered and reached at her.

"My God," she gasped. Events, days, and what she had just read began to arrange themselves in her mind, to explain one another and weave together into a complete picture, a puzzle solved. It was a tapestry of grisly horror, and she reacted in the only way she could, flinging the book from her as if it were burning her flesh. It flew over the seat and was lost somewhere in the shadows of her backseat, and she reached out with a trembling hand, jabbing the key into the ignition and firing the engine to life.

She pulled out of the little parking lot in a spray of gravel, completely ignoring the posted speed limits and stops, driving as if possessed. There was no time left for caution, no room left for sanity.

Glancing down at her watch, she saw that it was forty-five minutes past nine already. She had to get to Ken, to the television station, to catch him before he disappeared into the night. She pushed even harder on her gas pedal, barely making a yellow light and skidding onto Main Street recklessly.

What had pushed her to the limits, galvanized her to action so quickly and insistently, was the last chapter of what she had just read, the last rite of completion of *The Grand Sabbat*. The bits and pieces of the ritual were precise, planned and mapped in gory, insidious precision, including the timetable. It had to be performed perfectly, completely.

That meant unless she had read the thing wrong, and she knew from the words burned into her brain she had not, tonight was the night when the final rite had to be performed. Tonight the demon would be summoned: the demon who had presumably written the book, whose face had glared out at her from the yellowed parchment with such maleficent glee. Pamela didn't know if it was Satan or not, but it had to be something close, very close—close enough that the distinctions couldn't possibly matter.

She didn't even have the luxury of disbelief after having been trapped against her will among the pages of the filthy little book, held to its pages by unknown force. Something evil was going to happen, at least if that ritual was allowed to reach its completion. Whatever it was, it had to be stopped, could not be allowed to happen. There was another sacrifice to be offered.

Thoughts of Gretchen filled her mind, mingled with the grinning visage of the demon's malevolent face; and she shuddered violently. It was as if the thing were aware of her, mocking her.

Ahead she could just make out the huge letters that announced WTOK TV. She homed in on them without regard to safety, hers or anyone around her, weaving insanely through the downtown traffic. Somehow, she managed to reach the parking lot alive and stumble out of her car. It was nearly 10:00.

CHAPTER TWENTY

It was late, and lonely, and the light was very dim in the shack. Ruthie sat alone, huddled as deeply into Nick's beanbag chair as she could get, wishing with every ounce of concentration she could muster that someone else was there. Anyone. It was horrible waiting, not knowing what was happening on that horrid show, with no one available to share her fears. She hated it, but there was no other way.

She had wanted to wait, to come to the shack later with the others; but it wouldn't have been possible. Both of her parents were at home, and it would have taken nothing short of an act of God, considering all of the trouble that had been going on lately, to get her through the doors of her house after dark.

As it was, she'd had to lie; and she hated to lie to her parents. They were good people, and they loved her; it was just that they sometimes failed to understand the things that were really important to her. A good excuse was her only way out, something along the lines of a school function, dance class, an occasional night spent at a friend's house, set up and verified well ahead of time.

All of those would have been fine, good excuses, the type of thing a "proper young lady" might do with her evenings. Going to hang out in a converted chicken coop with boys like Nick, Flash, and Weasel, was not even close. It was hard for her to imagine a thing less likely to be cool with her father, so she had lied. At 7:00 p.m., an armload of books and notecards in her hands, she'd left—for the library. Never mind that the library was closed, she could deal with any trouble later. Tonight she had to be there for Nick; she just *had* to.

She'd brought one of her own tapes along, by the Steve Miller Band, and the mellow strains of the melody wafted about the small room softly, helping a little. Nick would listen to her music, on occasion, even claimed to like some of it. Steve Miller, he said, was "okay." If the other guys had ever caught him listening to it, she knew they would've laughed; but it was enough that he'd shared it with her. It was something she could cling to, something to hold her steady until he arrived.

She wasn't really playing it loud, not considering the decibel level the shack was accustomed to; but it was loud enough. When the three dark figures surrounded the outside of the building, she heard nothing. She was lost in thought, worried, and not a little bit frightened, considering all they'd been through lately. She didn't hear it when they began to crack the door open slightly. She was doing her best to blank her mind, to float off with the notes of the music and make the night just disappear.

The first thing that she noticed being different was the smell. It caught her attention, bringing a slight frown to her face. Flowers? She thought maybe it was jasmine. Snapping to awareness seconds too late, she tried to cry out and failed. Two of the figures slipped quickly and silently through the door and lunged at her. One of them clapped a strong hand over her mouth, sharply and roughly cutting off the scream that was building.

The other dived lower, wrapped his arms around her legs and lifted her from the chair so that she couldn't stand. In a desperate effort to free herself, Ruthie bit down on the hand that covered her mouth, squirming to one side and trying to get her sluggish body to react—to escape.

Her teeth got a grip on the hand, but it was ripped free, leaving behind a trace of skin and the salty taste of blood. The man barely flinched, grunting at the pain, and his grip on her face returned, tighter than ever, squeezing until the pain brought tears to her eyes. She squirmed and kicked out with her legs at the second robed figure. No good.

Within what must have been only seconds, a loop of strong twine had been wrapped quickly around her legs; and a bandanna flashed out, replacing the hand across her mouth in a blur of fear-tainted motion. The cloth was pulled around behind her ears and tightened, biting deeply into the corners of her mouth and immobilizing her jaws.

Through the haze of tears that poured from her eyes, Ruthie saw that a third figure had slipped through the door to join the others. This one took a small carpet from under one arm and unrolled it on the floor. Held and bound helplessly, Ruthie could only watch, eyes wild, trying to figure out what was happening to her.

"So," the newest intruder hissed at her, moving closer as the others lowered her onto the now flattened rug, "you will soon be food for the master. It is good, very good."

A slender hand snaked out of the figure's robe; Ruthie was startled to see that it was a woman's. It slid forward, unfastened the top button of Ruthie's blouse and slid inside, tracing a slow pattern over the shivering, heaving flesh of her breasts and lingering on her nipple.

Ruthie twisted to the side and tried to roll away from the touch, but it only made things worse, tearing loose another button and baring more of her flesh to the air.

Sobbing into the material of the gag, she pressed her eyes as tightly shut as she could make them go, tried to scream and managed only a soft gurgling sound. She tried to conjure images of home, of Nick, of anything that would screen out what was happening.

"Leave her alone," a second voice commanded. "There's no time."

Ruthie felt the hand reluctantly slide from her flesh, and she shuddered, gulping in what air she could around the cloth that filled her mouth.

She felt more hands on her then, rougher, masculine hands, but they did not prod or poke at her. They gripped her solidly, pulling her like a sack of flour to the edge of the rug. Before she realized what was happening they rolled her, a dizzying, disorienting sensation. Her arms were pressed solidly to her sides, the light faded away, and her air became close and dusty.

The scent of old carpet filled her nostrils, musty and damp;

and her eyes watered. She sneezed once, taking too much of the dust into her nose, and tried to control her breathing. Finally, as her heart raced and her lungs tried to shut down, the limited supply of oxygen that was reaching her brain sent her reeling away, shutting her into a world of soothing darkness.

Ignoring her, the three were back at the doors and the one window of the shack, checking the yard and the street beyond to make certain that they would not be seen. One of them reached over and turned the stereo up, then they dimmed the lights slightly more than they had been and cracked the door open once again. Seeing nothing, they lifted the now limp bundle they'd created and headed out into the shadowed yard, making their way hurriedly past the house on their way to the street beyond.

Oblivious to what had been happening in his back-yard, Weasel's dad looked up from the book he was reading. Something had crossed in front of the streetlight outside, creating a shadow, and it distracted him. He was just in time to see the figures cross his yard, three of them, and he slammed his book down with a curse and leapt to his feet.

He reached the front door on the run and slammed it open just as the three tossed some bundle they'd been carrying into the back end of a blue station wagon and ran for the doors.

"Hey!" he called out, grabbing the length of two-by-four he'd kept behind the door for years and heading barefoot into the yard, his hair flying in the wind. "Hey! Come back here, you assholes! Who the hell do you think you are?"

He never even made it to the edge of the porch before the car's engine roared into life, spitting gravel out behind it as it lurched into the street.

He glared after the disappearing taillights until they were completely out of sight around the corner of the block. He thought momentarily of calling the police. He knew that his son kept some valuable items out in that old shed, but he decided he'd better wait. He also knew, more even than his son realized—about the other activities that took place in that shack; and the last thing they needed was some rednecked cop finding a bag of pot in his yard.

Besides, he reasoned, the intruders might not have been in the shack at all. They could have just as easily been cutting through from the neighbor's yard. He shook his head, upset that they had gotten away cleanly, and went back to his house, depositing his makeshift club beside the door and returning to his book and his Led Zeppelin.

Several blocks away, slowed now to a law-abiding pace, the three kidnappers and their victim headed into the deeper shadows beyond the lights of town. The driver was tense, barely controlling the urge to speed off through the night, ignoring speed limits and traffic signals.

Nobody was to have seen them. On that matter their instructions had been explicit. Tonight was far too important for anything to interrupt—the final step toward the victory that would make everything else pale to unimportance.

Cursing under her breath, the driver turned at last onto the highway that led out of town, pressing her foot a little more solidly to the floor. The dirt road to the farmhouse was not that many miles away, and once they turned onto that, it was very unlikely they could be followed. Her rearview mirror remained empty, and the thrill of what was to come enveloped her once more. No one would follow them—it was their night.

Ruthie, unaware of anything that was taking place, was lost in a vast sea of darkness, dreaming fitfully as the car bounced her along. She dreamed of huge, slavering demon figures and odd creatures with bobbing, leering eyes. Hands ran themselves in sensuous waves over her skin, and she writhed beneath their touch. She whimpered, but she did not awake.

The lights of the city blinked to life behind them, filling the air with small glints like distant fireflies. Ahead, only darkness loomed, sliced here and there by the dim light of the moon, but not really intruding on the shadows.

Ahead, others were arriving, closing in on the old farmhouse in silence. The coming hour loomed vast, deep, and eternal.

CHAPTER TWENTY-ONE

If anything, the confusion and madness at the studio sur-
passed even Pamela's stricken state. The parking lot was alive
with moving bodies, screaming voices and clouds of smoke. She
thought, just for an instant, how odd it was that every single
person present should be smoking one thing or another, but
that passed quickly with the appearance of a grimy apparition,
stalking forward out of the smoke.

Pamela recognized him from what she'd seen of the show
earlier; it was The Mechanic. Close on his heels, coughing and
waving their arms about to clear enough air that they could
breathe, came Devon Storme, Gail Force, and Louie "Lightning"
Rivers, who was the only one apparently unaffected by whatever
disaster had just befallen them. He was launched into a nonstop, high-speed conversation with the boy, Nick Leatherman,
who grinned from ear to ear.

The next in line, and she nearly broke into tears of relief at
the sight, was a slightly amused Ken Straker. There was a big,
self-satisfied grin riding on his face, and she almost smiled herself, seeing it. It was not like any Ken Straker she'd yet come in
contact with.

All around the group, the staring, glaring eyes of studio
personnel followed them, mixtures of anger, disgust, and shock
mingling among their features. *Maelstrom* and their two com-
panions were paying the people no attention at all.

From deeper within the walls of the studio, loud cursing
and yelling could be heard over the din. Faintly, as a background to the madness, Pamela heard the insipid background
music to one of the local TV sitcoms floating through the air.

Obviously, the tide of the interview had swung a bit since she'd flipped off her television and launched into the night. It appeared that the "good guys" might have held their own after all.

Raising her arm and fighting her way through the growing crowd of people toward him, she called out. "Ken! Ken Straker!"

He turned, his smile widening as he caught sight of her, squirming her way through the teeming bodies. He couldn't see how upset she was from where he stood, and whatever personal victory he'd just experienced was still in control of his senses.

"Hey," he called out, "come on over here and meet these guys. You missed one hell of a show, Pam. I think we gave Mr. Clearwater something to think about for a long, long time to come."

She decided that there, in the midst of all those people, in particular people associated with the likes of Hector Clearwater, was not the place to tell him all that she had discovered. The last thing they needed was to be tailed by a bunch of television cameras.

Smiling back at him tentatively as she finally managed to make it to his side, she answered him. "You weren't too hard on him, were you?"

"Actually," he said, spinning to his left and dropping a large hand to rest on Devon Storme's shoulder, "this guy here was the star who stole the show. Clearwater never knew what hit him. You should have heard it."

Now that she was among friends, no longer trapped in her car with only that evil little book for a companion, it was easier to think; and she was truly curious. "But," she asked them, "how did you get that idiot to shut up? I was watching the first part of it, and it seemed like he cut you all off, just before you could say anything he didn't want to hear."

"Well," Louie Rivers drawled, breaking in quickly with a big grin. "The first thing that happened was that The Mechanic here gave old Clearwater the raspberry. The idiot asked what that was supposed to mean, so I told him it was 'up yours,' backwards masked. After that, it was cake."

"Well," Straker took the narrative back again, "it wasn't

exactly *that* simple, though that was a good start. What actually turned the tide was when Devon here managed to get his hands on a real microphone. You're right, Pam, he was cutting us off pretty short; and it was just starting to really piss me off when the fun started.

"It seems that while ol' Hector was jumping back and forth, trying his best to make us look stupid and evil, which by the way he was doing quite a job of, Mr. Storme was busy. He managed to fumble around beneath that desk and find the switch that cut off his microphone. A quick bit of under-the table rewiring with a paper clip, and he was on the air.

"Right about the time The Mechanic and Louie got him flustered, Devon kind of jumped in, just started talking in a calm, reasonable voice. You should have seen Clearwater's face when he pushed that damned button of his and nothing happened. I thought he was going to have an apoplectic fit there on the spot."

"But," Pamela asked, "What did you say?" She was smiling now, caught up in their enthusiasm, "Surely you didn't just thumb your nose at him and call him names?"

"No," Devon smiled at her, "I'd been planning what I wanted to say on this show ever since they called us—even had some notes written down for the occasion. I really never thought I'd get a chance to speak my mind, but I was prepared, just in case; and it's a good thing I was.

"What I did was to explain a little bit to Mr. Clearwater, his friend Hiram, and his studio audience about our lyrics. As usual in cases like this, he relied on cheap pyrotechnics and the common viewpoint on rock music to back him up here. He'd never heard our songs—not to where the words could get through.

"A lot of what we sing is spiritual in nature, closer to Christianity by far than to any sort of demon or Satan worship. I read him a few excerpts from songs we're working on, and from some of our older hits.

"Then I went ahead, since I had the floor and all, and talked about the music business in general. I told him we were both entertainers, and that the biggest difference between himself and I was that I didn't make my money off of the hardship of others, and wasn't he worried that kids would watch his show and grow up to be assholes?

"I guess it was about that time that the paper clip I used on the microphone got too hot. It started smoking, and before I noticed it the wiring had caught fire. I jumped up, said my good-byes, and we hustled on out of there. They'd started, by that time, running some backup tape they'd had ready, about some crime lord in Chicago, but I think I got my message across."

"Good for you," Pamela said. As the young man had been speaking, she'd taken a closer look at him, noting his deep, searching eyes and honest, friendly smile. It took a bit of imagination to cut through all of the makeup and the stage-hype, but she decided that Devon Storme was actually quite handsome.

Then, as though struck from behind, she recalled why she was there, all of it whipping through her mind in a whirlwind of urgent emotion. "Ken!" she cried out, turning back to the Inspector, "My God, with all the excitement, I almost forgot!"

The Ken she knew emerged in a flash, and he was gripping her shoulders tightly. "What? Have you found something?"

She quickly explained about the phone call from the book dealer and her immediate purchase. She then gave as detailed as possible an account of the odd happenings in her car after-ward, and of the conclusions she'd reached upon reading the ritual.

When she had finished, Straker didn't hesitate. It was crazy, but so was every other single thing involved in this case; and he wasn't about to let anyone else die, not while he was still around to do something about it.

Thinking quickly, he called out to Devon, "You up for a little adventure?"

"Why not?" the singer grinned back, echoed by the others in the band. "We're on a roll, why bust up the party?"

"Good. I thought you might feel that way. I'll fill you all in on what Nick can't later. For the moment, Pam and I have to go by the station house and arrange for some backup, just in case we run into more than we can handle. You take Nick to his house and wait for us there."

Nick looked at him gravely, then at Pam, and back. "It's

Goldbough, isn't it?" he asked, guessing what was going on. "Is it another ritual?"

"No time, Nick," Straker said, "but you're on the right track. See you guys in a few...very few."

He hurried with Pamela over to where she'd parked. "Mind if I drive?" he asked, not waiting for her answer before he leaped behind the wheel and fired the engine up.

Without a word, Pam jumped into the passenger seat beside him, a little miffed for having left the keys in the ignition. It was a strange night already, and she was fairly certain the strangeness had only just begun. At this point, she'd rather have the expert in charge, the steadier hand at the wheel. It might not "be" safer, but it certainly felt safer, and for the moment that was more than enough.

The memory of that leering face, glaring up from the yellowed parchment paper, still haunted her mind. It had seemed aware of her, and of the world. That was enough to send her shuddering into her bed to lift up the covers. Although it was warm, she wrapped her arms close about herself, grasping her shoulders and watched as the road fell away beneath them.

Straker's mind, meanwhile, was awhirl with feverish thought. Time was not their ally on this one; every single second that ticked off the clock was working against them, mocking them. Damn Goldbough, anyway. It had been a diversion. The whole thing had been that psycho minister's doing—a set up. He'd patted them all on the bottoms with a smile and sent them off to play on television, while he went out for games of his own.

Straker wondered if they were already at the graveyard, if they had a victim for the night, and if so, who it would be.

Goldbough was primed for something, that much was certain; and it was obviously going to be something big. He surely couldn't hope to have fooled them forever with this one; for some reason getting caught didn't seem to bother the man anymore, and that made him seem even more dangerous.

It was, in fact, what bothered Straker the most. He'd dealt with more than his share of psychos, directly and indirectly, and one thing they never seemed to want was to be caught.

They invariably wanted to prove they were better, smarter than those who hunted them. Goldbough was no fool. He had to know that they were on to him, that he would be brought to justice soon. So why the setup? It only served to confirm their suspicions of his guilt.

No, there was something missing. Something was expected of this night, something that stank of raw sewage and sawed at his heart like razor wire as he pressed against it, felt it out, worried it over in his mind.

He'd heard Pamela's account of what she'd read in the book, the account of the one ritual that remained; and there had been something in the way she'd related it, something in her eyes that had grabbed that razor wire working on his heart and yanked, helping it to cut deeper. She was scared.

He could understand her fear, could even empathize with it somewhat. Anyone in a position like this would be scared if they weren't crazy themselves. It wasn't just her fear, but the depth of it, the sheer animal terror that he'd glimpsed behind her veneer of calm.

There was a wild light in her eyes that had flashed like a warning beacon ever since she'd mentioned the ritual. It was like the flicker he'd seen once in the eyes of a deer he'd come upon in the woods and startled, one that had turned and looked at him, expression carved of accusation and terror, just before he'd squeezed the trigger and shot it.

That deer had made one last scramble before it died: crashing through trees, tripping over roots it could easily have avoided, mindlessly running from its fear. It was that sort of light he saw in Pamela's eyes, and it shouldn't have been there. She was a brave girl, had to be in her line of work; and yet this had her spooked. More was at work here than your average, run-of-the-mill psycho, that much was certain.

The two of them didn't speak as he sped along, watching the road melt beneath them. It wasn't far from the studio to the station house. Pamela was out her car door and at his side before he even had his halfway open, unwilling to wait for even a moment alone in the growing darkness. He led her quickly through the front doors and on to his office, ignoring the night dispatcher as they passed.

He'd said he was there for backup. Partly that was true. Unfortunately, what he didn't want was a lot of other cops on the scene just yet. It might still prove to be a false alarm, or Goldbough might have moved the whole damned business to another location.

He wanted a couple more guns, some ammo for the one he already carried, and maybe a small shot of the scotch he kept in his desk drawer for "emergencies." There was an uncomfortable rolling burn developing in the pit of his stomach, nagging at his thoughts. It was all just too damned crazy.

Even after all they'd just been through together, Nick started out the trip from the studio to his house a little overawed by the presence of Devon and the others. Dressed as they were in their makeup and costumes, just like on his posters, it was as though they'd walked straight off his MTV screen and into the car, planting themselves beside him and talking about the weather.

On his left sat Gail Force, and on his right was Louie "Lightning" Rivers. Devon rode up front with The Mechanic, who'd taken over as driver, handing a fifty to the limo man and promising to have the car back by the next day. It was all like some sort of wacked out dream—unbelievable.

When Louie reached into his inside jacket pocket and pulled loose an almost empty bottle of tequila, Nick gratefully took a swig, scowling heavily as the odd-tasting liquor flowed down his throat. Gail had given the guitarist a dirty look as he handed over the bottle, but Nick was in no mood to be coddled.

Seeing how nervous their new companion was, Devon began to talk to him, a steady flow of questions and quick answers, finally managing to put him at ease. He asked Nick what he thought of their music, and it was obvious from the tone of his voice and the look in his eyes that it really mattered, that his opinion made a difference.

Nick wasn't shy on that subject. He quickly listed his favorites among their songs, those he liked less, and why, and asked a few of the burning questions they left him with about the lyrics and the melodies. It was fun, light-hearted, and it took his mind, for the moment, off of the seriousness of the business at hand.

"So," Louie grinned, just as they were finally pulling into the Leatherman driveway, "I hear that the devil, and us, of course, have possessed you, Nickster. Tell me, what's all this about women being sacrificed?"

Seeing how Nick tensed up at the question, they listened closely as he related the incidents that had led up to this night. He started with the concert, not leaving out the acid this time, and moving quickly past that to the graveyard.

He told them about the Church of New Light, how he and his friends had broken in there and about the book they'd seen, the murder they'd nearly witnessed, and how he himself had come to be blamed, at the same time dragging them into it too. All of this he managed to get out from the time they hit the driveway to the time they reached the front door, and by then he had their interest completely.

"Your dad is gone too?" Gail asked, concern washing over her face. "How awful for you."

"Stepfather," Nick corrected her, turning his eyes away quickly. "You might think this is a shitty thing to say, but it's not really much of a loss, if you ask me. I mean, my mom's all torn up over it, although if she told the truth I think she's as relieved as I am; but I'm really not sorry he's gone. He had his moments, I guess, but he liked to beat on people too much, and he drank a lot."

Gail and Devon exchanged a glance, a blast of personal memory, and she replied softly, "Oh." She searched Nick's face, wondering what kind of a boy they'd been thrown in with, and in the end liking what she saw. He'd averted his eyes when he mentioned his stepfather, but she'd caught a flash of them as they passed, and in those few seconds they had sliced out at her like a knife. This boy had seen a lot of life that most adults never faced, but he seemed to be okay.

He had opened the front door by this time, and was calling out to the kitchen. "Mom, I'm home, and I brought company. This, you aren't going to believe."

"Is that you, Nick?" Jeanette hurried out of the kitchen and into the hall, a coffee cup in one hand and a paring knife in the other. She was dressed more casually than he could remember seeing her for some time, blue jeans and an old flannel shirt that he recognized as one of Ed's. Her eyes were bright, almost cheerful, and Nick found himself stopping to stare. He couldn't remember when he'd last seen her so full of energy.

She stopped as well, caught unaware by the invasion from outer space that had infiltrated her hallway, though she recovered quickly.

"Mom," Nick said unnecessarily, "This is *Maelstrom*." He waved his hand in a gesture that encompassed them all, wondering just how she was going to take it. Again she surprised him. She walked forward, popping the knife into the pocket of her shirt, and wiping the now free hand, extended it to Devon.

"That was a very impressive performance tonight, Mr. Storme," she said. "I've watched Clear it Up for years now, hoping against hope that something like this would finally happen to that creep. Other than the skinhead kids from Los Angeles and the interview he did a couple of years back with that serial killer, face to face, I don't think I've ever seen him lose his cool like he did tonight."

Louie turned to The Mechanic and winked, trying unsuccessfully to hide the tequila bottle behind his back. "You hear that, man? We've made it up there in the rankings with skinheads and serial killers! We're *in*, man, really there!"

Shaking his head at his companion's antics, and smiling in return, Devon took her hand and answered. "Call me Devon, please, Mrs. Leatherman. I'm just glad to have been given the opportunity. It seems like there are an awful lot of Hector Clearwaters out there, and someone needs to shake their cages and get them riled up from time to time."

Moving aside to let them all make their way toward the kitchen, Jeanette went on. "Call me Jeanette, then, Devon. Would you all like some coffee?"

Nick watched her with a grin spreading across his face he couldn't hide. There was decisiveness in her stride, a confidence in her voice that warmed his heart. He followed the others as they trailed her into the kitchen.

"Uh, Nick," Louie said, dragging him back a bit and whispering close up to his ear. "Me and The Mechanic, we aren't really coffee people, you know? I don't suppose anything resembling a beer would live here?"

Nick grinned at the man, pushing him on ahead into the kitchen. "No problem, man," he assured the guitarist. "Thanks to my stepfather, that's one thing we never run short of. It'll be kind of nice to have someone drinking it who isn't going to turn around later, scream at my mom and punch me."

"Scout's honor," Louie grinned. "If I feel like punching someone, I've always got The Mechanic."

They were settled around the table pretty quickly with his mom, Devon, and Gail drinking coffee, himself with a Pepsi, and The Mechanic and Louie gleefully popping the tops of the first of a twelve pack of Budweiser that had been in the refrigerator since Ed had left. The two had wandered down the hall to Nick's room, where they were sorting through the many albums, tapes, and compact discs while Lizzy, growling softly, watched them from a perch on Nick's bed, unsure of exactly what, or who, they might be.

The phone jangled, stopping the conversation momentarily, and Nick jumped up to grab it. It didn't take long for him to react to what he heard, slamming a hand down hard on the counter and exclaiming, "What? When?"

He slammed the phone down after this cryptic outburst, turning to the others with his eyes wide and frightened. "Mom, can you call Ruthie's mom and see if she came home tonight? I'd call, but her dad still doesn't think too much of me."

"Of course, Nick, but what's wrong? Has something happened to her?"

"She, Flash, and Weasel were all going to meet me later at the shack in Weasel's backyard. I guess Flash and Weasel were off taking care of something, and by the time they got there, Ruthie was gone. The music was still on the stereo, Steve Miller. She's the only one of us who plays that one," he explained, as this last comment drew a blank stare from his mother.

"And that's not all," he went on, his words stumbling one over the other in their haste to leap off his tongue. "They said it looks like somebody else might have been in there, someone we don't know. Weasel's dad said he saw someone sneaking around in the yard earlier, carrying off a long bundle—like a rug. He tried to stop them, but they were gone before he even got out of the house."

As his mother moved to the counter, taking the phone up quickly and dialing the number Nick gave her, there was a knock at the door; and Nick rushed down the hall to open it, letting Straker and Pamela Green into the hallway and leading them back to the group in the kitchen. As they walked, he filled Straker in on the events of the last few moments; and he heard the woman, Pamela, let out a little yelp of fear.

"Damn," Straker grated, his eyes going cold and slate-grey with shock. At that moment, Nick thought, he looked like a very angry and very dangerous man. It was good to be on the same side with him for a change. You could almost hear the whir and click of gears in the Inspector's head, piecing the facts together and shifting them about to form a plan.

"Damn," he repeated. "Nick, I want you to go and pick up your friends and that van of theirs—take Devon and the others too. We have to get out to that cemetery, and we have to be there *now*. You meet me there; I'm taking off now."

He swept his eyes quickly over those present, barking out quick commands. "Gail, Jeanette, you stay here—Pamela, how about you?"

"Just a minute, Ken," Jeanette piped up. "I'll be going along, too. I've lost a husband, though at this point that's a questionable evil; and I'm not losing my son, or my friends, while I sit here and wonder what the hell is going on. I'm coming with you."

"Me too," Gail chimed in. "I'm as into adventure as these other clowns, and a lot more sober than some of them. Pam and I will go with the kids, you two go on ahead. When we have the van and Nick's friends, we'll follow."

Straker looked around at the odd assortment of serious faces, considered what would happen to his pension if any of them got hurt, said fuck it, and nodded.

"All right then, there isn't any time for arguments. If we're right about what's going on out there now, we have less than an hour to stop this thing from happening."

"Just what is this 'thing'," Devon asked as they headed for the door, grabbing Louie and The Mechanic by their shirt collars and towing them along.

"It's pretty simple, really," Straker answered, his eyes dancing with a dangerous light. "Goldbough is trying to raise Satan—we have to get there before he does."

"Swell," Devon answered, grabbing one of the beers from Louie and swallowing quickly, tossing the can aside as they went. "Just freaking swell."

CHAPTER TWENTY-TWO

As Horace stepped from the interior of his car into the fetid, cloying thickness of the air in the old barn, it nearly drove him back into his seat. There was heaviness in the air, a rotting, overpowering stench. He glanced over at the mound of hay in the corner, wiping the tears from his eyes brought on by the smell.

Not unbearable, he admitted, after his senses had had a moment or two to adjust. Considering the amount of time the body had been lying there, and the heat at midday, it was surprisingly mild. For just a second he thought about wandering over to examine the remains, to see the final handiwork of that earlier night's triumph.

It seemed odd to him that there were no flies about. He'd always thought they would swarm hungrily, feeding on every fermented drop before the corpse decayed back into the earth that had spawned it. Horace had never actually seen a dead man before. Not one who had died and remained at the mercy of the Earth and her environment.

As minister, he'd seen endless strings of reconstructed dead bodies, snapped back together like a child's model with plastic and wax and deftly applied makeup caked to their features. They had never seemed truly dead to him, or perhaps it was just impossible, seeing them like that, to believe that they had ever truly been alive. They were more like department store mannequins, dummies from a wax museum.

They had never smelled like this. There was no stench of rot or of decay, only the timeless, decadent scent of formaldehyde and other chemicals, preserving the artist's recreations for posterity. It was a temptation to see just what would happen if Mother Nature was allowed to have her way with the dead flesh.

There was no time. As he stood there, the station wagon arrived with their little secret ingredient passed out in the back end; and it was time for him to take charge and galvanize the others into motion. There was plenty of time to check out the dead when the night's tasks were complete. Maybe he'd kill someone, Inspector Straker or Hector Clearwater, for example, and just watch as his or her remains wasted back into the earth. It was definitely worth considering.

As the others emptied out of their cars, a thrill ran through him, a jolt of anticipation of what would come. Little eddies of dark power ran along the hairs at the back of his neck and slipped down the insides of his arms and back up the center of his spine.

He remembered the sensations brought forth by the last sacrifice. They had been exquisite and powerful. This one would be much more, so much more that it was nearly beyond him to conceive of the consequences of it. He sensed it in the air, and in the darkness.

Throughout the rituals, even a short time before they'd actually started to perform them, he'd had momentary flashes and visions that allowed him glimpses into the immense darkness, the bottomless well of power he now served. As they progressed, as each step was completed and they drew nearer and nearer to completion, to the final ritual, these flashes grew more frequent, clearer and longer. In the back of his mind, bolstering his will and building on his confidence, there was a constant level of that dark energy resting, awaiting the ritual to awaken it.

As the final moments of completion neared, as his focus became clearer, he found that less and less of the mundane reality he had lived in and waded through for so many years held meaning for him. When things seemed to grow in importance, the visions would rise up, superimposing themselves as a moving portrait over what he saw, showing him what was to come—helping him to focus. It made him feel powerful, and that arrogance shone and danced in his eyes as he surveyed those around him.

The others swung open the back door of the station wagon, and between them they dragged forth a long, rolled bundle. There was no movement in that bundle, but Horace held no fear that they had harmed the girl. None among them would risk defeat at this late date.

He smiled as they moved to join the others, their burden borne easily between them, silently taking their places and awaiting his own next move. This had been the one point that was slightly beyond his control, the wild card that could have blown his hand completely. It was the kidnapping that had provided the only chance fate had had to blow up their plans, and they had eluded her safely.

Finding virgins wasn't as hard as one might think. The first one, Gretchen, had been something of a surprise. Gynecologists, though, knew things even the proverbial hairdresser did not. The woman living alone had been the final factor in their choosing her, that and her looks. Horace knew it was an unimportant aspect, a luxury he shouldn't have even taken into consideration, but she had been a knockout. It made the whole thing that much sweeter.

This one had proven a bit trickier. They had been uncertain whether or not they could find her alone, whether more drastic measures might be in order. Young people don't follow the same rules, the same established patterns that adults find so comfortable. Of course, they had been fully prepared to risk breaking and entering, slaughtering the entire family if the need presented itself; but it had not.

All of these were aspects of the problem that could have ended in disaster. He had worried, but not to the degree that Brenda had. She had wanted them to be more certain, to have an alternate planned in case of failure. It was just like a woman, he thought.

Ignoring her, as usual, Horace had gone on with his plans in his own way. He wanted *this* girl, had counted on it; and it had happened, just as everything else recently had gone the way he planned it. His confidence had paid off. Their night had arrived, in its entire dark, seductive splendor; and the girl had been taken with a minimum of trouble. At the same time he'd made sure that all of the others who might wish to interrupt the night's festivities were unavailable. It was just too perfect.

His smile broadened further as a flashing vision of Hector Clearwater, leering at Inspector Straker over a mass of dials and microphones, filled his head. In the background of the scene, he could hear the slow, plodding tones of Hiram Pierce's voice, proclaiming the kingdom of God in his monotonous baritone. They had all been duped so easily, so smoothly.

And the beauty of it was that none of them, even those who already suspected what was going on, had any real clue of the magnitude of what they were involved in. They might even figure it out and make a last ditch effort, miraculously deducing that they would be here tonight, completing what they had started; and still they couldn't stop it. It had come too far now, was beyond their puny abilities to cope with.

About now, Straker and the boy would be leaving the studio, their heads hanging in defeat, nursing the wounds that Clearwater, irate over Horace's own absence, would have inflicted. The next stop for the boy would either be home, or that shack where they'd found his girlfriend, for Straker, no doubt a coffee shop or a bar, maybe even bed to clear his head.

It was remotely possible that when the Leatherman boy found his girlfriend missing, he would put two and two together and contact someone for help. Who would listen? Even if he got someone's ear, how quickly could they organize something and react? It was a big, rich joke at everyone else's expense; and Horace loved it—feared none of it. It was his night.

Within the space of the next couple of hours, darkness would descend on Lavender like a swarm of locusts, a darkness that would be born in and of himself. He would serve that darkness, paying the price of mind, body, and soul, gladly, for the chance of being granted a large part of the control of its time upon the earth. The power of their Lord was deep, immense—it vibrated through the earth at their feet and slipped around them as they moved; it teased at their brains, and it was not even close to its full strength. It was reaching across barriers of time and space to aid them, to push them onward. The reality of its coming to the land would be profound.

In any case, the long-awaited victory could be savored at his leisure once it was reality. The all-important ritual would soon be upon them, and it was on this that his attention must remain focused. A mistake now would end all thoughts of any sort of future, though not of the darkness. Their Lord was not known for his patience or his mercy.

Signaling to the others to form up behind him, as they had on all the previous occasions, Horace snared Brenda with a glance and moved toward the door, waiting until all were in place. As he watched, glimmers and transient visions, phantom figures of odd shapes and sizes, moved in and about their group, figures that apparently only he could see. The barriers were weak between the worlds, ready to snap at his command.

Shadows moved, as well. He saw them as the group began the trek down the winding road toward the altar, detached slivers of darkness rose from unseen sources to glide among the surrounding trees at the very periphery of his vision. He strode purposefully through these visions, shielded in a dark haze of protection, a protection that somehow kept the growing chill of the air from settling into their hearts.

The gates, as always open and welcoming them to the gardens of Death, seemed somehow more symbolic than before, more ominous than he could ever remember seeing them. They beckoned with wrought iron talons, cold and glinting in the silver light of the moon for them to enter and achieve their destiny.

Horace stared at the spikes, an odd itching forming behind his eyes; and suddenly he saw something more—something hanging, impaled from the very tip of one of the iron spears. It was the figure of a man, a man wearing robes such as he now wore; and the man was hauntingly familiar. Then there were six more, impaled in the same manner, dark liquid dripping from their slowly slumping forms.

Horace closed his eyes tightly, unwilling to be distracted by the vision. He counted slowly to three, took measured steps and did not allow the shaking in his shoulders to become visible to those around him. He opened his eyes, and all that he saw were the spikes, naked metal poles. He quickly turned his gaze to the path before him, not giving the image time to return, or to solidify.

If it was a warning, it was certainly a powerful one. He shivered, trying not to think of how that metal stake would feel, impaling his chest and coming to rest in the soft flesh of his chin, holding his eyes up for all to see.

He tried to ignore another image that flashed through his mind: the gates; the bodies; the dripping blood; and the expression of stark, mindless terror that had graced the face of the man he now recognized as himself.

There was no wavering in the sensation of power that surrounded him, but his own smile slipped a notch, and his features trembled. Where a minute before he had been arrogant and filled with self-importance, planning a future of opulence and decadence, now he was serious—devoted to the moment. He prayed fervently to whatever power sustained him that nothing would happen, that there would be no failure in this challenge.

Brenda, walking directly behind him, was also aware of the figures that shot about their legs, moving just beyond their vision, aware and thrilled. To her they were old friends, old lovers back to play. Their touch was a fiery memory, their leering faces taunted her, fueling her desire until her skin ached and her eyes watered.

She noted the small jerk in Horace's step, the quick spin of his head toward the fence; but when she followed the direction of his gaze, she saw nothing. She was spared, or denied, the vision of the bodies sliding slowly and painfully down the spikes; but when she saw Horace waver, she began, again, to worry.

Something was wrong, though it might be only a small thing, something Horace had noted but would not share. Failure was not an option at this point—there was no alternative to success that could be considered without passing one's sanity into the abyss. The need rushed through her veins, the need for that otherworldly touch, sliding through her veins like hot lava. Her thoughts were tangled and feverish—obsessed.

If Horace faltered, if he fell away or failed them in any small detail, she would burn. Her mind would ignite, and the darkness would consume her. His steps steadied, and she shuddered with relief. As her breath seared through lungs that threatened to burst, coming in hot panting bursts, she followed. The minutes seemed to stretch to hours—to days, in her churning mind.

As they broke into the relative freedom of the clearing, they all moved at once, each knowing his or her part without the need for instruction or speech. The two carrying the rolled bundle moved toward the altar as the others began the intricate ritual of laying the circle and commenced the rites of banishing. At the points of the star, incense burst into smoky life, filling the air with the heady scent of jasmine.

There were prayers to the guardians of each gate, wards placed by each burning pyre. The protection of the circle depended on its perfection, and on this night of all nights, protection was first on their minds. None wanted to imagine what might happen if their Lord were allowed free reign with them—not until they had finished their part of the bargain and sealed themselves to his will, body and soul.

As the circle grew stronger, as the combined powers of the protective spells and incantations forced the weight of the darkness to recede, moving it behind invisible borders of power and flame, Horace sensed the building of the power. The pressure that was being exerted on them was building to levels greater than anything he'd ever experienced, beyond even his wildest imagination. It was like being a brick in a dam, watching helplessly as floodwaters built up on all sides of you, and knowing that the slightest slip of a stone, the slightest crack in the mortar that held you to the other bricks and they to each other, would drown you—pulverize you—crush you to dust in the torrent it brought down upon your head.

Mists rose in the clearing. At first he thought it was just the smoke from the incense, but it continued to rise, to thicken, surrounding them and isolating the clearing from the night and its moving, hungering demons. As the visions faded from his sight and the cloying sweetness of the jasmine slid through his senses, all doubt and independent thought slipped from Horace's mind as well. He sensed them beyond the barrier, faintly, but their menace no longer affected his concentration. He felt his heart-beat slowing in his chest, and the smile returned to his lips.

The chant rose to his lips and flowed from them to blast against the night, resounding through the clearing and echo-ing from the barriers. The words flew out: defiant, clear, over-powering. His eyes alight with the blooming of the power, with the sensation of otherworldly fingers playing the strings of his vocal chords like a familiar instrument, he raised his arms to the night; and the dance began. The final dance. The dance of completion.

Ruthie woke to a world of nightmare. The first thing she noticed, as in the shack, was the scent of jasmine, wafting about her and filling her senses. She wanted to ignore it, to clear her thoughts and wipe away the haze that clung to her mind. She wanted to sit up and shake her head, but she found to her dismay that she could not.

The darkness about her was nearly complete. The air was not only scented heavily with the cloying smoke, but also filled with dust, and it was hot—way too hot. The darkness felt heavy and solid: it held her tightly in place so that struggle was impos-sible. Her head rang from the resonant tones of someone chant-ing, loud and insistent syllables that jarred her thoughts loose before they could find purchase.

The words had a consciousness all their own; she felt a pres-ence behind them, watching her, and by some odd power all their own, dispersing her thoughts as she tried to form them. She was driven back into her mind, toward darkness and con-fusion. Her eyes would not fully open, no matter how hard she tried to force them. Her mind reeled from the lingering touch of some half-remembered fear, some memory that she couldn't quite bring back into focus.

She fought the urge to close them again, though they watered and itched, and fought to pry them open wider. When they opened fully, she screamed, or tried to. The bandanna was still stretched tightly across her mouth, and the horror of the last few hours snapped back with almost painful force.

The scream changed nothing. The muffled sound she'd been able to muster just seemed to blend in, to weave itself among the tones of the strange chanting, swept skyward and away from her like a macabre harmony to the sound already surrounding her.

Suddenly the world was awhirl, and she was rolling, breaking free into a cloudy, misty reality much worse even than the clinging darkness she had been trapped in. Evil figures, warped by the haze of her mind and surrounded by scented smoke, danced all about her.

The chant flowed around and over her, beneath and beside her, clinging to her skin and slipping about her. Her limbs were no longer bound, on some level she realized this, but she was still unable to move—held in place by some unseen force. Every time she moved, something opposed her. All she was allowed was a kind of writhing struggle that somehow seemed to make her movements a part of the dance, molding her to its pattern.

She sobbed in fear, and when she felt the cloth cut free from about her mouth, she screamed again, this time sending the sound carrying to the treetops. It made no impression on the chant or the rhythm of the dancers.

She felt hands brush lightly over her skin. She felt the clothing slide from her body. Nothing she did hampered them. The smoke and the words battered at her sanity, and her body refused her commands. Cool ointment was spread, starting from her feet, in a complete coating of her skin.

Where the lotion touched her, the skin tingled. Her pulse slowed, and the world shifted to a slow-motion dream speed. Her screams, though they continued, lost their force and their conviction. Fingers probed and kneaded, caressing her incessantly and taking possession of her senses. The chant droned on, and a last, forlorn cry sped skyward.

"Nick!" She screamed, even as her traitorous young body arched, dancing to the beat of the mystery fingers, even as her mind stopped fighting, began to seek the heat. The ointment had reached her breasts, and the tingling was becoming more of a pulse, a pulse that throbbed through her mind like a clock, keeping rhythm with the words—the grunting, monotonous tones, of the chant.

She became one with the darkness surrounding her, whimpering deep inside; and she closed off what was left of herself in a tiny shell, protecting it, praying for escape.

Down the road, at the entrance to the Shady Grove Cemetery, a car screeched to a halt. In the barn, lost among the empty shadows of expensive cars and clinging evil, the wind stirred the straw to a small whirlwind, dancing in the light of the waxing moon. It was 11:30.

CHAPTER TWENTY-THREE

The sight of the huge black limousine pulling up in front of Weasel's house would have been enough, on any normal day, to bring the entire neighborhood out in excitement. When it screeched to a halt, shooting gravel out of the street into the yard beyond it, and Nick jumped out, quickly followed by Devon Storme, Gail Force, Louie, The Mechanic, and Pamela Green, it was almost too much for Flash and Weasel to handle. Weasel managed to lift his jaw, which had dropped nearly to the sidewalk, to move and form sound, and summed it up quickly.

"Wow," he said.

Ignoring his two friend's bewilderment, Nick ran up to Flash, grabbed his arm and shook him, pulling him back to the moment. "Flash, where is she? Has anyone seen her yet? What the hell is going on?"

Stepping back slightly, still unable to pull his eyes free of Gail Force's worried face, Flash gulped in a lungful of air and managed to spit out an answer.

"No; nobody's heard a thing. We were both over at my place, watching you on the show, you know? Nobody knew she was going to come out here by herself, still don't know why she did. Guess her parents weren't going to let her out later."

"There's a lot of stuff shoved around in the shack," Weasel cut in, "but nothing is really missing. The Steve Miller was a dead giveaway, though..." He stopped, suddenly aware of his unfortunate choice of words, and stood there looking miserable.

"Weasel's dad saw someone out here earlier carrying a large bundle," Flash went on, "but he figured it was too late to catch them, thought it was just stereo equipment or something."

"Let's get going," Devon directed, grabbing Nick's arm and spinning him back toward the street.

Turning to Flash, he gave him his best stage grin. "How about you fire up that van I've been hearing so much about? We won't all fit in the limo, and Inspector Straker tells me that we have an appointment with the devil."

Unable to cope with a coherent answer, Flash turned immediately and ran up the street about half a block, where the "magic bus" was parked beneath a streetlight. The others, not wanting to wait for him to pull up, followed closely on his heels, Weasel staring openly at Gail and repeating, "Wow, wow!" under his breath like a mantra.

As Flash hit the driver's seat, firing the engine to life and revving it quickly, the others piled in around and behind him, filling the interior of the van quickly. It was a pretty tight fit, but with Pam and Gail in the middle, the others were certainly not going to complain about close quarters. The Mechanic slipped into the passenger seat beside Flash, slammed the door behind him and let out a rebel whoop that could be heard for several blocks. They tore off up the street, sliding around the first corner and heading out of town by the closest route.

The ice finally broke once they were on the road, and Weasel, coming a bit out of the coma Gail had produced, piped up first. "So, what's going on? I mean, if this is going to involve, like *weeks* or something, I'll need to phone my broker. I have a lot of big deals on the fire..."

"I'd like to know too," Gail chimed in, her eyes bright with the excitement of the moment. "Just where is it that we're going, and what has happened that has the whole world in an uproar?"

"Shady Grove," Nick told them, ripping his mind free of the visions he'd been caught up in: Ruthie in trouble; Ruthie on that altar, naked and screaming. "It's a ritual—not the first, either. These psychos, the same one's that killed the woman that got you all involved in this, may have Ruthie...at least that's what Straker thinks. I don't know exactly what they want, why they wanted her, but we have to save her...I..."

"It's a ritual, all right," Pam cut in, trying not to upset anyone further, but thinking it was time they all knew just what they might be facing in that graveyard. She'd had to drag her own mind free of some intriguing thoughts as well, like dwelling on the features of a certain lead singer who kept smiling at her across the van.

"I guess I would be the most qualified to explain this part... I read the damned book just this evening."

Nick's eyes snapped over to hers. "You broke into Goldbough's office too?"

"No; I bought my own copy," she said grimly, "but I wish I'd never seen the filthy thing. Anyway, there are a total of six rituals involved in what they're trying to pull off. It's called *The Grand Sabbat*, or *Great Sabbath*.

"The purpose of the rituals is to draw forth power, bit by bit, until in the last ritual you break through the borders between this world and the next and set free the devil, or *a* devil, anyway. The first five rituals are complete; this is the night of the sixth.

"My friend Gretchen was the fourth. They must have chosen Ruthie for the same reason they chose her. The last ritual is special, and it requires a virgin for completion. It is absolutely essential."

"But," Nick's eyes went wider, "but she's not, I mean..."

His face reddened. Memories of the previous few days haunted him, of the graveyard, the bloody body on the altar, of all they'd been through, and of the shed—of the time he'd spent there with Ruthie. He could even recall the music that had played, could almost hear the words and the melody ringing through his head.

There was no longer any doubt of one thing, not for him, or for anyone who took a long, serious look at him. He was in love, head over heels, out of his mind in love. Even with the prodigious temptations of Gail Force, whose body he'd worshipped from afar for years now, sitting scant inches from his thigh, he could think of only one thing: Ruthie. He ground his teeth together in frustration.

"But," Pam's eyes brightened noticeably, "how recently, I mean...how long has she been this way, Nick? This may be very important. I know it's personal, and I wouldn't ask, but what happens later tonight may depend on this."

"Less than a week," he mumbled, surprised that with all of them watching and listening so closely that he could speak at all. He started to go on, to tell them more, but he found that his throat was constricting, that his sight was blurring from the tears that would not stop flowing.

Any other time, any other place, what happened next might have been more than his adolescent libido could handle. Sensing his discomfort, the depth of his emotions, Gail laid her arm softly around his shoulder and pulled him over to sob quietly against her. Looking back at Pam, letting Nick work through it in his own time, she said, "But why would it matter? You think they need a virgin for what they're doing? I mean, is this all real, or are they crazy. I'm pretty confused here."

"I don't know," Pam answered, staring at the dirty carpet of the van as they sped along, "I really don't know." Her mind shifted back across the hours, strobing the image of that hideous, hand-scribbled face that had held her so easily from the dry yellow parchment that held it captive. She thought of the sensation of being trapped in the pages of the book, the sensation of being watched, and mocked; and her shoulders shook.

"I had to look at that book. These kids have seen the face in the front. I just can't pass it off as easily as I could have a week ago. If you'd asked me at the beginning of this I'd have said that the people who killed Gretchen were homicidal maniacs, that they should be shot or put away where they couldn't hurt anyone ever again, but I would not have believed they possessed any special powers beyond madness. Now I just don't know."

"What made you change your mind," Devon asked, his eyes bright with curiosity. "You all keep mentioning this book, you don't happen to have it handy, do you?"

She turned to him and met those eyes she'd been trying to avoid to clear her thoughts, then answered, her shoulders shaking with revulsion.

"I have a copy in the back of my car somewhere, but I wouldn't open it or look inside if someone else did, for any amount of money or power. It was filthy.

"Nothing in the rituals was human, not in any way that

we would recognize, not in any way that sanity would allow. If I had merely read the rituals, then my opinion would have probably stayed the same, though the magnitude of the insanity being dealt with would have been driven home a bit more clearly. There was more, though, much more. I'm really not sure how to describe it.

"It starts with the feel of the cover. It's some sort of leather, hand-cured, I'd guess; and it has this oily, unnatural feel to it. I wanted to pull my gloves out of my purse just to touch it, but there wasn't time.

"On the first page is this face. It's drawn by hand, really harsh strokes in some sort of dark, brownish ink; and it just glares out at you. It's as if it sees you, as if it knows you are there and is mocking your inability to pull your eyes away from it. I know how this sounds, and I know that it probably just spooked me, but I'd swear that book, or something beyond it, something working through it, was aware of its being read."

"Yeah," Weasel cut in, nodding in affirmation as he listened attentively. "We saw that book, too, in Goldbough's office. We found it inside a book safe, a fifth gospel. Pretty sick stuff, even for a psycho minister.

"We didn't read any of the pages though, not beyond the title. Something tells me, after hearing you tell about it, that I'm glad we didn't. That face alone was enough for me, man. I had nightmares about the damned thing for days—couldn't get it out of my mind. And the color—man, if I didn't think it was just too fuckin' crazy, I'd say it was drawn in blood. I mean, I've seen enough horror movies to know it when I see it."

"What do you mean in Goldbough's office?" Louie asked with a chuckle. "Don't tell me you're an altar boy—not with a name like Weasel."

"We found a pin that led us to his church that first night, the night I dropped my knife," Nick said, gathering his composure about him again and joining in. "We went there the day I found out about the Hector Clearwater show. I was afraid that they'd send me to jail or something, after they found my knife. I guess I didn't trust Straker enough then to help me work it all out. I wanted to find something there myself, something I could give him that would get me out of the picture completely.

"Maybe I should have given him a bit more credit," he said ruefully. "Anyway, we broke into the church in the middle of the night; well, actually it was unlocked. We searched his office, and Weasel found that book on his shelf."

He went on to relate their flight from the arrival of the old drunk and his subsequent return to his home, only to find Straker there ahead of him and his stepfather missing.

"Things have been happening a little fast around here lately," he concluded. "Now they seem to be out of hand completely. I wake up thinking, nothing could be worse than having to go on television in front of all those people and face an asshole like Hector Clearwater; and here I am running off to a graveyard to face Satan. See if *I* ever wonder how it could be worse again."

"Shady Grove," Flash called out, as the headlights sliced the large ornate sign that marked the turnoff from the main road. He mentioned nothing, this time, of hunting for ghosts or other strangeness. For Flash it had definitely been an uncharacteristically quiet journey. Besides, they all felt it without his urging: the odd, otherworldly tug of the place.

As they neared the large fence, they huddled as near to the center of the van, and to one another, as possible. Flash felt and fought an urge to spin the wheel recklessly and rush them back off into the night. He felt as if he were fighting against unseen hands for control, and sweat broke out on his brow as he exerted his will to its utmost.

Twice he was certain a ghostly shape had slipped out and been ground under the van's wheels, but there was no sound or impact. There was shifting movement all around them. No shadow seemed rooted in place, and no light would remain stationary. He concentrated on the gravel road, wished for an instant of relief in which to reach up and wipe the sweat away that was trickling down to burn his eyes. Still he said nothing. He had no energy to spare for conversation, and there was no way that the others could help him, anyway; it was his own struggle.

When they passed through the gates and turned down the left hand road, pulling to a halt in front of their usual tomb, the van was deathly quiet. Nobody moved at first, nobody spoke. They were all lost in their own separate visions.

"Christ," Louie exclaimed at last, lurching toward the door and prying it open, "you guys *party* here?" He grimaced, spinning to chase a flitting shadow with his eyes and losing it instantly in the surrounding gloom. It had melted back to darkness before he could pin it with his gaze. "What a trip."

They all piled out then. The spell of the place wasn't broken, but its hold over their limbs and voices was. Nick, Flash, and Weasel took the lead, heading immediately off toward the darker, older part of the cemetery.

"We've been coming here for years," Nick told them as they went. "It's never been like this, though. We always kidded about it, said we were here on a ghost hunt. It seemed fun then, like we were playing with mysterious forces or something. Now I wish I'd never seen the place."

Ahead the woods were alive with sounds, mists, voices and whipping winds, all blending in an eerie beat that shook them to the roots of their souls. It was primal, strengthened by the fear it brought on and feeding that emotion back into itself, creeping across their skins and down through their spines.

The mist rose to wisp about their legs as they ran; nothing around, beneath, or near them seemed in any way solid. They were not alone in those woods, either. All around them the shadows shifted; small dark forms danced and pranced just beyond their sight. Faces glowed from the mist, rising from the trunks of the surrounding trees.

All of this swayed, flowing back and forth, up and about to the awful, gut-wrenching rhythm of a stream of words they could now discern from somewhere ahead: a chant that rose up and offered itself to the bright, glittering face of the moon.

Sweating heavily and forcing himself to fight back a scream, Nick broke into a run. The others saw him, tried to call out to him or grab him, but they could not. Unwilling to leave him in that place alone, they followed, tripping and cursing their way through the overgrown graveyard, crying out and clinging to one another as the shapes grew bolder, came closer, slithered over skin and pressed against soft flesh.

They burst through the trees as a group, Nick in the lead, just as twin headlights behind them sliced the blackness of the gate and approached rapidly from the way they'd come.

With all of the others in danger, and with his own plans changed considerably, Straker had opted to stop one more time at the station house. He was in no mood for discussion when he hit the front door, and he had not even greeted the night dispatcher as he dove headlong over the desk to grab the microphone from her hand and called out for every available bit of backup to meet him as soon as possible at the Shady Grove Cemetery.

Fuck it, he thought. If there's nothing out there, I'll look like a fool; but if there is, by God we're going to stop it this time.

He stormed down the hall with Jeanette in tow, the two of them no doubt looking like the actual psychotics in the situation; and he took charge, ignoring the feeble protest of the duty officer who mumbled something about fucking regulations.

When he knew things were moving in the direction he wanted them, Ken turned them back and herded Jeanette quickly into his office, to his personal arsenal. He'd already gotten ammo for his pistol, but he decided to grab a shotgun too, and a belt loaded with double-ought shells. Almost as an afterthought, when he heard her heavy breathing at his shoulder, he turned to Jeanette and asked, "Can you use a gun?"

She nodded. The sight of her flinching had amused Ed, something he'd seen enough of, as his hand was traveling up and back. He'd learned at her first "shooting lesson" that having her try and use his guns was a sure fire way to make her nervous, and to see her afraid.

Those guns had been his babies, after all. Who more fit to handle them and to care for them? She hadn't actually hated that time, either. It had been one of those rare things they'd shared that didn't lead to anger or to more fighting.

He'd lined up old bottles and cans for her in the desert outside town, and the two of them had fired round after round at them. Jeanette knew that she would be considered a competent shot with a number of weapons, some of which would no doubt have surprised Straker greatly. It was maybe the one thing of worth she'd gotten from Ed that was not warped—not ruined.

Assessing her quickly, Straker nodded. He rummaged in the cabinet again for just a moment, and came up with a .38. She tucked it into her pocket after a quick check of the load. Ken smiled as he saw her efficient handling of the weapon, and told himself that once more he'd underestimated her. It all seemed so out of place in such a friendly, pretty woman.

There was no time to dwell on that kind of thing, and he moved them back out and through the station as quickly as possible. He had one arm protectively around her shoulder, and she wasn't protesting.

Nearly all of the rest of the Lavender Police Department were rushing about, making preparations for the first full-scale raid they'd had in years, as the two shot through, not even speaking a word to those around them. The entire building had galvanized into action. They would have more than enough backup for a few psychos, Straker thought.

Of course, his mind added, if Goldbough and company manage to raise this demon, if it isn't all bullshit and we get there too late to stop it, all the backup in the state of California may not be enough to help us. He mouthed a silent prayer, his first in years, as he hurried Jeanette back into the car and pulled out with a screech of tires.

He felt a strange sensation, then, as if something rotten was squirming around in the pit of his stomach and would not be still. He recognized it moments later with some surprise. It was the growing, gnawing bite of fear.

Fear itself was not new to him. Anyone who regularly took the risks that his job demanded faced the madness, death, and ignorance that roamed the streets so freely these days, was on intimate terms with fear. This was different.

He'd seen death enough to feel that he understood it, to feel that it was a part of him that was familiar and if not comfortable, at least bearable. He understood it in its spirit, and in its finality. Now he was faced with a different sort of proposition, a proposition based on the premise that most of what he'd learned over all the years of his life might not be the only reality possible.

It seemed that, no matter how much he might wish the

world to be cut and dried, for concrete answers to the problems that life presented him with, there might be more to it. Much, much more. It was beginning, for instance, to seem that death might not, after all, be the very worst thing a man could be faced with—might not even be the final thing.

There was something about this night, something about the very air he sucked through his lungs that seemed tainted, askew. It tingled down his arms with dark, electric energy. Visions passed behind his eyes, flashed in the periphery of his mind. Visions he'd previously managed to banish to infrequent viewings of cheap horror movies and even less frequent nightmares.

Jeanette seemed to feel it too. She scooted very close on the seat, her leg pressed tightly against his as if unwilling that there be even a fraction of an inch between them. Her eyes scanned the road ahead, shifting along the ditches that lined the way, and over the fields and trees. He sensed that every nerve in her body was on edge, every muscle taut; but he also saw strength in her, a determination in the set of her jaw.

She had the appearance of one who'd been pushed as far as they were willing to be pushed. He'd seen the same look often enough in the streets, as often as not cleaning the remains of the recipient of such a look off of the asphalt before all was said and done. Her presence, the touch of her leg brushing his, was comforting—stabilizing. Straker realized that he was very, very glad that he did not have to face what was ahead alone.

"Here we are," he said as they pulled beneath the overhanging gate, parking directly beside Flash's van. His voice sounded unnatural, breaking the long silence and slicing through the darkness with the cutting bite of an unwanted intruder.

Smiling at him nervously, Jeanette put her hand lightly on his arm, locked eyes with him and pooled their courage. Without further hesitation they slipped out of the car and stood there for just a moment, side by side, bathed in the glow of the moon's bright light.

Without speaking a word, they stared ahead into the waiting darkness, darkness that they were now aware was truly moving and swaying about them, shifting like a horror video reel from hell. Straker put his arm around her once more, a position he was beginning to find very comfortable, and he gave her a quick, reassuring hug. She turned to press against him, just for a moment, and laid her lips softly against his cheek, putting a finger over his own mouth to keep him from saying anything.

Then they were moving. They were surrounded by the same sounds as the others had been, though they had no way of knowing what had already taken place. The air was filled with it: chanting, moaning, and a barely discernible undercurrent of human voices.

They heard shouting, voices they recognized; and Straker hurried his steps, pulling her along as he broke into a steady run. He knew that the others must have reached the clearing by now. He cursed himself for sending them ahead—they were unarmed, and they were taking far too great a risk.

He pulled the .45 from his belt as he went, hoping fervently as he moved to chamber the first round, that it would not prove a waste of time. Not for the first time since the night had gone crazy on him, he wondered if what they were about to face might not be beyond any human means of defeat. He found his mind slipping back to his childhood and to a silver crucifix his mother had presented him with on his tenth birthday. He wished that he had that cross with him now—would have almost traded his gun for it.

It wasn't that far to the clearing. Straker's brain told him this over and over; and he ran headlong. Jeanette, trusting his sense of direction and his footing, ran lightly at his side. Branches whipped at their faces, stinging and leaving long painful welts and scratches in their skin; but they ignored it.

They heard the voices again, Nick's, then Devon's and several others that jumbled together in an indistinguishable garble of sound. There were screams as well, but they could not tell from whom, or what, the sound arose. Throughout it all, pounding in the background, shaking the earth beneath them and controlling the swaying, bobbing shadow creatures that paralleled their path, was the chanting. It was loud, so loud that it was impossible to believe it was achieved without sound equipment, without amplification. It seemed to grow louder and more powerful with every passing moment.

As they finally approached the clearing, something happened to the ground beneath them, something they could not have explained had they the time to consider it. The branches and roots beneath their feet rose, rippled and grasped at them, fighting to trip them and send them sprawling.

Where smooth ground had been seconds before, stones rose to trip them. Ahead, barely visible through the swirling mist and waving branches, there was light; but they could not seem to reach it.

Cursing and lowering his head like an angry bull, Straker lurched forward again, grabbing Jeanette tightly about the arm and charging. He moved, only scant inches at a time, but he moved, concentrating on the break ahead, the edge of the clearing. Sobbing in terror and frustration, Jeanette clung to him and struggled along at his side. She searched the shadows and mist ahead of them for her son.

It was 11:45.

CHAPTER TWENTY-FOUR

He had no name, not in the sense of Earth names, none that men could pronounce, though they'd called him by plenty of their own. For twice a century and beyond he'd lain in idle contemplation of events beyond his influence, awaiting the completion of the summons, awaiting the chance to walk again on the roads of Earth.

Beyond the planes, powers moved and shifted. The awakening of his thought stirred the ancient hunger. He felt the construction, the intricate balances created by those who neared the ritual completion, like the pieces of an ancient, gigantic puzzle that would culminate in a bridge between worlds. He could feel the heat of their world, of their own lust and greed, from his own, where frigid darkness ruled.

As his thought awakened, so too his memories. There was nothing he could do, beyond subtle force-lines that he'd already manipulated, to speed the completion. With no other means of satisfying the gnawing that itched at his senses, the hunger that had consumed him time and again throughout centuries of solitude, he drifted. He relived days long gone and hungers once sated, passed through boundaries in his mind that were barred in the reality of the present.

There had been a time when his world was not separate from that of the Earth. In those days, free and unhindered, he had roamed the channels of men's minds, feasting at leisure and taking what he wanted without thought.

Men were his toys: playthings and morsels of such insignificance that he controlled them as a child would its dolls, insinuating the threads of his own will among their thoughts, invading their minds and bending them to his whim.

His was not a physical reality in the plane of man's existence. He could, if he chose, take on such an aspect and manifest his power through it. It was an avenue he'd explored many times in many places. There were times when, weak as men were, the fastest way to gain control of them was through their physical world and their own hungers. It was certainly not necessary. He was capable of manifesting through dreams, walking the pathways of the thoughts of others and bringing them to their knees in worlds of nightmare and terror.

There had been a people, once, long before the creeping, crawling desolation that man called progress had swept across the world, before the great decay, who'd worshipped him as a God. In a way, they hadn't been totally mistaken. In comparison to their own puny essence, he was not unlike an angry, vindictive deity.

He had played their emotions, working through those most zealous; and they had fed his hunger, sated his needs. He had demanded sacrifices of them, forced upon them practices that they thought would elevate them, but that in reality only served to steal their humanity and weaken their minds. They'd answered these calls like dogs. Pain and fire had become their pleasures, and they had begged for his favor. In silence, gloating, he had answered their puny pleas, and he had fed.

He wasn't the greatest of the ancient powers of the universe, nor could he control the shifting of the planes, or the order of reality. Lines of force and pathways through dimensions shifted occasionally as the pattern of the universe continued to unfold, planes that once intersected no longer met, and parallel lines diverged. It was beyond his control.

One such shift had occurred near the last time he'd been fully "summoned" two centuries, give or take a little, in the past. Since then it had become more difficult each passing day to cross the planes. The routes necessary to reach certain aspects of the pattern had become impossibly complex; the rules governing barriers and shifts were themselves changed.

The result was that what had previously required a small thread of belief alone, an open channel of nightmare in a receptive mind, or a simple prayer by a follower, had come to require much, much more. The prayers continued, and he was still aware of them; the dreams went undisturbed, and the belief wavered beyond his control. As he continued to fail to appear, his "followers" gnashed their teeth and smote themselves, thinking that it was some failure on their own part, believing that he was merely displeased.

From his own realm, he struggled against the change. He wove patterns of his own creation and fought to impose the power of his will upon the barriers, to break free of the cosmic chains that bound him. It wasn't enough. Great as his powers were, there was a span of years during which he was utterly helpless and cut off from the planes that had fed his hunger for so long.

There were other powers that moved more freely on the earth after the shift, powers that he knew, and a few that were new to him and that he did not understand. These he merely watched, keeping a close eye on the progress of matters that might one day apply to him once more.

Some of these new powers were greater than he. Others were lesser in all except that they were free. Some of them were aware of other planes; others were blind to anything but their own existence. There was one who strode the earth, preferring most of the time the guise of a human: a physically manifested spirit that took notice of him, and took an interest in the shifts that had imprisoned him.

This one was indifferent to his hunger, cared not at all for his pleasure, or his rage. This power that walked as a man was powerful—watchful—ever ready to stir the mixing pot known as earth, with new change—reforming it in ways that suited its own interest.

It was with this other power he had begun a search that led through the folding patterns to another world, another means to sate his hunger. Then the contact came, and everything changed. Another shift.

When the other power reached through, it was not to taunt, or to prod, but to make an offer, for reasons obviously important only to itself. There was a way, it instructed, ignoring the rage the intrusion brought forth, a way between the planes that still existed, that could still be accessed.

The key, however, lay in the point of access. It was this that had shifted, this that had caused the barriers to stand so firmly. They key to his world was no longer his to hold, but depended on the very food he sought, upon the insignificant nothings that walked that world. The puny minds of those who had served him so easily, for so long, were the only tools he would have to break free. It was not an easy way. They were ignorant. They would have to be taught. He would have to make a change of his own; he would have to learn patience.

And that was the way it had progressed. They *had* learned. The other had taught them, still not caring to divulge reascns that would not have mattered in any case. All that mattered was the hunger. The humans learned, but it was a very slow, infuriating process. They failed often, maddeningly so, trying first one ritual, then another, seeking blindly for combinations that would bring forth their desired end.

As often as not, other, lesser powers were able to answer their calls. The barriers were not so strong between the worlds of these powers and his own, and he had taken matters in hand at that point, forcing his will outward by manipulating these lesser powers and forcing them to become teachers as well, forcing them to build the blocks of the ritual that would become his escape, his freedom. Forcing them to feed and relay that strength. To his followers, the new disciples of his need, he sent what visions, small powers, and wicked appetites he could force through, promising much, much more.

It had taken long, unbelievable years, but it had happened at last, not once, not twice, but in the last thousand years, the ritual had reached its final conclusion three times. Three times he had been freed to walk the earth, to feed freely and cast his dark dreams before him, laying waste to the world so long denied him.

Each time his own realm reached through the twisting bends of the trail between worlds and summoned him back again, closing the door behind him as solidly as it had been before opening. Still, for a time, he was free. Somehow, he knew, the other power had control of this. It did not matter. The ritual, the book, now existed; and the requirements could be met, were in fact being met as he watched, straining at his bonds, ready to burst free and to feed.

The other, lesser beings that inhabited his own realm pranced about the gates, sensing the immense pressure exerted by his concentration, basking in the energy of his pleasure and feeding off it. With the door so close to bursting open, small cracks were available to them. They were not so bound as he, being less attached to their existence in this realm, and less powerful. Already they faded in and out of the world beyond, straining in their own insignificant manners to break free completely.

They would be free as he would be. He felt the impact their half-presence made on the fabric of the world beyond, and read the reactions they caused. He tasted the fear their presence generated as it rippled through the cracks and splits that had appeared, but were not yet large enough, or complete enough, to allow escape.

It was time to shift his thoughts from the exhilaration of near freedom, and to sift through the thoughts of those who now held the key. It was time to regain contact with those he had so recently exposed to his will, and monitor their progress as they fitted the ritual key to the hole and readied themselves for the task of turning it.

He was not amused; it wasn't part of his nature. He sensed the arrogance of the leader. That arrogance was what allowed the words to flow forth, flowing from channels that led inward to the darkness, falsely believing in his own control of forces so far above his puny existence that full realization of them would melt his mind to madness.

The female, her individual spirit lost to the lesser spirits long before, realized perhaps better than the leader the impact of what was to come, and looked forward with hungry, ecstasy filled eyes to the coming of his fiery embrace. The two of them alone would make a small feast, the first feast.

Shifting his concentration through the others, lesser even than the two, he found the level of belief and concentration adequate and gave them no further thought. Each believed himself, or herself, in control of a destiny that they understood less than not at all. The destiny of food. Emotions like arrogance and stupidity were alien to him. Hunger was his nature, only that; all else was a means to that end.

The notch of the key that would turn the final tumbler lay on the altar, no longer struggling, but being dragged into the whirlpool of forces that led down to that point of power that would soon crack the dam. He allowed a feather touch of energy to slip through, to brush past the planes and focus on her form, risking a preview of the perfection to come. He caressed her young, tender flesh, setting a sheen of energy about her like an aura, plucking at her senses and her psyche for just a taste, a single touch of that spark that would set him free. He touched, and he searched, and he grew frantic, but it was not there.

Overcome with rage, he pushed harder, returning to her form yet again, though he knew he should wait—should not expend so much energy before the awakening. It must have been a shift in the planes, a mistake. It had to be. No. She was not pure, not perfect. Somehow it was all unraveling, would never reach completion. Despite his guidance, despite the visitations of the minor powers and the machinations of that other who followed his motions with such interest, despite the fact that the first five keys were in place, they were failing. Would fail. It was inevitable.

The sensation of being trapped closed in on all sides and wrapped itself about him, squeezing the sanity from his thoughts, shifting the rage to the fore and blending it with the biting clutches of the hunger. Power radiated unchecked from the very core of his being in a flash of rage that shook the planes, inside and out.

And, incredibly, that rage continued to grow, intensifying with each passing second, centering on one thought, a single focus of energy and hatred—those who had failed. They would share his fate, and they would die; as surely as his world was dark, empty, and void of anything that could sate his hunger, he would see it so.

He flexed his mind, exerting himself beyond all limits, and reached out. He avoided the focus of the circle, though it would have been simplest to manifest his rage there, sought beyond it, beyond those who had left him trapped by their own imperfection.

There was another. He recalled it, a vaguely remembered shell. This was what he sought. It was a key of a different sort, a physical shell he could inhabit, and that could walk in his stead. It would be a weapon, a weapon of vengeance and rage— or redemption.

The silence that reigned in the old barn was suddenly shattered. Winds gusted where there had been only stagnant air. Lights danced where there had been nothing but darkness. The straw scooted across the floor, then leapt into the air, blowing into a whirling vortex of energy, rising to a funnel that tapered down to nothing and beyond.

Flesh, soft and rotted from the irreversible effects of time and heat, flies and moisture, lay still, covered in the hay. The vortex swung clear of the floor, centered just above Ed's silent, empty brain and seeped inside. The body twitched. Maggots, disturbed by the movement, rolled from eye sockets burned empty in the blast of the other's eyes, from his gaping mouth. Drying bodily fluids were forced from within, pressed out as if from overripe fruit, until they lay over him in a glistening sheen—a milky film that coated him like some sort of grisly cocoon.

His hair blew wildly as the head lifted; the bones in the neck creaked and popped with the movement, shifting about his head and rippling in the grasp of the demon-wind. First one arm, then the other, in a jerky, marionette pantomime of human motion, pressed downward against the barn's floor and forced the body to stagger up, finally balancing upright. As a macabre puppet master pulled the strings from beyond human thought, Ed Leatherman rose and walked.

Straw, maggots, slime, and crumbling earth cascaded from his body as it moved, slowly, then more quickly, refamiliarizing limbs and appendages with the ways of life. Small trickles of energy, the remnant of the spirit that had been Ed Leatherman, rose to drain into the demon's mind in tiny wisps of data.

This was part of the cost of control, part of the price of

vengeance. He was constrained to act in accordance with what would come naturally to the shell. He would be forced to read the nature of this man like a book, memorize it and make no errors. It was something he was more suited to than his followers, and he did it without thought of failure. Any notable deviation from the nature of his host, and the planes would rip him back, sealing behind him as securely as a safe.

There would, of course, be deviation soon. When the host had carried him to his destination, when he breached the circle, setting them bare to the forces that swirled and chomped at the bit to reach them. When he had made his way to the center of the circle and was throttling the life from them, yes.

Then, then he would deviate. Then he would open his soul and feed. Tottering out the door, the pseudo-Ed zombie, to the consternation of the demon and feeding its anger, turned on unsteady feet and began a stumbling, halting climb up the hill toward the woods that overlooked the farm—away from the circle, away from his goal. Thrashing against the bonds that constrained it from turning this puny half-being about, but curious at the same time, the demon merely settled back and allowed the half-dead thoughts of the creature to control itself.

There was a flicker of memory, an insistent hunger that reminded it vaguely of its own, flashing through the man's dead and silent mind. The tongue, now blackened and shriveled, forced itself free of the upper flesh of the mouth and reached out, running across the rotted lips, dislodging a stubborn snail and several loose teeth that fell in its path. There was no reaction to this—no nerves carried pain or any other sensation to the puddled remains of the brain.

Ed was heading for his truck. A skeletal remnant of purpose clung to his limbs, an instinctive urge that drove him onward. There was something still to be done, something that needed finishing. Yep, ol' Ed had work to do.

When he flipped the lights on in the truck, they had little effect on the surrounding darkness. It seemed somehow thicker than was natural, dense and impenetrable. It didn't matter, not much, anyway. All that remained of Ed's eyes were the empty, burnt-out sockets the demon had left him as it fed. Flies and mice had long since chewed away the choicer bits that had remained, cleaning them hungrily and efficiently. Ed didn't need to see where he was going, though, not anymore.

The demon read the intent behind the curious actions, felt the drive, even beyond death, beyond another plane, for completion; and it felt the closest to a sensation of relief that was available to it. He and this shell, insignificant and infuriating as it was, were in perfect agreement. The vehicle would prove useful—might even be the key to the success of its revenge.

Forcing the dead body to walk the distance between the barn and the circle would have expended a great deal of energy, energy it was impossible to spare and maintain the tenuous bridge that made what was happening possible. The truck would not only lessen the amount of energy necessary, but would also cut down the time; and time was the one crucial element that was furthest beyond control, most likely to end it all in futility.

He could sense the actions of the others; even without the comforting pressure of his support, they were nearing the moment of completion, the false promise of their failure that would drive him back to his dark prison. When that moment came, when the fear leapt to their eyes and their puny systems lost control of things they had never truly controlled in the first place, when those fear-filled eyes rolled to white and the hideous, inhuman screams ripped free of their throats, he planned to be there to feast on it—to intensify it. It would not be the rampage of hunger satiating carnage he'd planned on, nor would it be enough—not nearly enough—but it would be his!

The engine, well tuned and maintained at peak perfection—always—fired to life at the first touch of the ignition by dead fingers. Flesh flayed from the bones as the sharp metal edges of the key dug through it, dangling uselessly as the force behind the motion moved inexorably on. The hand slipped off the key and reached up to grasp the steering wheel.

The other, in a motion so natural it happened almost smoothly, even in this dead state, reached down and to the side, clawing around the edges of the cardboard box and ripping free one of the remaining cans of Budweiser. The pressure of the tab as it was popped nearly took off the top joint of Ed's index finger, but it came open at last with a hissing pop, spraying lukewarm beer over the dash and the seat, soaking the remains of his clothing.

His mouth came open, the skin around the jaw and neck parting from the strain, wrinkles forming and spreading, widening to gashes of torn skin. Tipping the can back, he poured the beer down the ruined chute that had been a throat, leaking and sprinkling out from hundreds of openings that should not have been in its path, foaming and bubbling from the agitation of its plunge. Ignoring this, taking another swig, he reached down and rammed the truck into gear.

There was no road between the point where the truck was parked and the trail below. There was barely even a trail leading down toward the abandoned farm below, but such concerns were nothing to dead men, and the demon cared not at all. In any case, the truck was more than a match for such terrain. It would not be the first time it had forged its own road where none should have been, though it was likely to be the last.

Bobbing and lurching as the wheels covered the uneven ground, it roared downward, its grisly passenger clutching tightly to the wheel with one hand and balancing a nearly empty beer in the other. The demon was along for the ride at the moment, allowing the corpse its freedom of instinctual movement, conserving energy.

At that moment, there was very nearly a kinship between the two disparate spirits, the dead, galvanized man, and the trapped and furious demon. The demon was surprised to find such an adequate mirror of its own hatred in such an insignificant being, surprised to find that there were similarities of any sort.

Of course, all that truly remained of Ed Leatherman was this single-minded purpose, this final call of vengeance. Most of what had been the man had long since departed the plane. The demon could read the afterimage, the psychic imprint the man had left, the final moments of life that had possessed this form—imbedded in the flesh by the intensity of dying emotions.

This was not the first time the demon had made such use

of a human form, not the first set of impressions it had sifted through in its quest to quench its hunger. Usually though, the final thoughts, the final impressions, had dealt with fear. Ed had not been afraid, not in any normal sense. He had not been capable of such a weakness. He had wanted to kill, to wipe what he'd seen from the earth; but even faced with fiery demon eyes that looked out from the body of a human woman, he had not really died in fear. Frustration would have summed it up better, unrequited rage.

As the truck bottomed out, reaching the level ground at the foot of the hill and intersecting with the larger path that led toward the graveyard, the skeletal remnant of Ed Leatherman put the pedal to the metal, flooring it. Gravel and loose earth shot up in a spray from the tires, and the engine, guzzling gas at an ungodly rate, roared with life and power.

In jerky, weaving sprints—short stretches of flat ground and small ridges that sent it airborne, only to land heavily and jounce on ahead, the vehicle made it to the turn and scooted around the corner, nosing toward the back gates of Shady Grove and plowing on through the darkness.

The lights were dimmed now, still inconsequential, in any case. Rage drew the truck forward like a magnet, aiming the deadened skin and rotted flesh like a guided missile, an unstoppable automaton. The instincts that remained, the small bits and pieces of Ed that were at the demon's command, were more than adequate to operate the truck. It had been too much a part of the man's being, like an extension of his very existence. The motions were automatic.

With some relish, though the thought of being constrained to physical devices grated at its soul, the demon noted the .357 with interest and satisfaction. It might come in handy if there was too much resistance, or if they seemed to be arriving too late. The demon's power in this realm was far from complete, bound by endless laws and weighted by the binding strands that threatened to drag it back through the planes. Its destiny in this plane was locked to its joining with this puny mortal shell.

The gates loomed ahead. The memory-flicker of images it had generated, planted in the mind of its failing "priest" resurfaced, generating images that clung to the metal, sliding slowly and inexorably downward, impaled and bloody.

Ahead in the clearing, voices rose, not all in ritual chant; and there was activity everywhere. More movement than was correct. All was in shambles, the ritual undone.

There was something else there, as well, some other that dared interfere in its wrath. Perhaps, if enough time remained after it had claimed its feast, there would be a chance to teach these others as well. The rage of two centuries of hunger rushed in a surge of power through Ed's veins. The truck rushed ahead. It was 11:55.

CHAPTER TWENTY-FIVE

As he launched himself into the final sequence of the chant, and the ritual wound into its ultimate point of passion and release, Horace felt an enormous shift of power. Casting his eyes skyward, he strove to steady himself, awaiting the expected rush of energy, the instinctive flow of words and motions that would carry him through to the completion, the controlling force that would finish the ritual and change his world. It did not come. Nothing.

There was no lessening in the flow of power, nor did the growing darkness recede in any way. He knew the words well enough on his own, and he continued to force them forth, uninterrupted. There was no burst of supporting energy though, and the words no longer brought with them the euphoric sense of control that he had grown so accustomed to relying on. They fell from his lips, complete, but weak, at times seeming to wisp away before they were even there. Sweat beaded on his brow as the effort of concentrating fell on his shoulders alone, as the fading signals that triggered the rhythm became further and further removed from his thoughts with each passing second.

There was no slackening in the dance. The others continued, knowing their own parts intimately and oblivious to Horace's struggle. Their own motions were caught in the whirling imagery and energy, fluid, almost frantic steps that moved them over the earth as their puny human muscles drove them in the eerie patterns required, pushed them beyond their normal limits.

The twisting, near-impossible gyrations, borne of a sensual abandon that went past the realm of thought, beyond even instinct, held them easily. They could not have stopped had they desired it, and their faces, murky and fading, as if transposing themselves from one world to the next and back, were unclear. As they strobed in and out, back and forth, their forms were replaced alternately with grinning imp-forms and prancing, demonic creatures that skipped even faster, moved even more frantically, fighting for solidity in an existence that denied them. It was a kaleidoscopic miasma of desire and energy, fate and destiny, all woven of the pulsing fabric of Horace's words, words he chased madly through the whirling maelstrom that was now what remained of his brain.

He heard other sounds then, distractions. Other voices than his own rang out with cries that had no part in the chanting or the ritual, words that had no place in the circle, should not have been allowed past the wards. They were faint, indistinct and blown about by the curling tendrils of mist and power, but they were there all the same. They became another part of his struggle, another obstacle between him and completion.

The circle was inviolate, at least in that much he felt the remnants of his earlier confidence, even his arrogance. He knew that the magic they controlled with words and motion would protect, would still serve, as long as he maintained his cool, as long as he didn't make a mistake.

The problem was that these protections, these wards, were of an otherworldly nature—supernatural in focus and construction. The intruding voices that itched at his brain and threatened to shatter his concentration were not supernatural; they were achingly familiar and rooted in this world, the physical world. He didn't know how long the protection of the circle, even bolstered from beyond as it now was, might stand against a physical assault.

If they were found out, if the others had so soon figured out his ruse and come upon them, then there was precious little time remaining to him. The cries continued, and he was certain that they had moved, that they were coming closer, maybe no more than a few yards away. They threatened to confuse his words, insinuating themselves and the nervous fear their presence instilled into his consciousness.

Just as he was afraid the chant would falter, that his words would slip and fumble, he managed to pull himself together. Somehow he found the strength within himself to brush the distractions aside, ignore all interference and regain his concentration. There were only three more stanzas of the chant, thirty-six lines to be spoken; and they burned in his mind's eye like the pages of an open book. He would not fail. He tensed himself to plunge ahead with them, closing his eyes and screaming them to the skies.

On the altar, Ruthie had begun to slip back to awareness, to remember what was happening and who she was. She had been—gone. There was no other way to describe it, just gone. It had been like floating in a strange lake of invisible water, lost to normal thought by sensations that had riveted her, pushed her beyond emotional limits no human should ever reach. Then something had happened, some force had awakened her, stirred her thoughts and nudged her back toward the shell of her body, toward the reality that swirled so maddeningly about her form.

Confusion ruled her, galvanized by fear, and she felt her limbs becoming her own once more, felt the cold, clammy sheen of terror-born sweat that coated them. She couldn't move. Her arms and legs were bound to whatever it was that she lay upon, and she could not pull them free, despite her struggles. Her mind was a fuzzy mass of half-images and shocked nerves, a little bit like she felt when she was really stoned, but much more intense.

The hands were still there too, the hands that had sent her away with the intensity of their caresses. The ointment that had brought the tingling heat to her flesh had fused her to the sliding fingers. The strange faces that had danced so wildly before her, wild-eyed creatures that had pranced and minced and fondled her physically and mentally until she writhed in pleasure were gone.

In their place, dancing crazily, their rough, all-too-human hands roaming up and down her naked form, were the faces of men and women. She saw a lawyer her father worked with, another man who was her doctor, the waitress from the diner out on the coast road, all jumping and bouncing around as if crazed. They seemed inhuman, somehow, frightening in their madness. Their movements appeared to be controlled by some force beyond themselves, too fast, graceful, and—*wrong*—to be human.

And the words, the horrible, rhythmic, bone-chilling chant that swept about, these were still there as well, though worse, sounding sickly and more human, somehow. Weaker.

They chased her through her own mind, waited behind each thought to leap out at her and reach to regain the control she had snatched back from them. They floated down from somewhere above her that was beyond the limited field of her vision, from within the wisping mists and whirling smoke, controlling the cavorting maniacs. They even seemed to draw hypnotic designs in the swirling mist that spun crazily everywhere she looked.

Whimpering, biting her lip to use the pain as a focus, she closed her eyes tightly, trying to shut it all out and escape back into darkness with her sanity. The chant continued its ghastly paintings on the insides of her eyelids, denying her release, relentlessly pursuing her. Then they were parted, just for a moment, and she heard the scream: a single word that drew her back once more.

"Ruthie!"

It was faint. The flowing evil of the chant confused her almost instantly, stealing the word from her thoughts and replacing it with shadows, with half-traces of shattered hope; but then it came again, and she latched onto it like a drowning person to a floating log.

"Ruthie! Where are you?"

She knew who it was, who it must be; and though the odds seemed beyond the scope of possibility, she knew that he was coming, that he was making his way near to her. Would he be enough? Would there be anything he could do when he arrived beyond joining her in her helpless flight from the droning words?

She couldn't think straight. The drug from the ointment still held her in thrall, still warped her perceptions of her surroundings. It magnified her emotions, her senses, intensified her fear. He had to make it, and if that was to happen, she knew, she would have to find a way to help.

From the depths of her being, fighting madly against the constraining straps and the pressure on her mind, a scream of her own was born. It rose through her forever, floating up from the depths like a balloon from the bottom of a deep well, slowly at first, hanging suspended for inner eternities; then streaking up, exploding through the heavy mist and disrupting everything in its path, it erupted.

"Nick!"

Nick heard her clearly. Somewhere in the mad whirling before him, she was reaching out to him, needing him. He spun wildly, realized he could see neither what was ahead, nor behind to where he'd first entered the clearing. The forest, eerie and dark, had seemed to battle him every step of the way, to clutch at his legs and grasp at his feet; and each shadow had leaped into his vision, a new confusion.

He'd passed it all, forced his way through to the clearing, only to find an impassible void before him, a nearly physical barrier of darkness and mist that barred both sight and sound. He knew that Goldbough, and Ruthie, had to be inside it, but where, and how could he find them?

It was that point where Nick lost control, leaving the others behind and diving headlong into the madness. He screamed her name and waded through the thick soupy mist. It was like swimming through molasses or quicksand—his limbs felt weighed down, useless.

At the first, he heard Devon and Gail and the others, calling his name from somewhere behind, telling him to wait, to let them help. It was too late for that. Win or lose, live or die, he was going in; and the mists and swirling images clouded his sense of direction almost immediately. He wasn't about to try changing directions to find his way out and become even more lost.

He closed his eyes, since they seemed useless in any case, and pushed toward where he thought the altar must lie, calling out to Ruthie with each passing breath. He heard a buzzing, droning sound, a voice, he thought, and the dizzying whirlwind that raced about him seemed to move to its rhythm. It was like a gruesome MTV video for some rap song from hell. Then he heard Ruthie scream, and it all cleared—instantly.

Everyone in the clearing stopped at once as that single word ripped to the sky. The chanting, shattered and lost, faded like a distant echo. The release of power was bewildering. Nick was the first to recover, and the first, as well, to move. He saw Ruthie lying, naked and sobbing, on the stone altar; and he was at her side in seconds, working at her bonds.

As if waking from a dream, or being released from a nightmare, the robed dancers launched themselves at him crazily. They didn't see him, he thought, not really, only the object that had caused their failure, the focus of their undoing. They had no comprehension of the real reason for interruption, had yet to realize how they had lost, how utter was their defeat.

Rushing from behind like a wild-eyed, longhaired cavalry, Louie and The Mechanic hit the first two headlong, sending them flying. Devon, a bit slower to react, found himself face to face with two other robed figures. He grappled with the first, sidestepping to avoid the other. From his left he heard Pamela cry out in an anger that surprised and impressed even him, the king of the primal scream.

"Bastard! Filth!" A rock, large and well thrown, caught the second of his assailants squarely between the eyes, dropping him to the dirt.

Grinning, Devon let loose an uppercut right hand that sent his remaining opponent sprawling. He turned to look for more, but Weasel and Flash had double-teamed one of the two that Louie and The Mechanic had rushed, and all four of the attacking figures were grounded. The rest had run, leaving only Goldbough and a woman nobody recognized behind them.

Raising himself pompously, a rage that was beyond human burning in his eyes, Goldbough turned to face Nick, who had just managed to release the final bond that held Ruthie to the altar. As he slid her across the stone to him, leaving it between himself, the "Reverend," and the woman, Goldbough spat at him in fury.

"You have ruined everything!" he cried. "Two hundred years have passed, passed very slowly for the one we serve.

You, in your simpleminded meddling, have cost us—cost me—everything…"

"One step," the woman was mumbling brokenly, her eyes vacant as if the spirit behind them had already fled, "one step and it was ours. I was his…I."

"You're stupid," Nick told them, backing slowly away with Ruthie in tow. "You're too stupid to know you'd failed before you started. I read that book, man, the one in your office, you know? You needed a virgin, Goldbough; didn't you read that part? You would have killed Ruthie, and you would have failed anyway. You're an idiot."

"No!" Goldbough's fear had turned once more to rage. He looked wildly about him for the one who had assured them, the one responsible for the error; but there was no one there.

"Hold it," Straker's voice cut in as he and Jeanette stumbled from the forest, "hold it right there!" The .45 in his hand was an attention grabber, and the clearing fell once again to silence. That was when they heard the truck.

As they all turned, gaping in amazement, Ed's truck bounced down the rutted, overgrown trail at breakneck speed. It bore down on them at a frightening rate. Nick grabbed Ruthie tightly by the arm and dragged her away from the altar toward the safety of the trees. Horace didn't move, only stared, mouth wide, as the apparition approached, raising a hand, half in recognition, half in denial.

"Look out!" Straker screamed at him from the trees, a scream that blended in with Pamela's, who'd gotten a better look at the driver, what was left of him anyway.

Suddenly the mists that had died rose again and pushed them all from the clearing with incredible force, knocking them to the ground and obscuring the clearing from view. Moments, perhaps only seconds, later, an explosion rocked the earth, sending them sprawling and smashing through their minds with a wave of darkness.

When it had passed, they regained their senses slowly, and their sight returned. The mists surrounding the altar whirled more slowly, and then receded as if they'd never been.

CHAPTER TWENTY-SIX

The splintering crash of the hurtling truck colliding with the stone altar barely registered in Horace's mind. Shards of stone and mangled bits of glass and chromed metal cascaded to the sky, followed by a single, unopened can of Budweiser that broke on impact with the ground and sprayed white foam throughout the clearing.

It was a grinding cacophony that exploded through the air, terminating the silence with a shattering roar. It still didn't register in Horace's eyes. He watched the driver, looking in through the approaching windshield as the truck crashed through the trees. He had a good view, head-on, eye to eye.

Those eyes, devoid of such mundane things as eyeballs, burned him like twin lasers, pinning him in place. The crash was a slow-motion wash of surreality. Pieces of wreckage passed his line of sight, but could not deflect it, could not rip his gaze free from the spot in the darkness where he'd met, and been imprisoned by, those eyes. They glowed, alight with inner fire, burning with hatred.

Horace knew those eyes, had been transfixed by their power before, many times. They were the same that had stared back from the book, the same that Brenda had worn scant days earlier, after the fifth ritual; and they were the same that haunted his mind, waking and sleeping.

He was rooted to the spot, unable to move or to run, unable even to open his mouth and let loose the scream that threatened to burst forth and just keep coming, flowing out of him until there was nothing left to give. The mists were rising even further, drawing nearer and thicker, closing in around him and blocking the world beyond the clearing out.

At his side, trembling like a slender leaf in the wind, Brenda stood, also staring. She, as Horace himself, had met that gaze, had read the message of hunger, vengeance, and finality that awaited her there. She did not tremble in fear, though, not like Horace, whose fear was tangible and distinct, leaving a bitter tang in the air. She trembled in anticipation, in a need of her own that nearly echoed the hunger in those eyes.

As the mists rose, licking softly at the bare skin of her ankles, upward along the curves of her calves and thighs, she shuddered and dropped heavily to the earth on her knees. Her legs, seemingly cast from rubber, would no longer support her weight.

All of this took place in short seconds, eternal suspended moments. Control was slipping through the demon's grasp in that long second of time. When the chant had ended, had it not been for the truck, it would have truly ended. It would have staggered away and faltered, then been ripped from the existence it had forced itself upon with might beyond reckoning.

Already the dimension walls were reweaving themselves, the tears and small holes opened by the final ritual mending with uncanny speed. It was too soon. There was still revenge to complete, hunger to sate.

Even before the debris had settled, it leapt free of the wreckage and stood, wobbling on broken, recalcitrant limbs that fought to return to the soil. Its head lolled grotesquely to the side where the neck had snapped in the wreck, only the eyes lived. Raging pools of hatred, clearly visible through the clouding mist, piercing it like twin daggers, they stabbed out at the two who remained. Step by step it closed on Horace and Brenda, hissing evilly through rotted lips and vocal chords that no longer had the ability to create sound.

The mist was its final curtain call, the last bastion of its strength, holding out both its own world and that on which it trod, forcing the moment to last. Within the protective shell of cloudy energy it could maintain this presence for yet a few moments. It would be enough—had to be. It had taken two centuries to gain; it must not be wasted.

Drawn into the mist as to a vacuum, the lesser creatures whirled in a maelstrom of faces, fangs, claws and eyes, mirrors on a smaller scale of the glowing orbs shining from the ruins of Ed Leatherman's face. It was their energy that the demon fed on now, their essence. Probably most of them would be trapped as the dimensions finally snapped, crushed and ruined by the backlash of power. The demon cared not at all for their existence, one way of another. They were tools, a means to its end.

As the leering parody of humanity approached, plodding steps forcing rigidity to smashed and shattered bones, moving not by physical support but by the sheer power of the demon's hatred, Horace's mind cleared for a quick second, or so it seemed. His legs buckled, the strength that had held him upright failing as he wrenched his mind and gaze free from the demon.

Falling to his knees beside Brenda, scant yards from eternities of darkness, Horace Goldbough began to pray, to call up the golden words and powerful phrases, to resonate each word with power and surety. It was as he had done it so many times in the past, so many times over years of evangelical work. What escaped his lips, though, did not sound like the Horace Goldbough whose brilliant, eloquent prayers had built the Church of New Light.

They were choked, incomplete phrases, escaping his parched lips as a barely coherent stream of chaotic thought. He cried out to the Lord, begged for salvation. He exhorted powers he'd never believed in to come to his aid, to wipe the abomination he'd brought forth out of the bowels of hell itself, from the earth. To save him.

As he spoke, his mind seemed to return to his own control. He felt righteous fury burn through him and believed in a power great enough to save him. It was a golden moment, a moment of revelation.

Stumbling forward, the demon heard. Recognizing what the puny man in front of it was doing, seeing the confidence in another power that so easily replaced it in this one's mind, it came close to an understanding of the concept of amusement.

The hatred was too intense to allow anything but the hunger to truly shine through, though. It ate at the demon's heart, ripped at its being with searing talons of fire. A last surge of controlled energy brought it within reach, first of the woman.

Brenda, head back and eyes rolled into their sockets, panted her need, her mind a broken wasteland of lust. No thought remained; no reason ruled within those confines. There was only heat, an animal heat that consumed her from within. Her tongue moved wildly over her lips, remoistening drying skin where the heat evaporated it time and again. Her hands roved her own body shamelessly, rending the cloth that covered her form and tearing madly at the flesh beneath.

The demon sensed it, felt the waves of energy radiating from her. He fed on the power, on the ecstasy; the need within her, so close to the feeling of pain that it was indistinguishable, washed through it, teasing it to further limits of torture, yet not satisfying for an instant the cravings it sensed within her.

He fed her need from the fires of his own hatred, from memories snatched from her psyche of what he had promised, what she had failed to attain. He granted visions of times when heaving crowds of worshippers had knelt as she, groveling for the touch, the essence of pain that would set them free. Failed! After two hundred years, she had failed!

Reaching out with a broken, ruined claw-like hand, the demon grabbed her by the hair. Snatching the ebon tresses with far from human strength, it dragged her to her feet, then to her toes, writhing and squirming in its clutches. It forced her face to turn, her head to be still and forced her gaze to meet its own.

For a second, her eyes widened, her gaze met that of the living corpse and the raging fire that waited within them. Then they grew blank as she was drawn forth, ripped from her body, pulled inward toward the center of those dancing, maniacal flames. She screamed, then, loud and long, screamed in agony, desire, and pain; and nobody heard. Nobody, that is, except Horace.

His own eyes closed now, their lids forming the perfect screen for the casting of inner visions, he was busily convincing himself that he might survive. Surely, even though he'd lived a wrecked life, salvation could not be truly beyond him? His mind raced over the things he would do to earn it, over the repentance he would surely make if only the God he'd mocked throughout his life would save him, would make things right.

He felt something, like a glow from within himself, something different. He almost smiled. It had to be that he was succeeding. It stood to what little reason he still possessed that if one could perform rituals in a graveyard and raise a devil, just like in the old books and legends, one could surely pray and raise God in the same manner. And God must protect him. God was benevolent and good; surely he would wish Horace enough life to repent his many sins, to make good the evil he had caused...surely?

Then he heard Brenda scream. Horace did not want to open his eyes to that scream, did not want to acknowledge it at all. He tried to continue his prayer, to hold his eyelids closed by the sheer force of his will, and failed.

His tongue, in the midst of pleading, whining prayer, ceased to function properly. His words turned into a jumble, a strangled stream of incoherent babble. He was ripped free from within, a tearing sensation like no other. The words failed him because, though sound still emerged through his lips, there remained no connection between those lips and his brain. Horace was departing, and he had neither the time nor the energy to concentrate on his voice. He was approaching hell.

At the last second his eyes snapped open and he took in the grinning, leering, and decayed face that had been Ed Leatherman. Maggots squirmed and fled from the rotting hole that had been a mouth; flayed and putrid flesh dangled from broken and mangled limbs, hanging there like peeling wallpaper, or the skin on rotted fruit.

The hot core of those eyes had not changed, except that they burned with perhaps a trace more intensity, a bit more hatred. Horace was not to have the chance to consider this. His eyes had ripped loose from them again to take in what the thing held, to see firsthand the fate that awaited him.

Brenda's body, still squirming mindlessly, the tongue lolling from her mouth in obscene, strangled spasms, dangled from the creature's—the *abomination's*—hand. A steel grip of broken bone and rot held her, swinging like a pendulum, madly fondling herself and pressing forward toward it as though striving to become one with the corpse—as if begging to be consumed. No humanity remained in that shell.

Horace shot his eyes skyward then, searching for the salvation he craved, searching for evidence of the benevolent savior he'd scorned. Nothing was there but the mist, condensed now to a solid shell that covered the three of them, separating them even from the open sky of the night. The realization of darkness was complete—darkness deeper than that of the heavens.

Far too late, he made a scrambling move to the side. The free hand of Ed's ruined body shot out, dropped something it had been clutching and snatching at his hair. As with Brenda before, the grip was inhumanly strong, inexorable. Horace had a fleeting glimpse of what it had held as he was lost to thought, his last vision of anything earthly. It was a crushed and empty aluminum Budweiser can.

Then there was only the darkness. Horace did not have convenient long tresses for gripping, and the demon had no time to fumble with half-rotted fingers to get a grip. It plunged three of those fingers, cracking bone and popping already mangled joints, through Horace's temples, clutched his skull like a broken eggshell and hoisted him beside his still squirming partner in failure.

Time was gone. It felt the barriers slamming into place, and the pressure was enormous. Gathering a burst of energy such as it had not released in centuries, the demon slipped through the cracks, sending probing snaps of energy darting into the darkness to complete unfinished revenge.

The mists exploded with otherworldly power. They burst outward to crash into the night. As quickly as it had begun, it was over. When the mist cleared, wisping about the bases of the trees, nothing but the mangled remains of the truck and the stone altar remained. The breeze, slowly rippling through the leaves and grass, breathed reality back into the world through invisible lips. Midnight had passed.

CHAPTER TWENTY-SEVEN

Having been partially shielded from the blast by the trunk of a large tree, Devon was the first to stir. The first sensation that struck him was the unearthly silence: the utter, peaceful quietude that now surrounded them. Shaking his head from side to side slowly, he took in his surroundings carefully.

He'd never seen this place under any conditions that could be called normal, only through the chaotic, swirling mists that were now dissipating, and the impenetrable darkness that had cloaked the land scant moments before. It all seemed like some macabre dream now, except that he was awake and all too aware of the reality of the moment. He felt as if he were coming down from some ultimately bad trip.

As his thoughts cleared, he began to worry about the others. Pamela lay closest to him, so he went to her first. She seemed fine, though she was not yet conscious. He raised her head to rest in his lap and brushed stray strands of her hair aside, thinking that it was strange that he'd not noticed before how attractive she was.

He'd liked her attitude from the start, and her obvious courage and intelligence had impressed him. Now, with a quiet chance to get a better look at her features, he found that she was also beautiful.

Her eyelids fluttered, and a soft moan escaped her lips. When they opened, her eyes looked directly into his own; and she smiled tentatively.

"Heaven?" she asked, making no move to rise further. All around them the others were recovering as well, but for the moment, neither of them noticed.

"Maybe," he answered, returning her smile. On impulse, he leaned close and kissed her softly. She didn't resist.

"Oh, God," came a shaky voice to his left—Louie's. "Don't tell me two generations of hopeful, swooning groupies are about to start gnashing their teeth and tearing out their hair?"

Helping Pamela to sit up, Devon rose and turned, grinning widely. 'You're still available, man, so there's no problem. A bit ugly, sure, but they'll have to manage."

The two of them moved about the fringes of the clearing then, checking the others for broken bones, concussions, or whatever. Jeanette, curled up close to Straker, who was sitting up groggily and trying to reclaim his own thoughts, was gazing out into the clearing. She could still see that face, dead and staring, eyes blazing, driving the truck into the midst of the chaos.

It had been Ed, she knew that, but it had also been something else. Something more. She was certain, just as it hit the altar and the vehicle's front end crumpled, as the mists clouded her sight and the scream pushed all thoughts from her mind that it had looked at her—that *Ed* had looked, and that he had tried to smile. He'd raise his hand in mock salute, a Budweiser can held high; and then it had all ended in the longest, darkest blackness she'd ever seen—deeper than the pits of her worst nightmares.

Shivering, she rose shakily to her feet. With a nervous smile, she held out a hand to Straker, asking with her eyes for him to join her. Ignoring the raging turmoil in his gut, he complied. She turned slowly and entered the clearing, heading for the truck. Steam still escaped from the radiator, rising to dissipate in a slow, hissing geyser of mist.

"Mom" Nick's voice was soft, worried. "Mom, why?"

"I have to see, Nick," she answered. "Please understand. He may have been bad, but he loved me. I have to see."

Further protest dying on his lips, Nick turned back to Ruthie. He'd covered her naked body with his own shirt, which fell to her thighs, and he held her trembling form tightly against himself, gently running his hand over her hair as she sobbed into his shoulder.

"I'm going to call for help," Gail called after Straker. "Can I use the radio in your car?"

"Of course," he answered, "but take someone with you, though. None of us needs to be alone just yet."

Flash and Weasel, recovering with marvelous resiliency, both jumped to their feet in unison shouting, "We'll go!" Nick and Devon both laughed, Gail only smiled. Grabbing them, each by one hand, she started off through the woods. "Come on, then," she said. "Someone's got to show me the way, anyhow."

Turning back to the clearing, Straker and Jeanette slowly approached the truck. The front end was hopelessly mangled, bent and twisted around the now crushed stone of the altar in a wildly contorted jumble of metal and molten rubber. The windshield was cracked as well, a splintered starburst of cracks spiderwebbed it, snaking out from a point where something had obviously struck it with staggering force. There was a wet smear in the center, not really red or bloody, just a splatter of something soft and gooey.

Ignoring the windshield, Jeanette moved to the side door and reached out a trembling hand to steady herself against the open window frame. Straker placed a firm, reassuring hand on her shoulder and stood beside her in silence as she looked inside.

There was nothing—nobody, at least—inside. The floorboards, crumpled by the impact, had folded back against the edge of the seat. Shards of safety glass and shattered particles of the dash were sprinkled over the interior. On the passenger seat, on its side and still dribbling empty cans out its mouth, was the box-holder of a twelve pack of Budweiser. There was no sign of Ed at all. She turned slowly and caught Straker's eyes nervously.

They walked then, his arm circling her shoulders protectively, around the back end of the truck to the other side, where they'd last seen Goldbough and the woman. Nobody was in sight, nothing moved. Slowly, skimming the ground with a practiced eye for anything that might be a clue, they walked across the grassy clearing. There was nothing except a small scorched spot on the earth, blackened and charred as if from a thousand campfires. It was a circle about the size of a man's head. There was nothing to indicate what might have caused it,

but both of them knew that it must have had something to do
with the explosion that had blacked them all out.

Straker swore under his breath. What could cause such
force, such explosive power, and yet contain its destructive area
to such a small space? It defied logic. There was a great deal
he was coming to understand. A lot of things were taking on
deeper, and much less comfortable, connotations. Death, for
instance. It had always seemed so cut and dried, so logical and
predictable. Now he could no longer deny the possibility that
there might be a great deal more involved in their lives than
he'd previously believed.

Turning her head to the left, Jeanette caught a glitter in the
grass, a glint of moonlight off of some shiny object. Stooping,
she picked it up, recognizing it instantly and gasped, nearly letting it fall back to the earth. It was a plain gold band, no orna-
mentation, no engraving. It was Ed's wedding ring, his one
concession to commitment. A tear formed momentarily, but she
brushed it aside.

"He's really gone, isn't he?" she asked, not really needing
an answer. "This was his ring. He always wore it, I think." Her
eyes had grown far away, and Straker sensed that he should not
interrupt.

"He did love me, you know," she said, swiveling her eyes to
catch his, sparking slightly, as if expecting to have to defend her
statement. "I only wish I could be sad. I'm afraid I've wished
him gone for a very long time now, and that I'm just now real-
izing it. You know what I wonder?"

"No," he answered, not letting her gaze slip from his own,
"tell me."

"I wonder what I've missed," she said, moving a bit closer,
"what it might have been like if I'd never married Ed. Do you
think it's too late for me to find out?"

Straker didn't answer, not with words, anyway. Drawing her
slowly toward him, he bent, kissing her deeply and crushing
her against his chest. He met no resistance. She moved forward
and lifted herself onto her toes, returning the kiss passionately.

Nick's voice startled them both back to reality.

"Mom, Inspector?" he said softly. "We have to go. Ruthie's

been through a lot. I think they might have drugged her—we have to get her to a hospital."

Drawing apart, but only slightly, the two hurried back, leaving tingling touches on one another's lips. It was a strange night. Nick watched them as they walked together, noted how closely they remained, how their steps matched. He watched, considering it with the odd realization in mind that his mother, who had always been just that, a mother, was also a woman, and that she looked awfully happy next to Inspector Kendall Straker.

It was cool, he decided, breaking into a grin. He could think of worse prospective stepfathers, and he had a lot of experience in that area. He turned back to Ruthie, helping her to her feet and starting back through the woods with her, supporting her and holding her close. She was shivering but not from the cold, and he was worried.

They reached the others a few moments later, the sounds of sirens filling the air of the old graveyard and shattering the silence. The backup that Straker had requested earlier was arriving, spreading out and taking charge of the cleanup/rescue.

"Too weird," Devon commented as they gathered around Flash's van and Straker's cruiser to wait. "I never dreamed that an invitation to a television show would end up like this!"

"It'll make some killer songs," Louie added. "I thought we were pretty awesome until I saw that, that—*Maelstrom*—back there. Can't think of a better word for it. I mean, there were fucking *faces*, uh," he noticed the women around and blushed, "I mean there were faces in those clouds, things dancing and grinning. What the hell was that?"

Nobody even tried to answer him, but Gail put in dryly, "If that was a Maelstrom, I want no part of it. It did give me a lot to think about, though, a lot to write about. I can't wait to get to my guitar."

Devon, off to one side now, was holding Pamela's hand. He showed no sign that he was in any hurry to go anywhere.

Flash, who'd been silent since they'd left the clearing, basking in the nearness of his idols, slipped inside the van. Now that the excitement was dying down, he felt the need for release of a different kind. He slipped a tape into the deck and fired up the stereo. He turned the volume just loud enough that it could be heard clearly outside without jangling anyone's frayed nerves.

It was, of course, *Maelstrom*, that he played. The song that began the tape was one of Gail's haunting, slow ballads, "Purest White." Her voice, captured for posterity on Memorex, rose clear and clean, soaring through the notes with a fluidity that was nearly inspirational.

For once, everybody present, Straker, Jeanette, Pamela, even the band, just listened, hearing the lyrics, feeling them move through their minds. It was not a love song. The words had come to Gail one night as she sat and daydreamed, flowing from the pen in rhyming sequence as if she were copying them from some unearthly source. They spoke of balance, courage, and dreams. They spoke to the heart, and her voice awakened them for all to hear.

"That's beautiful, Nick," Jeanette breathed as the words began, finally, to fade. "Who was that?"

Nick only smiled and pointed at Gail, who blushed furiously. "It's off one of those albums of 'horrible noise' you always complain about," he said.

As the officers from the squad cars began moving back toward the woods, having evacuated the clearing and performed a perfunctory search, Straker heaved a heavy sigh and moved off to join them. Before he left, he turned to Jeanette.

"Get the girl to the hospital, and everyone else to your house. They'll all have to file reports later. I guess you'd better make some coffee."

She smiled. He sounded like a husband already, she thought, not displeased by the image. Stepping forward impulsively, she kissed him. "I'll take care of it," she promised. "And I'll see you there."

Now it was Straker's turn to blush, and he turned gruffly away to join the waiting officers, now grinning at him, though curiously. It was going to be one *hell* of a long night.

As the others piled into the Magic Bus, somehow managing to fit everyone, he motioned to the waiting officers to follow him in, explaining as much as he dared as they went. He left out all mention of moving shadows, dead men driving Jeeps, and the explosion. They could draw their own conclusions. His mind was in enough of a turmoil sorting itself out. He needed no lengthy investigations launched on his own sanity.

They trooped noisily through the overgrown graves at the rear of the cemetery, entered the clearing briskly and professionally. No branches snagged at their feet, and nothing moved in morning mist. The truck, after several colorful strings of creative profanity proclaimed the wonder of its condition, was gone over with a fine-toothed comb. Prints were dusted, samples of cloth were found, even a bit of the goo from the cracked windshield was removed and carefully packed away for later study by the technicians at the lab. Straker hoped the boy, Bates, would have a field day with it.

Then they combed the clearing itself, finding little, as Straker had known they would, but being very thorough, just the same. He stood to the side, thoughts scrambling up from his mind to badger him with new questions, questions he could not ignore.

If his count had been right, there had been at least six of the robed figures dancing around that clearing when they'd first arrived. Some had run almost immediately, others had disappeared when the mist rose again and blocked it all from sight. Where had they gone? They couldn't be allowed to remain loose; that much was certain.

"Truck came from the old back road," he said, "let's go on down there and see what we can find. There's a farmhouse there, and an old barn, remember it from when I was a kid."

"Right," Lt. Chapman spoke up. He was a young, lean-muscled officer, new to the area, and was obviously in charge of the detail. Straker smiled at him grimly.

Not speaking, he started down the gravel trail at a brisk pace. It was getting late—or early—in a few hours he would see the rose-hued dawn rising over the hills in the distance. Then he saw something else, and he stopped in his tracks, causing those behind him to stumble against him and curse.

"What?" Chapman barked, reaching for his gun. When the younger man raised his eyes to follow Straker's gaze, his jaw clamped shut so fast he nearly bit through his own tongue.

Silhouetted against the backdrop of darkness, skewered

from groin to head atop the rusted spikes of the huge, wrought iron fence, six robed figures dangled. The barbed top of each spike protruded about five inches past the top of the skull it transfixed. Blood had dripped from each, running in rivulets of crimson down the poles to pool on the ground at the base of the fence.

Lurching to the side, Lt. Chapman, and most of the men who had moved up beside them, lost what food they'd carried in their stomachs. Straker just stared, glassy-eyed with horror. He turned away at last, brushed the sweat from his brow and muttered under his breath. "Jesus."

They found the cars in the barn when control returned, enough evidence, along with the bodies, to identify all involved, all except Goldbough and the woman, of whom they found no trace. Straker was questioned at length on how the bodies might have gotten where they were, but he steadfastly refused to offer a guess.

"I have no more idea than you," he lied, "and I'm not sure, when I think about it, that I want to know, either. We got all we're going to get, that much I'm sure of. Let it go."

When he finally finished clearing up all the details he could think of, Straker prepared to depart the Leatherman home and get some sleep. Everyone else, having filled out their statements, was already gone, *Maelstrom* to a hotel downtown, all except for Devon, who'd been invited to Pam's apartment. Straker was happy for them. As he turned to leave, he felt a hand come gently to rest on his shoulder.

"Ken?" Jeanette's voice mirrored his own weariness, but there was something else in it that drew his tired eyes a bit wider open as he turned back to her. "Don't go."

He almost declined the invitation, almost told her that she was only upset, and that he wasn't going to push things. Almost. Somehow, it didn't feel as though she were jumping into anything; and it had been a long time since any woman had taken more than a passing interest in him. When he met her eyes, what he saw there removed the last of his doubt. She reached out more firmly, taking his hand in her own, and removing it from the door handle.

No further words were exchanged, but soon the last of the lights darkened in the house. Watching curiously from the hall, Lizzie eyed the two, Straker and Jeanette, as they entered the master bedroom and the door closed softly behind them. A movement from Nick's room caught her attention, and, with a whimper she moved inside, nuzzling him gently.

"It's okay, girl," he told her. "I think this time it's really okay." He let his head drop back onto the pillow and was asleep almost immediately. With a final look at the dark, lonely hall, Lizzy leapt to the foot of the bed and laid her head on her front paws with a sigh. For once the house was both dark and peaceful. She closed her eyes, and she slept.

SPECIAL BONUS STORY

THE HAUNTING OF VICTOR DRAHOS

Flash wheeled his van, "The Magic Bus," out of the convenience store parking lot and onto the highway toward San Valencez with practiced ease, merging with the light Saturday morning traffic. Nick Leatherman watched the road and fiddled with the radio, trying to find something that didn't involve angsty young women or tired classic rock. He turned a final time and WKROK out of San Valencez snapped to life. The song was Dragon's Breath, one of his favorite Maelstrom tunes, and he smiled.

"Better?" Flash asked, glancing over at him.

"Good as it can be working on a Saturday before noon," Nick said.

Flash laughed. From the back of the van, Weasel chimed in. "Early bird gets the ten bucks an hour, dude. We're lucky my dad got us this gig. Old Victor is cool. Bet he has the stereo cranked... probably *The Doors* and spends half the time telling us stories about the old days.

"If he doesn't mind me napping through half of it, I'm in," Nick said. "I was up too late last night."

"Doing what?" Flash asked. "Isn't Ruthie still down at the beach with her grandparents?"

"Yeah, it wasn't anything like that," Nick said. "I was talking with Ken...can't quite call him dad, but...it was pretty cool. He's seen a lot for a guy who never really moved away from here."

They were all quiet for a while. They'd known one another

since kindergarten, and they'd all known Nick's stepdad, Ned. Ned was the stereotypical redneck nightmare of every teenage boy, too much drink, violence as a social activity; now Ned was dead, but not forgotten. The shift from those days to the present, where Nick's mom was living with - and probably going to marry – Inspector Ken Straker had been positive and life-changing for all of them. The fact they were headed out to a job on Saturday morning instead of sitting in their clubhouse pounding out their brains one note at a time with Weasel's Frankenstein Monster of a stereo was a good indicator.

"He's a good guy," Flash said at last.

That settled it, and they kicked back to enjoy the music, and the ride.

They turned off the main highway and followed a smaller, private rode in past the sign reading Blackhall Shores. The community was a mix of smaller and larger homes, spread out over many decades of growth. On the right, they faced out into San Valencez Bay. The community had been built on an inlet, off the main water, but with good boat access and backyard beaches. It wasn't a cheap place to live, but at the same time, there was a sort of "decadent" decayed feel to many of the homes. Some of them were empty. Others still housed families that had been in the area so long that the richer families moved in around them, like the south and north bearing Yak's from the Dr. Seuss story.

Victor Drahos owned several homes in the area. His own was a big, sprawling place that had once belonged to a banker. Instead of upgrading and moving into a bigger home as his financial status grew, the man had simply added on sections and walls. It was an oddly laid out mansion with a sort of time-machine feel to the rooms. Some were stucco; others had siding on the outside and dark wood paneling within. Even the floor levels rose and dropped from segment to segment.

In the garage, two old cars rested side by side in various states of rebirth. One was a very old Buick Electra, candy-apple red, the convertible top down. Leather covers were draped over the fenders, and the hood was open. Beside it, mostly hidden by a tarp, was an old Thunderbird.

"Why are we here again?" Flash asked. He parked in the

driveway behind the Electra and turned to Weasel.

"He bought another house," Weasel said. It's got a garage built up underneath it, and it's full of all kinds of stuff. We have to help clear it all out. He said he didn't even know for sure what we might find in there."

Nick groaned and rolled his eyes. He'd heard that tone in Weasel's voice before. If there was junk to go through, Weasel was there. Anything with a wire, speaker, or component board was fair game.

"I hope he's paying in cash, and not junk," Nick said. He opened the door and stepped out onto the driveway. Flash did the same and Weasel climbed out over the front seat and joined them.

"Watch the seats," Flash said. "You could use the back door like everyone else."

Weasel only grinned.

They followed a stone walk around to the front door of Victor's house. Weasel reached out to bang the old, decorative knocker, but before he could do it, the door swung open with a creak. Victor Drahos stood in the opening. He wore only a pair of old khaki shorts and leather sandals. His hair was disheveled, and he stared at them as if barely aware anyone was present. His eyes were wide, and his face was pale.

"Jesus," Weasel said. "Mr. Drahos, are you okay?"

The man shook his head slowly, like a great shaggy dog, and then glanced down at his three visitors, as if finally recognizing he wasn't alone.

"No," he said. "No, I don't think I am. He turned, suddenly, gazing straight into Nick's eyes with an almost hungry expression on his face. "Tell me," he said, "do you believe in ghosts?"

Ten minutes later they were seated on Victor's old leather couch. Weasel was in the kitchen, banging pots around looking for coffee. Flash had managed to get the radio going. There was an actual cassette player on the thing, and it worked. When Flash hit play, Jim Morrison began singing about Strange Days, and with a shrug, Flash joined Nick and Victor Drahos on the couch.

"What happened?" Nick asked.

Victor stared at his hands for a minute, then shook his head again.

"It doesn't make any sense," he said. "The more I think about it the sillier it sounds, but…"

"Try us," Flash said. "You'd be surprised what we'd believe."

Victor didn't look up, but he talked.

"I was over at the new place. I picked it up cheap, and part of the reason is that everything this guy owned seems to still be packed away inside. The rooms are full of boxes, there's an attic… the closets are packed."

"Like a hoarder?" Weasel called from the kitchen.

"No, not at all," Victor said. "Everything is clean, neat, and well-packed. Some of it's just junk, but a lot of it is pretty nice stuff. I'm going to be hauling most of it to the auction house over in Lavender, some to the Goodwill, and the rest to the dump. I really have no idea what's in there."

"But what …"

"I'm getting to that," Drahos said. "I was over there last night going through it all and trying to mount a plan of attack for today. It was pretty dark upstairs, but I had my truck with me, and the garage is sort of tucked up under the house. I figured I'd leave the headlights on and work under there a little, sort things out so we could get in and out quicker when you were here to help."

"What did you find?" Weasel asked. He had a small tray in his hand, easily balancing four cups of hot coffee. It was one of his many oddball talents, learned from carrying trays of snacks and drinks from his kitchen to their clubhouse, ducking down through the half-concealed doorway, and weaving among the snarled bird's nest of wires and cables that powered the stereo.

"I didn't get a chance to find anything," Victor said. "I pulled the truck around and snapped on the lights. I wasn't really paying attention – I was trying to get something to come in on the radio. When I looked up, they were just… there."

"Who was there?" Flash said.

"I… I don't know. I don't even know if 'who' is the right word. Maybe what? I saw what looked like two men. They were wearing tattered clothes, their hair was matted – it looked like they'd just crawled out of the bay. I even thought I saw sea-weed on one of their shoulders...."

"What did you do?" Nick asked.

Drahos took a sip of his coffee, then glanced up. "What could I do? I got out to ask what they wanted, and to see if I could help. They looked pretty rough."

"And?" Weasel asked.

"And," Victor said, "When I got out and turned toward that garage, they just... this is going to sound weird... they just flew at me. I heard a sound like a rocket whistling. There was a really bright light. Those three faces just seemed to shoot straight at me... and then through me... and they... they were just gone. It was loud... and bright. By the time it was over, I'd fallen, took a pretty good shot to the hip when I fell. I was there maybe a minute. When I got up, the lights were shining in on all those boxes, and I was alone. Something stank, though, like dead fish, or a beach when the tide goes out and leaves a lot of seaweed behind.

"Then I drove home. I got up off that ground, hip hurting like hell, and I got in the truck and drove. I came here. I tried to sleep, but...."

"But where did they go?" Flash asked. "I mean, what were they, homeless guys?"

"I don't know who, or what they were," Victor said. "I know when I got up, they were gone, and as quick as I could manage it, I did the same."

They sat in silence. None of the boys knew what to say. Finally Drahos glanced around at them, frowned, and put down his coffee cup.

"You don't believe me," he said.

"I don't know what to think," Weasel said. "I've been out here lots of times. You know I'd help you work on almost any-thing. These guys," he pointed a thumb first at Flash, and then at Nick, "are my best friends. We've seen some things a lot cra-zier than what you described, but all I can think is... why?"

"I don't know," Victor said.

"I bet if we get over there and start going through that garage we'll find out," Nick said. "It seems pretty obvious that whoever they were, or whatever, they didn't want you going in there."

"I guess you're right," Drahos said. "At the very least, I need to get that place cleaned out."

"You want to start in the garage?" Weasel asked.

"No, I don't think so. I had this all planned out. The power's not on yet, so we need to clear out the interior while we can. If you boys want to stick around this evening, we can make another run at the garage. I'll feel better about it someone else is there."

The three boys glanced at one another, Nick shrugged, and Weasel grinned. "It's not like we have really full dance cards," he said. "I'm in. Flash?"

Flash nodded. "I'll have to call home and explain, but sure. I've always been a Scooby Doo fan… why not?"

Victor drained his coffee mug and stood. The color had returned to his face, and he seemed steadier on his feet than when they'd arrived.

"We'd better get started then," he said. "We've already burned part of our morning."

They followed him out and clambered into the back of his pickup truck, leaving the van in the driveway. It was only a couple of blocks to the other house. Vincent drove slowly and carefully, barely faster than they could have walked the distance. He pulled around the side of the house and parked facing into the basement garage.

The boys climbed out. Vincent cut the engine, climbed out, and stared. There were several boxes torn and scattered across the driveway. Some rags, a small pile of books, and some broken glass littered the ground.

"Was it like that last night?" Flash asked.

"I honestly don't remember," Drahos replied. "Like I said I saw those… things… come at me, and then they were gone. I didn't stay to look around. I got the hell out of here. It could have been like this."

"Looks like you interrupted something," Nick said, stepping forward and picking up one of the books. He thumbed through it, then turned and tossed it to Victor. "Your previous owner had good taste.

"Stephen King?" Drahos said, frowning.

"All of them," Nick said, turning back to the books. "Most of his older books are here. You should probably check the publication dates on those. Some of them are worth money."

Drahos laid the book on the hood of the truck.

"Let's get upstairs," he said. "We have a lot to get through before we can concentrate on this."

They climbed the winding stair that led up and around to the front of the house. For the next five hours they hauled boxes, old furniture, mattresses, and boxes out to the front yard. About noon Victor drove into town and returned with a large U-Haul trailer. They piled everything they'd pulled from the old home inside. It was nearly 18 feet long, and by the time they were done, it was packed floor to ceiling, and the rooms of the house, for the most part, were bare.

"Did the guy who owned this place die?" Weasel asked, wiping sweat from his brow and brushing his long brown hair out of his eyes. He stared into the trailer. "He left everything. Clothes, stereo, records, books...."

"He left town," Drahos said. "The realtor wasn't too clear. When he lived here, I don't remember seeing him more than once or twice, and then only in passing. He drove a beat up old VW, and now and then I saw him headed into town. He was a sort of thin, nervous looking guy. Then one day, the newspapers started piling up on the steps. A week later, the 'For Sale' sign was in the yard, and I called. The realtor told me he got a certified letter. It was postmarked Texas, but no return address. It contained power of attorney and everything necessary to sell the house... along with everything in it. The price was good."

"Maybe," Nick said. "I guess that might depend on what's in that garage. Do we go down there now?"

Drahos glanced at the trailer.

"I have to drive this to the auction house, and the rest over to The Hope House Thrift Store. We can't fit any more in there, and the garage is full. One of you come with me to help me unload this, the other two can wait at the house. Give us an hour, and then order pizza. We'll pick it up on the way back."

"Tony's" Flash asked.

"Where else," Drahos said, grinning.

"I'll go," Flash said. "Andrea is working tonight."

Nick laughed. "Fine with me. I'm ready for some ice tea and a piece of floor to lie down on."

"Don't recommend that," Drahos said. "King will be all over you."

Victor had a dog named King. Weasel had asked once, given the man's fascination with Jim Morrison and The Doors, if the dog was named after the Lizard King.

"Nope," Victor had said. "There's only one King, and Vicki won't let me call him Elvis."

Victor and Flash climbed into the cab of the U-Haul trailer, and a moment later it pulled away. Nick and Weasel walked the short distance to Drahos' home and went inside. The door had been open all day so they could get to the kitchen and the bathroom. King waited for them at the door, and Weasel scratched between the dog's ears. He was an old, scruffy half shepherd.

"Dibs on the couch," Nick said, slipping past and making a dash for the family room. Cursing, with King on his heels, Weasel followed.

As it turned out, Nick detoured to the bathroom, and by the time he returned, Weasel was sprawled across the couch, eyes closed, with King plopped happily on his chest.

"I called that," Nick muttered.

Weasel didn't move. Nick crossed the room and about half-way across, he heard the telltale rumble of a snore.

"Damn," he said. "Just like that. It's like a super power...."

He glanced around the room. There were several comfortable seats, and he briefly considered dropping into one of them and trying to catch a nap of his own while they waited. He wasn't sleepy, though, and though they'd been working all day, he still felt hyped up from the coffee.

He glanced at the bookshelves, and walked over. He briefly considered cranking the stereo and driving Weasel back into the world of the living as rudely as possible, then thought better of it.

There were a lot of books on the shelves, but nothing that

caught his eye immediately. Besides, it felt a little bit weird going through Victor's things, even if they had been invited in. He was reconsidering the nap, when he remembered the books in the garage at the other house. If there was Stephen King in there, who knew what he might find. He'd read all the King that was out, but when someone collected one author he liked, it stood to reason they might have something else. He was pretty sure Victor wouldn't care about those books, so he decided to run back over and have another look. As he headed out, he turned back. King glanced up at him, drooling happily, and Nick chuckled.

"You two deserve one another, he said. He closed the door behind himself and headed back down the street.

It was just starting to get dark as Nick slipped around back to the open garage. The pile of paperbacks was right where they'd left it, tumbling free of one of the boxes to the left side of the garage. Nick moved to it, thumbed through the books in the box quickly, and smiled. He'd read most of them, Koontz, Clive Barker, a few more obscure hardcovers. He made a note to mention the value of a few of them to Vincent when he got back. There were several more boxes behind the first, so he scooted it out and kept digging. He'd just spotted a Joe Lansdale novel that he hadn't read in the rear box, when he saw the gravestone.

Leaning against the worn leg of a wooden workbench behind the boxes of books, he saw a plain, gray tombstone. It was deep in the shadows, and he couldn't make out the inscription carved into it.

He tugged out the last box and lifted the tombstone free. There wasn't much light outside, and suddenly, standing alone in that garage after what he'd heard from Vincent about the night before, he felt alone and vulnerable. Books forgotten, he tucked the tombstone up under his arm and hurried back around the side of the house and up to the street. He made it back to Vincent's home without incident and stumbled in the door. When he entered the living room, King sat up and woofed at him. Weasel opened his eyes, caught sight of the tombstone, and sat up.

"What the hell, dude?"

"I found it in that garage," Nick said. "I went back to get a book and...."

Just then, a car door slammed, and they heard Vincent and Flash talking and laughing outside. Nick leaned the tombstone against the wall beside the stereo. Weasel kept staring at it.

"It was just in there with the books?" he asked.

Nick nodded. He squatted and brushed his fingers over the lettering. It was obviously old, and the lettering was somewhat faded. It said.

"Bunting Miles – 1857 - 1892" There was no other message. The stone was slightly worn and crumbled at the edges.

Victor and Flash walked in, Victor with two large Pizza boxes in his hand and Flash carrying a pair of two-liter Pepsi bottles. They stopped, staring at Nick, and the stone leaning on the wall.

Victor put the pizza boxes on the coffee table and stared at the tombstone.

"My memory isn't what it used to be," he said, "but that wasn't there when we left."

Nick filled him in quickly.

"So you brought it here?" Victor asked.

"I didn't want to just leave it, and that place started to freak me out. Sorry. I guess I wasn't thinking."

"It's fine," Victor said. He leaned down and read the inscription. "Bunting Miles? What kind of name is that?"

"Not sure," Nick said. "He was around during the Civil War though. What I wonder is, what was his tombstone doing in a garage, tucked in behind an old pile of books?"

"Better question," Victor said. "What is Lil going to say when she comes home and finds it leaning on my wall? I can't keep it here."

"I'll take it," Nick said, not sure why. "Maybe Ken can suggest how we can find out who's it is?"

"Fine with me," Victor said. "Tell you guys what, let's eat this pizza and call it a night. We can hit up the garage in the daylight, and I think we'll all feel better about it. Now that you've dragged that thing out, I'm afraid of what we'll find."

"Bodies!" Weasel called out. He started to wander around the room, arms out and eyes blank. "Brains... BRAINS...."

"Yeah, that's *exactly* what you need," Flash said, shaking his head. He flipped open the first pizza box and they all dug in.

A half hour later, full and tired, they clambered into the van, and Flash headed back toward Lavender. They had one more day of weekend, and they'd all agreed to gather back at Victor's the following day to tackle the contents of the garage.

"You're really taking that thing home?" Flash asked, nodding at the tombstone on the floor beneath Nick's feet. "Your mom is gonna *freak*."

"Nah," Nick said, "this is tame compared to other things in my room. I really want to know what Ned says. There's something about this name that keeps itching at the back of my mind."

"Still sounds like a baseball player who can't hit the short ball to me," Weasel said, laughing. "Bunting Miles? Doesn't even sound real.'

"Yeah," Nick said, "not nearly as real as Weasel...."

Nick lugged the tombstone down the hall to his room, bumped the door open with his knee, and leaned it against his bed. It was clearly visible from the doorway, and he stood for a moment staring at it. Footsteps sounded in the hall, and he turned. His mother, smiling, walked down from the kitchen.

"Hey mom," Nick said. He gave her a quick hug. "Is Ken around? I need to show him something."

"He's working late," she said, "but...."

She saw the tombstone and her hand rose to cover her mouth. Nick stepped close and supported her. He laughed.

"Easy mom. I haven' t been grave robbing. It came from the garage in the house we're cleaning out for Mr. Drahos – Weasel's Dad's friend?"

"But...why is it here?"

"His wife would have killed him if he kept it, and there's something about it that bothers me. The name. It's weird, and I've heard it before, but I can't place it. I thought maybe Ken would know how to track down where it belongs...."

His mom relaxed visibly.

"You're probably right." She stepped closer and leaned down, reading the name. Then she stood up very quickly.

"My God," she said.

"Mom? What is it?"

"Bunting Miles. Are you telling me," she turned to him, one eyebrow raised, "that you expect me to believe you have Bunting Miles' tombstone in your bedroom? Is this some sort of joke?"

Nick gaped at her.

She watched him, waiting for him to crack a smile or betray the joke. When he only stood and stared, she backed up and leaned against the frame of his door.

"My God," she repeated. "You don't know... so it's not a joke. Nicky, where did you say this came from? Do you not remember where you've heard that name?"

"It sounds familiar," he admitted, "but no. I don't remember. It was behind a bunch of boxes in a garage full of junk. The guy who owned it disappeared and left everything behind, and something weird is going on. Mr. Drahos, Victor, last night he got the crap scared out of him by someone – or something – going through that garage."

"Come into the kitchen," she said. "I'll tell you the story while we wait for Ken. He's going to want to hear this all right. This would be the coldest case in Lavender history."

Over coffee, Nick's mom told him a story, and as she spoke, he started to remember.

"Bunting Miles was a North Carolina Freedman just after the end of the Civil War," she said. "He worked as a laborer until he was eighteen, and then, when he saw how things would be for a black man in the southeast, he struck out on his own. He had saved some money, and he used it to buy a wagon and a mule. He drove that rig all the way from North Carolina to what is now Lavender, California."

"I'm starting to remember," Nick said. "Didn't he strike it rich? Gold?"

"Exactly," his mom said. "He came out here, found a rich vein, and mined it. He kept it to himself, and he worked it slow.

He and his wife built their own cabin, not that far from here. It's still standing. He raised goats. He had a small farm, and a fruit orchard, and all that time... he was mining gold. No one knows how much he pulled out of that mine before the cat got out of the bag, but when all was said and done...."

"He founded a town," Nick said, smacking himself on the forehead. And... he named it after his mule."

His mom smiled and nodded. "A mule named Lavender. When Bunting Miles died, other people took over. His story was forgotten. Even out here on the west coast, he was a black man, and a successful one – it sat less and less well with the rest of the town as people migrated from coast to coast. His family died, or left him, and he ended up a miser... alone. No one knows what he did with all the gold. There are stories, legends, but no facts. Most people believe...."

"That he was buried with it," Nick said, staring back down the hallway toward the door to his room. "Jesus Christ!"

"Nick!"

"Sorry mom but... Jesus."

She let it slide. Just then the door opened, and Ken Straker walked in. He had Nick's dog Lizzy on a leash, and at the sight of her owner, the dog turned into a quivering shaking ball of energy.

"Hold on," Ken chuckled. "He isn't going anywhere."

Lizzy, who'd spent the afternoon being groomed and a rare afternoon away from home on a rug in the corner of Ken's office, was more than ready to be home. She launched from about four feet away, and only experience and good balance kept Nick from going down under her tongue-first assault.

"Lizzy!" his mom cried out, laughing.

Nick picked the big dog up and gave her a hug, then put her down and gave her a quick and very thorough greeting.

"You'd think she hadn't seen you for a week," Ken said, laughing. "She's been a bundle of nerves ever since we started for home."

When Lizzy had settled, Nick took Ken down the hall to his room. On the way, he explained what he had, and how he'd come by it. Ken knelt and inspected the old gravestone, ran his fingers through the carved numbers and letters, and shook his head.

"Makes no sense," he said. "Miles was buried in Shady Grove. It's a big tomb, and well tended. We've had several attempts to break through it and open the grave by would-be treasure hunters."

"Isn't that for show?" Nick's mom said. "I've lived here all my life, and it seems I remember hearing that, when they thought they'd use the legend and story of a town named after a mule to draw in tourists. When they couldn't actually find his grave, they made that fancy headstone for Bunting Miles."

"I hadn't heard that," Ken said, "but I'll admit local legends aren't my forte. If that's true... then this is a major find. It's definitely old, and even if it turns out that Miles was buried beneath the fancy stone out at Shady Grove... doesn't mean this marker wasn't important. It could have been marking the location of the gold."

They all looked at one another, excitement growing.

"Tell you what," Ken said. "Let me take this in to the office tomorrow. I'll have the boys in the lab give it a once over. We should be able to date it, at the very least, and if we get really lucky with some soil trace, maybe we can pinpoint the area it came out of."

"That would be great," Nick said. "We're going to help Mr. Drahos finish cleaning out the garage tomorrow. I guess I'd better keep my eyes open for a map."

The next morning, the three boys were back at the Drahos home. They found Victor wide awake and eager to start, much different from the previous day.

"I left it alone after you took off," he told them. "I figured it could wait until today, and it would be better if I got some sleep."

Nick filled him in quickly on what he'd learned at home. Victor listened attentively, his eyes widening hear the end of the tale.

"Really? They named Lavender after a mule?"

Nick nodded. "I learned about it in school, but I forgot. All of us did. If my mom hadn't remembered...."

"Weird," Victor said. "I'm not from Lavender. I came here when I was stationed at Long Beach in the Navy. I never heard a thing about it. Always thought Lavender was a strange name for a town. But... if there's a big tombstone at Shady Grove, what did we find here last night?"

"I'm hoping we'll find out when we clear that garage," Nick said. "Ken said maybe the big memorial was just that – a memorial for tourists, hoping the story of gold and mules would attract tourists, and that what you had in that garage was the real tombstone. The other thought was, it was the marker for where he buried the gold."

Victor shook his head. "Strange. Well, let's get started then. If you want to pull out those old horror novels and take them, you're welcome to those, too. If you hadn't gone back for them, we might never have known about the stone at all."

The boys walked this time, hurrying over to the empty house, while Victor followed more slowly with his pickup. He had a flat trailer hitched to the back of it that they could load up with anything worth taking to the auction or the thrift store. The rest they'd take on a second trip to the dump.

When they got to the garage, all the boys could do was stare. A moment later, when Vincent backed in, parked, and joined them, he whistled.

"Damn."

The garage looked as if it had been hit by a small tornado. Boxes had been torn, their contents strewn all over the driveway. Cartons were tipped and dumped. It was a mess.

"I have a pile of old empty boxes at the house," Victor said. "They just need to be folded back together and taped. I think we'd better go through this more carefully than whoever was here last night did... maybe if they didn't find what they were after, we will. Nick, come on back with me and we'll bring them."

Flash and Weasel started out by gathering up the already dumped boxes. They stood them up and started piling in books and papers, scattered clothing and nick-nacks. Nothing very interesting came up in the first few feet of the garage, but by the time Nick and Victor returned with the boxes and tape, there was a path into the garage that made it slightly easier to work.

"They made a pretty big mess," Nick said, poking dubiously through a stack of rubber storage bins.

"Yes," Victor said, "but they must not have had enough light, or someone disturbed them again. They didn't really scratch the surface. If there's something in here, I'm betting they didn't find it."

They all dug in with vigor then, hauling boxes, stacking and re-packing things for the various destinations, and all the time with the thought in mind that the next thing they touched could be it. A box, or a picture, a map or a letter. Something scrawled in the back of an old diary. When Nick gave a cry, the rest of them came running.

He lifted up a framed print and held it where the rest of them could see it. It was an old tourist map. At the bottom, in Gothic Script, were the words "Shady Grove," and across the top it read "Bunting Miles, and his Mule Lavender" 1857-1892." Beneath that it read "Visit the historic tomb".

"How old is that thing?" Flash asked. "No one goes out there anymore. Not since...."

He fell silent. The three boys exchanged a look, and Nick shook his head.

"It's from the 1940s," Nick said. "That's not what's important."

He flipped the frame around, and they could all see that the lining on the rear had torn and curled down. On the inside, just the corner showing, there was another paper. Nick handed the map to Victor, who quickly tore away the remaining lining. On the back, faded and yellowed, was another map of Shady Grove. It was much older. Many of the landmarks showing on the front were missing, and a lot of the land that now comprised the place lay beyond the scrawled outline of a fence that surrounded it all.

There was a single red "X" near the back of the graveyard. Nick pulled back.

"No way, man," he said.

"What?" Weasel asked.

"Look where that 'X' is."

Weasel did, and then Flash.

"Holy crap!" Flash said, backing away.

"What?" Victor asked. "What is it?"

Nick turned and left the garage, heading out to fresh air. Weasel followed. Flash turned to Victor.

"You remember all that crap that happened at Shady Grove a couple of years back, when Nick's stepdad Ned died, and the Minister disappeared?"

"Of course," Victor said, "but..."

"That place," Flash said, stabbing his forefinger onto the red "X" on the map, "is where it happened. That's where that freaking altar was set up. Hell, for all I know, that tombstone we pulled out of here was one of those that held it up."

"Jesus," Victor said. "I mean, what are the odds?"

"Odds don't really figure into it," Flash said. "If I tried to tell you everything that happened there – what really went down – you wouldn't believe me. Trust me when I say, I don't much believe in coincidences anymore."

"Well, we'll take this to Ken Straker," Victor said. "He'll know what to do with it. For now, we're almost done in here. Let's see if the other two are going to help finish."

They all worked in silence. Along the way, they found an old leather doctor's case filled with folders and papers. Several of them seemed to be antique legal documents, and at least one of them bore the name Miles. When they were done, Victor packed the map, the papers, and three boxes of horror novels into the van with the boys.

"You take this and the map back and see what Ken has to say," he told Nick. "We'll get to the bottom of it. You boys don't worry about the rest. I'll take the boxes in myself, and the guys at the auction house can unload them. I'll leave as soon as you're out of here. Let me know what you find out?"

"Sure," Nick said, staring at the papers suspiciously. "I'm starting to be afraid we *will* find something."

Nick, his mom, and Ken sat around the kitchen table, the papers spread out between them, separated into stacks. The map of

Shady Grove, the older map on the back showing, leaned against the wall nearby.

"It's not one of the stones that were part of the altar," Ken said, scratching his head. "We had those removed. Both of them belonged to a very old San Valencez family by the name of Johndrow, and they were returned to their proper gravesites this past spring. I think they took the stone that was on top of the table to the dump."

"So... maybe it was all set up over the top of a grave?" Nick's mom said. "Could the stone in your room be the one that was meant to be there?"

Nick was poring over some of the old papers. He glanced up.

"I supposed it's possible. They have been looking for this gold for a very long time. If the person who removed the tombstone did so before the altar was put into place, it would have helped hide it all this time. Kind of weird that they would pick that spot...."

"Maybe not," Ken said. "Considering all that was involved in that... if there is a fortune or a mystery buried in Shady Grove, maybe it gave off some sort of aura they picked up on? Who knows?"

"Some of these are bank records," Nick said. "They show accounts for the Miles family. This one," he turned it so Ken could see, "seems to be around the time of his death. It shows the amounts that were left to his children, about $10,000 apiece. There's another number on the sheet, at the bottom. It's written in different script, but seems old. It says '$2,000,000 – unaccounted for'"

"$2,000,000?" Ken said. He took the paper and scanned it quickly.

"That's a lot of money," Nick's mom said.

"Enough to try and steal, for sure," Nick said. "And don't forget, if it was worth $2,000,000 back then, and it's gold bullion that is buried there, the price of gold is a lot higher now."

Ken whistled.

"We need to get some people out there tomorrow," he said. "If that's really the second gravesite for Bunting Miles, it's of historic interest and it's a good enough reason for an exhumation order. I'm going to drive down to the office and get it all put in motion tonight. We might be able to give Victor some answers by late tomorrow, if I get lucky."

They all stood up. Nick turned and called to Lizzy, who came lumbering down the hall from his room. It was just a ruse so he wouldn't have to watch Ken and his mom say goodbye. He liked Ken, and it was growing to be more than that, but he still wasn't used to the idea that the man shared his mom's bed. A moment later, Ken passed by on his way out.

"See you later," he said, turning and smiling. Nick smiled back, and Lizzie trotted over to lick Ken's hand.

Then Ken was out the door, and the Nick turned back to the kitchen to put the papers away. He and his mom worked together, keeping the files organized and leaving the most significant find on the table. They had just tucked away the last page when Lizzy, who'd been laying at their feet, leapt up and started growling. She shot down the hall toward the front door, and Nick stared after her in shock. There was a knock on the door, and he started forward, just as the back door to the kitchen burst in, kicked off its hinges, and a pair of masked men rushed into the room, guns drawn.

"What the...?" Nick said. He backed toward his mom, putting himself between her and the intruders. He grabbed Lizzy by the collar, barely able to hold her back.

"Where is it," a muffled voice asked.

"Where's what?" Nick asked, trying not to stare at the table.

"Don't get funny with me kid," the second intruder snarled. He stepped forward like he was going to swing his gun at Nick's head but stopped short of Lizzy's snapping jaws. Barely.

"The map," the first voice said, "where's the freaking map?"

Nick glanced at the frame by the wall, dragged his eyes away, and knew it was too late. They'd seen it. The second man stepped over, snatched the framed map, and backed toward the door.

"You'll never get there in time," Nick said. "The cops already know where it's at."

"Sure they do," the second man said. He looked down at

the papers on the table, then back at Nick. "I see they took all the evidence down to the station. You take that dog, and get down the hall. You too lady."

They were forced down to where Nick's bedroom door stood open, and then inside. Once they were in, the door was closed, and the first man spoke a final time.

"You count to a hundred before you open that door. I see you, your dog, anyone before I'm out of sight, I'm shooting. I don't want to hurt you, but I will. You got it?"

Nick didn't answer, but his mother called out, "Yes, we understand."

There was no answer. A moment later, they heard the kitchen door slam and Nick bolted for his bedroom door.

"Nick!" his mother called.

But he was already out the door and down the hall. He grabbed the phone and dialed without hesitation, and a moment later, Ken answered.

"Nick? What is it?" Ken asked.

Nick told him quickly what had happened. "I'm worried about Victor, too," he said. "They probably went there before they came here."

"I'll get someone out there," Ken said. "And I'll get someone over to the house."

"No," Nick said, "They're gone from here. They took the map. We have to make sure they don't get to that grave before you do."

There was a hesitation.

"You stay there with your mom, Nick, okay? I'll come by and get you both once I make sure everything is under control. I'm counting on you."

"I will," Nick said. He didn't want to. He wanted to call Weasel and Flash and rush out to Shady Grove, but things were different now. More even than he wanted the adventure, he realized, he wanted Ken Straker to trust him. "We'll be right here."

"You think that kid was tellin' the truth?" Marty Hampton asked, pushing aside a small tree branch and shining his light onto the overgrown graves at the rear of Shady Grove Cemetery.

"You think the cops will be out here?"

"Don't know, and don't care." Bill Preston, Marty's partner, was a tall man. He never smiled, and he only spoke when he had something to say. At least, that's what he claimed.

"It's gonna take time to dig up a grave," Marty said.

"It's gonna take longer if you keep yapping about it. Keep moving. We have to be in and out of here quick. If that kid had the map, he knows where it leads. There might not have been cops on the way before, but there will be now."

"How we gonna dig it out then?" Marty asked. "I mean, no way we can do this in just a few minutes."

"We going to make some changes," Bill said. "We'll slide some stones around, move some brush – hide the 'right' spot so they don't find it. Then we'll come back in a few days, when things have died down, and do our digging."

"Oh," Marty said. It made sense, and he felt silly for not thinking of it himself. Of course, Marty didn't think much... that was Bill's job. Always had been. Ever since they'd met in the can and Marty had told him about the missing gold. Bill had been a history teacher once. He'd gotten caught stealing from his university and put away, but he still 'had it' when it came to research. Not long after Marty told him about the mule, Lavender, and the old guy who they said had been buried with his gold, Bill had found references in the prison library. They'd been at it ever since.

The first stroke of luck had been finding Kevin Kane. The guy had been living out here in that house by the bay for years, collecting artifacts, chasing maps... he'd found the treasure first, years back, but he didn't have the nerve to dig it up. Christ, the guy had even stolen the tombstone. When they called him, he wouldn't tell them anything. When they threatened him, he didn't believe them. Then bad things started happening around his house, and the guy just freaking disappeared. That hadn't been the plan. They had only wanted to scare the guy into giving them the map. When he left and sold everything, it all started falling apart, and now here they were, tramping around an old graveyard in the middle of the night, wondering whether the cops would be onto them at any second.

"What you think happened to that guy Kane?" Marty asked, distracted by his own train of thought.

"What?" Bill asked. "Christ, Marty, get your head on straight. We have work to do. Who gives a fart in the wind about Kane?"

"Just thinkin'," Marty said.

They came to a clearing, and Bill stopped. They'd pulled the map out of the frame, and he held it up to the moonlight to get a better look. Just to the left and in front of them was an angel memorial the height of a man. Bill bent, read the inscription, and grunted.

"This is it," he said. "This clearing. Not sure why it's a clearing – there should be," he read quickly, "about three graves in this spot… but where are the stones? I know Kane took Miles' stone, but the others?"

"I don't know," Marty said. "This place gives me the creeps though. Why is it round?"

Bill glanced around, as if noticing the large, cleared circle for the first time. It was out of place in the middle of an overgrown cemetery, and he frowned.

"Weird," he said. "Makes this easier though.

He paced out ten steps from the angel, then glanced up, and grinned. Straight ahead a thick, Celtic cross canted off to the right side. He stomped his foot.

"Right here," He said. "This is the spot. Come on. Help me."

Bill made a quick circuit of the clearing, and at last, he found what he wanted. It was a thick concrete headstone, not too large, that had fallen over on its side.

"Help me with this," He said. "We'll plant it right on top of that spot. Then we'll scoot some leaves around and cover up our tracks. If they come looking, they aren't going to look in someone else's grave. When they don't find anything, they'll leave. We can come back in a week or so. We've waited this long…"

Just as he leaned down to pick up the stone, a thin figure melted from the shadows. Before Bill could react, something hard and heavy smacked into the side of his head and sent him reeling. He went down, and did not get back up.

"Wh… who is that?" Marty called out. He moved cautiously

over to where his friend had fallen. "Bill?"

"He's not getting up," a voice grated from the shadows. "He's never getting up. This is the end of the line...."

Marty wavered. He saw his friend on the ground, not moving, and he saw the shadowy intruder advancing. Whoever it was wasn't very big, but he'd taken Bill down with one shot, and Marty wasn't armed.

"Who are you?" he said. "What do you want.'"

"Get OUT!" the figure growled. With a lurch and swing, the guy came at him, and Marty, barely ducking the blow, turned and started to run. He only got a few steps before sudden, glaring light filled the clearing.

"Nobody move," Straker called. "I see you both, there are officers at every exit. You have nowhere to run. Do not move."

The thin man turned and bolted back through the graves. Marty stood very still as Ken Straker and two deputies moved cautiously forward, guns drawn and bright flashlights illuminating the clearing.

"Keep your hands where I can see them," Straker said. He knelt and felt the pulse on Bill's neck, then turned to one of the deputies.

"Get dispatch to send out an ambulance. He's going to be okay, but there's a hell of a knot on his head."

Ken flashed the light up into Marty's face.

"Who were you talking to?" he said.

"I don't know!" Marty said. "Christ, I don't know. Guy came outta nowhere. He hit Bill, he..."

"Get after him," Straker barked. "Remember, there's a back gate. It should be locked, but if he came in that way he may have cut it."

"Yes sir," the deputy said. He took off at a slow trot, swinging his flashlight from side to side.

Straker and the other deputy cuffed Marty. The whine of a siren sounded in the distance.

"Get him back to the car," Straker said. "Call for more backup. I'll wait here for the medics, and to see what McMullan finds at the back gate.

The deputy nodded. He grabbed Marty by his cuffed arms

and started him back through the cemetery. A moment later, Ken stood alone in the clearing with an unconscious man, and that clearing. He shivered. It hadn't been long enough. It would never be long enough to erase the incidents that had first brought him to that place. He wasn't even certain that a treasure in gold was worth taking a shovel to the ground. He'd seen something there. Something he'd never be able to accept or explain.

He heard a moan, and he stepped over to where his second prisoner was starting to come around. As the man sat up groggily, Ken drew his weapon. He aimed the gun, and his light, directly into the man's eyes, blinding him.

"Christ," Bill said. "What hit me?"

"Not what, who," Straker said. "I have a man trying to chase the guy down now. Your partner is in custody. You want to tell me why you broke into my house, and just what the hell you think you're doing out here."

"If you're here, you already know the answer to that."

"Humor me," Straker said.

Bill shook his head slowly, then stopped, as if the motion caused more pain.

"The gold. We're here looking for Bunting Miles' gold. We didn't hurt anyone, we just needed the map."

"How did you know there was a map?" Straker asked.

"We didn't. We guessed. We've been searching for this a long time. When we found out that kook Kane had the tombstone, we figured he must have left some kind of map... or found one. How else would he have found it? Your kid – Christ, it has to be a cop's kid? He took the tombstone, so we figured he was onto the secret, and then he left with those boxes."

"Who is Kane?" Straker asked. "The tombstone was in the garage of a man named Drahos... Victor Drahos."

"Yeah, but Kane's the guy who put it there," Bill said. "We were trying to scare him into giving us the map when he disappeared. Guy just took off and never came back. We figured we'd get in and out after the house was sold, but that new guy, Drahos... he got there too quick."

There was a crunch of footsteps, and more lights bobbed

through the brush. A moment later two medics with a stretcher came into sight, as well as two more deputies.

"Get this guy out of here," Straker said. "I want a perimeter roped off around this clearing, and digging equipment brought in. Call the judge and get an order of exhumation, just in case someone's actually buried here. We're going on a treasure hunt."

The phone rang, and Nick answered. It was Victor.

"What's going on in there, Nick?" he said. "There was a squad car out here a few minutes ago. We went down to the other house, but the garage is pretty well clear now, and we didn't see anything. It's been quiet here."

Nick filled him in quickly.

"So… they actually broke into your house?" Victor asked. "Are you okay? Your mom?"

"We're fine," Nick said. "They took the map, but I called Ken. I'm sure he's out there by now… we're waiting for him to call."

"I just wanted to clean out my garage," Victor said.

"I know, Mr. Drahos, I…"

Drahos grunted and then cursed.

"What?" Nick said "Victor what is it?"

"I don't know. King just raced out the front door, banged through the screen like it wasn't there… I have to go. He looks like he's headed down toward the other house."

The line went dead, and Nick turned to his mom.

"We have to go help him," he said. "I'll call Flash, you see if you can get Ken on his cell phone."

"'Nick, He told us to stay here…." his mom said. Her voice was nervous, and her eyes wide. Nick put his hand on her shoulder.

"He's not Ned, mom. He'll understand. Call him. I have to get hold of Flash."

His mom shook off the cobwebs and ran to the kitchen table for her purse and her phone. Nick dialed again, and a moment later Flash answered.

"Get Weasel… get over here," Nick said. "No time for

questions. We have to get to Victor's house now!"

Flash hung up without answering. They'd all been friends long enough to know when it was cool to mess around, and when it was time to act. They'd been through crazy and back together. Nick thought, just for a second, about calling Ruthie, then shook his head. She'd only just gotten back into town, and he didn't want to drag her into anything dangerous. She'd be mad, but he'd have a story to tell, and Ruthie would forgive him.

When he turned, his mom was already headed toward the door.

"He's got someone on the way," she said. "They're going to meet us there."

They patted Lizzy on the head, locked the door behind themselves, and waited out front for Flash and the "Magic Bus" to arrive. When he pulled up to the curve, Nick's mom took the front seat, and Nick piled in back with Weasel.

"Get us to Victor's," Nick said. "Fast."

Flash floored it, and Nick tumbled over Weasel, who cursed, and then apologized to Nick's mom, who laughed. It felt comfortable.

They made the drive quickly, though Flash was careful to keep it just under the speed limit. Nick filled them in on everything he knew.

"That's crazy!" Weasel said. "I mean, they broke into your house? They didn't know Ken ... I mean, Mr. Straker ... is a cop?"

"I don't think they're from around here," Nick said. "Not recently... but those guys are in custody."

"Then who is out at Victor's?" Flash asked.

"Good question, genius," Nick said. They laughed. "I guess we're about to find out."

When they pulled up in front of Victor's house, there were flashing lights up and down the street. They parked and went straight to Victor's door. They were met by a young officer Nick new, Debbi Smith. She smiled when she saw them.

"He's in the living room," she said. "He's kind of shaken up."

"What happened?" Nick asked.

"I'm sure he'll fill you in," Officer Smith said. "I have to get down to the other place. We have a ... situation."

She brushed past them without further explanation, and Nick hurried on into the living room. The others trailed after.

When Victor saw them, he smiled. He was pale, and he held a tumbler of what must have been whiskey in shaking hands.

"What happened?" Nick repeated.

"Someone's in there," Victor said. "The house. I followed King out the door, had to run just to keep up. I heard the door slam, but when I got there, the place was locked tight from the inside. I didn't have the key with me, but I rang the bell, banged on the door, yelled. Nothing. Then, all of a sudden someone dropped a plant from the second story. It landed right next to me, almost hit King. That pot exploded, and I got the hell out. Came back here, and before I could even call for help... there were sirens."

"You don't know who it is?" Nick asked.

Victor shook his head. "I met the police at the street, told them what happened, and they sent me in here."

There were more car doors slamming outside, and Weasel, who'd been watching the street from the front door, called out, "Ken is... I mean, Mr. Straker, is here..."

Nick hurried out past his friend toward the street. Ken was climbing out of a cruiser and headed down the street. There was yellow tape cordoning off the other house. Nick stopped at the tape and watched as Ned approached the front of the place. Nick started to call out, then held back. He watched Ken as he questioned the officers on duty. He liked the way they deferred to him. He liked Ken's confidence. A moment later, Ken looked up, caught him staring, and smiled. In that second he was glad he hadn't called out.

Ken walked over to the tape.

"The guy is locked in," he said. "He's claiming he has a gun, but I'm thinking not. Drahos said the place was locked, so whoever it is has a key."

"The previous owner?" Nick asked.

Ken nodded. I think so. Just can't figure out why.

There was a commotion by the front door, it opened, and a moment later a thin young black man was being cuffed and led away from the home, straight toward Ken and Nick. He wore thick framed glasses and his hair was disheveled. His eyes were wild, but he didn't struggle.

Something flashed in Nick's brain clicked. His mouth opened, closed, and then he spoke.

"Oh my god," he said.

"What?" Ken asked, turning to him and frowning. "What is it Nick?"

"Miles," Nick said. "That guy is a dead ringer for the picture of Bunting Miles I found online. It's like... it's like his ghost...."

The man was led over to where Ken and Nick stood, staring at him. He kept his eyes on the ground, and his face was set in a sullen, if slightly frightened expression.

"Mr. Kane, I presume?" Ken said.

The man looked up defiantly.

"Or should I say... Miles?"

That did it. The man crumbled back into the arms of the officers, nearly collapsing on the ground. They hurried him past the tape and got him seated in the back seat of Ken's cruiser. He sat there, gulping in the night air as if he'd been oxygen deprived, and Ken waited.

"It's mine," the man said finally, his voice coming out thin and reedy. He cleared his throat. When he spoke again, it was clearer. "Mine."

"I assume you mean the gold," Ken said. "If so, there's probably some contest on that, particularly since you chose to steal a gravestone, and assault a man in a cemetery, as well as breaking and entering as your method of retrieving it. Just who are you, anyway?"

"Denton Miles," he said. "Bunting Miles was my great grandfather. My grandfather, Bunting's son, took off for San Francisco. He was the only surviving relative."

"And you waited until now to show up? Didn't your grandfather get his inheritance?"

"He got *an* inheritance," Miles said. "It wasn't much. The thing is the will stated that he got a percentage. Half was to go to his father, and half to his aunt, Lydia Miles, who also left Lavender around the same time. Unfortunately, she died without marrying. Neither child ever returned, and since then, all there have been are rumors and some old papers floating around. I'm the last that I know of, and I got the papers from my father. I moved down here almost fifteen years ago to see if I could find the treasure. I'm a computer programmer, I worked from home. When I could afford it, I moved out here where I thought people would leave me alone."

"Seems like you were searching with some success," Ken said. "I still don't get, after you knew where it was, why you decided to steal the tombstone instead of just coming forward to try and get an exhumation order for the grave site. You probably wouldn't have had any trouble."

"I was getting phone calls," Miles said. "They were threatening me. They'd researched and found that I had gathered all the information and somehow they knew who I was. They tried to break into my house. They flattened the tires on my car, and they said if I went to the police – no one would believe me. They said the town would take the money, and all I'd be is the great grandson of a guy who loved his mule more than his family. I didn't know that to do. Then they took a shot at me when I was out walking... I left town. I figured no amount of gold was worth that, and I thought the minute I was gone they'd break in, get what they wanted, and leave me alone. I guess I wasn't actually thinking very straight at all."

"You got that right," Ken said, shaking his head. "At this point, you better hope that there *is* some gold, and that they let you keep it. You're going to have some fines to pay, and I'm guessing a lawyer or two before you're done."

Miles hung his head. "Not to mention all my stuff is gone," he said. "God, my great grandfather is probably turning over in his grave..."

"Question is," Nick cut in, "which grave?"

In the end, it turned into quite the local "happening". At the advisement of his attorney, Denton Miles agreed that, if the city would allow him to excavate his great grandfather's second grave to either confirm the old man was there, or that the gold wasn't a myth, that he would donate ten percent of whatever he found to the city parks and recreation committee. All charges against him were dropped, including the assault in the cemetery. Bill and Marty agreed not to press charges, and in return their own charges were dropped to parole violations. They headed back to prison, but not for too long, and no one was sorry to see them go.

On the day of the exhumation, Nick, his girlfriend Ruthie, his mom, Ken, Weasel, Flash and Victor Drahos stood together in the shade of an old Elm tree, watching the proceedings with interest. Not far off, surrounded by a small group of city councilmen and reporters, Denton Miles waited. He wore a suit, despite the heat, and looked like a rumpled schoolboy.

"I hope it's there," Nick said. "That guy could use a break."

"I know a good house he can have cheap," Victor said, chuckling. "What a mess."

The digging began with a small back-hoe that had been carefully rolled in through the back gate. It scraped one small layer at a time from the grave site. Nick held his breath. He couldn't get the image of what had once stood on that spot out of his head. He hugged Ruthie to his side, and she shivered a little. Then he glanced over at Ken, and knew that whatever happened, it was going to be all right.

There was a scraping sound, and the back-hoe rolled away a few feet. Men with shovels jumped down into the hole and began excavating more carefully.

"Something's here," one man called. "It's metal, and it's big. Bigger than a coffin ought to be."

They worked by hand for nearly three hours. Then, they used the back-hoe to lift the metal box using a series of blocks and tackles and a wooden framework that creaked and groaned, and slid wooden slats beneath the load, backing the big machine up so that it slid the case onto solid ground. When it was done, Denton Miles and the city fathers gathered in a semicircle around the brass padlock that dangled from the huge container's hasp. It was a square box nearly four feet on each side, and another four deep. Like a giant dirt-coated metal cube.

With exaggerated effort, one of the deputies cut the lock with a large pair of bolt cutters. It gave with a snap; Denton leaned forward and yanked the broken lock free. With the help of two councilmen and the deputy, he pried the top open and heaved the heavy lid up. The four men stepped back. Denton cried out. The deputy cursed. From where Nick stood, he saw a glint of brilliant yellow, and he knew the gold was there.

"What is it?" Ruthie asked. "Why are they all backing away?"

Nick started forward, moving with the crowd. Even as Miles and the city fathers backed away, those who'd not yet seen what was inside surged forward. The deputy saw, too late, what was happening and raised his hands in an effort to stop them, but the crowd reached the lip of the box, and since he was in front, Nick was one of the first to look.

The bottom of the crate was lined with several feet of solid gold, carefully molded into bricks. It was more wealth than he'd ever imagined seeing at one time. For all that, it wasn't the gold that caught his eye.

Laid out on top was a decayed, rotted skeletal body. It was long and deep chested. On the head, pierced by the tattered remnant of two long ears, was an old straw hat. There was a saddle carefully tucked in beside it, and despite the horror of what he saw, Nick started laughing, and found that he couldn't stop. He pulled back, dragging Ruthie behind him, and collapsed against a tree, trying to get his breathing under control.

Victor, who had not joined the surge, stood staring at him.

"What?" he said. "For God's sake, what's in that box?"

Nick drew himself up straight, forced a serious expression to remain in place long enough for him to speak, and answered.

"The city will be happy to know," he said solemnly, "that along with enough money to build a couple of hundred parks, give or take, their ten percent of today will include one tenth of the last remains of a mule named Lavender... and his hat."

Victor started at him, then glanced at the box, where a beleaguered Ken Straker and a squad of deputies were finally managing to force back the crowd, half of whom were shocked or sickened, and the other half, like Nick, taken by gales of laughter.

"Come on," Nick said, grabbing Ruthie by the arm. "Let's get back to the van. I think I've had about all of this place I can take."

Ruthie nodded and followed, and slowly the others trickled after them, leaving Denton Miles and the city fathers to figure out how to get half a ton of gold bricks and a dead mule out of the cemetery without breaking any other tombstones. As they went, Victor called out from behind.

"Hey Nick," he said. "Know anyone who's looking for a house?"

ABOUT THE AUTHOR

DAVID NIALL WILSON has been writing and publishing horror, dark fantasy, and science fiction since the mid-eighties. Once President of the Horror Writers Association and multiple recipient of the Bram Stoker Award, his novels include *Maelstrom, The Mote in Andrea's Eye, Deep Blue*, the Grails Covenant Trilogy, *Star Trek Voyager: Chrysalis, Except You Go Through Shadow, This is My Blood, Ancient Eyes, On the Third Day, The Orffyreus Wheel*, The DeChance Chronicles, including *Heart of a Dragon, Vintage Soul, My Soul to Keep, Kali's Tale, A Midnight Dreary* and the stand-alone spinoff *Nevermore—A Novel of Love, Loss & Edgar Allan Poe*. His novels in the O.C.L.T. series include *The Parting, Crockatiel*, and the novella *The Temple of Camazotz*. He is also the author of the memoir / cookbook American Pies: Baking with Dave the Pie Guy. His brand new series, HOODS, debuts in January of 2020 with "Hoods: The Beginning". David can be found at http://www.davidniallwilson.com and can be reached by e-mail at David@Davidniallwilson.com

Curious about other Crossroad Press books?
Stop by our site:
http://store.crossroadpress.com
We offer quality writing
in digital, audio, and print formats.